By James Purdy

Novels

63: Dream Palace (1956)
Malcolm (1959)
The Nephew (1960)
Cabot Wright Begins (1964)
Eustace Chisholm and the Works (1967)
Jeremy's Version (1970)
I Am Elijah Thrush (1972)
The House of the Solitary Maggot (1974)
In a Shallow Grave (1976)
Narrow Rooms (1978)
Mourners Below (1981)
On Glory's Course (1984)
In the Hollow of His Hand (1986)
Garments the Living Wear (1990)

Stories & Plays

Don't Call Me by My Right Name (1956)
Color of Darkness (1957)
Children Is All (1962)
A Day After the Fair (1977)
Proud Flesh (1980)
The Candles of Your Eyes (1987)

Poetry

An Oyster Is a Wealthy Beast (1967)
The Running Sun (1971)
Sunshine Is an Only Child (1973)
Lessons and Complaints (1978)
Collected Poems (1990)

James Purdy

63: DREAM PALACE

SELECTED STORIES

1956 - 1987

BLACK SPARROW PRESS
SANTA ROSA - 1991

The author would like to thank New Directions Publishing Corp., Penguin Books and Grove Weidenfeld who published some of these stories in previous collections.

Black Sparrow Press books are printed on acid-free paper.

LIBRARY OF CONGRESS CATALOGING-IN-PUBLICATION DATA

Purdy, James.
   63, dream palace : selected stories. 1956-1987 / James Purdy.
     p.   cm.
ISBN 0-87685-845-0 :   — ISBN 0-87685-846-9 (signed) :
   — ISBN 0-87685-844-2 (pbk.) :
   I. Title.
PS3531.U426A615   1991
813'.54 — dc20

                                                   91-27119
                                                   CIP

for Edith Sitwell

• TABLE OF CONTENTS •

63: DREAM PALACE

SELECTED STORIES 1956-1987

• COLOR OF DARKNESS •

SOMETIMES he thought about his wife, but a thing had begun of late, usually after the boy went to bed, a thing which *should* have been terrifying but which was not: he could not remember now what she had looked like. The specific thing he could not remember was the color of her eyes. It was one of the most obsessive things in his thought. It was also a thing he could not quite speak of with anybody. There were people in the town who would have remembered, of course, what color her eyes were, but gradually he began to forget the general structure of her face also. All he seemed to remember was her voice, her warm hearty comforting voice.

Then there was the boy, Baxter, of course. What did he know and what did he not know. Sometimes Baxter seemed to know everything. As he hung on the edge of the chair looking at his father, examining him closely (the boy never seemed to be able to get close enough to his father), the father felt that Baxter might know everything.

"Bax," the father would say at such a moment, and stare into his own son's eyes. The son looked exactly like the father. There was no trace in the boy's face of anything of his mother.

"Soon you will be all grown up," the father said one night, without ever knowing why he had said this, saying it without his having even thought about it.

"I don't think so," the boy replied.

"Why don't you think so," the father wondered, as surprised by the boy's answer as he had been by his own question.

The boy thought over his own remark also.

"How long does it take?" the boy asked.

"Oh a long time yet," the father said.

"Will I stay with you, Daddy," the boy wondered.

The father nodded. "You can stay with me always," the father said.

11

The boy said *Oh* and began running around the room. He fell over one of his engines and began to cry.

Mrs. Zilke came into the room and said something comforting to the boy.

The father got up and went over to pick up the son. Then sitting down, he put the boy in his lap, and flushed from the exertion, he said to Mrs. Zilke: "You know, I am old!"

Mrs. Zilke laughed. "If you're old, I'm dead," she said. "You must keep your youth," she said almost harshly to the father, after a pause.

He looked up at her, and the boy suddenly moved in his father's arms, looking questioningly at his father. He kissed his father on the face.

"He's young yet," the boy said to Mrs. Zilke.

"Why, of course. He's a young man," she said. "They don't come no younger for fathers."

The father laughed and the boy got up to go with Mrs. Zilke to his bed.

The father thought about Mrs. Zilke's remark and he listened as he heard her reading to the boy from a story-book. He found the story she read quite dry, and he wondered if the boy found anything in it at all.

It was odd, he knew, that he could not remember the color of his wife's eyes. He knew, of course, that he must remember them, and that he was perhaps unconsciously trying to forget. Then he began to think that he could not remember the color of his son's eyes, and he had just looked at them!

"What does he know?" he said to Mrs. Zilke when she came downstairs and sat for a moment with the newspaper. She lit a cigarette and blew out some smoke before she replied to him. By then he was looking out the window as though he had forgotten her presence and his question.

"He knows everything," Mrs. Zilke said.

The father came to himself now and looked at her gently.

"They all do now, don't they," the father said, meaning children.

"It seems so," the woman said. "Yes," she said, thinking. "They know everything."

"Everybody seems forty years old to me," the father said. "Even children maybe. Except they are complete mysteries to me. I don't know what to say to any of them. I don't know what they know, I guess."

"Oh, I understand that. I raised eight kids and I was always thinking the same thing."

"Well, that relieves me," he told Mrs. Zilke.

She smiled, but in her smile he thought he saw some thought reserved, as though she had not told everything.

"Of course we never know any other human being, do we?" he told Mrs. Zilke, hesitating as though to get the quotation right.

She nodded, enjoying her cigarette.

"Your son is lonely," she said suddenly.

The father did not look at her now.

"I mean by that," she went on, "it's too bad he's an only child."

"Doesn't he have other children over here, though. I thought—"

"Oh, it's not the same," Mrs. Zilke said. "Having in other youngsters like he does on Saturday and all. It's not enough."

"Of course I am gone a good deal."

"You're gone all the time," she said.

"That part can't be helped, of course. You see," he laughed, "I'm a success."

Mrs. Zilke did not return his laughter, he noticed, and he had noticed this before in plain strong old working women of her kind. He admired Mrs. Zilke tremendously. He was glad she had not laughed with him.

"No one should have just the one child," she told him.

"You know," he said, confidentially, "when you have just your work, as I do, people get away from you."

He looked at the bottle of brandy on the bookshelf.

"Would you have a pony of brandy with me, Mrs. Zilke."

She began to say no because she really didn't like it, but there was such a pleading look on his young face, she nodded rather regally, and he got up and poured two shots.

"Thank you for drinking with me," he said suddenly, as though to brush away something that had come between his words and his memory.

"Quite a bouquet," she said, whiffing first.

"You are really very intelligent," he told Mrs. Zilke.

"Because I know the bouquet," she said coldly.

"Oh, that and a lot of other things."

"Well, I don't know anything," Mrs. Zilke said.

"You know everything," he remarked. "All I have is my work."

"That's a lot. They need you," she said.

He sat down now, but he did not touch the brandy, and Mrs. Zilke having smelled the bouquet put her tiny glass down too.

They both sat there for a moment in silence as though they were perhaps at communion.

"I can't remember the color of my wife's eyes," he said, and he looked sick.

Mrs. Zilke sat there as though considering whether this had importance, or whether she might go on to the next topic of their talk.

"And tonight, would you believe it, I couldn't remember the color of his!"

"They're blue as the sea," Mrs. Zilke said rather gruffly, but with a kind of heavy sad tone also in her voice.

"But what does it matter about those little things," she said. "You're an important man!"

He laughed very loud at this, and Mrs. Zilke suddenly laughed too. A cord of tension had been snapped that had existed between them earlier.

The father lifted his glass and said the usual words and Mrs. Zilke took her glass with a slight bored look and sipped.

"I can taste the grapes in that, all right," she said.

"Well, it's the grapes of course I buy it for," he replied in the tone of voice he might have used in a men's bar.

"You shouldn't care what color their eyes are or were," Mrs. Zilke said.

"Well, it's my memory about people," he told her. "I don't know people."

"I know you don't," she said. "But you have other things!"

"No, I don't. Not really. I could remember people if I wanted to."

"If you wanted to," Mrs. Zilke said.

"Well, why can't I remember my wife's eyes," he brought the whole thing out. "Can you remember," he wanted to know, "the color of eyes of all those in your family."

"All forty-two of them," she laughed.

"Well, your husband and your sons and daughters."

"Oh, I expect I can," she was rather evasive.

"But you do, Mrs. Zilke, you know you do!"

"All right, but I'm just a woman about the house. You're out in the world. Why should you know the color of people's eyes! Good grief, yes!"

She put her glass down, and picked up some socks she had been darning before she had put the boy to bed.

"I'm going to work while we talk," she said with a firmness that seemed to mean she would be talking less now and that she would probably not drink the brandy.

Then suddenly closing his own eyes tight he realized that he did not know the color of Mrs. Zilke's eyes. But suddenly he could not be afraid anymore. He didn't care, and he was sure that Mrs. Zilke would not care if he knew or not. She would tell him not to care. And he remembered her, which was, he was sure, more important. He remembered her kindness to him and his son, and how important they both were to him.

"How old *are* you?" Baxter asked him when he was sitting in his big chair with his drink.

"Twenty-eight, I think," the father said vaguely.

"Is that old enough to be dead?" the son wondered.

"Yes and no," the father replied.

"Am I old enough to be dead?"

"I don't think so," the father replied slowly, and his mind was on something else.

"Why aren't we all dead then?" the son said, sailing a tiny paper airplane he had made. Then he picked up a bird he had made out of brown paper and sailed this through the air. It hit a philodendron plant and stuck there in it, as though it were a conscious addition.

"You always think about something else, don't you?" the boy said, and he went up and stared at his father.

"You have blue eyes," the father said. "Blue as the sea."

The son suddenly kissed his father, and the father looked at him for a long time.

"Don't look funny like that," the boy said, embarrassed.

"Like what?" the father said, and lowered his gaze.

The son moved awkwardly, grinding his tiny shoes into the carpet.

"Like you didn't know anything," the boy said, and he ran out into the kitchen to be with Mrs. Zilke.

After Mrs. Zilke went to bed, which was nearly four hours after the boy had gone, the father was accustomed to sit on downstairs thinking about the problems in his work, but when he was at home like this he often thought about *her,* his wife of long ago. She had run off (this was almost the only term he used for her departure) so long ago and his marriage to her had been so brief that it was almost as though Baxter were a gift somebody had awarded him, and that as the gift increased in value and liability, his own relation to it was more and more ambiguous and obscure. Somehow Mrs. Zilke seemed more real to him than almost anybody else. He could not remember the color of her eyes either, of course, but she was quite real. She was his "mother," he supposed. And the boy was an infant "brother" he did not know too well, and who asked hard questions, and his "wife," who had run off, was just any girl he had gone out with. He could not remember her now at all.

He envied in a way Mrs. Zilke's command over everything. She understood, it seemed, everything she dealt with, and she remembered and could identify all the things which came into her view and under her jurisdiction. The world for her, he was sure, was round, firm, and perfectly illuminated.

For him only his work (and he remembered she had called him a man of importance) had any real meaning, but its relationship to everything else was tenuous.

As he went upstairs that night he looked into his son's room. He was surprised to see that the boy was sleeping with an enormous toy crocodile. The sight of the toy rather shocked him. For a moment he hesitated whether or not to remove the toy and then deciding not to disturb him, he went to his room, took off all his clothes, and stood naked, breathing in front of the opened window. Then he went quickly to bed.

"It's his favorite doll," Mrs. Zilke said at breakfast. "He wouldn't part with it for the world." She referred to the toy crocodile.

"I would think it would give him nightmares," the father said.

"He don't have nightmares," Mrs. Zilke said, buttering the toast. "There you are, sir!" and she brought him his breakfast.

The father ate silently for a while.

"I was shocked to see that crocodile in his bed," he told Mrs. Zilke again.

"Well, that's something in you, is all," she said.

"I expect. But why couldn't it have been a teddy bear or a girl doll."

"He has those too. It just happened to be crocodile night last night," Mrs. Zilke said, restless now in the kitchen.

"All right," the father said, and he opened the newspaper and began to read about Egypt.

"Your boy needs a dog," Mrs. Zilke said without

warning, coming in and sitting down at the table with him. Her hands still showed the traces of soap suds.

"What kind?" the father said.

"You're not opposed to it, then?" Mrs. Zilke replied.

"Why would I oppose a dog?" He continued to look at the newspaper.

"He's got to have something," Mrs. Zilke told him.

"Of course," the father said, swallowing some coffee. Then, having swallowed, he stared at her.

"You mean he doesn't have anything?"

"As long as a parent is living, any parent, a child has something. No, I didn't mean *that*," she said without any real apology, and he expected, of course, none.

"I'd rather have him sleeping with a dog now than that crocodile."

"Oh, that," Mrs. Zilke said, impatient.

Then: "All right, then," he said.

He kept nodding after she had gone out of the room. He sat there looking at his old wedding ring which he still wore. Suddenly he took the ring off his finger for the first time since he had had it put on there by the priest. He had left it on all these years simply because, well, he wanted men to think he was married, he supposed. Everybody was married, and he had to be married somehow, anyhow, he knew.

But he left the wedding ring lying on the table, and he went into the front room.

"Sir," Mrs. Zilke called after him.

"Just leave the ring there," he said, thinking she had found it.

But on her face he saw something else. "You'll have to take the boy to buy the dog, you know. I can't walk on hard pavements anymore, remember."

"That will be fine, Mrs. Zilke," he said, somehow relieved at what she said.

The dog they bought at the shop was a small mongrel with a pitifully long tail, and—the father looked very close: brown eyes. Almost the first thing he did was to make a puddle near the father's desk. The father insisted on cleaning it up, and Baxter watched, while Mrs. Zilke muttered to herself in the kitchen. She came in finally and poured something white on the spot.

The dog watched them too from its corner, but it did not seem to want to come out to them.

"You must make up to your new little friend," the father said.

Baxter stared but did not do anything.

"Go to him," the father said, and the son went over into the corner and looked at the pup.

The father sat down at his desk and began to go through his papers.

"Did you have a dog?" Baxter asked his father.

The father thought there at the desk. He did not answer for a long time.

"Yes," the father finally said.

"What color was it," the son asked, and the father stirred in his chair.

"That was so long ago," he said almost as though quoting himself.

"Was it gray then?" the boy wanted to know.

The father nodded.

"A gray dog," the son said, and he began to play with his new pet. The dog lifted its wet paw and bit the boy mildly, and the boy cried a little.

"That's just in fun," the father said absentmindedly.

Baxter ran out into the kitchen, crying a little, and the small dog sat in the corner.

"Don't be afraid of the little fellow now," Mrs. Zilke said. "Go right back and make up to him again."

Baxter and Mrs. Zilke came out of the kitchen and went up to the dog.

"You'll have to name him too," Mrs. Zilke said.

"Will I have to name him, Daddy?" the boy said.

The father nodded.

After supper all three sat in the front room. Baxter nodded a little. The father sat in the easy chair smoking his pipe, a pony of brandy near him. They had gathered here to decide what name to choose for the dog, but nobody had any ideas, it seemed, and the father, hidden from them in a halo of expensive pipe smoke, seemed as far away as if he had gone to the capital again.

Baxter nodded some more and Mrs. Zilke said, "Why, it still isn't bedtime and the little man is asleep!"

From below in the basement where they had put the pup they could all hear the animal's crying, but they pretended not to notice.

Finally, Mrs. Zilke said, "When he is housebroken you can sleep with him, Baxter."

Baxter opened his eyes and looked at her. "What is that?" he said.

"When he learns to take care of himself, not make puddles, you can have him in bed with you."

"I don't want to," the boy said.

Mrs. Zilke looked stoically at the father.

"Why don't you want to, sweetheart," she said, but her words showed no emotion.

"I don't want anything," the boy said.

Mrs. Zilke looked at the father again, but he was even more lost to them.

"What's that hanging loose in your mouth," Mrs. Zilke suddenly sprang to attention, adjusting her spectacles, and looking at the boy's mouth.

"This." The boy pointed to his lips, and blushed slightly. "Gum," he said.

"Oh," Mrs. Zilke said.

The clock struck eight.

"I guess it *is* your bedtime," Mrs. Zilke said.

She watched the boy.

"Do you want to go to bed, Baxter," she said, abstractedly.

The boy nodded.

"Say goodnight to daddy and kiss him," she told him perfunctorily.

The boy got up and went over to his father, but stopped in front of the rings of smoke.

"Goodnight," the boy lisped.

"What's that in his mouth," the father addressed his remark to Mrs. Zilke and his head came out of the clouds of smoke.

Mrs. Zilke got up painfully now and putting on her other glasses looked at the boy.

"What are you sucking?" Mrs. Zilke said, and both of them now stared at him.

Baxter looked at them as though they had put a net about him. From his long indifference to these two people a sudden new feeling came slowly into his dazed, slowly moving mind. He moved back a step, as though he wanted to incite them.

"Baxter, sweetheart," the old woman said, and both she and the father stared at him as though they had found out perhaps who he was.

"What do you have in your mouth, son," the father said, and the word *son* sounded queer in the air, moving toward the boy with the heaviness and suggestion of nausea that the dog puddle had given him earlier in the afternoon.

"What is it, son," the father said, and Mrs. Zilke watched him, her new understanding of the boy written on her old red face.

"I'm chewing gum," the boy told them.

"No, you're not now, Baxter. Why don't you tell us," Mrs. Zilke whined.

Baxter went over into the corner where the dog had been.

"That dog is bad, isn't he," Baxter giggled, and then he suddenly laughed loudly when he thought what the dog had done.

Meanwhile Mrs. Zilke and the father were whispering in the cloud of tobacco smoke.

Baxter sat down on the floor talking to himself, and

playing with a broken piece of Tinker Toy. From his mouth still came sounds of something vaguely metallic.

Then Mrs. Zilke came up stealthily, a kind of sadness and kindness both in her face, like that of a trained nurse.

"You can't go to sleep with that in your mouth, sweetheart."

"It's gum," the boy said.

Mrs. Zilke's bad legs would not let her kneel down beside the boy on the floor as she wished to do. She wanted to have a close talk with him, as she did sitting by his bed in the nursery, but instead now, standing over him, so far away, her short heavy breathing sounding obnoxiously in the room, she said only, "You've never lied to me before, Baxter."

"Oh yes I have," Baxter said. "Anyhow this is gum," and he made the sounds again in his mouth.

"I'll have to tell your father," she said, as though *he* were already away in Washington.

"It's gum," the boy said in a bored voice.

"It's metal, I think," she said looking worriedly at the boy.

"It's just gum." The boy hummed now and played with the Tinker Toy.

"You'll have to speak to him," Mrs. Zilke said.

The father squatted down with the son, and the boy vaguely realized this was the first time the father had ever made the motion of playing with him. He stared at his father, but did not listen to what he was talking about.

"If I put my finger in your mouth will you give it to me?" the father said.

"No," the boy replied.

"You wouldn't want to swallow the thing in your mouth," the father said.

"Why not," the boy wondered.

"It would hurt you," the father told him.

"You would have to go to the hospital," Mrs. Zilke said.

"I don't care where I go," the boy said. "It's a toy I have in my mouth."

"What sort of toy," the father wondered, and he and Mrs.

Zilke suddenly became absorbed in the curiosity of what Baxter had there.

"A golden toy," the boy laughed, but his eyes looked glassy and strange.

"Please," the father said, and he put his finger gently on the boy's lips.

"Don't touch me!" the son called out suddenly. "I hate you!"

The father drew back softly as though now he would return to his work and his papers, and it was Mrs. Zilke who cried out instead: "Shame!"

"I do hate him," the boy said. "He's never here anyhow."

"Baxter," the father said.

"Give your father what's in your mouth or you will swallow it and something terrible will happen to you."

"I want it right where it is," the boy said, and he threw the Tinker Toy at Mrs. Zilke.

"Look here now, Baxter," the father said, but still sleepily and with no expression.

"Shut your goddamn face," the boy spat out at his father.

The father suddenly seized the boy's chin and jaw and forced him to spit out what he had.

His wedding ring fell on the carpet there, and they all stared at it a second.

Without warning the son kicked the father vigorously in the groin and escaped, running up the stairs.

Baxter stepped deliberately from the safety of the upper staircase and pronounced the obscene word for his father as though this was what he had been keeping for him for a long time.

Mrs. Zilke let out a low cry.

The father writhing in pain from the place where the boy had kicked him, managed to say with great effort: "Tell me where he learned a word like that."

Mrs. Zilke went over to where the ring lay now near the Tinker Toy.

"I don't know what's happening to people," she said, putting the ring on the table.

Then, a weary concern in her voice, she said, "Sir, are you hurt?"

The tears fell from the father's eyes for having been hit in such a delicate place, and he could not say anything more for a moment.

"Can I do anything for you, sir?" Mrs. Zilke said.

"I don't think right now, thank you," he said. "Thank you." He grunted with the exquisite pain.

"I've put your ring up here for safekeeping," she informed him.

The father nodded from the floor where he twisted in his pain.

• You May Safely Gaze •

DO we always have to begin on Milo at these Wednesday lunches," Philip said to Guy. Carrying their trays, they had already picked out their table in the cafeteria, and Philip, at least, was about to sit down.

"Do I *always* begin on Milo?" Guy wondered, surprised.

"You're the one who knows him, remember," Philip said.

"Of course, Milo is one of the serious problems in our office, and it's only a little natural, I suppose, to mention problems even at one of our Wednesday lunches."

"Oh, forget it," Philip said. Seated, he watched half-amused as Guy still stood over the table with his tray raised like a busboy who would soon now move away with it to the back room.

"I don't dislike Milo," Guy began. "It's not that at all."

Philip began to say something but then hesitated, and looked up at the cafeteria clock that showed ten minutes past twelve. He knew, somehow, that it was going to be Milo all over again for lunch.

"It's his attitude not just toward his work, but life," Guy said, and this time he sat down.

"His life," Philip said, taking swift bites of his chicken à la king.

Guy nodded. "You see now he spares himself the real work in the office due to this physical culture philosophy. He won't even let himself get mad anymore or argue with me because that interferes with the development of his muscles and his mental tranquillity, which is so important for muscular development. His whole life now he says is to be strong and calm."

"A muscle ascetic," Philip laughed without amusement.

"But working with him is not so funny," Guy said, and Philip was taken aback to see his friend go suddenly very pale. Guy had not even bothered to take his dishes off his tray but

25

allowed everything to sit there in front of him as though the lunch were an offering he had no intention of tasting.

"Milo hardly seems anybody you and I could know, if you ask me," Guy pronounced, as though the final decision had at last been made.

"You forget one of us *doesn't*," Philip emphasized again, and he waved his fork as though they had finally finished now with Milo, and could go on to the real Wednesday lunch.

But Guy began again, as though the talk for the lunch had been arranged after all, despite Philip's forgetfulness, around Milo.

"I don't think he is even studying law anymore at night, as he was supposed to do."

"Don't tell me that," Philip said, involuntarily affecting concern and half-resigning himself now to the possibility of a completely wasted hour.

"Oh, of course," Guy softened his statement, "I guess he goes to the law library every night and reads a little. Every waking hour is, after all, not for his muscles, but every real thought, you can bet your bottom dollar, *is*."

"I see," Philip said, beginning on his pineapple snow.

"It's the only thing on his mind, I tell you," Guy began again.

"It's interesting if that's the only thing on his mind, then," Philip replied. "I mean," he continued, when he saw the black look he got from Guy, "—to know somebody who is obsessed . . ."

"What do you mean by that?" Guy wondered critically, as though only he could tell what it was that Milo might be.

"You said he wanted to devote himself to just this one thing." Philip wearily tried to define what he had meant.

"I tried to talk to Milo once about it," Guy said, now deadly serious, and as though, with all preliminaries past, the real part of his speech had begun. Philip noticed that his friend had still not even picked up his knife or fork, and his food must be getting stone cold by now. " 'Why do you want to look any stronger,' I said to Milo. He just stared at me, and I said,

'Have you ever taken a good look in the mirror the way you
are now,' and he just smiled his sour smile again at me. 'Have
you ever looked, Milo?' I said, and even I had to laugh when
I repeated my own question, and he kind of laughed then too
. . . Well, for God's sake, he knows after all that nobody but
a few freaks are going to look like he looks, or will look, if he
keeps this up. You see he works on a new part of his body
every month. One month he will be working on his pectorals,
the next his calf muscles, then he will go in for a period on his
latissimus dorsi."

Philip stopped chewing a moment as though seeing these
different muscle groups slowly developing there before him.
Finally, he managed to say, "Well at least he's interested in
something, which is more than . . ."

"Yes, he's interested in *it,* of course," Guy interrupted,
"—what he calls being the sculptor of his own body, and you
can find him almost any noon in the gym straining away while
the other men in our office do as they please with their lunch
hour."

"You mean they eat their lunch then." Philip tried
humor.

"That's right," Guy hurried on. "But he and this Austrian
friend of his who also works in my office, they go over to this
gym run by a cripple named Vic somebody, and strain their
guts out, lifting barbells and throwing their arms up and
around on benches, with dumbbells in their fists, and come
back an hour later to their work looking as though they had
been in a rock mixer. They actually stink of gym, and several
of the stenographers have complained saying they always
know when it's exercise day all right. But nothing stops those
boys, and they just take all the gaff with as much good humor
as two such egomaniacs can have."

"Why egomaniacs, for God's sake," Philip wondered, putting his fork down with a bang.

"Well, Philip," Guy pleaded now. "To think of their own
bodies like that. These are not young boys, you know. They
must be twenty-five or so, along in there, and you would think

they would begin to think of other people, other people's bodies, at least." Guy laughed as though to correct his own severity before Philip. "But no," he went on. "They have to be Adonises."

"And their work suffers?" Philip wondered vaguely, as though, if the topic had to be continued, they might now examine it from this aspect.

"The kind of work young men like them do — it don't matter, you know, if you're good or not, nobody knows if you're really good. They do their work and get it out on time, and you know their big boss is still that old gal of seventy who is partial to young men. She sometimes goes right up to Milo, who will be sitting at his desk relaxed as a jellyfish, doing nothing, and she says, 'Roll up your sleeves, why don't you, and take off your necktie on a warm day like this,' and it will be thirty degrees outside and cool even in the office. And Milo will smile like a four-year-old at her because he loves admiration more than anything in the world, and he rolls up his sleeves and then all this bulge of muscle comes out, and the old girl looks like she'd seen glory, she's that gone on having a thug like that around."

"But you sound positively bilious over it," Philip laughed.

"Philip, look," Guy said with his heavy masculine patience, "doesn't it sound wrong to you, now seriously?"

"What in hell do you mean by wrong, though?"

"Don't be that way. You know goddamn well what I mean."

"Well, then, no, I can't say it is. Milo or whatever his name."

"You know it's Milo," Guy said positively disgusted.

"Well, he is, I suppose, more typical than you might think from the time, say, when you were young. Maybe there weren't such fellows around then."

"Oh there were, of course."

"Well, now there are more, and Milo is no exception."

"But he looks at himself all the time, and he has got himself tattooed recently and there in front of the one mirror in the office, it's not the girls who stand there, no, it's Milo and this Austrian boy. They're always washing their hands or combing their hair, or just looking at themselves right out, not sneaky-like the way most men do, but like some goddamn chorus girls. And oh, I forgot, this Austrian fellow got tattooed too because Milo kept after him, and then he was sorry. It seems the Austrian's physical culture instructor gave him hell and said he had spoiled the appearance of his deltoids by having the tattoo work done."

"Don't tell me," Philip said.

Guy stared as he heard Philip's laugh, but then continued: "They talked about the tattoo all morning, in front of all the stenogs, and whether this Austrian had spoiled the appearance of his deltoid muscles or not."

"Well, it *is* funny, of course, but I couldn't get worked up about it the way you are."

"They're a symbol of the new America and I don't like it."

"You're terribly worked up."

"Men on their way to being thirty, what used to be considered middle age, developing their bodies and special muscles and talking about their parts in front of women."

"But they're married men, aren't they?"

"Oh sure," Guy dismissed this. "Married and with kids."

"What more do you want then. Some men are nuts about their bowling scores and talk about that all the time in front of everybody."

"I see you approve of them."

"I didn't say that. But I think you're overreacting, to use the phrase . . ."

"You don't have to work with them," Guy went on. "You don't have to watch them in front of the one and only office mirror."

"Look, I've known a lot of women who griped me because they were always preening themselves, goddamn narcissists too. I don't care for narcissists of either sex."

"Talk about Narciss-uses," said Guy. "The worst was last summer when I went with Mae to the beach, and there *they* were, both of them, right in front of us on the sand."

Philip stiffened slightly at the prospect of more.

"Milo and the Austrian," Guy shook his head. "And as it was Saturday afternoon there didn't seem to be a damn place free on the beach and Mae wanted to be right up where these Adonises or Narciss-uses, or whatever you call them, were. I said, 'We don't want to camp here, Mae,' and she got suddenly furious. I couldn't tell her how those birds affected me, and they hardly even spoke to me either, come to think about it. Milo spit something out the side of his mouth when he saw me, as though to say *that for you.*"

"That was goddamn awful for you," Philip nodded.

"Wait till you hear what happened, for crying out loud. I shouldn't tell this during my lunch hour because it still riles me."

"Don't get riled then. Forget them."

"I have to tell you," Guy said. "I've never told anybody before, and you're the only man I know will listen to a thing like this. . . . You know," he went on then, as though this point were now understood at last between them, "Mae started staring at them right away. 'Who on earth are they?' she said, and I couldn't tell whether she was outraged or pleased, maybe she was a bit of both because she just fixed her gaze on them like paralyzed. 'Aren't you going to put on your sun tan lotion and your glasses?' I said to her, and she turned on me as though I had hit her. 'Why don't you let a woman relax when I never get out of the house but twice in one year,' she told me. I just lay back then on the sand and tried to forget they were there and that she was there and that even I was there."

Philip began to light up his cigarette, and Guy said, "Are you all done eating already?" and he looked at his own plate of veal cutlet and peas which was nearly untouched. "My God, you are a fast eater. Why, do you realize how fast you eat," he told Philip, and Philip said he guessed he half-realized it. He said at night he ate slower.

"In the bosom of your family," Guy laughed.

Philip looked at the cafeteria clock and stirred unceremoniously.

"But I wanted to finish telling you about these boys."

"Is there *more?*" Philip pretended surprise.

"Couldn't you tell the way I told it there was," Guy said, an indeterminate emotion in his voice.

"I hope nothing happened to Mae," Philip offered weakly.

"Nothing ever happens to Mae," Guy dismissed this impatiently. "No, it was them, of course. Milo and the Austrian began putting on a real show, you know, for everybody, and as it was Saturday afternoon, as I said, nearly everybody from every office in the world was there, and they were all watching Milo and the Austrian. So, first they just did the standard routine, warm-ups, you know, etc., but from the first every eye on the beach was on them, they seemed to have the old presence, even the lifeguards were staring at them as though nobody would ever dare drown while they were carrying on, so first of all then they did handstands and though they did them good, not good enough for that many people to be watching. After all somebody is always doing handstands on the beach, you know. I think it was their hair attracted people, they have very odd hair, they look like brothers that way. Their hair is way too thick, and of course too long for men of our generation. . . ."

"Well, how old do you think I am?" Philip laughed.

"All right, of *my* generation, then," Guy corrected with surliness. He went on, however, immediately: "I think the reason everybody watched was their hair, which is a peculiar kind of chestnut color, natural and all that, but maybe due to the sun and all their exercising had taken on a funny shade, and then their muscles were so enormous in that light, bulging and shining with oil and matching somehow their hair that I think that was really what kept people looking and not what they did. They didn't look quite real, even though in a way they are the style.

"I kept staring, and Mae said, 'I thought you wasn't going to watch,' and I could see she was completely held captive by their performance as was, I guess, everybody by then on the goddamn beach.

" 'I can't help looking at freaks,' I told Mae, and she gave me one of her snorts and just kept looking kind of bitter and satisfied at seeing something like that. She's a great woman for sights like that, she goes to all the stock shows, and almost every nice Sunday she takes the kids to the zoo. . . .''

"Well, what finally did come off?" Philip said, pushing back his chair.

"The thing that happened, nobody in his right mind would ever believe, and probably lots of men and boys who saw it happen never went home and told their families."

"It should have been carried in the papers then," Philip said coolly and he drank all of his as yet untouched glass of water.

"I don't know what word I would use to describe it," Guy said. "Mae has never mentioned it to this day, though she said a little about it on the streetcar on the way home that afternoon, but just a little, like she would have referred to a woman having fainted and been rushed to the hospital, something on that order."

"Well, for Pete's sake now, what did happen?" Philip's ill humor broke forth for a moment, and he bent his head away from Guy's look.

"As I said," Guy continued quietly, "they did all those more fancy exercises then after their warm-ups, like leaping on one another's necks, jumping hard on each other's abdomens to show what iron men they were, and some rough stuff but which they made look fancy, like they threw one another to the sand as though it was a cross between a wrestling match and an apache dance, and then they began to do some things looked like they were out of the ballet, with lots of things like jumping in air and splits, you know. You know what kind of trunks that kind of Narciss-uses wear, well these were tighter than usual, the kind to make a bullfighter's pants look baggy and oversize, and as though they had planned it, while doing one of their big movements, their trunks both split clear in two, at the same time, with a sound, I swear, you could have heard all over that beach.

"Instead of feeling at least some kind of self-consciousness, if not shame, they both busted out laughing and hugged one another as though they'd made a touchdown, and they might as well both been naked by now, they just stood there and looked down at themselves from time to time like they were alone in the shower, and laughed and laughed, and an old woman next to them just laughed and laughed too, and all Mae did was look once and then away with a funny half-smile on her mouth, she didn't show any more concern over it than the next one. Here was a whole beach of mostly women, just laughing their heads off because two men no longer young, were, well, exposing themselves in front of everybody, for that's all it was."

Philip stared at his empty water glass.

"I started to say something to Mae, and she nearly cut my head off, saying something like *why don't you mind your own goddamn business* in a tone unusually mean even for her. *Don't look damn you if you don't like it* was what my own wife said to me."

Suddenly Philip had relaxed in his chair as though the water he had drunk had contained a narcotic. He made no effort now to show his eagerness to leave, to hurry, or to comment on what was being said, and he sat there staring in the direction of, but not at, Guy.

"But the worst part came then," Guy said, and then looking critically and uneasily at Philip, he turned round to look at the cafeteria clock, but it showed only five minutes to one, and their lunch hour was not precisely over.

"This old woman," he continued, swallowing hard, "who had been sitting there next to them got out a sewing kit she had, and do you know what?"

"I suppose she sewed them shut," Philip said sleepily and still staring at nothing.

"That's exactly correct," Guy said, a kind of irritated disappointment in his voice. "This old woman who looked at least eighty went right up to them the way they were and she

must have been a real seamstress, and before the whole crowd
with them two grown men laughing their heads off she sewed
up their tights like some old witch in a story, and Mae sat there
as cool as if we was playing bridge in the church basement, and
never said boo, and when I began to really let off steam, she
said *Will you keep your big old ugly mouth shut or am I going to have
to hit you over the mouth with my beach clogs.* That's how they had
affected my own wife.

"So," Guy said, after a pause in which Philip contributed
nothing, "this country has certainly changed since I grew up
in it. I said that to Mae and that was the final thing I had to
say on the subject, and those two grown men went right on
lying there on the sand, every so often slapping one another
on their muscles, and combing their hair with oil, and
laughing all the time, though I think even they did have sense
enough not to get up and split their trunks again or even they
must have known they would have been arrested by the beach
patrol."

"Sure," Philip said vacantly.

"So that's the story of Milo and the Austrian," Guy said.

"It's typical," Philip said, like a somnambulist.

"Are you sore at me or something," Guy said, picking up
his and Philip's checks.

"Let me pay my own, for Christ's sake," Philip said.

"Listen, you *are* sore at me, I believe," Guy said.

"I have a rotten headache is all," Philip replied, and he
picked up his own check.

"I hope I didn't bring it on by talking my head off."

"No," Philip replied. "I had it since morning."

• Don't Call Me by My Right Name •

HER new name was Mrs. Klein. There was something in the meaning that irritated her. She liked everything about her husband except his name and that had never pleased her. She had fallen in love with him before she found out what his name was. Once she knew he was Klein, her disappointment had been strong. Names do make a great difference, and after six months of marriage she found herself still not liking her name. She began using more and more her maiden name. Then she always called herself on her letters Lois McBane. Her husband seldom saw the mail arrive so perhaps he did not know, and had he known she went by her old name he might not have cared enough to feel any particular hurt.

Lois Klein, she often thought as she lay next to her husband in bed. It is not the name of a woman like myself. It does not reflect my character.

One evening at a party when there had been more drinking for her than usual, she said offhand to him in the midst of some revelry: "I would like you to change your name."

He did not understand. He thought that it was a remark she was making in drink which did not refer to anything concrete, just as once she had said to him, "I want you to begin by taking your head off regularly." The remark had meant nothing, and he let it pass.

"Frank," she said, "you must change your name, do you hear? I cannot go on being Mrs. Klein."

Several people heard what it was she said, and they laughed loudly so that Lois and Frank would hear them appreciating the remark.

"If you were all called Mrs. Klein," she said turning to the men who were laughing, "you would not like to be Mrs. Klein either."

35

Being all men, they laughed harder.

"Well, you married him, didn't you," a man said, "and we guess you will have to keep his name."

"If he changed his name," another of the men said, "what name would you have him change it to?"

Frank put his hand on her glass, as though to tell her they must go home, but she seized the glass with his hand on it and drank quickly out of it.

"I hadn't thought what name I did want," she said, puzzled.

"Well, you aren't going to change your name," Frank said. "The gentlemen know that."

"The gentlemen do?" she asked him. "Well, I don't know what name I would like it changed to," she admitted to the men.

"You don't look much like Mrs. Klein," one of the men said and began to laugh again.

"You're not friends!" she called back at them.

"What are we, then?" they asked.

"Why don't I look like Mrs. Klein?" she wanted to know.

"Don't you ever look in the mirror?" one of the men replied.

"We ought to go, Lois," her husband said.

She sat there as though she had heard the last of the many possible truths she could hear about herself.

"I wonder how I will get out of here, Frank," she said.

"Out of where, dear?" he wondered. He was suddenly sad enough himself to be dead, but he managed to say something to her at this point.

"Out of where I seem to have got into," she told him.

The men had moved off now and were laughing among themselves. Frank and Lois did not notice this laughter.

"I'm not going to change my name," he said, as though to himself. Then turning to her: "I know it's supposed to be wrong to tell people when they're drunk the insane whim they're having is insane, but I am telling you now and I may tell the whole room of men."

"I have to have my name changed, Frank," she said. "You know I can't stand to be tortured. It is too painful and I am not young anymore. I am getting old and fat."

"No wife of mine would ever be old or fat," he said.

"I just cannot be Mrs. Klein and face the world."

"Anytime you want me to pull out is all right," he said. "Do you want me to pull out?"

"What are you saying?" she wanted to know. "What did you say about pulling out?"

"I don't want any more talk about your changing your name or I intend to pull up stakes."

"I don't know what you're talking about. You know you can't leave me. What would I do, Frank, at my age?"

"I told you no wife of mine is old."

"I couldn't find anybody now, Frank, if you went."

"Then quit talking about changing our name."

"*Our* name? I don't know what you mean by *our* name."

He took her drink out of her hand and when she coaxed and whined he struck her not too gently over the mouth.

"What was the meaning of that?" she wanted to know.

"Are you coming home, Mrs. Klein?" he said, and he hit her again. Her lip was cut against her teeth so that you could see it beginning to bleed.

"Frank, you're abusing me," she said, white and wide-eyed now, and as though tasting the blood slightly with the gin and soda mix.

"Mrs. Klein," he said idiotically.

It was one of those fake dead long parties where nobody actually knows anybody and where people could be pushed out of windows without anybody's being sure until the morrow.

"I'm not going home as Mrs. Klein," she said.

He hit her again.

"Frank, you have no right to hit me just because I hate your name."

"If you hate my name what do you feel then for me? Are you going to act like my wife or not."

"I don't want to have babies, Frank. I will not go through that at my age. Categorically not."

He hit her again so that she fell on the floor, but this did not seem to surprise either her or him because they both continued the conversation.

"I can't make up my mind what to do," she said, weeping a little. "I know of course what the safe thing is to do."

"Either you come out of here with me as Mrs. Klein, or I go to a hotel room alone. Here's the key to the house," he said, and he threw it on the floor at her.

Several of the men at the party had begun to notice what was really going on now. They thought that it was married clowning at first and they began to gather around in a circle, but what they saw had something empty and stiff about it that did not interest and yet kept one somehow watching. For one thing, Mrs. Klein's dress had come up and exposed her legs, which were not beautiful.

"I can't decide if I can go on with his name," she explained from the floor position to the men.

"Well, it's a little late, isn't it, Mrs. Klein," one of the men said in a sleepy voice.

"It's never too late, I don't suppose, is it?" she inquired. "Oh, I can't believe it is even though I feel old."

"Well, you're not young," the same man ventured. "You're too old to be lying there."

"My husband can't see my point of view," she explained. "And that is why he can't understand why his name doesn't fit me. I was unmarried too long, I suppose, to suddenly surrender my own name. I have always been known professionally and socially under my own name and it is hard to change now, I can tell you. I don't think I can go home with him unless he lets me change my name."

"I will give you just two minutes," Mr. Klein said.

"For what? Only two minutes for what?" she cried.

"To make up your mind what name you are going out of here with."

"I know, men," she said, "what the sensible decision is,

and tomorrow, of course, when I'm sober I will wish I had
taken it."

Turning to Frank Klein, she said simply, "You will have
to go your way without me."

He looked hurriedly around as though looking for an exit
to leave by, and then he looked back to her on the floor as
though he could not come to a decision.

"Come to your senses," Frank Klein said unemphatically.

"There were hundreds of Kleins in the telephone direc-
tory," she went on, "but when people used to come to my
name they recognized at once that I was the only woman going
under my own special name."

"For Jesus Christ's sake, Lois," he said, turning a peculiar
green color.

"I can't go with you as Mrs. Klein," she said.

"Well, let me help you up," he said.

She managed to let him help her up.

"I'm not going home with you, but I will send you in a
cab," he informed her.

"Are you leaving me?" she wanted to know.

He did not know what to say. He felt anything he said
might destroy his mind. He stood there with an insane emptiness on his eyes and lips.

Everyone had moved off from them. There was a silence
from the phonograph and from the TV set which had both
been going at the same time. The party was over and people
were calling down to cabs from all the windows.

"Why won't you come home with me?" she said in a
whisper.

Suddenly he hurried out the door without waiting for her.

"Frank!" she called after him, and a few of the men from
the earlier group came over and joked with her.

"He went out just like a boy, without any sense of responsibility," she said to them without any expression in her voice.

She hurried on out too, not waiting to put her coat on
straight.

She stood outside in the fall cold and shivered. Some

children went by dressed in Hallowe'en costumes.

"Is she dressed as anybody?" one of the children said pointlessly.

"Frank!" she began calling. "I don't know what is happening really," she said to herself.

Suddenly he came up to her from behind a hedge next to where she was standing.

"I couldn't quite bring myself to go off," he said.

She thought for a minute of hitting him with her purse which she had remembered to bring, but she did nothing now but watch him.

"Will you change your name?" she said.

"We will live together the way we have been," he said not looking at her.

"We can't be married, Frank, with that name between us."

Suddenly he hit her and knocked her down to the pavement.

She lay there for a minute before anything was said.

"Are you conscious?" he said crouching down beside her. "Tell me if you are suffering," he wanted to know.

"You have hurt something in my head, I think," she said, getting up slightly on one elbow.

"You have nearly driven me out of my mind," he said, and he was making funny sounds in his mouth. "You don't know what it means to have one's name held up to ridicule like this. You are such a cruel person, Lois."

"We will both change our names, if you like," she said.

"Why do you torture me?" he said. "Why is it you can't control your power to torture?"

"Then we won't think about it, we will go home," she said, in a cold comforting voice. "Only I think I am going to be sick," she warned.

"We will go home," he said in a stupid voice.

"I will let you call me Mrs. Klein this one evening, then tomorrow we will have a good talk." At the same moment she fell back on the walk.

Some young men from the delicatessen who had been doing inventory came by and asked if there was anything they could do.

"My wife fell on the walk," he said. "I thought she was all right. She was talking to me just a moment ago."

"Was it your wife, did you say?" the younger man leaned down to look at her.

"Mrs. Klein," Frank replied.

"You are Mr. Klein, then?"

"I don't understand," the older of the two young men said. "You don't look somehow like her husband."

"We have been married six months."

"I think you ought to call a doctor," the younger man said. "She is bleeding at the mouth."

"I hit her at a party," Frank said.

"What did you say your name was?" the older man asked.

"Mr. Klein. She is Mrs. Klein," Frank told them.

The two men from the delicatessen exchanged looks.

"Did you push her?" the one man asked.

"Yes," Frank said. "I hit her. She didn't want to be Mrs. Klein."

"You're drunk," the one man ventured an opinion.

Lois suddenly came to. "Frank, you will have to take me home," she said. "There is something wrong with my head. My God," she began to scream, "I am in awful pain."

Frank helped her up again.

"Is this your husband?" the one man asked.

She nodded.

"What is your name?" he wanted to know.

"It's none of your business," she said.

"Are you Mrs. Klein?" he asked.

"No," Lois replied. "I don't happen to be Mrs. Klein."

"Come on, J.D., we can't get mixed up in this," the younger man said. "Whatever the hell their names are."

"Well, I'm not Mrs. Klein, whoever you are," she said.

Immediately then she struck Frank with the purse and he fell back in surprise against the building wall.

"Call me a cab, you cheap son of a bitch," she said. "Can't you see I'm bleeding?"

• Eventide •

MAHALA had waited as long as she thought she could;
after all, Plumy had left that morning and now here it was
going on four o'clock. It was hardly fair if she was loitering,
but she knew that certainly Plumy would never loiter on a day
like this when Mahala wanted so to hear. It was in a way the
biggest day of her whole life, bigger than any day she had ever
lived through as a girl or young woman. It was the day that
decided whether her son would come back to live with her or
not.

And just think, a whole month had rolled past since he
left home. Two months ago if anyone had said that Teeboy
would leave home, she would have stopped dead in her tracks,
it would have been such a terrible thing even to say, and now
here she was, talking over the telephone about how Teeboy
had gone.

"My Teeboy is gone," that is what Mahala said for a long
time after the departure. These words announced to her mind
what had happened, and just as an announcement they gave
some mild comfort, like a pain-killer with a fatal disease.

"My Teeboy," she would say, like the mother of a dead
son, like the mother of a son who had died in battle, because
it hurt as much to have a son missing in peacetime as to have
lost him through war.

The room seemed dark even with the summer sunshine
outside, and close, although the window was open. There was
a darkness all over the city. The fire department had been
coming and going all afternoon. There were so many fires in
the neighborhood—that is what she was saying to Cora on the
telephone, too many fires: the fire chief had just whizzed past
again. No, she said to Cora, she didn't know if it was in the
white section of town or theirs, she couldn't tell, but oh it was
so hot to have a fire.

43

Talking about the fires seemed to help Mahala more than anything. She called several other old friends and talked about the fires and she mentioned that Teeboy had not come home. The old friends did not say much about Teeboy's not having returned, because, well, what was there to say about a boy who had been practicing to leave home for so long. Everyone had known it but her blind mother love.

"What do you suppose can be keeping my sister Plumy?" Mahala said to herself as she walked up and down the hall and looked out from behind the screen in the window. "She would have to fail me on the most important errand in the world."

Then she thought about how much Plumy hated to go into white neighborhoods, and how the day had been hot and she thought of the fires and how perhaps Plumy had fallen under a fire truck and been crushed. She thought of all the possible disasters and was not happy, and always in the background there was the fresh emotion of having lost Teeboy.

"People don't know," she said, "that I can't live without Teeboy."

She would go in the clothes closet and look at his dirty clothes just as he had left them; she would kiss them and press them to her face, smelling them; the odors were especially dear to her. She held his rayon trousers to her bosom and walked up and down the small parlor. She had not prayed; she was waiting for Plumy to come home first, then maybe they would have prayer.

"I hope I ain't done anything I'll be sorry for," she said.

It was then, though, when she felt the worst, that she heard the steps on the front porch. Yes, those were Plumy's steps, she was coming with the news. But whatever the news was, she suddenly felt, she could not accept it.

As she came up the steps, Plumy did not look at Mahala with any particular kind of meaning on her face. She walked unsteadily, as if the heat had been too much for her.

"Come on in now, Plumy, and I will get you something cool to drink."

Inside, Plumy watched Mahala as if afraid she was going

to ask her to begin at once with the story, but Mahala only waited, not saying anything, sensing the seriousness of Plumy's knowledge and knowing that this knowledge could be revealed only when Plumy was ready.

While Mahala waited patiently there in the kitchen, Plumy arranged herself in the easy chair, and when she was once settled, she took up the straw fan which lay on the floor.

"Well, I seen him!" Plumy brought the words out.

This beginning quieted the old mother a little. She closed her mouth and folded her hands, moving now to the middle of the parlor, with an intentness on her face as if she was listening to something high up in the sky, like a plane which is to drop something, perhaps harmless and silver, to the ground.

"I seen him!" Plumy repeated, as if to herself. "And I seen all the white people!" she finished, anger coming into her voice.

"Oh, Plumy," Mahala whined. Then suddenly she made a gesture for her sister to be quiet because she thought she heard the fire department going again, and then when there was no sound, she waited for her to go on, but Plumy did not say anything. In the slow afternoon there was nothing, only a silence a city sometimes has within itself.

Plumy was too faint from the heat to go on at once; her head suddenly shook violently and she slumped in the chair.

"Plumy Jackson!" Mahala said, going over to her. "You didn't *walk* here from the white district! You didn't walk them forty-seven blocks in all this August heat!"

Plumy did not answer immediately. Her hand caressed the worn upholstery of the chair.

"You know how nervous white folks make me," she said at last.

Mahala made a gesture of disgust. "Lord, to think you walked it in this hot sun. Oh, I don't know why God wants to upset me like this. As if I didn't have enough to make me wild already, without havin' you come home in this condition."

Mahala watched her sister's face for a moment with the same figuring expression of the man who comes to read the

water meter. She saw everything she really wanted to know on
Plumy's face: all her questions were answered for her there, yet
she pretended she didn't know the verdict; she brought the one
question out:

"You did see Teeboy, honey?" she said, her voice changed
from her tears. She waited a few seconds, and then as Plumy
did not answer but only sank deeper into the chair, she continued: "What word did he send?"

"It's the way I told you before," Plumy replied crossly.
"Teeboy ain't coming back. I thought you knowed from the
way I looked at you that he ain't coming back."

Mahala wept quietly into a small handkerchief.

"Your pain is realer to me sometimes than my own,"
Plumy said, watching her cry. "That's why I hate to say to you
he won't never come back, but it's true as death he won't."

"When you say that to me I got a feeling inside myself like
everything had been busted and taken; I got the feeling like I
don't have nothing left inside of me."

"Don't I know that feeling!" Plumy said, almost angrily,
resting the straw fan on the arm of the chair, and then suddenly fanning herself violently so that the strokes sounded like
those of a small angry whip. "Didn't I lose George Watson of
sleeping sickness and all 'cause doctor wouldn't come?"

Plumy knew that Mahala had never shown any interest in
the death of her own George Watson and that it was an
unwelcome subject, especially tonight, when Teeboy's never
coming back had become final, yet she could not help mentioning George Watson just the same. In Mahala's eyes there really had never been any son named George Watson; there was
only a son named Teeboy and Mahala was the only mother.

"It ain't like there bein' no way out to your troubles: it's
the way out that kills you," Mahala said. "If it was goodbye
for always like when someone dies, I think I could stand it better. But this kind of parting ain't like the Lord's way!"

Plumy continued fanning herself, just letting Mahala run
on.

"So he ain't never coming back!" Mahala began beating

her hands together as if she were hearing music for a dance.

Plumy looked away as the sound of the rats downstairs caught her attention; there seemed to be more than usual tonight and she wondered why they were running so much, for it was so hot everywhere.

Her attention strayed back to Mahala standing directly in front of her now, talking about her suffering: "You go through all the suffering and the heartache," she said, "and then they go away. The only time children is nice is when they're babies and you know they can't get away from you. You got them then and your love is all they crave. They don't know who you are exactly, they just know you are the one to give them your love, and they ask you for it until you're worn out giving it."

Mahala's speech set Plumy to thinking of how she had been young and how she had had George Watson, and how he had died of sleeping sickness when he was four.

"My only son died of sleeping sickness," Plumy said aloud, but not really addressing Mahala. "I never had another. My husband said it was funny. He was not a religious man, but he thought it was queer."

"Would you like a cooling drink?" Mahala said absently.

Plumy shook her head and there was a silence of a few minutes in which the full weight of the heat of evening took possession of the small room.

"I can't get used to the idea of him *never* comin' back!" Mahala began again. "I ain't never been able to understand that word *never* anyhow. And now it's like to drive me wild."

There was another long silence, and then, Mahala suddenly rousing herself from drowsiness and the heat of the evening, began eagerly: "How did he look, Plumy? Tell me how he looked, and what he was doing. Just describe."

"He wasn't doin' nothin'!" Plumy said flatly. "He looked kind of older, though, like he had been thinking about new things."

"Don't keep me waiting," Mahala whined. "I been waitin' all day for the news, don't keep me no more, when I tell you

I could suicide over it all. I ain't never been through such a hell day. Don't you keep me waitin'."

"Now hush," Plumy said. "Don't go frettin' like this. Your heart won't take a big grief like this if you go fret so."

"It's *so* unkind of you not to tell," she muffled her lips in her handkerchief.

Plumy said: "I told you I talked to him, but I didn't tell you where. It was in a drinking place called the Music Box. He called to me from inside. The minute I looked at him I knew there was something wrong. There was something wrong with his hair."

"With his hair!" Mahala cried.

"Then I noticed he had had it all made straight! That's right," she said looking away from Mahala's eyes. "He had had his hair straightened. 'Why ain't you got in touch with your mother,' I said. 'If you only knowed how she was carryin' on.'

"Then he told me how he had got a tenor sax and how he was playing it in the band at the Music Box and that he had begun a new life, and it was all on account of his having the tenor sax and being a musician. He said the players didn't have time to have homes. He said they were playing all the time, they never went home, and that was why he hadn't been."

Plumy stopped. She saw the tenor sax only in her imagination because he had not shown it to her, she saw it curved and golden and heard it playing far-off melodies. But the real reason she stopped was not on account of the tenor sax but because of the memory of the white woman who had come out just then. The white woman had come out and put her arm around Teeboy. It had made her get creepy all over. It was the first time that Plumy had realized that Teeboy's skin was nearly as light as the white people's.

Both Teeboy and the woman had stood there looking at Plumy, and Plumy had not known how to move away from them. The sun beat down on her in the street but she could not move. She saw the streetcars going by with all the white people pushing one another around and she looked around on the scorched pavements and everyone was white, with Teeboy looking just as white as the rest of them, looking just as white as if he had come out of Mahala's body white, and as if Mahala had been a white woman and not her sister, and as if Mahala's mother and hers had not been black.

Then slowly she had begun walking away from Teeboy and the Music Box, almost without knowing she was going herself, walking right on through the streets without knowing what was happening, through the big August heat, without an umbrella or a hat to keep off the sun; she could see no place to stop, and people could see the circles of sweat that were forming all over her dress. She was afraid to stop and she was afraid to go on walking. She felt she would fall down eventually in the afternoon sun and it would be like the time George Watson had died of sleeping sickness, nobody would help her to an easy place.

Would George Watson know her now? That is what she was thinking as she walked through the heat of that afternoon. Would he know her—because when she had been his mother she had been young and her skin, she was sure, had been lighter; and now she was older looking than she remembered her own mother ever being, and her skin was very black.

It was Mahala's outcries which brought her back to the parlor, now full of the evening twilight.

"Why can't God call me home?" Mahala was asking. "Why can't He call me to His Throne of Grace?"

Then Mahala got up and wandered off into her own part of the house. One could hear her in her room there, faintly kissing Teeboy's soiled clothes and speaking quietly to herself.

"Until you told me about his having his hair straightened, I thought maybe he would be back," Mahala was saying from the room. "But when you told me that, I knew. He won't never be back."

Plumy could hear Mahala kissing the clothes after she had said this.

"He was so dear to her," Plumy said aloud. It was necessary to speak aloud at that moment because of the terrible feeling of evening in the room. Was it the smell of the four o'clocks, which must have just opened to give out their perfume, or was it the evening itself which made her uneasy? She felt not alone, she felt someone else had come, uninvited and from far away.

Plumy had never noticed before what a strong odor the four o'clocks had, and then she saw the light in the room, growing larger, a light she had not recognized before, and then she turned and saw *him,* George Watson Jackson, standing there before her, large as life. Plumy wanted to call out, she wanted to say *No* in a great voice, she wanted to brush the sight before her all away, which was strange because she was always wanting to see her baby and here he was, although seventeen years had passed since she had laid him away.

She looked at him with unbelieving eyes because really he was the same, the same except she did notice that little boys' suits had changed fashion since his day, and how that everything about him was slightly different from the little children of the neighborhood now.

"Baby!" she said, but the word didn't come out from her mouth, it was only a great winged thought that could not be made into sound. "George Watson, honey!" she said still in her silence.

He stood there, his eyes like they had been before. Their beauty stabbed at her heart like a great knife; the hair looked so like she had just pressed the wet comb to it and perhaps put a little pomade on the sides; and the small face was clean and sad. Yet her arms somehow did not ache to hold him like her heart told her they should. Something too far away and too strong was between her and him; she only saw him as she had always seen resurrection pictures, hidden from us as in a wonderful mist that will not let us see our love complete.

There was this mist between her and George Jackson, like the dew that will be on the four o'clocks when you pick one of them off the plant.

It was her baby come home, and at such an hour.

Then as she came slowly to herself, she began to raise

herself slightly, stretching her arms and trying to get the words to come out to him:

"George Watson, baby!"

This time the words did come out, with a terrible loudness, and as they did so the light began to go from the place where he was standing: the last thing she saw of him was his bright forehead and hair, then there was nothing at all, not even the smell of flowers.

Plumy let out a great cry and fell back in the chair. Mahala heard her and came out of her room to look at her.

"What you got?" Mahala said.

"I seen *him!* I seen *him!* Big as life!"

"Who?" Mahala said.

"George Watson, just like I laid him away seventeen years ago!"

Mahala did not know what to say. She wiped her eyes dry, for she had quit crying.

"You was exposed too long in the sun," Mahala said vaguely.

As she looked at her sister she felt for the first time the love that Plumy had borne all these years for a small son Mahala had never seen, George Watson. For the first time she dimly recognized Plumy as a mother, and she had suddenly a feeling of intimacy for her that she had never had before.

She walked over to the chair where Plumy was and laid her hand on her. Somehow the idea of George Watson's being dead so long and yet still being a baby a mother could love had a kind of perfect quality that she liked. She thought then, quietly and without shame, how nice it would be if Teeboy could also be perfect in death, so that he would belong to her in the same perfect way as George Watson belonged to Plumy. There was comfort in tending the grave of a dead son, whether he was killed in war or peace, and it was so difficult to tend the memory of a son who just went away and never came back. Yet somehow she knew as she looked at Plumy, somehow she would go on with the memory of Teeboy Jordan even though he still lived in the world.

As she stood there considering the lives of the two sons Teeboy Jordan and George Watson Jackson, the evening which had for some time been moving slowly into the house entered now as if in one great wave, bringing the small parlor into the heavy summer night until you would have believed daylight would never enter there again, the night was so black and secure.

• WHY CAN'T THEY TELL YOU WHY? •

PAUL knew nearly nothing of his father until he found the box of photographs on the backstairs. From then on he looked at them all day and every evening, and when his mother Ethel talked to Edith Gainesworth on the telephone. He had looked amazed at his father in his different ages and stations of life, first as a boy his age, then as a young man, and finally before his death in his army uniform.

Ethel had always referred to him as *your father,* and now the photographs made him look much different from what this had suggested in Paul's mind.

Ethel never talked with Paul about why he was home sick from school and she pretended at first she did not know he had found the photographs. But she told everything she thought and felt about him to Edith Gainesworth over the telephone, and Paul heard all of the conversations from the backstairs where he sat with the photographs, which he had moved from the old shoe boxes where he had found them to two big clean empty candy boxes.

"Wouldn't you know a sick kid like him would take up with photographs," Ethel said to Edith Gainesworth. "Instead of toys or balls, old photos. And my God, I've hardly mentioned a thing to him about his father."

Edith Gainesworth, who studied psychology at an adult center downtown, often advised Ethel about Paul, but she did not say anything tonight about the photographs.

"All mothers should have pensions," Ethel continued. "If it isn't a terrible feeling being on your feet all day before the public and then having a sick kid under your feet when you're off at night. My evenings are worse than my days."

These telephone conversations always excited Paul because they were the only times he heard himself and the photographs discussed. When the telephone bell would ring he would run to the backstairs and begin looking at the photographs and then as the conversation progressed he often ran into the front room where Ethel was talking, sometimes carrying one of the photographs with him and making sounds like a bird or an airplane.

Two months had gone by like this, with his having attended school hardly at all and his whole life seemingly spent in listening to Ethel talk to Edith Gainesworth and examining the photographs in the candy boxes.

Then in the middle of the night Ethel missed him. She rose feeling a pressure in her scalp and neck. She walked over to his cot and noticed the Indian blanket had been taken away. She called Paul and walked over to the window and looked out. She walked around the upstairs, calling him.

"God, there is always something to bother you," she said. "Where are you, Paul?" she repeated in a mad sleepy voice. She went on down into the kitchen, though it did not seem possible he would be there, he never ate anything.

Then she said *Of course,* remembering how many times he went to the backstairs with those photographs.

"Now what are you doing in here, Paul?" Ethel said, and there was a sweet but threatening sound to her voice that awoke the boy from where he had been sleeping, spread out protectively over the boxes of photographs, his Indian blanket over his back and shoulder.

Paul crouched almost greedily over the boxes when he saw this ugly pale woman in the man's bathrobe looking at him. There was a faint smell from her like that of an uncovered cistern when she put on the robe.

"Just here, Ethel," he answered her question after a while.

"What do you mean, *just here,* Paul?" she said going up closer to him.

She took hold of his hair and jerked him by it gently as though this was a kind of caress she sometimes gave him. This gentle jerking motion made him tremble in short successive starts under her hand, until she let go.

He watched how she kept looking at the boxes of photographs under his guard.

"You sleep here to be near them?" she said.

"I don't know why, Ethel," Paul said, blowing out air from his mouth as though trying to make something disappear before him.

"You don't know, Paul," she said, her sweet fake awful voice and the stale awful smell of the bathrobe stifling as she drew nearer.

"Don't, don't!" Paul cried.

"Don't what?" Ethel answered, pulling him toward her by seizing on his pajama tops.

"Don't do anything to me, Ethel, my eye hurts."

"Your eye hurts," she said with unbelief.

"I'm sick to my stomach."

Then bending over suddenly, in a second she had gathered up the two boxes of photographs in her bathrobed arms.

"Ethel!" he cried out in the strongest, clearest voice she had ever heard come from him. "Ethel, those are my candy boxes!"

She looked down at him as though she was seeing him for the first time, noting with surprise how thin and puny he was, and how disgusting was one small mole that hung from his starved-looking throat. She could not see how this was her son.

"These boxes of pictures are what makes you sick."

"No, no, Mama Ethel," Paul cried.

"What did I tell you about calling me Mama," she said, going over to him and putting her hand on his forehead.

"I called you Mama Ethel, not Mama," he said.

"I suppose you think I'm a thousand years old." She raised her hand as though she was not sure what she wished to do with it.

"I think I know what to do with these," she said with a pretended calm.

"No, Ethel," Paul said, "give them here back. They are my boxes."

"Tell me why you slept out here on this backstairs where you know you'll make yourself even sicker. I want you to tell me and tell me right away."

"I can't, Ethel, I can't," Paul said.

"Then I'm going to burn the pictures," she replied.

He crawled hurrying over to where she stood and put his arms around her legs.

"Ethel, please don't take them, Ethel. Pretty please."

"Don't touch me," she said to him. Her nerves were so bad she felt that if he touched her again she would start as though a mouse had gotten under her clothes.

"You stand up straight and tell me like a little man why you're here," she said, but she kept her eyes half closed and turned from him.

He moved his lips to answer but then he did not really understand what she meant by *little man*. That phrase worried him whenever he heard it.

"What do you do with the pictures all the time, all day when I'm gone, and now tonight? I never heard of anything like it." Then she moved away from him, so that his hands fell from her legs where he had been grasping her, but she continued to stand near his hands as though puzzled what to do next.

"I look is all, Ethel," he began to explain.

"Don't bawl when you talk," she commanded, looking now at him in the face.

Then: "I want the truth!" she roared.

He sobbed and whined there, thinking over what it was she could want him to tell her, but everything now had begun to go away from his attention, and he had not really ever understood what had been expected of him here, and now everything was too hard to be borne.

"Do you hear me, Paul?" she said between her teeth, very close to him now and staring at him in such an angry way he closed his eyes. "If you don't answer me, do you know what I'm going to do?"

"Punish?" Paul said in his tiniest child voice.

"No, I'm not going to punish this time," Ethel said.

"You're not!" he cried, a new fear and surprise coming now into his tired eyes, and then staring at her eyes, he began to cry with panicky terror, for it seemed to him then that in the whole world there were just the two of them, him and Ethel.

"You remember where they sent Aunt Grace," Ethel said with terrible knowledge.

His crying redoubled in fury, some of his spit flying out onto the cold calcimine of the walls. He kept turning the while to look at the close confines of the staircase as though to find some place where he could see things outside.

"Do you remember where they sent her?" Ethel said in a quiet patient voice like a woman who has endured every unreasonable, disrespectful action from a child whom she still can patiently love.

"Yes, yes, Ethel," Paul cried hysterically.

"Tell Ethel where they sent Aunt Grace," she said with the same patience and kind restraint.

"I didn't know they sent little boys there," Paul said.

"You're more than a little boy now," Ethel replied. "You're old enough. . . . And if you don't tell Ethel why you look at the photographs all the time, we'll have to send you to the mental hospital with the bars."

"I don't know why I look at them, dear Ethel," he said now in a very feeble but wildly tense voice, and he began petting the fur on her houseslippers.

"I think you do, Paul," she said quietly, but he could hear her gentle, patient tone disappearing and he half raised his hands as though to protect him from anything this woman might now do.

"But I don't know why I look at them," he repeated, screaming, and he threw his arms suddenly around her legs.

She moved back, but still smiling her patient, knowing, forgiving smile.

"All right for you, Paul." When she said that *all right for you* it always meant the end of any understanding or reasoning with her.

"Where are we going?" he cried, as she ushered him through the door, into the kitchen.

"We're going to the basement, of course," she replied.

They had never gone there together before, and the terror of what might happen to him now gave him a kind of quiet that enabled him to walk steady down the long irregular steps.

"You carry the boxes of pictures, Paul," she said, "since you like them so much."

"No, no," Paul cried.

"Carry them," she commanded, giving them to him.

He held them before him and when they reached the floor of the basement, she opened the furnace and, tightening the cord of her bathrobe, she said coldly, her white face lighted up by the fire, "Throw the pictures into the furnace door, Paul."

He stared at her as though all the nightmares had come true, the complete and final fear of what may happen in living had unfolded itself at last.

"They're Daddy!" he said in a voice neither of them recognized.

"You had your choice," she said coolly. "You prefer a dead man to your own mother. Either you throw his pictures in the fire, for they're what makes you sick, or you will go where they sent Aunt Grace."

He began running around the room now, much like a small bird which has escaped from a pet shop into the confusion of a city street, and making odd little sounds that she did not recognize could come from his own lungs.

"I'm not going to stand for your clowning," she called out, but as though to an empty room

As he ran round and round the small room with the boxes of photographs pressed against him, some of the pictures fell upon the floor and these he stopped and tried to recapture, at the same time holding the boxes tight against him, and making, as he picked them up, frothing cries of impotence and acute grief.

Ethel herself stared at him, incredulous. He not only could not be recognized as her son, he no longer looked like a child, but in his small unmended night shirt like some crippled and dying animal running hopelessly from its pain.

"Give me those pictures!" she shouted, and she seized a few which he held in his fingers, and threw them quickly into the fire.

Then turning back, she moved to take the candy boxes from him.

But the final sight of him made her stop. He had crouched on the floor, and, bending his stomach over the boxes, hissed at her, so that she stopped short, not seeing any way to get at him, seeing no way to bring him back, while from his mouth black thick strings of something slipped out, as though he had spewed out the heart of his grief.

• MAN AND WIFE •

HOW could it happen to you in good times if you didn't do nothing wrong?" Peaches Maud said.

"Peaches, I am trying to tell you," Lafe replied. "None of the men in the plant ever liked me." Then as though quoting somebody: "I am frankly difficult."

"Difficult? You are the easiest-to-get-along-with man in the whole country."

"I am not manly," he said suddenly in a scared voice, as though giving an order over a telephone.

"Not manly?" Peaches Maud said and surprise made her head move back slightly as though the rush of his words was a wind in her face.

"What has manly got to do with you being fired?" She began walking around the small apartment, smoking one of the gold-tipped cigarettes he bought for her in the Italian district.

"The foreman said the men never liked me on account of my character," Lafe went on, as though reporting facts he could scarcely remember about a person nearly unknown to him.

"Oh, Jesus," Maud said, the cigarette hanging in her mouth and a thin stream of smoke coming up into her half-closed eyes. "Well, thank God we live where nobody knows us. That is the only thing comes to mind to be grateful for. And for the rest, I don't know what in hell you are really talking about, and my ears won't let me catch what you seem to be telling."

"I have done nothing wrong, Peaches Maud."

"Did you ever do anything right?" She turned to him with hatred.

"I have no character, Maud," he spoke slowly, as though still quoting from somebody.

It was true, Maud thought, puffing vigorously on the Italian cigarette: he had none at all. He had never found a character

61

to have. He was always about to do something or start something, but not having a character to start or do it with left him always on the road to preparation.

"What did the men care whether you had a character or not?" Maud wanted to know.

For nearly a year now she had worn corsets, but this afternoon she had none, and, it being daylight, Lafe could see with finality how fat she was and what unsurpassed large breasts stuck out from her creased flesh. He was amazed to think that he had been responsible so long for such a big woman. Seeing her tremendous breasts, he felt still more exhausted and unready for his future.

"They told me in the army, Peaches, I should have been a painter."

"Who is this *they?*" she inquired with shamed indignation.

"The men in the mental department."

Lafe felt it essential at this moment to go over and kiss Maud on the throat. He tasted the talcum powder she had dusted herself with against the heat, and it was not unwelcome in his situation. Underneath the talcum he could taste Maud's sweat.

"All right, now." Maud came down a little to him, wiping his mouth free of the talcum powder. "What kind of a painter did these mental men refer to?"

"They didn't mean somebody who paints chairs and houses," Lafe said, looking away so that she would not think he was criticizing her area of knowledge.

"I mean why did they think you was meant for a painter?" Maud said.

"They never tell you those things," he replied. "The tests test you and the mental men come and report the findings."

"Well, Jesus, what kind of work will you go into if it ain't factory work?"

Lafe extracted a large blue handkerchief dotted with white stars and held this before him as though he were waiting for a signal to cover his face with it.

"Haven't you always done factory work?" Peaches Maud

summarized their common knowledge in her threatening voice.

"Always, always," he replied in agony.

"Just when you read how the whole country is in for a big future, you come home like this to me," she said, suddenly triumphant. "Well, I can tell you, I'm not going back to that paint factory, Lafe. I will do anything but go back and eat humble pie to Mrs. Goreweather."

"I don't see how you could go back." He stared at her flesh.

"What meaning do you put in those words?" she thundered. Then when he stared at her uncomprehending: "You seem to lack something a husband ought to have for his wife."

"That's what everything seems to be about now," he said. "It's what I lack everywhere."

"Stop that down-at-the-mouth talk," she commanded evenly.

"All the way home on the streetcar I sat like a bedbug." He ignored her.

"Lafe, what have I told you?" She tried to attract his attention now back to herself.

"I have always lacked something and that lack was in my father and mother before me. My father had drink and my mother was easily recognized as . . ."

She pulled his arm loosely toward her: "Don't bring that up in all this trouble. She was anyhow a mother. . . . Of course, we could never afford for me to be a mother. . . ."

"Maybe I should go back and tell the men all the things I lack they still don't know about."

"You say things that are queer, all right," Maud said in a quieter voice, and then with her old sarcasm: "I can kind of see how you got on the men's nerves if you talked to them like you talk at home."

"You're beginning to see, you say, Peaches?" Lafe said, almost as though he were now the judge himself, and then he began to laugh.

"I wish you would never laugh that way," Maud corrected him. "I hate that laugh. It sounds like some kid looking through a bathroom window. Jesus, Lafe, you ought to grow up."

He continued to laugh for a few moments, giving her the chance to see he had already changed a little for her. It was his laughing that made her pace up and down the room, despite the heat of July, and listen with growing nervousness to the refrigerator make its clattering din.

"I can see what maybe the men meant," she said in her quiet-triumph-tone of voice, and at the same time putting rage into her eyes as they stared at the refrigerator.

"Christ, I hated every goddamn man."

"You can't afford to hate nobody! You can't go around hating men like that when you earn your bread with them."

"You hated Mrs. Goreweather."

"Look how unfair! You know Mrs. Goreweather had insanity in her family, and she pounced on me as a persecution target. You never even hinted there was any Mrs. Goreweather character at the factory."

"I was *her!*"

"Lafe, for Jesus' sake, in all this heat and noise, let's not have any of this mental talk, or I will put on my clothes and go out and get on the streetcar."

"I'm telling you what it was. The company psychiatrist told me I was the Mrs. Goreweather of my factory."

"How could he know of her?"

"I told him."

"No," she said stopping dead in the room. "You didn't go and tell him about her!" She picked up a large palm straw fan from the table and fanned with angry movements the large patches of sweat and talcum powder on her immense meaty body. As Lafe watched her move the fan, he thought how much money had gone to keep her in food these seven peculiar years.

"I am not a normal man, Peaches Maud," he said without conviction or meaning. He went over to her and touched her shoulder.

"I'll bet that psychiatrist isn't even married," Maud

said, becoming more gentle but suddenly more worried.

"He wasn't old," Lafe said, the vague expression coming over his face again. "He might be younger than me."

"If only that damn refrigerator would shut up," she complained, not knowing now where to turn her words.

She went over to the bed and sat down, and began fanning the air in his direction, as though to calm him or drive away any words he might now say.

"You have no idea how the refrigerator nags me sometimes when you can be gone and away at work. I feel like I just got to go out when I hear it act so."

"Maud," he said, and he stopped her arm from fanning him. "I have never once ceased to care for you in all this time and trouble."

"Well, I should hope," she said, suddenly silly, and fanning her own body now more directly.

"You will always attract me no matter what I am."

"Jesus, Lafe!" And she beat with the fan against the bedpost so that it shook a little.

Then they both noticed that the refrigerator was off.

"Did I jar it still?" she wondered.

But the moment she spoke it began again, louder and more menacing.

"I am not a man to make you happy," Lafe touched her shoulder again.

"I thought I told you I couldn't stand that mental talk. I have never liked having you say you felt like a bug or any other running of yourself down. Just because you lost your job don't think you can sit around here with me in this heat and talk mental talk now."

"Maud, I feel I should go away and think over what it is I have done to myself. I feel as though everything was beginning to go away from me."

"What in Jesus' name would you go away on?" she exclaimed, and she threw the fan in the direction of the refrigerator.

"I realize now how much of me there is that is not right,"

he said, as though he had finally succeeded in bringing this fact
to his own attention.

"Jesus! Jesus!" she cried. "How much longer do I, an old
married woman, have to listen to this?"

"Peaches Maud!" he said, standing up and looking down
at her squatting bulk on the bed. "There's no point me
postponing telling you. Why I am without a job should be no
sort of mystery for you, for you are after all the woman I married. . . . Have you been satisfied with me?"

"Satisfied?" she said, becoming quiet again, and her hand
rising as though still in possession of the fan. "Lafe, listen a
moment." Peaches spoke quickly, holding her finger to her
face, as though admiring a strain of music. "Did you ever hear
it go so loud before? I swear it's going to explode on us. Can
they explode, do you suppose?"

He stood there, his face and body empty of meaning, not
looking where she pointed to the refrigerator.

Maud broke a piece of chewing gum in two and, without
offering him the other piece, began to unfold the tin foil and
then to chew the gum industriously but with a large frown between her eyes as though she could expect no pleasure from
what she had put into her mouth.

"You never let me show you nothing but the outside," he
said, his face going white and his eyes more vacant.

"Well, that's all anybody human wants to hear," she
shouted, but she felt a terrible excitement inside, and her
mouth went so dry she could hardly chew the gum.

"Peaches Maud, you have to listen to what I am trying to
tell you." He touched her jaws as though to stop her chewing.
"First of all you must answer my first question. Have you been
satisfied with me?"

Peaches Maud felt welling up within her for the first time
in seven years a terrible tempest of tears. She could not explain
why or from where these tears were coming. She felt also,
without warning, cold and she got up and put on her kimono.

"Don't tell me no more now." She faced him, drawing the
kimono sash about her.

The refrigerator clattered on in short unrhythmic claps as though to annihilate all other sound.

"Answer my question, Peaches." He took her hand up from the folds of the kimono.

"I bought this for you in Chinatown." He made an effort to raise his voice.

"I don't want to hear no memory talks, Lafe, for the love of Christ!" And she looked down at him suddenly as though she had gone up above him on a platform.

"Maud," he coaxed, putting a new and funny hopeful tone into his voice, "I can forget all that mental talk like you say. I did before anyhow. The men in the army tried to make me feel things too, with their tests, and here I went and married you."

"Stop it now," she began to make crying sounds. "I can't bear to hear no more of that talk, I tell you. Put it off for later. I don't feel up to hearing it, I tell you."

"We both quick change and make up our minds, don't we?" he said, briefly happy. He kissed her on the face.

"Don't kiss me when I feel like I do," she said peevishly.

Then without any warning, shouting as though something had stung her: "What did the company psychiatrist tell you?"

"You got to answer my first question first," Lafe said, a kind of mechanical strength coming to him.

"I can't answer until I hear what he told you," she said.

"Peaches," he pleaded with her.

"I mean what I said now." She began to sob a little.

"No, don't tell me after all, Lafe." Her face was open now and had a new empty weak quality he had never seen on it before. "I feel if it's what I am fearing I'd split open like a stone."

"How could it be that bad?" he seemed to ask himself this question.

"I can tell it is because you keep making it depend on me being satisfied. I know more than you think I know."

Then she began to scream at him again as though to stop any tears that might have force enough to fall.

"What did you do at the factory that wasn't human? Oh, I thank Jesus we don't live in the same neighborhood with them men that work for you. This apartment may be hell with nothing but foreigners around us and that busted refrigerator and no ventilation but heat from the roof, but thank Jesus nobody don't know us."

"You won't answer me, then?" he said, still as calm and empty in his movements as before.

"You're not a woman," she told him, "and you can't understand the first question can't be answered till I know what you done."

"I asked the psychiatrist if it was a crime."

"Well, what did he tell you?" Peaches Maud raised her voice as though she saw ahead some faint indication of escape.

"He said it depended. It was what the men thought where you had to work."

"Well, what in the name of Christ did the men think?"

"They thought it was a crime."

"Was it a boy you were stuck on?" Peaches Maud said, making her voice both empty and quiet, and at the same time all the tears came onto her face as though sprayed there by a tiny machine, in one second.

"Did the psychiatrist call you up, Peaches?" he said, and he took hold of the bedpost and stared away from her.

Then, when she did not answer, he went over to her: "Did he, Peaches?" He took her by the hands and waited for her to answer.

"You leave loose of me, Lafe Krause. Do you hear? Leave loose of my hands."

"Peaches," he called in a voice that seemed to come from under the floor.

"Don't call me that old love name," she wept. "I'm an old fat woman tied down to a . . ."

She waited before she said the word, listening as though for any sound that might rescue them there both together.

"Did he call you up?" Lafe kept on, but his voice carried

now no real demand, and came as though at a still greater distance from under where they stood.

Listening sharply, Maud felt it was true: the refrigerator had stopped again, and the silence was high and heavy as the sky outside.

"*Did he call you, Maud, did he?*"

"No," she answered, finally, still feeling he had to be addressed at some depth under where she was standing. "It was your mother. She told me before we got married. I said I would take a chance."

"The old bitch told you," he reflected in his exhausted voice.

"Considering the way the son turned out, the mother can hardly be blamed," Maud said, but her voice was equally drained of meaning.

"Peaches," he said, but as if not addressing the word to her at all, and going rapidly over to the refrigerator and opening up the door.

"The little light is out that was on here," he said dully.

"There ain't no point in fussing with it now," she remarked.

"Maybe I could fix it," he said.

"I doubt that. I doubt you could, Lafe Krause. I don't think I would want you to fix it anyhow, even if you could. . . ."

"Don't you want me to do nothing for you then anymore?" He turned with a slight movement toward her, his eyes falling on her breasts.

"I can't stand the pressure, I can't," she shouted back at him. "Why did you have to go and do it?"

"I didn't do nothing," he explained, as though trying to remember what had been said and what had not. "That's why it's so odd. They just felt I looked like I was going to, and they fired me."

"Jesus, I don't understand," she said, but without any tears on her face now. "Why did this have to happen to me when I can't bear to hear about anything that ain't human."

But her husband was not listening to her words or noticing whether she had tears or not. He was looking only at what was she, this fat, slightly middle-aged woman. She looked as though she had come to her permanent age, and he knew then that though he was but twenty-eight, he might as well be sixty, and the something awful and permanent that comes to everybody had come at last to him. Everything had come to an end, whether because he had looked at boys, or whether because the men had suddenly decided that yes, there was something odd in his character.

"Peaches," he said, and as he paused in his speech, the name he had always called her seemed to move over into the silence and vacancy of the broken refrigerator. "I will always stand by you anyhow, Peaches Maud."

• You Reach for Your Hat •

PEOPLE saw her every night on the main street. She went out just as it was getting dark, when the street lights would pop on, one by one, and the first bats would fly out round Mrs. Bilderbach's. That was Jennie. Now what was she up to? everyone would ask, and we all knew, in company and out. Jennie Esmond was off for her evening walk and to renew old acquaintances. Now don't go into details, the housewives would say over the telephone. Ain't life dreary enough without knowing? They all knew anyhow as in a movie they had seen five times and where the sad part makes them cry just as much the last showing as the first.

They couldn't say too much, though. Didn't she have the gold star in the window, meaning Lafe was dead in the service of his country? They couldn't say too much, and, after all, what did Jennie do when she went out? There wasn't any proof she went the whole hog. She only went to the Mecca, which had been a saloon in old World War days and where no ladies went. And, after all, she simply drank a few beers and joked with the boys. Yes, and well, once they told that she played the piano there, but it was some sort of old-fashioned number and everybody clapped politely after she stopped.

She bought all her clothes at a store run by a young Syrian. Nobody liked him or his merchandise, but he did sell cheap and he had the kind of things that went with her hair, that dead-straw color people in town called angel hair. She bought all her dresses there that last fall and summer, and they said the bargain she got them for no one would ever believe.

Then a scandalous thing. She took the gold star out of the window. What could it mean? Nobody had ever dreamed of such a thing. You would have thought anyone on such shaky ground would have left it up forever. And she took it down six

71

months after the sad news. It must mean marriage. The little foreign man. But the janitor said nobody ever called on her except Mamie Jordan and little Blake Higgins.

She went right on with her evening promenades, window-shopping the little there was to window-shop, nodding to folks in parked cars and to old married friends going in and out of the drug store. It wasn't right for a woman like Jennie to be always walking up and down the main street night after night and acting, really acting, as if she had no home to go to. She took on in her way as bad as the loafers had in front of the court house before the mayor ordered the benches carried away so they couldn't sit down. Once somebody saw her in the section around the brewery and we wondered. Of course, everyone supposed the government paid her for Lafe's death; so it wasn't as if she was destitute.

Nobody ever heard her mention Lafe, but Mamie Jordan said she had a picture of him in civilian clothes in her bedroom. He wasn't even smiling. Mamie said Jennie had had such trouble getting him to go to Mr. Hart's photography studio. It was right before his induction, and Jennie had harped on it so long that Lafe finally went, but he was so mad all the time they were taking him he never smiled once; they had to finish him just looking. Mamie said Jennie never showed any interest in the picture and even had toilet articles in front of it. No crepe on it or anything.

Mamie didn't understand it at all. Right after he was reported missing in action she went down to offer her sympathy and Jennie was sitting there eating chocolates. She had come to have a good cry with her and there she was cool as a cucumber. You'd never have known a thing had happened. It made Mamie feel so bad, because she had always liked Lafe even if he never would set the world on fire, and she had burst out crying, and then after a little while Jennie cried too and they sat there together all evening weeping and hugging each other.

But even then Jennie didn't say anything about Lafe's going really meaning anything to her. It was as though he had been gone for twenty years. An old hurt. Mamie got to thinking about it and going a little deeper into such a mystery. It came back to her that Lafe had always gone to the Mecca tavern and left Jennie at home, and now here she was out there every night of her life.

Mamie thought these things over on her way to the movie that night. No one had ever mentioned Jennie's case lately to her, and, truth to tell, people were beginning to forget who Lafe was. People don't remember anymore. When she was a girl they had remembered a dead man a little longer, but today men came and went too fast; somebody went somewhere every week, and how could you keep fresh in your memory such a big list of departed ones?

She sighed. She had hoped she would run into Jennie on her way to the movie. She walked around the court house and past the newspaper office and she went out of her way to go by the drygoods store in hopes she would see her, but not a sign. It was double feature night; so she knew she would never get out in time to see Jennie after the show.

But the movie excited her more than ever, and she came out feeling too nervous to go home. She walked down the main street straight north, and before she knew it she was in front of the Mecca. Some laboring men were out front and she felt absolutely humiliated. She didn't know what on earth had come over her. She looked in the window and as she did so she half expected the men to make some underhanded move or say something low-down, but they hardly looked at her. She put her hands to the glass, pressing her nose flat and peering in so that she could see clear to the back of the room.

She saw Jennie all right, alone, at one of the last tables. Almost before she knew what she was doing, she was walking through the front door. She felt herself blushing the most terrible red ever, going into a saloon where there were no tables for ladies and before dozens of coarse laboring men, who were probably laughing at her.

Jennie looked up at her, but she didn't seem surprised.

"Sit down, Mamie." She acted just as cool as if they were at her apartment.

"I walked past," Mamie explained, still standing. "I couldn't help noticing you from outside."

"Sweet of you to come in," Jennie went on. Something in the dogged, weary quality of her voice gave Mamie her chance. She brought it right out: "Jennie, is it because you miss him so that you're . . . here?"

The old friend looked up quickly. "Dear Mame," she said, laughing, "that's the first time I've heard you mention him in I don't know how long."

Jennie simply kept on looking about as if she might perhaps find an explanation for not only why she was here but for the why of anything.

"I wish you would let me help you," Mamie continued. "I don't suppose you would come home with me. I suppose it's still early for you. I know my 'Lish always said time passed so fast with beer."

Jennie kept gazing at this frowsy old widow who was in turn gazing at her even more intently. She looked like her dead mother the way she stared.

"I understand," Mamie repeated. She was always saying something like that, but Jennie didn't weigh her friend's words very carefully. She wasn't quite sure just who Mamie was or what her friendship stood for, but she somehow accepted them both tonight and brought them close to her.

"You may as well drink. May as well be sheared for a sheep as a lamb."

"I believe I will," Mamie said, a kind of belligerence coming into her faded voice.

"Charley," Jennie called, "give Mamie some bottle beer."

The "girls" sat there laughing over it all.

The smile began to fade from Jennie's mouth. She looked at her old friend again as if trying to keep fresh in her mind that she was really sitting there, that she had come especially. Mamie had that waiting look on her face that old women always have.

The younger woman pulled the tiny creased photograph from her purse. Mamie took it avidly. Yes, it was coming, she knew. At last Jennie was going to pour herself out to her. She would know everything. At last nothing would be held back. In her excitement at the thought of the revelation to come, she took several swallows of beer. "Tell me," she kept saying. "You can tell old Mamie."

"He wasn't such a bad looker," Jennie said.

The friend leaned forward eagerly. "Lafe?" she said. "Why, Lafe was handsome, honey. Didn't you know that? He was." And she held the picture farther forward and shook her head sorrowfully but admiringly.

"If he had shaved off that little mustache, he would have been better looking. I was always after him to shave it off, but somehow he wouldn't. Well, you know, his mouth was crooked. . . ."

"Oh, don't say those things," Mamie scolded. "Not about the dead." But she immediately slapped her hand against her own mouth, closing out the last word. Oh, she hadn't meant to bring that word out! We don't use that word about loved ones.

Jennie laughed a little, the laugh an older woman might have used in correcting a little girl.

"I always wondered if it hurt him much when he died," she said. "He never was a real lively one, but he had a kind of hard, enduring quality in him that must have been hard to put out. He must have died slow and hard and knowing to the end."

Mamie didn't know exactly where to take up the thread from there. She hadn't planned for this drift in the conversation. She wanted to have a sweet memory talk and she would have liked to reach for Jennie's hand to comfort her, but she couldn't do it now the talk had taken this drift. She took another long swallow of beer. It was nasty, but it calmed one a little.

"I look at his picture every night before I climb in bed," Jennie went on. "I don't know why I do. I never loved him, you know."

"Now, Jennie, dear," she began, but her protest was scarcely heard in the big room. She had meant to come forward boldly with the "You did love him, dear," but something gray and awful entered the world for her. At that moment she didn't quite believe even in the kind of love which she had seen depicted that very night in the movies and which, she knew, was the only kind that filled the bill.

"You never loved him!" Mamie repeated the words and they echoed dully. It was a statement which did not bear repeating; she realized that as soon as it was out of her mouth.

But Jennie went right on. "No, I never did love Lafe Esmond."

"Closing time!" Charley called out.

Mamie looked around apprehensively.

"That don't apply to us," Jennie explained. "Charley lets me stay many a night until four."

It was that call of closing time that took her back to her days at the cigar factory when fellows would wait in their cars for her after work. She got to thinking of Scott Jeffreys in his new Studebaker.

She looked down at her hands to see if they were still as lovely as he had said. She couldn't tell in the dim light, and besides, well, yes, why not say it, who cared about her hands now? Who cared about any part of her now?

"My hands were lovely once," Jennie said aloud. "My mother told me they were nearly every night and it was true. Nearly every night she would come into my bedroom and say, 'Those lovely white hands should never have to work. My little girl was meant for better things.' "

Mamie swallowed the last of the bottle and nodded her head for Jennie to go on.

"But do you think Lafe ever looked at my hands? He never looked at anybody's hands. He wasn't actually interested in woman's charm. No man really is. It only suggests the other to them, the thing they want out of us and always get. They only start off by complimenting us on our figures. Lafe wasn't

interested in anything I had. And I did have a lot once. My
mother knew I was beautiful."

She stopped. This was all so different from anything
Mamie had come for. Yes, she had come for such a different
story.

"Lafe married me because he was lonesome. That's all. If
it hadn't been me it would have been some other fool. Men
want a place to put up. They get the roam taken out of them
and they want to light. I never loved him or anything he did
to me. I only pretended when we were together.

"I was never really fond of any man from the first."

Mamie pressed her finger tightly on the glass as if begging
a silent power in some way to stop her.

"I was in love with a boy in the eighth grade and that was
the only time. What they call puppy love. Douglas Fleetwood
was only a child. I always thought of forests and shepherds
when I heard his name. He had beautiful chestnut hair. He left
his shirt open winter and summer and he had brown eyes like
a calf's. I never hardly spoke to him all the time I went to
school. He was crippled, too, poor thing, and I could have
caught up with him any day on the way home, he went so
slow, but I was content to just lag behind him and watch him.
I can still see his crutches moving under his arms."

Mamie was beginning to weep a little, a kind of weeping
that will come from disappointment and confusion, the slow
heavy controlled weeping women will give when they see their
ideals go down.

"He died," Jennie said.

"When Miss Matthias announced it in home economics
class that awful January day, I threw up my arms and made
a kind of whistling sound, and she must have thought I was
sick because she said, 'Jennie, you may be excused.'

"Then there were those nice boys at the cigar factory, like
I told you, but it never got to be the real thing, and then Lafe
came on the scene."

Here Jennie stopped suddenly and laughed rather loudly.
Charley, who was at the other end of the room, took this for

some friendly comment on the lateness of the hour and waved and laughed in return.

Mamie was stealthily helping herself to some beer from Jennie's bottle.

"Drink it, Mame," she said. "I bought it for you, you old toper." Mamie wiped a tear away from her left eye.

"As I said, I was tired of the cigar factory and there was Lafe every Friday at the Green Mill dance hall. We got married after the big Thanksgiving ball."

"Why, I think I remember that," Mamie brightened. "Didn't I know you then?"

But Jennie's only answer was to pour her friend another glass.

"He went to the foundry every morning after I had got up to cook his breakfast. He wouldn't go to the restaurants like other men. I always had such an ugly kimono to get breakfast in. I was a fright. He could at least have given me a good-looking wrapper to do that morning work in. Then there I was in the house from 4:30 in the A.M. till night waiting for him to come back. I thought I'd die. I was so worn out waiting for him I couldn't be civil when he come in. I was always frying chops when he come."

She took a big drink of beer.

"Everything smelled of chops in that house. He had to have them."

Charley began again calling closing time. He said everybody had to clear the place.

"It ain't four o'clock, is it?" Mamie inquired.

"No, not yet. I don't know what come over Charley tonight. He seems to want to get rid of us early. It's only one-thirty. I suppose some good-lookin' woman is waiting for him."

Yes, the Mecca was closing. Jennie thought, then, of the places she had read about in the Sunday papers, places where pleasure joints never closed, always open night and day, where you could sit right through one evening into another, drinking and forgetting, or remembering. She heard there were places like that in New Orleans where they had this life, but mixed up with colored people and foreigners. Not classy at all and nothing a girl would want to keep in her book of memories.

And here she was all alone, unless, of course, you could count Mamie.

"I was attractive once," she went on doggedly. "Men turned around every time I went to Cincinnati."

Mamie, however, was no longer listening attentively. The story had somehow got beyond her as certain movies of a sophisticated slant sometimes did with her. She was not sure at this stage what Jennie's beauty or her lack of it had to do with her life, and her life was not at all clear to her. It seemed to her in her fumy state that Jennie had had to cook entirely too many chops for her husband and that she had needed a wrapper, but beyond that she could recall only the blasphemies against love.

"My mother would have never dreamed I would come to this lonely period. My mother always said that a good-looking woman is never lonely. 'Jennie,' she used to say, 'keep your good looks if you don't do another thing.' "

The craven inattention, however, of Mamie Jordan demanded notice. Jennie considered her case for a moment. Yes, there could be no doubt about it. Mamie was hopelessly, unbelievably drunk. And she was far from sober herself.

"Mamie Jordan," she said severely, "are you going to be all right?"

The old friend looked up. Was it the accusation of drink or the tone of cruelty in the voice that made her suddenly burst into tears? She did not know, but she sat there now weeping, loudly and disconsolately.

"Don't keep it up anymore, Jennie," she said. "You've said such awful things tonight, honey. Don't do it anymore. Leave me my little mental comforts."

Jennie stared uncomprehendingly. The sobs of the old woman vaguely filled the great empty hall of the drinking men.

It was the crying, she knew, of an old woman who wanted something that was fine, something that didn't exist. It was the crying for the idea of love like in songs and books, the love that wasn't there. She wanted to comfort her. She wanted to take her in her arms and tell her everything would be all right. But she couldn't think of anything really convincing to say on that score. She looked around anxiously as if to find the answer written on a wall, but all her eyes finally came to rest on was a puddle of spilled beer with Lafe Esmond's picture swimming in the middle.

No, you can't really feel sorry for yourself when you see yourself in another, and Jennie had had what Mamie was having now too many times, the sorrow with drink as the sick day dawned.

But the peculiar sadness evinced by Mamie's tears would not go away. The sore spot deep in the folds of the flesh refused to be deadened this time, and it was this physical pang which brought her back to Lafe. She saw him as if for a few illumined seconds almost as though she had never seen him before, as though he were existing for her for the first time. She didn't see exactly how the dead could know or Lafe could be in any other world looking down on her, and yet she felt just then that some understanding had been made at last between them.

But it was soon over, the feeling of his existing at all. Lafe wasn't coming back and nobody else was coming back to her either. If she had loved him she would have had some kind of happiness in looking at his photograph and crying like Mamie wanted her to. There would be consolation in that. Or even if they had brought him home to her so she would be able to visit the grave and go through the show and motions of grief. But what was him was already scattered so far and wide they could never go fetch any part of it back.

Clasping Mamie by the arm, then, and unfolding the handkerchief to give to her, she had the feeling that she had been to see a movie all over again and that for the second time she had wept right in the same place. There isn't anything to say about such private sorrow. You just wait till the lights go on and then reach for your hat.

• A GOOD WOMAN •

MAUD did not find life in Martinsville very interesting, it is true, but it was Mamie who was always telling her that there were brighter spots elsewhere. She did not believe Mamie and said so.

Mamie had lived in St. Louis when her husband was an official at the head office of a pipeline company there. Then he had lost his job and Mamie had come to Martinsville to live. She regretted everything and especially her marriage, but then she had gradually resigned herself to being a small town woman.

Mamie was so different from Maud. "Maud, you are happy," she would say. "You are the small town type, I guess. You don't seem to be craving the things I crave. I want something and you don't."

"What is it you want?" Maud asked.

The two women were sitting in Hannah's drug store having a strawberry soda. Mamie was reminded, she said, of some old-fashioned beer parties she and her husband had been invited to in Milwaukee when they were younger.

Mamie did not know what it was she wanted. She felt something catch at her heart strings on these cool June days and she would purposely remind herself that summer would soon be over. She always felt the passing of summer most keenly before it had actually begun. Fall affected her in a strange way and she would almost weep when she saw the falling maple leaves or the blackbirds gathering in flocks in deserted baseball parks.

"Maud, I am not young," Mamie would say, thinking of how bald and whitish and grubby her husband was getting.

Maud put down her ice-cream spoon, the straw hanging half out of the dish, and looked at her. Maud was every bit three years younger than Mamie, but when her best friend talked the way she did, Maud would take out her purse mirror and stare wonderingly through the flecks of powder on the glass. Maud had never been beautiful and she was getting stout. More and more she was spending a great deal of money on cosmetics that Mr. Hannah's young clerk told her were imported from a French town on the sea coast.

"If I could only leave off the sweets," Maud said, finishing her soda.

"Maud, are you happy?" Mamie sighed. But Maud did not answer. She had never particularly thought about happiness; it was Mamie who was always reminding her of that word. Maud had always lived in Martinsville and had never thought much about what made people happy or unhappy. When her mother died, she had felt lonely because they had always been companions. For they were not so much like mother and daughter as like two young women past their first youth who knew what life was. They had spent together many a happy afternoon saying and doing foolish young things, in the summer walking in the parks and fairgrounds and in the winter making preserves and roasting fowl for Thanksgiving and Christmas parties. She always remembered her mother with pleasure instead of grief. But now she had Mamie for a friend and she was married to Obie.

Her marriage to Obie had been her greatest experience, but she did not think about it much anymore. Sometimes she almost wished Obie would go away so that she could remember more clearly the first time she had met him when he was an orchestra leader in a little traveling jazz band that made one-night stands near the airport in Martinsville. Obie had been so good-looking in those days, and he was still pretty much the same Obie, of course, but he was not Obie the bandleader anymore. But once he had quit playing in orchestras and had become a traveling salesman, Maud's real romance had ended and she could only look out her window on to the muddy Ohio River and dream away an afternoon.

Obie and Mamie had talks about Maud sometimes. "We spend too much," Obie would say to her. He said he lived on practically nothing on the road. They both agreed she was not very practical. And she spent too much on cosmetics and movies. Mamie did not say so much about the movies because she knew she was the cause there of Maud's spending more than her income allowed, but then it was not Mamie surely who advised her the night of the carnival to buy that imported ostrich plume fan with the ruby jewels in the center and a good many other things of the same kind. And how could Maud give up the pleasure of the movies, or the ice cream or perfumes she got at Mr. Hannah's drug store? And what would Mr. Hannah do for star customers, for that was what Mamie said she and Maud were. They were actually out of all Martinsville his star customers, though they never purchased anything in his pharmaceutical department.

"Maud," Mamie said, "what do we get out of life anyway?"

Maud was not pleased with Mamie's taking this turn in the conversation. She did not like to get serious in the drug store as it spoiled her enjoyment of the ice cream and she had to think up an answer quickly on account of Mamie's impatience or Mamie would not be pleased and would think she was slow-witted, and she was sure Mamie thought she was slow-witted anyhow.

When Maud left Mamie that day she began to think it over. She walked slowly down the street, going north away from Mr. Hannah's drug store.

Mr. Hannah was standing by his green-trimmed display window, watching her as she walked to her yellow frame house over the river.

"What do we get out of life anyway?" Mamie's words kept humming about in her mind but she was so tired from the exhaustion of the warm dusty day that she did not let herself think too much about it. She did not see why Mamie had to keep thinking of such unpleasant things. It depressed her a little, too, and she did not like the feeling of depression. She did not want to think of sad things or whether life was worth living. She knew that Mamie always enjoyed the sad movies with unhappy endings, but she could never bear them at all. Life is too full of that sort of thing, she always told Mamie, and Mamie would say, pouting and giving her a disappointed look, "Maud, you are like all small town housewives. You don't know what I am feeling. You don't feel things down in you the way I feel them."

As she sauntered along she saw Bruce Hauser in front of his bicycle shop. Bruce was a youngish man always covered with oil and grease from repairing motorcycles and machines. When he smiled at Maud she could see that even his smile was stained with oil and car paint and she found herself admiring his white teeth.

She heard some school boys and girls laughing and riding over the bridge on their bicycles and she knew that school was out for the summer and that was why they were riding around like they were. It had not been so very long since she had gone to school, she thought, and for the second time that day she remembered her mother and the warm afternoons when she would come home from school and throw her books down on the sofa and take down her red hair, and her mother and she would eat a ripe fruit together, or sometimes they would make gooseberry preserves or marmalade. It was all very near and very distant.

The next day she felt a little easier at finding Mamie in a better humor and they went to a movie at the Bijou. It was a comedy this afternoon and Maud laughed quite a lot. On the way home Mamie complained that the movie had done nothing to her, had left her, she said, like an icicle, and she felt like asking for her money back.

When they sat down in Hannah's drug store, they began reading the *Bill of Fair with Specialties* — for though they had sat in the same booth for nearly five years and knew all the dishes and drinks, they still went on reading the menu as if they did not know exactly what might be served. Suddenly Mamie said, "Are you getting along all right with Obie, Maud?"

Maud raised her too heavily penciled eyebrows and thought over Mamie's question, but instead of letting her answer, Mamie went on talking about the movie, and when they were leaving the drug store, Maud told Mr. Hannah to charge her soda.

"Why don't you let me pay for yours?" Mamie said, pulling her dress which had stuck to her skin from the sticky heat of the day.

Maud knew that Mamie would never pay for her soda even if she happened to be flat broke and hungry. She knew Mamie was tight, but she liked her anyway. Maud owed quite a bill at Mr. Hannah's and nearly all of it was for strawberry sodas. If Obie had known it, Maud would have been in trouble all right, but she always managed to keep Obie from knowing.

"I know," Mamie said on the way home, "I know, honey, that you and Obie don't hit it off right anymore."

Maud wondered how Mamie knew that, but what could she say to deny it? She said, "Obie has to work out of town too much to be the family man I would like him to be."

When Maud got home that night she found that Obie had arrived. He was a little cross because she had not prepared dinner for him.

"I was not sure you was coming," Maud said.

She prepared his favorite dinner of fried pork chops and French fried potatoes with a beet and lettuce salad and some coffee with canned milk and homemade preserves and cake.

"Where was you all day?" Obie asked at the table, and Maud told him she usually went to a movie with Mamie Sucher and afterwards she went to the drug store and got a soda.

"You ought to cut down on the sweets," Obie said, and Maud remembered having caught a reflection of herself that day in the hall mirror, and she knew she was a long way from having the same figure she had had as a girl. For a moment she felt almost as depressed as Mamie said she was all the time.

While Maud was doing the dishes, Obie told her that he had some good news for her, but she knew from the first it was not really good news. Obie told her that he had quit his traveling job and was going to sell life insurance now. He said he was getting too old to be on the road all the time. He wanted to have a little home life for a change, and it wasn't right for Maud to be alone so much.

Maud did not know what to say to him. The tears were falling over her hands into the dishwater, for she knew Obie would never make as much money selling life insurance as he had made on the road as a traveling salesman, and she knew there wouldn't be any more money for her for a long while. And all of a sudden she thought of the time when she had first begun getting stout and the high school boys had quit asking her for dances at the Rainbow Gardens and didn't notice her anymore.

The next time Maud saw Mamie was a week later, and Mamie was curious to know everything and asked how Obie was getting along these days.

"He quit his sales work," Maud said, and she felt the tears beginning to come, but she held them back by breathing deeper.

"I'm not a bit surprised," Mamie said. "I saw it coming all the time."

They walked over to the movie, and it was a very sad one. It was about a woman who had led, as Maud could see, not a very virtuous life. She had talked with three or four such women in her lifetime. The woman in the picture gave up the man she was in love with and went away to a bigger town. Mamie enjoyed it very much.

On the way home Mamie wanted Maud to come and have a soda.

"A strawberry soda?" Maud said, putting on some more lipstick and looking in at the green display windows with their headache ads and pictures of cornplasters. "I can't afford it."

"What do you mean, you can't afford it?" Mamie said.

"Obie has to make good at his insurance first," Maud told her.

"Come on in and I will buy you one," Mamie said in a hard firm voice, and though Maud knew Mamie did not want to spend money on her, she couldn't bear to go home to an empty house without first having some refreshment, so she went in with her.

As soon as they had finished having their sodas, Mr. Hannah came over to Maud and said he would like to have a few words in private with her.

"I am paying for this," Mamie said as if she suspected trouble of some sort.

Maud made a motion with her hand and started to walk with Mr. Hannah toward the pharmacy room.

"Do you want me to wait outside?" Mamie said, but she got no reply.

An old woman with white gloves was sitting in a booth looking at Maud and Mr. Hannah. Maud knew her story and kept looking at her. She was to have married a young business man from Baltimore, but the day before the wedding the young man had died in a railroad accident. Ever since then, the old woman had not taken off her white wedding gloves.

"Well, Maud," said Mr. Hannah, his gray old eyes narrowing under his spectacles, "I've been meaning to talk over with you the little matter of your bill and have been wondering whether or not . . ."

Maud could feel the red coming up over her face. She knew the old woman with the white gloves was hearing all of it. Maud feared perhaps she had put on too much rouge, for Mr. Hannah was giving her peculiar looks.

"How much is the bill?" she managed to say.

Mr. Hannah looked over his books, but he did not need to look to know how much Maud owed.

"Thirty-five dollars," he said.

Maud moved slightly backwards. "Thirty-five?" she repeated without believing, and she looked over on the books where her account was listed in black purplish ink. "Surely," Maud said, "that must be a mistake."

"Well, you have been having sodas on credit for more than six months," Mr. Hannah said, grinning a little.

"Not surely thirty-five dollars' worth," Maud told him, working the clasp on her purse, "because," she said, "I can't pay it, Obie isn't making full salary and I can't give it to you now at all."

"No hurry to collect yet," Mr. Hannah said and there was a little warmth coming into his voice. "Ain't no hurry for that," he said.

Suddenly Maud could not control her tears. They were falling through her fingers into a small handkerchief embroidered with a bluebird and a rosebush.

"Now, Maud," Mr. Hannah said, "I will be real easy on you. Maybe you would like to talk it all over in the pharmacy room," he said taking her arm, and before she knew her own mind he had led her into the back room.

"Don't in any case," Maud begged him, sobbing a little, "don't in any case, Mr. Hannah, tell my husband about this bill."

"No need at all, no need at all," he said, turning on the light in the pharmacy room. Mr. Hannah was staring at her. Maud was not beautiful, really. Her powder-spotted mirror told her that, and she had a receding chin and large pores. But Mr. Hannah was looking. She remembered now how he had led a singing class at the First Presbyterian Church and he had directed some girls to sing "America the Beautiful" in such a revised improper way that the elders had asked him to leave the church, and he had, and soon after that his wife had divorced him.

As Mamie Sucher was not there to prompt her, Maud did not know what more to say to him. She stood there looking at the bill. She knew it could not be thirty-five dollars. She knew she was being cheated and yet she could not tell him to his face he was lying. It was the only drug store in town where she could get sodas on credit. All the other stores made you pay on leaving or before you drank your soda. Maud stood there paralyzed, looking at the bill, and her face felt hot and sticky.

Then Mr. Hannah said something that pleased her. She did not know why it pleased her so much. "Maud, you beautiful girl, you," he said.

He was holding her hand, the hand with her mother's

ruby ring. "Why don't you ever come into the pharmacy room," he said. "Why do you have to wait for an invitation, good friends like us?" And he clasped her hand so tightly that the ring pressed against her index finger, painfully. She had never been in the pharmacy room before but she did not like the whiffs of drugs and the smell of old cartons of patent medicines that came from there. "Maud, you beauty," he said.

Maud knew that she should say something cold and polite to Mr. Hannah, but suddenly she could not. She smiled and as she smiled the rouge cracked a little on her lips. Mr. Hannah was saying, "Maud, you know you don't have to stand on form with an old friend of the family like me. You know, Maud, I knowed you when you was only a small girl. I knowed your mother well, too."

She laughed again and then she listened to the flies on the screen, the flies that were collecting there and would be let in.

She tried to take the bill from his hand. "I will give it to my husband," she said.

"He will be very mad," Mr. Hannah warned her.

"Yes," Maud breathed hard. It wasn't possible for a man like Obie to believe that she could come into this drug store of Mr. Hannah's and buy only strawberry sodas and make that large a bill, and she knew Obie would never believe her if she told him.

"Well, give me the bill, Mr. Hannah," she said, but Mr. Hannah was still muttering about how dangerous such little things were to the happiness of young married people. Maud thought right then of a time when her mother had gone walking with her and Maud had a new pink parasol and all of a sudden a dirty alley cur had jumped on her as if to spoil her new parasol, not purposely but only in play, and she had said, "Oh, hell," and to hear her swear for the first time had given her mother a good laugh. And now she said so that Mr. Hannah could scarcely hear, "Oh, hell," and he laughed suddenly and put his arm around her.

She had thought everything like that was over for her and here was Mr. Hannah hugging her and calling her "beauty."

She knew it was not proper for her to be in this position with an old man like Mr. Hannah, but he wasn't doing anything really bad and he was so old anyhow, so she let him hug her and kiss her a few times and then she pushed him away.

"I ain't in no hurry to collect, you know that, Maud," Mr. Hannah said, and he had lost his breath and was standing there before her, his old faded eyes watering.

"Of course, my husband ought to see this bill," Maud said, but she just couldn't make the words have any force to sound like she meant it.

"You just go home and forget about it for a while, why don't you, Maud," he said.

She kept pushing a black imitation cameo bracelet back and forth on her arm. "You know how my husband would feel against it," she said.

Then Mr. Hannah did something that was even more surprising. He suddenly tore up the bill right in front of her.

Maud let out a little cry and then Mr. Hannah moved closer to her and Maud said, "No, Mr. Hannah, no, you let me make this right with you because Obie will soon be getting a check." She became actually frightened then with him in the dark, stale-smelling pharmacy room. "Some day," she said, "some day I will make this right," and she hurried out away from Mr. Hannah and she walked quickly, almost unconsciously, to the screen door where the flies were collecting before a summer thunder shower.

"I will make this right," she said, and the old druggist followed her and shouted after her, "You don't need to tell him, Maud."

"Don't call me Maud," she gasped.

She stopped and looked at him standing there. She laughed. The screen door slammed behind her and she was in the street.

It was getting a little late and Mamie was gone and the street was almost empty. She felt so excited that she would have liked to talk to Mamie and tell her what had happened to her, but she was too excited to talk to anyone and she hurried straight toward her house near the river.

Just as she got to the bridge she saw Bruce Hauser. She said, "Good evening, Bruce, how are you?" She could not say any more, she was that excited, and without waiting a minute to talk to Bruce, she took out her key and unlocked the door. As she was about to go up the stairs, she caught a reflection of herself in the hall mirror. She stared into it. Maud felt so much pleasure seeing herself so young, that she repeated Mr. Hannah's words again, "Maud, you beauty, you beauty." She was as pretty and carefree this June day as she had been that time when she and her mother had walked with the new pink parasol—long before she had met Obie—and they had joked together, not like mother and daughter, but like two good girl chums away at school.

• PLAN NOW TO ATTEND •

FRED Parker had not seen Mr. Graitop since college days and yet he recognized him at once. Mr. Graitop's face had not changed in twenty years, his doll-small mouth was still the same size, his hair was as immaculately groomed as a department story dummy. Mr. Graitop had always in fact resembled a department store dummy, his face wax-like, his eyes innocent and vacant, the doll-like mouth bloodless and expressionless, the body loose and yet heavy as though the passions and anguish of man had never coursed through it.

Fred on the other hand felt old and used, and he was almost unwilling to make himself known to Mr. Graitop. The fact that he remembered him as Mr. Graitop instead of by his first name was also significant. One did not really believe that Mr. Graitop had a first name, though he did and it was Ezra. Fred had remembered him all these years as Mister. And now here he was like a statue in a museum, looking very young still and at the same time ancient, as though he had never been new.

"Mr. Graitop!" Fred cried in the lobby of the hotel. The hotel was said to be one of the world's largest, perhaps the largest, and Fred felt somehow the significance of his meeting the great man here where they were both so dwarfed by physical immensity, their voices lost in the vastness of the lobby whose roof seemed to lose itself in space indefinitely.

Mr. Graitop's face broke into a faint but actual smile and his eyes shone as though a candle had been lghted behind his brain.

"You are *him*," Fred said with relief. He was afraid that perhaps there was another man in the world who looked like Graitop.

"Yes, you are not deceived in me," Mr. Graitop said, pale and serious.

Fred was going to say *twenty years,* but he decided this was not necessary. He was not sure that Graitop would know it was twenty years, for he had always denied facts of any kind, changing a fact immediately into a spiritual symbol. For instance, in the old days if Fred had said, "It has been twenty minutes," Graitop would have said, "Well, *some* time has passed, of course." He would have denied the twenty because they were figures.

"You are just the same, Mr. Graitop," Fred said, and almost at once he wished he had not called to him, that he had hurried out of the world's largest hotel without ever knowing whether this was the real Graitop or only his twenty-year-younger double.

As they were at the entrance of the Magnolia Bar, Fred ventured to ask him if he would have a drink, although it was only ten o'clock in the morning.

Mr. Graitop hesitated. Perhaps because he did remember it was twenty years, however, he nodded a quiet assent, but his face had again emphasized the bloodless doll expresion, and one felt the presence of his small rat-terrier teeth pressed against the dead mouth.

"Mr. Graitop, this is unbelievable. Really not credible."

Mr. Graitop made odd little noises in his mouth and nose like a small boy who is being praised and admonished by the teacher at the same time.

Fred Parker already felt drunk from the excitement of having made such a terrible mistake as to renew acquaintance with a man who had been great as a youth and was now such a very great man he was known in the movement as the great man.

"What is your drink now, Mr. Graitop?" Fred spoke as though on a telephone across the continent . . . "After twenty years," he explained, awkwardly laughing.

Mr. Graitop winced, and Fred felt that he did so because he did not like to be called by his last name even though he would not have liked to be called by his first, and perhaps also he did not like the twenty years referred to.

As Graitop did not answer immediately but continued to make the small-boy sounds in his nose and throat, Fred asked in a loud voice, "Bourbon and water, perhaps?"

"Bourbon and water," Mr. Graitop repeated wearily, but at the same time with a somewhat relieved note to his voice as though he had recognized his duty and now with great fatigue was about to perform it.

"I can't tell you how odd this is," Fred said nervously emphatic when they had been served.

"Yes, you said that before," Mr. Graitop said and his face was as immobile as cloth.

"But it is, you know. I think it's odd that I recognized you."

"You do?" Mr. Graitop sipped the drink as though he felt some chemical change already taking place in his mouth and facial muscles and perhaps fearful his changeless expression would move.

Then there was silence and strangely enough Mr. Graitop broke it by saying, "Your name is Fred, isn't it."

"Yes," Fred replied, paralyzed with emotion, and with his drink untouched. He suddenly noticed that Graitop had finished his.

"Graitop, won't you have another?" Fred asked, no invitation in his voice.

Graitop stared at him as though he had not understood actually that he had already finished one.

"Don't you drink, sir?" Fred said, surprised at once to hear his own question.

"No," Graitop replied.

"Another bourbon and water," Fred told the bartender.

"You know," Fred began, "this reminds me of one semester when we were roommates and we neither of us went to the football game. We could hear the crowd roaring from our room. It sounded like some kind of mammoth animal that was being punished. It was too hot for football and you tried to convert me to atheism."

Mr. Graitop did not say anything. Everybody had heard

of his great success in introducing "new Religion" to America so that when many people thought of "new Religion" they thought immediately of Graitop.

It was a surprise to Fred to remember that Graitop had been a practicing atheist in the college quadrangles, for he remembered it only this instant.

"You were one, you know," Fred said almost viciously.

"We are always moving toward the one path," Graitop said dreamily, drinking his second drink.

Although Fred was a hard drinker, he had swiftly lost all his appetite for it, and he knew that it was not the early hour. Very often at this hour, setting out as a salesman, he was completely oiled.

"Is it the new religion that keeps you looking so kind of embalmed and youthful," Fred said, as though he had had his usual five brandies.

"Fred," Mr. Graitop said on his third drink, with mechanical composure, "it is the only conceivable path."

"I liked you better as an infidel," Fred said. "You looked more human then, too, and older. I suppose you go to all the football games now that you're a famous man."

"I suppose I see a good many," Graitop said.

"Fred," Mr. Graitop said, closing his eyes softly, and as he did so he looked remarkably older, "why can't you come with us this time?"

Fred did not know what to say because he did not exactly understand the question.

"There is no real reason to refuse. You are a living embodiment of what we all are without *the* prop."

"I'm not following you now," Fred replied.

"You are, but you won't let yourself," Graitop said, opening his eyes and finishing his third drink. He tapped the glass as though it had been an offering for Fred.

Fred signaled for another drink for Graitop just as in the past he would have for himself. His own first drink remained untouched, which he could not understand, except he felt nauseated. He realized also that he hated the great man and had always hated him.

"Well, what am I?" Fred said as he watched Graitop start on his fourth drink.

"The embodiment of the crooked stick that would be made straight," the great man replied.

"You really do go for that, don't you. That is," Fred continued, "you have made that talk part of your life."

"There is no talk involved," Mr. Graitop said. "No talk, Fred."

I wonder why the old bastard is drinking so much, Fred nearly spoke aloud. Then: "Graitop, nobody has ever understood what makes you tick."

"That is unimportant," his friend replied. "It, too, is talk."

"Nobody ever even really liked you, though I don't suppose anybody ever liked St. Paul either."

"Of course, Fred, you are really with us in spirit," Graitop said as though he had not heard the last statement.

Fred looked at his drink which seemed cavernous as a well.

"Graitop," he said stonily, "you discovered Jesus late. Later than me. I'd had all that when I was twelve. . . ."

"You're part of the new movement and your denying it here to me only confirms it," Mr. Graitop informed him.

"I don't want to be part of it," Fred began and he tasted some of his drink, but Graitop immediately interrupted.

"It isn't important that you don't want to be part: you are part and there is nothing you can do about it. You're with us."

"I couldn't be with you," Fred began, feeling coming up within him a fierce anger, and he hardly knew at what it was directed, for it seemed to be larger than just his dislike, suspicion, and dread of Graitop.

Then Mr. Graitop must have realized what only the bartender had sensed from the beginning, that he was not only drunk but going to be sick. Fred had not noticed it at all, for he felt that he had suddenly been seized and forced to relive the impotence and stupidity of his adolescence.

With the bartender's help, he assisted Mr. Graitop out of the bar. In the elevator, Graitop grew loud and belligerent and shouted several times: "It's the only path, the only way."

"What is your room number?" Fred said hollow-voiced as they got out of the elevator.

"You are really part of our group," Graitop replied.

Fred took the key out of Graitop's pocket and nodded to the woman at the desk who stared at them.

"You are completely oiled," Fred informed Graitop when the latter had lain down on the bed. "And yet it doesn't convince me any more than your preaching."

"I wonder if I had appointments," Graitop said weakly. "I was to speak to some of our people. . . ."

"I wonder which of us feels more terrible," Fred replied. "This meeting after twenty years (and he shouted the number) has been poison to both of us. We hate one another and everything we stand for. At least I hate you. You are probably too big a fraud to admit hate. I'm saying this cold sober, too, although I guess just the inside of a bar oils me up."

"You are a living embodiment of sin and sorrow and yet you are dear to us," Graitop said, looking at the ceiling.

"What the hell are you the living embodiment of, what?" Fred said and he began loosening his friend's clothing. Before he knew it, he had completely undressed Mr. Graitop as mechanically as he undressed himself when drunk. As his friend lay there, a man of at least forty, Fred was amazed to see that he looked like a boy of sixteen. Almost nothing had touched him in the world. So amazed and objective was Fred's surprise that he took the bed lamp and held it to his face and body to see if he was not deceived and this forty-year-old man was not actually a palimpsest of slightly hidden decay and senility. But the light revealed nothing but what his eye had first seen—a youth untouched by life and disappointment.

He looked so much like God or something mythological that before he knew what he was doing Fred Parker had kissed him dutifully on the forehead.

"Why did you do that?" Mr. Graitop said, touching the place with his finger, and his voice was almost human.

Fred Parker sat down in a large easy chair and loosened his necktie. He did not answer the question because he had not heard it. He felt intoxicated and seriously unwell.

"How in hell do you live, Graitop?" he said almost too softly to be heard. "Are you married and do you have kids?"

"Yes, yes," Graitop replied, and he began to drivel now from his mouth.

Fred got up and wiped off his lips, and put the covers over him.

"A missionary," Fred Parker said. "But of what?"

"Don't be a fool," Graitop said sleepily. Suddenly he was asleep.

Fred Parker watched him again angrily from the chair.

"Who in hell are you, Graitop?" he shouted from the chair. "Why in hell did I run into you. Why in hell did I speak to you. . . . Why don't you look and act like other men?"

Fred called room service for ice, whiskey, and water. He began immediately the serious drinking he should not have been without all morning.

"When the bastard is conscious, I will ask him who he is and what he means to do."

"It's all right, Fred," Mr. Graitop said from time to time from the bed. "You are really with us, and it's all all right."

"I wish you wouldn't use that goddamn language, Graitop," he said. "You don't have the personality for a missionary. Too young and dead looking. Too vague."

From the bed there came sounds like a small boy sleeping.

• Sound of Talking •

IN the morning Mrs. Farebrother would put her husband in the wheelchair and talk to him while she made breakfast. As breakfast time came to an end he would sink his thumb into the black cherry preserves or sometimes he would take out an old Roman coin he had picked up from the war in Italy and hold that tight. In the summertime it helped to watch the swallows flying around when the pain was intense in his legs, or to listen to a plane going quite far off, and then hear all sound stop. There was a relief from the sound then that made you almost think your own pain had quit.

This morning began when Mrs. Farebrother thought of her trip to the city the day before, how she stared at the two young men on the bus, for they reminded her of two brothers she had known in high school, and of course her visit to the bird store.

As her husband's pain grew more acute, which happened every morning after breakfast, she would talk faster, which she knew irritated him more, but she felt that it distracted him more from his pain than anything else. Her voice was a different kind of pain to him, and that was diversion. For a while he held on to an iron bar when he had suffered, then he had pressed the Roman coin, and now he dabbed in the cherry preserves like a child.

"You know what I would like?" Mrs. Farebrother said. "I almost bought one yesterday in the bird store."

She moved his wheelchair closer to the window before telling him. "A raven."

"Well," he grunted, not letting his pain or anger speak this early. He hated birds, even the swallows which he watched from the kitchen were not silent enough for him.

"Ever since I was a little girl those birds have fascinated me. I never realized until the other day that I wanted one. I was walking down the intersection and I heard the birds' voices being broadcast from that huge seed store, all kinds of birds broadcasting to that busy street. I thought a bird might be a kind of amusement to us."

Here Mrs. Farebrother stopped talking as she moved him again, her eyes trying to avoid looking at his legs. Many times she did not know where to look, she knew he did not like her to look at him at all, but she had to look somewhere, and their kitchen was small and what one saw of the outdoors was limited.

"Do you need your pill," she said with too great a swiftness.

"I don't want it," he answered.

"I have plenty of nice ice water this morning," she said, which was a lie. She didn't know why she lied to him all the time. Her anguish and indecision put the lies into her mouth like the priest giving her the wafer on Sunday.

"Tell me about the bird store," he said, and she knew he must be in unusual pain and she felt she had brought it on him by telling about her outing. Yet if she had made him begin to suffer, she must finish what had started him on it, she could not let him sit in his wheelchair and not hear more.

"I went up two flights to where they keep the birds," she began, trying to keep her eyes away from his body and not to watch how his throat distended, with the arteries pounding like an athlete's, his upper body looking more muscular and power-ful each day under the punishment that came from lower down. But his suffering was too terrible and too familiar for her to scrutinize, and in fact she hardly ever looked at him carefully: all her glances were sideways, furtive; she had found the word in the crossword puzzles one evening, *clandestine*; it was a word which she had never said to anybody and it described her and haunted her like a face you can't quite remember the name for which keeps popping up in your mind. When they lay together in bed she touched him in a clandestine way also as though she might damage him; she felt his injuries were somehow more sensitive to her touch than they were to the hand of the doctor. She slept very poorly, but the doctor insisted that she sleep with him. As she lay in the bed with him, she thought of only two things, one that he could not approach her and the other when would he die.

Thinking like this, she had forgotten she was telling a story about the bird store. It was his contemptuous stare that brought her back to her own talking: "It was a menagerie of birds," she said, and stopped again.

"Go on," he said as though impatient for what could not possibly interest him.

"Vergil," she said looking at his face. "Verge."

She did not want to tell the story about the raven because she knew how infuriating it was to him to hear about pets of any kind. He hated all pets, he had killed their cat by throwing it out from the wheelchair against a tree. And all day long he sat and killed flies with a swiftness that had great fury in it.

"The men up there were so polite and attentive," she said, hardly stopping to remember whether they were or not, and thinking again of the young men on the bus. "I was surprised because in cities you know how people are, brusque, never expecting to see you again. I hadn't gone up there to see anything more than a few old yellow canaries when what on earth do you supose I saw but this raven. I have never seen anything like it in my life, and even the man in the shop saw how surprised and interested I was in the bird. What on earth is that? I said, and just then it talked back to me. It said, *George is dead, George is dead*."

"George is *what?*" Vergil cried at her, and for a moment she looked at him straight in the face. He looked as though the pain had left him, there was so much surprise in his expression.

"George is dead," she said and suddenly by the stillness of the room she felt the weight of the words which she had not realized until then. Sometimes, as now, when the pain left his face all her desire came back for him, while at night when she lay next to him nothing drew her to him at all; his dead weight seeming scarcely human. She thought briefly again about the hospital for paraplegics the doctor had told her about, in California, but she could never have mentioned even *paraplegic* to Vergil, let alone the place.

"What was the guy in the bird shop like?" he said, as though to help her to her next speech.

"Oh, an old guy sixty or seventy," Mrs. Farebrother lied. "He said he had clipped the bird's tongue himself. He started to describe how he did it, but I couldn't bear to hear him. Anything that involves cutting or surgery," she tried to stop but as though she had to, she added, "Even a bird . . ."

"For Christ's sake," Vergil said.

"I have never seen such purple in wings," Mrs. Farebrother went on, as though a needle had skipped a passage on the record and she was far ahead in her speech. "The only other time I ever saw such a color was in the hair of a young Roumanian fellow I went to high school with. When the light was just right, his hair had that purple sheen. Why, in fact, they called him the raven; isn't that odd, I had forgotten. . . ."

"Let's not start your when-I-was-young talk."

She thought that when he grunted out words like this or when he merely grunted in pain he sounded like somebody going to the toilet, and even though it was tragic she sometimes almost laughed in his face at such moments. Then again when sometimes he was suffering the most so that his hair would be damp with sweat, she felt a desire to hit him across the face, and these unexplained feelings frightened her a great deal.

But today she did not want him to suffer, and that is why she did not like to tell about the raven; she knew it was hurting him somehow — why she did not know, it was nothing, it bored her as she told it, and yet he insisted on hearing everything. She knew that if he kept insisting on more details she would invent some; often that happened. He would keep asking about the things that went on outside and she would invent little facts to amuse him. Yet these "facts" did not seem to please him, and life described outside, whether true or false, tortured him.

"Oh, Verge, I wished for you," she said, knowing immediately what she had said was the wrong thing to say; yet everything was somehow wrong to say to him.

"Then I said to the man in charge, doesn't the raven ever say anything but George is . . ." She stopped, choking with laughter; she had a laugh which Vergil had once told her sounded fake, but which somehow she could not find in her to change even for him.

"Then the man gave me a little speech about ravens," Mrs. Farebrother said.

"Well?" he said impatiently. His insistence on details had made her tired and gradually she was forgetting what things had happened and what things had not, what things and words could be said to him, what not. Everything in the end bore the warning FORBIDDEN.

"He said you have to teach the birds yourself. He said they have made no effort to teach them to talk." Mrs. Farebrother stopped trying to remember what the man had said, and what he had looked like.

"Well, he must have taught the bird to say *George is dead,*" Vergil observed, watching her closely.

"Yes, I suppose he did teach him that," she agreed, laughing shrilly.

"Had there been somebody there named George?" he said, curious.

"I'm sure I don't know," she said abstractedly. She began dusting an old picture-frame made of shells. "I imagine the bird just heard someone say that somewhere, maybe in the place where they got it from."

"Where did they get it from?" he wondered.

"I'm sure nobody knows," she replied, and she began to hum.

"*George is dead,*" he repeated. "I don't believe it said that."

"Why, Verge," she replied, her dust rag suddenly catching in the ruined shells of the frame. Tired as her mind was and many as the lies were she had told, to the best of her knowledge the bird had said that. She had not even thought it too odd until she had repeated it.

"Maybe the old man's name was George," Mrs. Farebrother said, not very convincing. A whole whirlwind of words waited for her again: "I asked him the price then, and do you know how much he wanted for that old bird, well not old, perhaps, I guess it was young for a raven, they live forever. . . . Fifty dollars!" she sighed. "Fifty dollars without the cage!"

He watched her closely and then to her surprise he drew a wallet out from his dressing gown. She had not known he kept a wallet there, and though his hands shook terribly, he insisted on opening it himself. He took out five ten-dollar bills, which oddly enough was all that was in it, and handed them to her.

"Why, Verge, that isn't necessary, dear," she said, and she put her hands to her hair in a ridiculous gesture.

"Don't talk with that crying voice, for Christ's sake," he said. "You sound like my old woman."

"Darling," she tried to control her tears, "I don't need any pet like that around the house. Besides, it would make you nervous."

"Do you want him or don't you," he said furiously, pushing up his chest and throat to get the words out.

She stopped in front of the wheelchair, trying to think what she *did* want; nearly everything had become irrelevant or even too obscure to bear thinking about. She fingered the five ten-dollar bills, trying to find an answer to please both of them. Then suddenly she knew she wanted nothing. She did not believe anybody could give her anything. One thing or another or nothing were all the same.

"Don't you want your raven," he continued in his firm strong male voice, the voice he always used after an attack had passed so that he seemed to resemble somebody she had known in another place and time.

"I don't really want it, Vergil," Mrs. Farebrother said quietly, handing him the bills.

He must have noticed the absence of self-pity or any attempt to act a part, which in the past had been her stock-in-trade. There was nothing but the emptiness of the truth on her face: she wanted nothing.

"I'll tell you what, Verge," she began again with her laugh and the lies beginning at the same time, as she watched him put the money back in his wallet. Her voice had become soothing and low, the voice she used on children she sometimes stopped on the street to engage in conversation. "I'm afraid of that bird, Vergil," she confessed, as though the secret were out. "It's so large and its beak and claws rather frightened me. Even that old man was cautious with it."

"Yet you had all this stuff about ravens and Roumanians and high school," he accused her.

"Oh, high school," she said, and her mouth filled with saliva, as though it was only her mouth now, which, lying to him continually, had the seat of her emotions.

"It might cheer things up for you if something talked for you around here," he said.

She looked at him to determine the meaning of his words, but she could find no expression in them or in him.

"It would be trouble," she said. "Birds are dirty."

"But if *you* want him, Verge," and in her voice and eyes there was the supplication for hope, as if she had said, If somebody would tell her a thing to hope for maybe she would want something again, have desire again.

"No," he replied, turning the wheel of the chair swiftly, "I don't want a raven for myself if you are that cool about getting it."

He looked down at the wallet, and then his gaze fell swiftly to the legs that lay on the wheelchair's footrest. She had mentioned high school as the place where life had stopped for her; he remembered further back even than Italy, back to the first time he had ever gone to the barbershop, his small legs had then hung down helplessly too while he got his first haircut; but they had hung *alive*.

"Of course you could teach the bird to talk," she said, using her fake laugh.

"Yes, I enjoy hearing talk so much," and he laughed now almost like her.

She turned to look at him. She wanted to scream or push him roughly, she wanted to tell him to just *want* something, anything for just one moment so that she could want something for that one moment too. She wanted him to want something so that she could want something, but she knew he would never want at all again. There would be suffering, the suffering that would make him swell in the chair until he looked like a god in ecstasy, but it would all be just a man practicing for death, and the suffering illusion. And why should a man practicing for death take time out to teach a bird to talk?

"There doesn't seem to be any ice after all," Mrs. Farebrother said, pretending to look in the icebox. It was time for his medicine, and she had quit looking at anything, and their long day together had begun.

• CUTTING EDGE •

MRS. Zeller opposed her son's beard. She was in her house in Florida when she saw him wearing it for the first time. It was as though her mind had come to a full stop. This large full-bearded man entered the room and she remembered always later how ugly he had looked and how frightened she felt seeing him in the house; then the realization it was someone she knew, and finally the terror of recognition.

He had kissed her, which he didn't often do, and she recognized in this his attempt to make her discomfort the more painful. He held the beard to her face for a long time, then he released her as though she had suddenly disgusted him.

"Why did you do it?" she asked. She was, he saw, almost broken by the recognition.

"I didn't dare tell you and come."

"That's of course true," Mrs. Zeller said. "It would have been worse. You'll have to shave it off, of course. Nobody must see you. Your father of course didn't have the courage to warn me, but I knew something was wrong the minute he entered the house ahead of you. I suppose he's upstairs laughing now. But it's not a laughing matter."

Mrs. Zeller's anger turned against her absent husband as though all error began and ended with him. "I suppose he likes it." Her dislike of Mr. Zeller struck her son as staggeringly great at that moment.

He looked at his mother and was surprised to see how young she was. She did not look much older than he did. Perhaps she looked younger now that he had his beard.

"I had no idea a son of mine would do such a thing," she said. "But why a beard, for heaven's sake," she cried, as though he had chosen something permanent and irreparable which would destroy all that they were.

109

"Is it because you are an artist? No, don't answer me," she commanded. "I can't stand to hear any explanation from you. . . ."

"I have always wanted to wear a beard," her son said. "I remember wanting one as a child."

"I don't remember that at all," Mrs. Zeller said.

"I remember it quite well. I was in the summer house near that old broken-down wall and I told Ellen Whitelaw I wanted to have a beard when I grew up."

"Ellen Whitelaw, that big fat stupid thing. I haven't thought of her in years."

Mrs. Zeller was almost as much agitated by the memory of Ellen Whitelaw as by her son's beard.

"You didn't like Ellen Whitelaw," her son told her, trying to remember how they had acted when they were together.

"She was a common and inefficient servant," Mrs. Zeller said, more quietly now, masking her feelings from her son.

"I suppose *he* liked her," the son pretended surprise, the cool cynical tone coming into his voice.

"Oh, your father," Mrs. Zeller said.

"Did he then?" the son asked.

"Didn't he like all of them?" she asked. The beard had changed this much already between them, she talked to him now about his father's character, while the old man stayed up in the bedroom fearing a scene.

"Didn't he always," she repeated, as though appealing to this new hirsute man.

"So," the son said, accepting what he already knew.

"Ellen Whitelaw, for God's sake," Mrs. Zeller said. The name of the servant girl brought back many other faces and rooms which she did not know were in her memory. These faces and rooms served to make the bearded man who stared at her less and less the boy she remembered in the days of Ellen Whitelaw.

"You must shave it off," Mrs. Zeller said.

"What makes you think I would do that?" the boy wondered.

"You heard me. Do you want to drive me out of my mind?"

"But I'm not going to. Or rather it's not going to."

"I will appeal to him, though a lot of good it will do," Mrs. Zeller said. "He ought to do something once in twenty years at least."

"You mean," the son said laughing, "he hasn't done anything in that long."

"Nothing I can really remember," Mrs. Zeller told him.

"It will be interesting to hear you appeal to him," the boy said. "I haven't heard you do that in such a long time."

"I don't think you ever heard me."

"I did, though," he told her. "It was in the days of Ellen Whitelaw again, in fact."

"In *those* days," Mrs. Zeller wondered. "I don't see how that could be."

"Well, it was. I can remember that much."

"You couldn't have been more than four years old. How could you remember then?"

"I heard you say to him, *You have to ask her to go.*"

Mrs. Zeller did not say anything. She really could not remember the words, but she supposed that the scene was true and that he actually remembered.

"Please shave off that terrible beard. If you only knew how awful it looks on you. You can't see anything else but it."

"Everyone in New York thought it was particularly fine."

"Particularly fine," she paused over his phrase as though its meaning eluded her.

"It's nauseating," she was firm again in her judgment.

"I'm not going to do away with it," he said, just as firm.

She did not recognize his firmness, but she saw everything changing a little, including perhaps the old man upstairs.

"Are you going to 'appeal' to him?" The son laughed again when he saw she could say no more.

"Don't mock me," the mother said. "I will speak to your father." She pretended decorum. "You can't go anywhere with us, you know."

He looked unmoved.

"I don't want any of my friends to see you. You'll have to stay in the house or go to your own places. You can't go out with us to our places and see our friends. I hope none of the neighbors see you. If they ask who you are, I won't tell them."

"I'll tell them then."

They were not angry, they talked it out like that, while the old man was upstairs.

"Do you suppose he is drinking or asleep?" she said finally.

"I thought he looked good in it, Fern," Mr. Zeller said.

"What about it makes him look good?" she said.

"It fills out his face," Mr. Zeller said, looking at the wallpaper and surprised he had never noticed what a pattern it had before; it showed the sacrifice of some sort of animal by a youth.

He almost asked his wife how she had come to pick out this pattern, but her growing fury checked him.

He saw her mouth and throat moving with unspoken words.

"Where is he now?" Mr. Zeller wondered.

"What does that matter where he is?" she said. "He has to be somewhere while he's home, but he can't go out with us."

"How idiotic," Mr. Zeller said, and he looked at his wife straight in the face for a second.

"Why did you say that?" She tried to quiet herself down.

"The way you go on about nothing, Fern." For a moment a kind of revolt announced itself in his manner, but then his eyes went back to the wallpaper, and she resumed her tone of victor.

"I've told him he must either cut it off or go back to New York."

"Why is it a beard upsets you so?" he wondered, almost to himself.

"It's not the beard so much. It's the way he is now too.

And it disfigures him so. I don't recognize him at all now when he wears it."

"So, he's never done anything of his own before," Mr. Zeller protested suddenly.

"Never done anything!" He could feel her anger covering him and glancing off like hot sun onto the wallpaper.

"That's right," he repeated. "He's never done anything. I say let him keep the beard and I'm not going to talk to him about it." His gaze lifted toward her but rested finally only on her hands and skirt.

"This is still my house," she said, "and I have to live in this town."

"When they had the centennial in Collins, everybody wore beards."

"I have to live in this town," she repeated.

"I won't talk to him about it," Mr. Zeller said.

It was as though the voice of Ellen Whitelaw reached her saying, *So that was how you appealed to him.*

She sat on the deck chair on the porch and smoked five cigarettes. The two men were somewhere in the house and she had the feeling now that she only roomed here. She wished more than that the beard was gone that her son had never mentioned Ellen Whitelaw. She found herself thinking only about her. Then she thought that now twenty years later she could not have afforded a servant, not even her.

She supposed the girl was dead. She did not know why, but she was sure she was.

She thought also that she should have mentioned her name to Mr. Zeller. It might have broken him down about the beard, but she supposed not. He had been just as adamant and unfeeling with her about the girl as he was now about her son.

Her son came through the house in front of her without speaking, dressed only in his shorts and, when he had got safely beyond her in the garden, he took off those so that he was completely naked with his back to her, and lay down in the sun.

She held the cigarette in her hand until it began to burn her finger. She felt she should not move from the place where she was and yet she did not know where to go inside the house and she did not know what pretext to use for going inside.

In the brilliant sun his body, already tanned, matched his shining black beard.

She wanted to appeal to her husband again and she knew then she could never again. She wanted to call a friend and tell her but she had no friend to whom she could tell this.

The events of the day, like a curtain of extreme bulk, cut her off from her son and husband. She had always ruled the house and them even during the awful Ellen Whitelaw days and now as though they did not even recognize her, they had taken over. She was not even here. Her son could walk naked with a beard in front of her as though she did not exist. She had nothing to fight them with, nothing to make them see with. They ignored her as Mr. Zeller had when he looked at the wallpaper and refused to discuss their son.

"You can grow it back when you're in New York," Mr. Zeller told his son.

He did not say anything about his son lying naked before him in the garden but he felt insulted almost as much as his mother had, yet he needed his son's permission and consent now and perhaps that was why he did not mention the insult of his nakedness.

"I don't know why I have to act like a little boy all the time with you both."

"If you were here alone with me you could do anything you wanted. You know I never asked anything of you. . . ."

When his son did not answer, Mr. Zeller said, "Did I?"

"That was the trouble," the son said.

"What?" the father wondered.

"You never wanted anything from me and you never

wanted to give me anything. I didn't matter to you."

"Well, I'm sorry," the father said doggedly.

"Those were the days of Ellen Whitelaw," the son said in tones like the mother.

"For God's sake," the father said and he put a piece of grass between his teeth.

He was a man who kept everything down inside of him, everything had been tied and fastened so long there was no part of him anymore that could struggle against the stricture of his life.

There were no words between them for some time; then Mr. Zeller could hear himself bringing the question out: "Did she mention that girl?"

"Who?" The son pretended blankness.

"Our servant."

The son wanted to pretend again blankness but it was too much work. He answered: "No, I mentioned it. To her surprise."

"Don't you see how it is?" the father went on to the present. "She doesn't speak to either of us now and if you're still wearing the beard when you leave it's me she will be punishing six months from now."

"And you want me to save you from your wife."

"Bobby," the father said, using the childhood tone and inflection. "I wish you would put some clothes on too when you're in the garden. With me it doesn't matter, you could do anything. I never asked you for anything. But with her . . ."

"God damn *her*," the boy said.

The father could not protest. He pleaded with his eyes at his son.

The son looked at his father and he could see suddenly also the youth hidden in his father's face. He was young like his mother. They were both young people who had learned nothing from life, were stopped and drifting where they were twenty years before with Ellen Whitelaw. Only *she*, the son thought, must have learned from life, must have gone on to some development in her character, while they had been tied to the shore where she had left them.

"Imagine living with someone for six months and not speaking," the father said as if to himself. "That happened once before, you know, when you were a little boy."

"I don't remember that," the son said, some concession in his voice.

"You were only four," the father told him.

"I believe this is the only thing I ever asked of you," the father said. "Isn't it odd, I can't remember ever asking you anything else. Can you?"

The son looked coldly away at the sky and then answered, contempt and pity struggling together, "No, I can't."

"Thank you, Bobby," the father said.

"Only don't *plead* anymore, for Christ's sake." The son turned from him.

"You've only two more days with us, and if you shaved it off and put on just a few clothes, it would help me through the year with her."

He spoke as though it would be his last year.

"Why don't you beat some sense into her?" The son turned to him again.

The father's gaze fell for the first time complete on his son's nakedness.

Bobby had said he would be painting in the storeroom and she could send up a sandwich from time to time, and Mr. and Mrs. Zeller were left downstairs together. She refused to allow her husband to answer the phone.

In the evening Bobby came down dressed carefully and his beard combed immaculately and looking, they both thought, curled.

They talked about things like horse racing, in which they were all somehow passionately interested, but which they now discussed irritably as though it too were a menace to their lives. They talked about the uselessness of art and why people went into it with a detachment that would have made an outsider think that Bobby was as unconnected with it as a jockey or oil magnate. They condemned nearly everything and then the son went upstairs and they saw one another again briefly at bedtime.

The night before he was to leave they heard him up all hours, the water running, and the dropping of things made of metal.

Both parents were afraid to get up and ask him if he was all right. He was like a wealthy relative who had commanded them never to question him or interfere with his movements even if he was dying.

He was waiting for them at breakfast, dressed only in his shorts but he looked more naked than he ever had in the garden because his beard was gone. Over his chin lay savage and profound scratches as though he had removed the hair with a hunting knife and pincers.

Mrs. Zeller held her breast and turned to the coffee and Mr. Zeller said only his son's name and sat down with last night's newspaper.

"What time does your plane go?" Mrs. Zeller said in a dead, muffled voice.

The son began putting a white paste on the scratches on his face and did not answer.

"I believe your mother asked you a question," Mr. Zeller said, pale and shaking.

"Ten-forty," the son replied.

The son and the mother exchanged glances and he could see at once that his sacrifice had been in vain: she would also see the beard there again under the scratches and the gashes he had inflicted on himself, and he would never really be her son again. Even for his father it must be much the same. He had come home as a stranger who despised them and he had shown his nakedness to both of them. All three longed for separation and release.

But Bobby could not control the anger coming up in him, and his rage took an old form. He poured the coffee into his saucer because Mr. Zeller's mother had always done this and it had infuriated Mrs. Zeller because of its low-class implications.

He drank vicious from the saucer, blowing loudly.

Both parents watched him helplessly like insects suddenly swept against the screen.

"It's not too long till Christmas," Mr. Zeller brought out. "We hope you'll come back for the whole vacation."

"We do," Mrs. Zeller said in a voice completely unlike her own.

"So," Bobby began, but the torrent of anger would not let him say the thousand fierce things he had ready.

Instead, he blew savagely from the saucer and spilled some onto the chaste white summer rug below him. Mrs. Zeller did not move.

"I would invite you to New York," Bobby said quietly now, "but of course I will have the beard there and it wouldn't work for you."

"Yes," Mr. Zeller said, incoherent.

"I do hope you don't think I've been . . ." Mrs. Zeller cried suddenly, and they both waited to hear whether she was going to weep or not, but she stopped herself perhaps by the realization that she had no tears and that the feelings which had come over her about Bobby were likewise spent.

"I can't think of any more I can do for you," Bobby said suddenly.

They both stared at each other as though he had actually left and they were alone at last.

"Is there anything more you want me to do?" he said, coldly vicious.

They did not answer.

"I hate and despise what both of you have done to yourselves, but the thought that you would be sitting here in your middle-class crap not speaking to one another is too much even for me. That's why I did it, I guess, and not out of any love. I didn't want you to think that."

He sloshed in the saucer.

"Bobby," Mr. Zeller said.

The son brought out his *What?* with such finished beauty of coolness that he paused to admire his own control and mastery.

"Please, Bobby," Mr. Zeller said.

They could all three of them hear a thousand speeches. The agony of awkwardness was made unendurable by the iciness of the son, and all three paused over this glacial control which had come to him out of art and New York, as though it was the fruit of their lives and the culmination of their twenty years.

• 63: DREAM PALACE •

DO you ever think about Fenton Riddleway?" Parkhearst Cratty asked the greatwoman one afternoon when they were sitting in the summer garden of her "mansion."

Although the greatwoman had been drinking earlier in the day, she was almost sober at the time Parkhearst put this question to her.

It was a rhetorical and idle question, but Parkhearst's idle questions were always put to her as a plea that they should review their lives together, and she always accepted the plea by saying nearly the same thing: "Why don't you write down what Fenton did?" she would say. "Since you did write once," and her face much more than her voice darkened at him.

Actually the eyes of the greatwoman were blackened very little with mascara and yet such was their cavernous appearance they gaped at Parkhearst as though tonight they would yield him her real identity and why people called her great.

"Fenton Riddleway is vague as a dream to me," the greatwoman said.

"That means he is more real to you than anybody," Parkhearst said.

"How could it mean anything else?" she repeated her own eternal rejoinder. Then arranging her long dress so that it covered the floor before her shoes, she began to throw her head back as though suffering from a feeling of suffocation.

It was her signal to him that he was to leave, but he took no notice of her wishes today.

"I can't write down what Fenton did because I never found out who he was," Parkhearst explained again to her.

"You've said that ever since he was first with us. And since he went away, a million times."

121

She reached for the gin; it was the only drink she would have since the days of Fenton.

"Not that I'm criticizing you for saying it," she said. "How could I criticize you?" she added.

"Then don't scratch and tear at me, for Christ's sake," he told her.

Her mouth wet from the drink smiled faintly at him.

"What Fenton did was almost the only story I ever really wanted to write," Parkhearst said, and a shadow of old happiness came over his thin brown face.

Grainger's eyes brightened briefly, then went back into their unrelieved darkness.

"You can't feel as empty of recollection as I do," Grainger mumbled, sipping again.

Parkhearst watched the veins bulge in his hands.

"Why are we dead anyhow?" Parkhearst said, bored with the necessity of returning to this daily statement. "Is it because of our losing the people we loved or because the people we found were damned?" He laughed.

One never mentioned the "real" things like this at Grainger's, and here Parkhearst had done it, and nothing happened. Instead, Grainger listened as though hearing some two or three notes of an alto sax she recalled from the concerts she gave at her home.

"This is the first time you ever said you were, Parkhearst. Dead," she said in her clearest voice.

He sat looking like a small rock that has been worked on by a swift but careless hammer.

"Are you really without a memory?" she asked, speaking now like a child.

He did not say anything and she began to get up.

"Don't get up, or you'll fall," he said, almost not looking in her direction.

The greatwoman had gotten up and stood there like some more than human personage at the end of an opera. Parkhearst closed his eyes. Then she advanced to a half-fall at the feet of her old friend.

"Are those tears?" she said looking up into his face.

"Don't be tiresome, Grainger. Go back and sit down," he said, with the petulance of a small boy.

Pushing her head towards his face, she kissed him several times.

"You're getting gray," she said, almost shocked. "I didn't know it had been such a long time."

"I try never to think about those things," he looked at her now. "Please get up."

"Do you think Fenton Riddleway would know you now, Parkhearst?" the greatwoman asked sullenly but without anything taunting in her voice.

"The real question is whether we would know Fenton Riddleway if we saw him."

"We'd know him," she said. "Above or beneath hell."

As evening came on in the "mansion" (*mansion* a word they both thought of and used all the time because Fenton had used it), they drank more and more of the neat Holland gin, but drunkenness did not take: was it after all, they kept on saying, merely the remembrance of a boy from West Virginia, that mover and shaker Fenton, that kept them talking and living.

"Tell me all about what he did again," Grainger said, seated now on her gold carved chair. The dark hid her age, so that she looked now only relatively old; it almost hid the fact that she was drunk, drunk going on to ten years, and her face was shapeless and sexless.

"Tell me what he did all over again, just this last time. If you won't write it down, Parkhearst, you'll have to come here and tell it to me once a month. I had always hoped you would write it down so I could have it read to me on my bad nights. . . ."

"Your memory is so much better than mine," Parkhearst said.

"I have no memory," the greatwoman said. "Or only a grain of one."

She raised her glass threateningly, but it had got so dark

in the room she could not see just where Parkhearst's tired voice was coming from. It was like the time she had called Russell long distance to his home town, the voice had wavered, then had grown, then had sunk into indistinguishable sounds. Parkhearst would take another drink of the gin, then his voice would rise a bit, only to die away again as he told her everything he could remember.

"Are you awake?" Parkhearst questioned her.

"Keep going," she said. "Don't stop to ask me a single thing. Just tell what he did, and then write it all down for me to read hereafter."

He nodded at her.

There was this park with a patriot's name near the lagoon. Parkhearst Cratty had been wandering there, not daring to go home to his wife Bella. He had done nothing in weeks, and her resentment against him would be too heavy to bear. Of course it was true, what he was later to tell Fenton himself, that he was looking for "material" for his book. Many times he had run across people in the park who had told him their stories while he pretended to listen to their voices while usually watching their persons.

In this section of the park there were no lights, and the only illumination came from the reflection of the traffic blocks away. Here the men who came to wander about as aimless and groping as he were obvious shades in hell. He always noticed this fact as he noticed there were no lights. Parkhearst paid little attention to the actual things that went on in the park and, although not a brave or strong young man, he had never felt fear in the park itself. It was its atmosphere alone that satisfied him and he remained forever innocent of its acts.

It was August, and cool, but he felt enervated as never before. His marriage pursued him like a never-ending nightmare, and he could not free himself from the obsession that "everything was over."

Just like children, he and the greatwoman Grainger

longed, and especially demanded even, that something should happen, or again Parkhearst would cry, "A reward, I must have a reward. A reward for life just as I have lived it."

It was just as he had uttered the words *a reward* that he first saw Fenton Riddleway go past, he remembered.

In the darkness and the rehearsed evil of the park it was odd, indeed, as Parkhearst now reflected on the event, that anyone should have stood out at all that night, one shadow from the other. Yet Fenton was remarkable at once, perhaps for no other reason than that he was actually lost and wandering about, for no other reason than this. Parkhearst did not need to watch him for more than a moment to see his desperation.

Parkhearst lit a cigarette so that his own whereabouts would be visible to the stranger.

"Looking for anybody?" Parkhearst then asked.

Fenton's face was momentarily lighted up by Parkhearst's cigarette: the face had, he noted with accustomed uneasiness, a kind of beauty but mixed with something unsteady, unusual.

"Where do you get out?" the boy asked.

He stood directly over Parkhearst in a position a less experienced man than the writer would have taken to be a threat.

Parkhearst recognized with a certain shock that this was the first question he had ever had addressed to him in the park which was asked with the wish to be answered: somebody really wanted out of the park.

"Where do you want to go?"

Fenton took from his pocket a tiny dimestore notebook and read from the first page an address.

"It's south," Parkhearst replied. "Away from the lagoon."

Fenton still looked too unsure to speak. He dropped the notebook and when he stooped to pick it up his head twitched while his eyes looked at the writer.

"Do you want me to show you?" Parkhearst asked, pretending indifference.

Fenton looked directly into his face now.

Those eyes looked dumb, Parkhearst saw them again, like

maybe the eyes of the first murderer, dumb and innocent and getting to be mad.

"Show me, please," Fenton said, and Parkhearst heard the Southern accent.

"You're from far off," Parkhearst said as they began to walk in the opposite direction from the lagoon.

Fenton had been too frightened not to want to unburden himself. He told nearly everything, as though in a police court, that he was Fenton Riddleway and that he was nineteen, that he had come with his brother Claire from West Virginia, from a town near Ronceverte, that their mother had died two weeks before, and that a friend of his named Kincaid had given him an address in a rooming house on Sixty-*three* Street . . .

"You mean Sixty-*third*," Parkhearst corrected him, but Fenton did not hear the correction then or when it was made fifty times later: "A house on Sixty-three Street," he continued. "It turns out to be a not-right-kind of place at all. . . ."

"How is that?" Parkhearst wondered.

They moved out of the middle section of the park and into a place where the street light looked down on them. Fenton was gazing at him easily but Parkhearst's eyes kept to his coat pocket, which bulged obviously.

"Is that your gun there?" he said, weary.

Fenton watched him, moving his lips quickly.

"Don't let it go off on yourself," Parkhearst said ineffectively as the boy nodded.

"But what were you saying about that house?" the writer went back to his story.

"It's alive with something, I don't know what. . . ."

Fenton's thick accent, which seemed to become thicker now, all at once irritated Parkhearst, and as they drew near the part of the city that was more inhabited and better lighted, he felt himself surprised by Fenton's incredibly poor-fitting almost filthy clothes and by the fact that his hair had the look of not ever perhaps having been cut or combed. He looked more or less like West Virginia, Parkhearst supposed, and then Parkhearst always remembered he had thought this, he looked not only just West Virginia, he looked himself, Fenton.

"What's it alive with, then?" Parkhearst came back to the subject of the house.

"I don't mean it's got ghosts, though I think it maybe does." He stopped, fishing for encouragement to go on and when none came he said: "It's a not-right house. There ain't nobody in it for one thing."

"I don't think I see," Parkhearst said, and he felt not so much his interest waning as his feeling that there was something about this boy too excessive; everything about him was too large for him, the speech, the terrible clothes, the ragged hair, the possible gun, the outlandish accent.

"All the time we're alone in it, I keep thinking how empty it is, and what are we waiting for after all, with so little money to tide us over, if he don't show up. Claire cries all the time on account of the change. The house don't do *him* any good."

"Can you find your way back now, do you think?" Parkhearst asked, as they got to a street down which ordinary people and traffic were moving.

A paralysis had struck the writer suddenly, as though all the interest he might have had in Fenton had been killed. He was beginning to be afraid also that he would be involved in more than a story.

Fenton stopped as if to remind Parkhearst that he had a responsibility toward him. His having found the first person in his life who would listen to him had made him within ten minutes come to regard Parkhearst as a friend, and now the realization came quickly that this was only a listener who having heard the story would let him go back to the "not-right house."

"Here's fifty cents for you," Parkhearst said.

He took it with a funny quick movement as though money for the first time had meaning for him.

"You won't come with me to see Claire?"

Parkhearst stared. This odd boy, who was probably wanted by the police, who had come out of nothing to him, had asked him a question in the tone of one who had known him all his life.

"Tomorrow maybe," Parkhearst answered. He explained lamely about Bella waiting for him and being cross if he came any later.

The boy's face fell.

"You know where to find the house?" Fenton said, hoarse.

"Yes," Parkhearst replied dreamily, indifferent.

Fenton looked at Parkhearst, unbelieving. Then: "How can you find it?" he wondered. "I can't ever find it no matter how many times I go and come. How can you then?"

The sorrow on Fenton's face won him over to him again, and he felt Bella's eyes of reproach disappear from his mind for a moment.

"Tomorrow afternoon I'll visit you at the house," he promised. "Two o'clock."

A moment later when Fenton was gone, Parkhearst looking back could not help wait for the last sight of him in the street, and a new feeling so close to acute sickness swept over him. It was the wildness and freedom Fenton had, he began to try to explain to himself. The wildness and freedom held against his own shut-in locked life. He hurried on home to Bella.

Bella listened vaguely to the story of Fenton Riddleway. There had been, she recalled mechanically, scores, even hundreds, of these people Parkhearst met in order to study for his writing, but the stories themselves were never put in final shape or were never written, and Parkhearst himself forgot the old models in his search for new ones.

"Is Fenton to take the place of Grainger now?" Bella commented on his enthusiasm, almost his ecstasy.

There was no criticism in her remark. She was beyond that. Bella Cratty had resigned herself to her complete knowledge of her husband's character. There was, furthermore, no opposing Parkhearst; if he were opposed he would disintegrate slowly, vanish before her eyes. He was a child who must not be crossed in the full possession of his freedom, one who must be left to follow his own whims and visions.

She had married him without anyone knowing why, but everyone agreed she had done so with the full knowledge of what he was. If she had not known before, their married life had been a continuous daily rehearsal of Parkhearst's character; he was himself every minute, taking more and more away from what was *her* with each new sorrow he brought home to her. He became more and more incurable and it was his incurable quality which made him essential to her.

She was not happy a second. Had she seen the wandering men in the park after whom Parkhearst gazed, she might have seen herself like them, wandering without purpose away from the light. And though she tried to pretend that she wanted Parkhearst to have friends no matter what they were, no matter what they would do, she never gave up suffering, and each of the "new" people he met and "studied" cost her an impossible sacrifice.

There was something at once about the name Fenton Riddleway that made her feel there was danger here in his name as Grainger was in hers. Only there was something in the new name more frightening than in Grainger's.

As two o'clock approached the following day (an evil hour in astrology, Parkhearst had noticed covertly, for Bella objected to his interest in what she called "the moons"), both of them felt the importance of his departure. He had tried to get her "ready" from the evening before so that she would accept this as Fenton's day, when as a writer he must find out all there was to know about this strange boy. Parkhearst used the word *material* again, though he had promised himself to give up using the word.

"I suppose in the end you will let Grainger have Fenton," Bella remarked, a sudden hostility coming over her face as she sat at the kitchen table drinking her coffee.

Parkhearst stopped his task of sewing on a button on his old gray-green jacket.

It was only when his wife said that that he understood he did not wish to share Fenton with anyone, until, he lied to himself, he had found out everything Fenton had done. And then he corrected this lie in his own mind: he simply did not want to share Fenton with anybody. Grainger would spoil him, would take him over, if she were interested, and he knew of course that she was going to be.

"Grainger won't get him," he said finally.

Bella laughed a very high laugh, ridden with hysteria and shaky restraint. "You've never kept anybody from one another as long as you've been friends," she reviewed their lives. "What would happen," she went on bitterly, "if you couldn't show one another what you take in, what you accomplish. If there was no competition!"

"Fenton is different," Parkhearst said, pale with anger. Then suddenly, so shaken by fear of what she said, he told her a thing which he immediately realized was trivial and silly: "He has a gun, for one thing."

Bella Cratty did not go on drinking coffee immediately, but not due to anything Parkhearst had said except his pronouncing of Fenton's name. There had, of course, in their five years of marriage and in their five years of Grainger, been people with guns, and people whom he had found in streets, in parks, in holes, who had turned out to be all right, but now she suddenly felt the last outpost of safety had been reached. Their lives had stopped suddenly, and then were jerked ahead out of her control at last. She felt she was no longer *here*.

"Maybe Grainger *should* meet him," she said in a tone unlike herself, because there was no hysteria or pretending in it, just dull fear, and then she finished the coffee at the same moment her husband finished sewing the button on his coat.

Still holding his needle and thread, he advanced to her and kissed her on the forehead. "I know you hate all this," he said, like a doctor or soldier about to perform an heroic act. "I know you can't get used to all this. Maybe you aren't used to what is me."

Bella had not waited this time for the full effect of the kiss.

She got up and quickly went into the front room and began looking out the window with the intensity of one who is about to fly out into space. He followed her there.

"Do you hate me completely?" Parkhearst asked, happy with the sense she had given him permission to go for Fenton.

It was nearly two o'clock, he noted, and she did not give him goodbye and the word to leave.

"Just go, dear," she said at last, and it was not the fact she had put on a martyr's expression in her voice, the voice was the only one that could come from her having chosen, as she had, the life five years before.

"I can't go when you sound like this," he complained. His voice told how much he wanted to go and that it was already past two o'clock.

Yet somehow the strength to give him up did not come to her. He had to find it in her for himself and take it from her.

"Go now, go," she said when he kissed the back of her neck.

"I will," he said, "because I know I'm only hurting you by staying."

Bella nodded.

When he was gone, she watched for him onto the street below. From above she could see him waving and throwing a kiss to her as he moved on down toward Sixty-third Street. He looked younger than Christ still, she said. A boy groom . . . Sometimes people had half-wondered, she knew, if she was his very young mother. She stood there in that stiff height so far above him and yet felt crawling somewhere far down, like a bug in a desert, hot and sticking to ground, and possibly not even any more alive.

As necessary as Bella was to his every need for existence, his only feeling of life came when he left her, as today, for a free afternoon. And this afternoon was especially free. There was even the feeling of the happiness death might give. It was only later that life was to be so like death that the idea of dying was meaningless to him, but tonight, he remembered, he had thought of death and it was full of mysterious desirability.

It was one of those heavy days in the city when a late riser is not certain it is getting light or dark, an artificial twilight in which the sounds of the elevated trains and trucks weight darkness the more. Parkhearst hurried on down the interminable street, soon leaving the white section behind, and into the beginning of the colored district. People took no notice of him, he was no stranger to these streets, and besides he was dressed in clothes which without being too poor made him inconspicuous.

He was not looking at the street anyhow today, whose meanness and filth usually gave his soul such satisfaction. His whole mind was on Fenton. Fenton was a small-town boy, and yet all his expression and gestures and being made it right that he should live on this street, where no one really belonged or stayed very long.

It was difficult, though, to see Fenton living in a house, even in the kind of house that would be near Sixty-third Street. There must be some kind of mistake there, he thought.

He went on, pursued by the memory of Fenton's face. Was there more, he wondered out loud, in that face than poverty and a tendency to be tricky if not criminal? What were those eyes conveying, then, some meaning that was truthful and honest over and above his deceit and rottenness?

He was late. He hurried faster. The dark under the elevated made him confuse one street for another. He stopped and in his indecision looked back east toward the direction of the park where he had met Fenton: he feared Fenton had played a trick on him, for there was nothing which resembled a house on the street. He stood in front of a fallen-in building with the handwritten sign in chalk:

The Come and See Resurrection Pentecostal Church. Reverend Hosea Gulley, Pastor.

Then walking on, he saw near a never-ending set of vacant lots the house he knew must contain Fenton. It was one of those early twentieth-century houses that have survived by oversight but which look so rotten and devoured that you can't believe they were ever built but that they rotted and mushroomed into existence and that their rot was their first and last growth.

There was no number. It was a color like green and yellow. Around the premises was a fence of sharp iron, cut like spears.

He began knocking on the immense front door and then waiting as though he knew there would be no answer.

As nobody stirred, he began calling out the name of his new friend. Then he heard some faint moving around in the back and finally Fenton, looking both black and pale, appeared through the frosted glass of the inner door and stared out. His face greeted Parkhearst without either pleasure or recognition, and he advanced mechanically and irritably, as though the door had blown open and he was coming to close it.

"No wonder you had trouble finding it," Parkhearst said when Fenton unlocked the door and let him in.

"He's having a bad spell, that's why I'm in a hurry," Fenton explained.

"Who?" Parkhearst closed the door behind him.

"Claire, my brother Claire."

They went through a hallway as long as a half city block to a small room in which there was a dwarf-like cot with a large mattress clinging to it and a crippled immense chest of drawers supported by only three legs. The window was boarded up and there was almost no light coming from a dying electric bulb hung from the high ceiling.

On the bed lay a young boy dressed in overall pants and a green sweater. He looked very pale but did not act in pain.

"He says he can't walk now," Fenton observed. "Claire, can't you say *hello* to the visitor?" Fenton went over to the bed and touched Claire on the shoulder.

"He keeps asking me why we can't move on. To a real house, I suppose," Fenton explained softly to Parkhearst.

"And that worries him. There are several things that worry him," Fenton said in a bored voice.

"Look," Claire said cheerfully and with energy, pointing to the wall. There were a few bugs moving rather rapidly across the cracked calcimine. "Sit down in this chair," Fenton said and moved the chair over to Parkhearst.

"Do you really think," Fenton began on the subject that was closest to him too, "that we're *in* the right house maybe?"

Parkhearst did not speak, feeling unsure how to begin. For one thing, he was not positive that the small boy who was called Claire was not feebleminded, but the longer he looked the more he felt the boy was reasonably intelligent but probably upset by the kind of life he was leading with Fenton. He therefore did not reply to Fenton's question at once, and Fenton repeated it, almost shouting. He had gotten very much more excited since they had met in the park the evening before.

Parkhearst was noticing that Claire followed his brother with his eyes around the room with a look of both intense approval and abject dependence. It was plain that between him and nothing there was only Fenton.

"We've come to the end of our rope, I guess," Fenton said, almost forgetting that Parkhearst had not replied to his question.

"No," Parkhearst said, but Fenton hardly heard him now, talking so rapidly that his spit flew out on all sides of his mouth. He talked about their mother's funeral and how they had come to this house all because Kincaid had known them back in West Virginia and had promised them a job here. Then suddenly he picked up a book that Claire had under the bedclothes and showed it to Parkhearst as though it was both something uncommon and explanatory of their situation. The book, old and ripped, was titled *Under the Trees,* a story about logging.

"Doesn't anybody else live here?" Parkhearst inquired at last.

"We haven't heard nobody," Fenton replied. "There's so

many bugs it isn't surprising everybody left, if they was here," he went on. "But Claire says there is," he looked in the direction of his brother. "Claire feels there is people here."

"I hear them all the time," Claire said.

"No, there is nobody here," Parkhearst assured both of them. "This is a vacant house and you must have made a mistake when you came in here. Or your friend Kincaid played a joke on you," he finished, seeing at once by their expression he should not have added this last sentence.

"Anyhow," Parkhearst continued awkwardly while Fenton stared at him with his strange eyes, "it's no place for you, especially with Claire sick. I think I have a plan for you, though," Parkhearst said, as though thinking through a delicate problem.

Fenton walked over very close to him as though Parkhearst were about to hand him a written paper which would explain everything and tell him and Claire what to do in regard to the entire future.

"I think Grainger will give you the help you need," he explained. He had forgotten that Fenton knew nothing about her.

Fenton turned away and looked out the boarded window. Evidently he had expected some immediate help, and Parkhearst had only spoken a name like a matchbox, Grainger, adding later that was the last name of a wealthy woman that nobody ever called by her first name. This was discouraging because of course Fenton knew he could never do anything to please anybody with such a name.

"Grainger will like you," Parkhearst went on doggedly, knowing he was not moving Fenton at all.

"You would be interested in going to her mansion at least," he said.

Claire, following Fenton's example, showed likewise no interest in the "great woman."

"If you promise me you will go with me to the house of the 'great woman,'" Parkhearst said (using that phrase preciously and purposely just as he had mentioned Grainger without explaining who she was or that she was a woman), "I assure you we'll be able to help you between us. Really help."

He had not finished this speech when he remembered what Bella had told him about his handing over Fenton to Grainger.

Fenton turned now from the boarded window and faced him. His whole appearance had grown surprisingly ominous as though Parkhearst had destroyed some great promise and hope.

"We don't have no choice," Fenton said, his words more gentle than his expression, and he looked at Claire, although he addressed his words to no one.

"I don't know what I'll do in the house of a greatwoman," Fenton went on. "Why do you call her *great?*"

"Oh I don't know," Parkhearst replied airily. "Of course she isn't, really. But is anybody? Was anybody ever?"

"I never did hear anybody called that," Fenton said. He looked at Claire as though he might have heard someone called that.

"Why is she great?" he wondered aloud again.

Parkhearst felt flustered despite his years of looking and collecting the "material" and talking with the most intractable of persons.

"If you come tomorrow, I feel you'll understand," Parkhearst told him, getting up. "I don't see why you act like this when you're in trouble." Then: "Where's your gun," he said irritably.

Fenton put his hand quickly to his pocket. "Fuck you," he said, feeling nothing there.

"Don't think I can get offended," Parkhearst said. "Neither your talk nor your acts. You just seemed a bit young to have any gun."

"Young?" Fenton asked, as though this had identified his age at last. His face flushed and for the first time Parkhearst noticed that there was a scar across his lip and chin.

"Please come, Fenton, when we want to help you," he said, almost as soft as some sort of prayer.

"I don't like to go in big houses. You said she was rich,
too. Claire and me don't have the clothes for it. . . . Say, are
you trying to make us a show for somebody?" Fenton asked,
as though he had begun to understand Parkhearst. His face
went no particular color as this new thought took hold of him.
"Or use us? You're not trying to *use* us, are you?"

When he asked that last question, Parkhearst felt vaguely
a kind of invisible knife cut through the air at him. He could
not follow the sources of Fenton's knowledge. At times the boy
talked dully, oafish, and again he showed a complete and in-
tuitive knowledge of the way things were and had to be.

"I want to help you," Parkhearst finally said in a
womanish hurt voice.

"Why?" Fenton said in an impersonal anger. Then quickly the fight in him collapsed. He sat down on the cheap kitchen
chair occupied a moment before by Parkhearst Cratty.

"All right, then, I'll come for your sake. But Claire has to
stay here."

"All right, then, Fenton. I'll be here for you."

They argued a little about the hour.

Fenton did not look at Parkhearst as he said goodbye, but
Claire waved to him as though seated in a moving vehicle, his
head constantly turning to keep sight of the visitor.

"Who is that, Fenton?" Claire asked as soon as his brother
had returned from closing the front door.

"He's a man who writes things about people," Fenton
said. "He wants me to tell him things so he can write about
me."

Fenton looked up at the high sick ceiling; the thought of
the man writing or listening to him in order to write of him
was too odd ever to be understood.

"Like you write in your little note papers?"

"No," Fenton answered, and turned to look at Claire. "I
only put things down there to clear up in me what we are going
to do next. Understand?"

"Why can't I see them, then, Fenton?"

"Because you can't, hear?"

"I want to read your little note papers!"

Fenton began to slap Claire, rather gently at first, and then with more force. "Don't mention it again," he said, hitting him again. "Hear?"

Claire's weeping both hurt Fenton deeply and gave him a kind of pleasure, as though in the hitting the intense burden of Claire was being lightened a little.

He had written once in the "note papers" a thought which had caused him great puzzlement. This thought was that just as he had wished Mama dead, so that he felt the agent of her death, so now he wanted Claire to be dead, and despite the fact that the only two people in the world he had loved were Mama and Claire.

Then he had to realize that the thing which stung him most about Claire when they were with strangers was his brother's not being quite right and that when he had been with the writer he had not felt this pain. There was this about the man who had turned up in the park, you did not feel any pain about telling him things, things almost as awful as those he had put down in the note papers.

"Why is it?" Fenton asked, raising his voice as though addressing a large group of people, "when I am so young I am so pissed-off feeble and low?"

Claire shook his head as he was accustomed to when Fenton put these questions to him. He had never answered any of them, and yet Fenton asked more and more of them when he knew that Claire did not know the answers.

Then Claire, seeing his chance, watching his brother narrowly, said, without any preparation: "I heard God again in the night."

Fenton tried to quiet himself in the tall room. It was always much easier to calm yourself outdoors or in a farmhouse, but in a small but high room like this when sorrow is heard it is hard to be quiet and calm. Fenton nevertheless made his voice cool as he said, "Claire, what did I tell you about talking like that?"

"I did." Claire began to cry a little.

"Are you going to quit talking like that or ain't you?" Fenton said, the anger welling up in him stronger than any coolness he had put into his voice.

"Don't hit me when I tell you, Fenton," Claire cried on. "Don't you want to know I hear Him?"

Fenton's hands loosened slightly. He felt cramps in his insides.

"I told you those was dreams," Fenton said.

"They ain't! I hear it all day when I don't dream. . . ."

"Maybe somebody lives here, that's all." Fenton waited as though to convince himself. "I could forgive you if you dreamed about Mama and she come running to you to say comforting things to you. But you always talk about God. And I strongly doubt . . ."

"Don't say it again, Fenton, don't say it again!" Claire sat up in bed.

". . . not only strongly doubt but know He's not real. . . ."

Claire let out a strange little cry when he heard the blasphemy and fell back on the bed. Claire fell so awkwardly it made Fenton laugh.

After this, Fenton felt the cramps again and he knew he must go out and get a drink. Yet because neither of them had had anything to eat since morning he feared that if he began drinking now he would not remember to get Claire anything to eat.

He began to rub Claire's temples gently. If only they were safe from trouble he would always be kind to Claire, but trouble always made him mean.

"It's so crappy late out!" he began again, moving away from Claire. "Why does it have to feel so late out everywhere?" This was one of the things which he had written on the note papers so he wouldn't feel so burned up and dizzy. "Even the writer says I am so young," Fenton muttered on, "yet why do I feel I only got two minutes more to do with?"

"It's late, all right," Claire said, still weeping some, but with a happy look on his face now. The small boy had gotten up out of bed and was walking over to where Fenton now stood near the window.

"You heard me tell you to stay in bed, didn't you. . . . Didn't you hear, crapface?"

The boy paused there in the middle of the room, his mouth open disgustingly. But he had already turned his mind away from Claire. He whirled out of the room and was gone.

"He forgot his gun," Claire said looking out into the awful night of the hall. "He don't know how to use it anyhow," he finished and went back to the little bed.

Everything had changed so much since he had been Mama's son, nothing as little as forgetting a gun was remarkable.

"He's gone, he's gone," Claire kept repeating to himself. "Fenton's gone," he repeated on and on until he had fallen asleep again.

Fenton had soon found the taverns where his existence aroused no particular interest or comment. People occasionally noticed his accent or his haircut, but generally they ignored him. There was such an endless row of taverns and the street itself was so endless he could always choose a different tavern for each day and each drink. In the end he went to the places that served both colored and white. It would have been unreal of him to Mama had she known, but this kind of tavern made him feel the easiest, perhaps it was more like home.

He knew now (he began all over again) that Kincaid was not coming to find them in the house. And as he went on with his drink he knew that nobody was ever coming to the house because it was the "latest" time in his life and maybe the "latest" in the world.

"Then where will we end up?" he said quickly, aloud. He felt that some of the customers must have looked at him, but when he said nothing more nobody came over to him or said anything. He got out a pencil stub and wrote something on the note papers.

"Things don't go anywhere in our lives," he wrote. "Sometimes somebody like Mama dies and the whole world stops or begins to move backwards, but nothing happens to us, even her dying don't get us anywhere except maybe back. Yet you have to go on waiting, it's the one thing nobody lets up on you for. Like now we're doing for Kincaid and for what?"

Someone had left a newspaper on the bar, open to the want ad section. Fenton began reading these incomprehensible notifications of jobs. Someone once had told him, perhaps Kincaid, that nobody was ever hired this way, they were only put in there because the employers had to do it, and actually, this somebody had told him, they were really all hired to begin with, probably when you read about them.

Fenton remembered again that he did not know how to do anything. He had no skills, no knowledge. That was why the big old house with tall rooms was getting more ghosty for him, it was so much like the way he was inside himself, the house didn't work at all, and he was all stopped inside himself too just like the house. That was why it was like a trap, he said.

As he drank a little more he decided he must move on to another drinking place because the bartender had begun to watch him write in the note papers too much and it scared him.

He went on in search of the next place, but before he reached it he saw the *All Night Theater,* a movie house that never closed. Instead of choosing another drinking place, he decided to choose this, for the price of admission was nearly the same as that of a beer.

There was the same sad smell inside, a faint stink from old men and a few boys who had been out in the open, standing or lying on the pavement during part of the night. The seats did not act as though they were required to hold you off the floor. Faces twisted around to look at you, or somebody's hand sometimes came out of the dark and touched you as though to determine whether you were flesh or not.

Fenton did not notice or care about any of these things. He scarcely looked at the picture, and half the audience must have been sleeping or looking at the floor, at nothing.

He did not know what time he woke up in the *All Night Theater.* The audience had thinned out a little. The screen showed a horse and a man crossing a desert, walking as though they were not going to go much longer if they didn't find some water or perhaps just a cool place to stop.

It was then that Fenton remembered Parkhearst Cratty and the greatwoman. For the first time he began to think about them as having some slight meaning, some relationship to himself. That is, they knew about him, and he existed for them. He had gotten as far down in the dumps as possible and still be alive, and now he began to come up a little out of where he was and to think about what Parkhearst Cratty was jawing about.

The thought that anybody called the greatwoman should want to see him struck him suddenly as so funny that he laughed out loud. Then he stopped and looked around him, but nobody was looking at him. The dead world of the shadows on the screen seemed to look at him just then more than the men around him.

Fenton sat a little while longer in the *All Night Theater,* holding his notebook down to a little of the light at the end of the aisle so that he might write down some more of what he was thinking. Then having written a little more, he gazed at the want ads again that he had carried along with him and saw the words MEN MEN MEN under the difficult light.

Finally he got hungry and walked out into the gray street. It was six o'clock in the morning and it would be a long day until night came and brought Parkhearst Cratty and his plans.

Fenton went into a cafe called *Checker* where some colored men were drinking orange pop. He ordered a cup of black coffee, and then drinking that, he ordered another. Then he ordered some rolls and ate part of those. After that he ordered some coffee and rolls to take out, and started home to Claire.

Just before getting to the house, he went back to a small tavern he had missed before and had a whiskey.

It was funny, he reflected, that before coming here to the city with its parks and vacant houses he had almost never had a drink, and now he had it, quite a bit.

Claire stared at him, his face red and swollen from bites. Fenton had him get up and they began going through the mattress looking for the bugs.

"Where was you?" Claire wanted to know.

"*All Night Movie.*"

This answer perfectly satisfied Claire.

"Why don't you drink the coffee I brought you and eat those rolls?"

"I ain't hungry, Fenton."

"Drink the coffee like I tell you."

Fenton kept looking at the mattress. "I don't see any of the bastards," he said. "They must be inside the fucking mattress."

"Fenton," Claire soothed him. "I didn't dream last night at all or hear anything."

"So?" Fenton spoke crossly. He set the mattress down and then lazily began eating the rolls Claire had not touched.

"I didn't even feel the bugs biting," Claire said, pushing his face close to Fenton to show him, but his voice trailed off as he saw Fenton's heavy lack of interest in what he had done and thought.

Then all at once Fenton saw his brother's face, which was almost disfigured from the bites. Fenton's own fear and amazement communicated themselves frightfully to Claire.

"You look Christ awful," Fenton cried.

"Don't scare me now, Fenton," Claire began to whimper.

"I don't aim to scare you," Fenton said with growing irritability. "Have you been crying over Mama or is your face just swelled from bugs?"

"I don't know," Claire said, and he quit whimpering.

There was something terribly old and pinched now in Claire's small face.

Fenton took him by the hands and looked at his face closer.

"Ain't you well or what?" he said, the irritation coming and going in his voice, but finally yielding to a kind of sadness. "Why don't you tell me what is bothering you?" he went on.

He put his mouth on the top of Claire's head, and half-opened his lips noticing the funny little boy smell of his hair.

"You can tell me if you have been thinking about God now, if you want to, Claire."

"I ain't been thinking about Him," he said.

"Well," Fenton said, "you can if you want to. It don't matter anyhow."

"I don't think about Him," Claire said, as if from far off.

"I think I'll go to bed now," Fenton complained, looking at the cruelly narrow cot. "You slept some, didn't you, Claire."

"Yes," Claire said, a tired sad duty in his voice.

"Can I walk around outdoors now?" Claire asked, watching Fenton's oblivious brooding face.

"Yes," Fenton replied slowly. "I guess it's all right if the house is open when it's daylight. Nobody ain't coming in anyhow.

"Don't get lost, though," Fenton went on quietly as Claire began to go out.

"What's going on inside the little thing's mind?" Fenton said to himself. He loosened his heavy belt and lay down on the cot.

Fenton thought about how Claire thought about Mama. He himself thought a lot about her when actually he wasn't very aware even that he was thinking about her. Maybe he thought about her all the time and didn't even know it. But he never thought she was waiting for him on some distant star as Claire did.

"Claire," he said, beginning to sleep, "why is it one of us is even weaker than the other. When West Virginia was tough why did we come clear over here? . . ."

Even though it was day it was night really, always, in this city and night like night in caves here in the house.

Fenton lay thinking of the long time before Parkhearst Cratty would come. He thought of Parkhearst as a kind of magicman who would show different magic tricks to him, but he knew not one would take on him.

"No damn one," he said, becoming asleep.

It was even darker somehow when he awoke, and he knew at once that Parkhearst Cratty was there, shaking him.

"Wake up, West Virginia," Parkhearst was saying.

Fenton's mouth moved as though to let out laughter but none came, as though there were no more sound at all in him now.

"She's waiting for us," Parkhearst said.

Fenton said quiet obscene words and Parkhearst waited a little longer, situated as though nowhere in the dark.

"Where's Claire?" Parkhearst wondered vaguely.

"Ain't he here?" Fenton said.

"No," Parkhearst said, a kind of uneasiness growing in him again.

"Claire went out, but he'll be back," Fenton said, remembering.

Then when Parkhearst did not say anything in reply, Fenton said rather angrily: "I said he'd be back."

"Well, let's go, then," Parkhearst said lightly. "She gets cross when people are late," he explained.

Fenton held on to his belt as though that were what was to lift him out of bed, then got up, and turned on the light.

"You're dressed up!" He looked at Parkhearst and then down at himself.

They suddenly were both looking at Fenton's shoes, as though they couldn't help it, and as they both saw they were so miserable and ridiculous, they had to look at them objectively as horrors.

"I'm not really dressed up," Parkhearst said weakly,

feeling the weakness come over him again which he always felt in Fenton's presence. "But come on, Fenton," he said, thinking of the boy's toes slightly coming through the shoes. "She's sent a taxi for us, and it's waiting."

Fenton threw a look back at the room. "So long, house," he said, and he actually waved at the room, Parkhearst noted.

They said almost nothing on the way to the greatwoman's house. Fenton kept his head down as though he were praying or sick in his stomach. He did not look out even when Parkhearst pointed out things that might have had a personal interest to him: the sight of the park where they had met, or the police station.

At last the taxi came to the house. Fenton hesitated, as though he might not get out after all. "Is this a mansion?" he asked.

Parkhearst looked at him closely. Fenton's words always had an ambiguousness about them, but there could be no ambiguousness when you studied his face: he meant just what he said, and perhaps that made the words odd.

They could hear the music from the outside.

"That is the new music the musicians are playing," Parkhearst explained. "Grainger doesn't really listen to it, but she has the musicians come because there is nothing else left to do, and it draws her circle of people to her."

Without knocking, they entered what was the most immense room Fenton had ever seen. It was almost as dark, however, as the house where he and Claire had been waiting, and the ceiling was no taller. There were a number of people sitting in corners except for one large corner of the room where some colored musicians were playing.

At the far end of the room on a slightly raised little platform, in a mammoth chair, Grainger, the greatwoman, sat, or rather hung over one side of the arm.

"My God, we're late after all," Parkhearst exclaimed. "She's too drunk to know us, I'm afraid."

Fenton began to feel a little easier once he was inside the mansion. No one had paid him the least attention. It was, in fact, he saw with relief, not unlike the *All Night Theater,* for whatever the people were doing here in the mansion, they were paying absolutely no attention to him or Parkhearst or perhaps to anything. Yet they must have seen him, for he could see their heads move and hear their voices as they talked softly among themselves. And again like the *All Night Theater,* they were about half colored and half white.

Parkhearst was not doing anything as Fenton's attention returned slowly to him. They were in the middle of the great room, and his guide merely stood there watching Grainger. Finally, as though after a struggle with himself, he took Fenton's hand angrily and said, "Come over here, we have to go through with this."

They went up to the woman in the chair. She was possibly forty and her face was still beautiful although her mouth was slightly twisted and her throat was creased now and fat. Her eyes, although not focused on the two young men who were standing in front of her, were extremely beautiful and would have been intelligent had they not been so vacant. Whenever Parkhearst addressed her, she would immediately turn her head in the other direction.

"Grainger, I have brought Fenton Riddleway here to see you, just as you told me to do."

She did not say a word, although Parkhearst knew that she had heard him.

"She's angry," Parkhearst said, like a radio commentator assigned to a historical event which is hopelessly delayed. He sighed as though he could no longer breathe in this atmosphere.

"Everything is getting to be more difficult than anything is really worth," he pronounced.

"Please look at Fenton at least and we will leave then," he addressed Grainger.

Suddenly the greatwoman laughed and took Parkhearst's hands in her very small ones. Parkhearst gave a sound expressing relief, though his face did not lose the agonized look it had assumed the moment he recognized she was drunk.

"Are you going to be good now?" he inquired in a calmer voice.

She laughed cheerfully, like a young girl.

Fenton thought that she looked beautiful at that moment and he looked at her dress which was the kind he felt a princess in old books might have worn; it was so frighteningly white and soft and there was so much of it, it seemed to fill the little platform on which they were now all standing.

Then as Grainger's eyes moved away from Parkhearst they settled slowly and gloomily upon Fenton. They immediately expressed hostility or a kind of sullen anger. Then looking away from both of them, she picked up a drink she had placed on the floor by the chair and took a swallow so deep that she seemed to be talking to someone in the end of the glass.

"Haven't you had enough, tonight?" Parkhearst said gently. "It's that Holland stuff, too, and you promised me you wouldn't ever take that again."

"Cut that, Parkhearst, cut that," she said suddenly. "You've been boring me for a year now and I'm not listening to any more."

This was said in a tone that was tough and which was hard to connect with the soft long dress and the fine eyes.

"Well, give us something to drink then," Parkhearst retorted. "If you're sobered up enough now to be ugly, you can remember your duties as the hostess."

Grainger pointed contemptuously to a table where there were bottles and glasses. Then her gaze returned to Fenton, and the same hostility and suspicion crossed her face.

"Who is this?" she said, putting her hand on his face as one might touch what is perhaps a door in a dark house.

Fenton could only stand there, allowing her hand to be on him and looking down at her dress. He found that her gaze and touch were not unlike the soft glances that the characters on the screen of the *All Night Theater* had given him last night, looking down while he wrote what he had to write in the note papers.

His meekness and his quiet partially calmed the anger of her expression.

"Don't you like Fenton, Grainger?" Parkhearst said, returning with drinks for himself and Fenton.

"Why didn't you fill mine up too?" she said, turning bitterly to Parkhearst.

"Because you've had enough. And I'm taking the drink you now have away from you," he said, reaching for her glass.

Grainger smiled at this and put the glass into his hand.

"Now, Grainger, wake up, clear awake, and look at this boy I brought to meet you. You're always wanting to meet new people and then when I bring them to you, you get into a state like this and don't even know me when I come in. This is Fenton Riddleway."

"I saw him," the greatwoman said. She kept eyeing her drink, which Parkhearst had set on the table near her.

"How do you feel about the musicians tonight?" she inquired suddenly.

"I've heard them when they sounded more advanced," Parkhearst said. "But I wasn't listening to them at all. . . . Anyhow, the new music sounds only like its name to me now. It was only new that first night."

"So you brought Fenton to see me," she said, looking now for the first time without hostility at the guest.

Fenton had finished half his drink and both he and Parkhearst had sat down on the floor at the feet of Grainger.

She began to grow quiet now that they were both with her and both drinking. *If everything,* she had said once a long time ago, *could be a garden with the ones you always want and with drinking for ever and ever.*

"Do you think you're going to like Fenton?" Parkhearst began again.

"If you want me to, I guess I can," Grainger answered. She looked at her drink on the table but then evidently gave up the struggle to have it.

"He looks a little like Russell," Grainger said without any preparation for such a statement.

The remark made Parkhearst go a little white because Russell had been everything. Russell had been her first husband, the one who when he died, people said, made her go off the deep end and drink for ten years, to end up the way she was now.

"Only he's *not*," Grainger added. But she added this only because she saw Parkhearst change color. "Nobody could quite be Russell again," she said.

When Parkhearst did not reply, holding his face in a wounded quivering expression, the greatwoman flared up. "I said, could they, Parkhearst?"

"Just nobody could resemble Russell," Parkhearst said.

"Well, all right, then, why didn't you say that before?" she scolded.

She ignored his contemptuous silence and acted happy. "Russell was the last of any men that there were," she began, turning to Fenton. "He didn't love me, of course, but I couldn't live without him, every five minutes having to touch him or see him coming somewhere near me. . . ."

"That isn't true, Grainger, and you know it. Why do you lie to this boy, making out that Russell wasn't crazy about you? . . ." Then he stopped as he realized how deadly it was going to be ever to get started on Russell all over again.

Upstairs, he wanted to tell Fenton, there was that memorial room to him everybody has heard about somewhere but never seen, a shrine to his being, with hundreds of immense photographs, mementos, clothes, and everywhere fresh flowers every day. Grainger herself never went into the shrine, and Negro women kept the flowers fresh and the holy places dusted.

"Crazy . . . about *me?*" Grainger shot at him and a look of unparalleled meanness came over her face, so that she resembled at that moment a stuffed carnivore he had once seen in a museum. "Nobody was ever crazy about me. The only reason anybody's here now is I have more money than anybody else in town to slake them."

Parkhearst looked up at the word *slake*; he could not ever remember hearing her use it before.

"Look at them!" she shouted, pointing to the dim figures in the next room. "Nobody was ever crazy about me."

Both Fenton and Parkhearst gazed back at the people in the next room as though to see them, in the greatwoman's word, being *slaked*.

Then her anger subsided, and she gave Fenton a brief oversweet smile. Growing a bit more serious and commanding, she said: "Come over here, Fenton Riddleway."

Parkhearst gave a severe nod with his head for Fenton to go to her.

Fenton had hardly gotten to her chair when she reached out and took his hand in hers and held it for a moment. She laughed quietly, kissed his hand in so strange a manner that the action had no easy meaning, and then released it.

Parkhearst had risen meanwhile and poured himself and Fenton another shot of gin.

"You think I should have more?" Fenton said in a way that recalled Claire.

"Well naturally, yes," Parkhearst said, and trembled with nervousness. The comparison of Fenton with Russell did not augur too well. He felt a kind of throbbing jealousy as well as fear. It was the biggest compliment that Grainger had ever given to any of the men he had brought to her house. He felt suddenly that he had given Grainger too much in giving her Fenton and Fenton too much in giving him to her.

Parkhearst realized with a suddenness which resembled a break in his reason that he needed both Grainger and Fenton acutely, and that if he lost them to each other, he would not survive this time at all.

In the midst of his anguish, his eye fell upon both of them coolly, almost as though he had not seen either of them before. It was outrageous, rather sad, and frightening all at once; not so much because she had a dress that was too fine for royalty and Fenton looked somehow seedier than any living bum, but because something about the way they were themselves, both together and apart, made them seem more real and less real than anybody living he had ever known.

"He's Russell!" Grainger said finally, without any particular emphasis.

"No, he's not," Parkhearst replied firmly but with the anger beginning to come to make his words shake in his mouth.

"He is," she said, louder.

"No, Grainger, you know these things don't happen twice. Nothing does."

"Just for tonight he is," Grainger replied, staring at Fenton.

"Not even for tonight. He just isn't Russell, Grainger. Look again."

"I'm going to have a drink now," she threatened him. Half to her own surprise she saw Parkhearst make no attempt to prevent her. She walked rigidly, balancing herself with outstretched hands, over to the little table, filled her glass with a tremendous drain of the bottle, and drank half the draught at once.

"Grainger!" Parkhearst was frightened, forgetting he had permitted her to get up at all.

"All right, he isn't Russell, then. Or he is Russell. What difference! He can stay here, though. . . . Does he need anything?"

The drink, Parkhearst thought, perhaps has sobered her.

She sat down in the great chair and began staring at Fenton again. Then his clothes at last caught her attention.

"Would you accept a suit?" she began. "One of Russell's suits," the greatwoman said, turning her face away from Parkhearst as though to shield her words from him and give them only to Fenton.

Fenton in turn looked at Parkhearst for a clue, and Parkhearst could only look down, knowing that Fenton would never understand the generosity that was being offered, the giving away of the clothes of the dead young Christ.

"Why don't you go upstairs?" She turned in rage now on

Parkhearst. "Why don't you go upstairs with your jealous eyes and give him one of Russell's suits?"

As her face lay back in the chair, burning with rage, Parkhearst saw how mistaken he had been about her ever being sobered up by a drink. At that very moment the musicians stopped playing the new music for the evening, the hostess fell over, slightly, upsetting her drink, and then with almost no noise slipped to the floor and lay perfectly still, her drinking glass near her hand, without even a goodnight, lying there, as Parkhearst observed, looking a little too much like Hamlet's mother.

"We may as well go to my house now," Parkhearst said, after they had got one of Russell's suits on Fenton.

"What shall we do with my old clothes?" Fenton wondered, looking at them with almost as much wonder now as other people had.

Parkhearst hesitated. "We'll take them," he said. "This way."

They went downstairs away from the "shrine" and walked past the room where Grainger was lying on an immense silver bed with red coverings. She had her clothes still on. Parkhearst hesitated near the bed.

"I suppose we should say goodnight to her, in case she's conscious."

They both stood there in dead silence while Parkhearst tried to make up his mind.

"Grainger!" he called. Then he suddenly laughed as he saw the serious expresion on Fenton's face.

"She's just out, she won't be up and around for God knows when," Parkhearst explained in his bored tone. "When she gets in these states she lies till she gets up or until they find her. I will have to come over here tomorrow and see how things are. . . ."

Then for the first time since they had been in the "shrine," Parkhearst gave Fenton a more critical look. Russell's suit had

been a close enough fit all right; the greatwoman had not been
too drunk to understand the relative sizes of the two men,
although the trousers were a bit too short in the legs. The suit
made a tremendous change, of course, and yet the boy who
looked out from this absurdly rich cloth seemed to belong in
it, despite the expression of pain mingled with rage imprinted
on his mouth. He was a Russell of some kind in the clothes.

Parkhearst gave him a last look directly in the eye.

"My wife will be asleep," Parkhearst told him in a rather
cross voice, "but if we speak low, she won't hear us. Anyhow
we have to have coffee."

Parkhearst's home was an apartment on the fifth floor of
a building that leaned forward slightly as if it would bend
down to the street.

"I forgot you had a wife," Fenton remarked, looking at
him vaguely. "I never thought of you as married."

"A lot of people can't," Parkhearst admitted. "I suppose
it's because I never had a job, never worked."

Parkhearst observed with some satisfaction that this made
no impression on Fenton. He believed that if he had said he
had murdered someone, for instance, Fenton would have accepted this statement with the same indifferent air.

That, as Parkhearst was beginning to see more and more,
was the main thing about Fenton, his being able to accept
nearly anything. For one so young it was unusual. He accepted the immense dreariness of things as though there were
no other possibility in the shape of things.

A cat came out of the door as they entered the apartment.
They proceeded down a long hallway to a kitchen.

"I'll throw your old clothes on this bench," Parkhearst
said. Then he began to fumble with the coffee can.

Before he began to measure out the coffee he stopped as
though he thought somebody was calling to him from the front
of the apartment. Then when he did not hear his wife's voice,
he began to boil the water for the coffee.

Fenton put his head down on the tiny kitchen table before which he sat.

"Don't go to sleep, Fenton. You can't spend the night here. My wife would die. . . . And Claire must be worrying about you."

"Not Claire," Fenton mumbled. "I thought I told you that we sleep at different times, on account of the bed being so small, and the bugs and all. There are hundreds of bugs." He began to think of the anguish they cause. "They crawl up and down, sometimes they go fast, and you can never find them when they bite. They stink like old woodsheds."

"Bugs are awful," Parkhearst agreed. "But," he went on, "about Claire. He may not miss you, but is he safe alone?"

"I'm too sick to care," Fenton said, his head on the table now.

"How are you sick?" Parkhearst wondered.

"Inside," Fenton replied, still not taking his head off the table and talking into the wood like a colored fortune teller Parkhearst had once known. "Where your soul's supposed to be," he spoke again.

Parkhearst stared at him.

"If there was a God," Fenton said quickly, raising his head from the table and giving Parkhearst an accusing look, "none of this would happen."

"Oh, it might, Fenton," Parkhearst answered. "You don't think He's all-powerful, do you?"

"Do you believe in Him?" Fenton wondered.

"I don't believe but I'm always thinking about it somehow."

"Do you believe Claire is dying?" Fenton said quickly.

"No," Parkhearst answered.

"I keep seeing him dead," Fenton said.

Parkhearst handed Fenton a cup of coffee. Then he sat down, facing Fenton. They both drank their coffee without continuing the discussion. Parkhearst from time to time would listen intently to see if Bella called to him, but there was no sound, no matter how many times he stopped to listen.

"I want to be dead like a bug," Fenton said and laid his head down on the table again.

"Drink all of that coffee and then I'll get you some more."

Parkhearst watched the thick hair come loose from the head and creep over the table's edge like a strange unfolding plant.

"Is this the first time you've ever been drunk?" Parkhearst's voice came from far away.

"I drink nearly all the time," Fenton said, and some coffee began to trickle down the side of his mouth. "When I go home," he went on, "Claire will be dead. I will be happy, like a great load has been taken off my neck, and then I will probably fly into a thousand pieces and disappear. I am sick of him just the same, dead or alive. He makes it too hard for me, just like Mama did. Both him and her talked too much about God and how we would all meet at His Throne on the Final Day. . . . Do you disbelieve in the Throne too?" he looked up at Parkhearst.

The writer watched him, silent.

Fenton was watching him also, almost as though from behind his thick disheveled hair.

"Keep drinking the coffee," Parkhearst said in a soft voice. He felt weak lest Bella should get up and see this. Then he began to feel irritated seeing Fenton in Russell's clothing.

"Grainger is an idiot," Parkhearst said.

"Are you in love with me too?" Fenton asked Parkhearst, but the writer merely sat there drinking, as though he had not heard.

Fenton did not say any more for a long time. Perhaps ten minutes passed this way in the silence of the city night; that is a silence in which although one cannot really say *this is a sound I am hearing now,* many little contractions and movements like the springs of a poorly constructed machine make one feel that something will break with a sudden crash and perhaps destroy everyone.

Fenton knocked his cup off the table and it broke evenly in two at Parkhearst's feet.

"What did you think of the *church* Grainger has for Russell?" Parkhearst said, getting up for another cup.

He poured coffee into the cup and handed it to his friend. "Drink this."

Fenton half sat up and gulped down some more of the coffee.

"Did you hear what I asked about her *church* for him?" Parkhearst began again.

"Why did she love Russell so?" Fenton asked, and the whites of his eyes suddenly extinguished his pupils so that he looked like a statue.

"He was nothing," Parkhearst said. "Rather beautiful. His mind worked all right, I guess. He was nothing. He had so little personality he looked all right in all kinds of clothes. I think he had millions of life insurance policies. He was a blank except for one thing. He loved Grainger. I think maybe he was the one started calling her by her last name, and now nobody calls her by her first. Grainger didn't love him, but he told her he loved her every ten minutes. It was funny, I could never figure it out, why he loved her. I used to stare at him to try to understand who he was. I think I know who Grainger is, but not Russell. Then he died in his car one night. Nobody knows what from. They said his heart. And he had all these life insurance policies. He was rich though before, owned factories and mines and patents and things. After that Grainger never had to think about work. But I think she's spent nearly all she has. When she has spent the last of it she will have to die too. . . ."

Parkhearst's voice ended with a little sound like an old phonograph record stopping but still running. He had not given the speech for any reason except the pleasure he took in telling it. "The way they found him in the car is so beautiful. He had been out drinking all night, and of course he and Grainger together. He said goodbye to her from that car he had from Italy, and she went dragging into her bedroom, not very much like Shakespeare but like the girl in Shakespeare, they threw kisses into and out of the balcony, and then

Grainger fell down dead drunk on her bed, and Russell still sat out there in the Italian car, trying to call somebody because he suddenly, I suppose, felt sick; the coroner said he had felt sick, Russell had opened his vest, and had blown the horn that only sounded like a small chime (the neighbors told about that), and the next morning there he sat in the sun under her house, dead as time. Grainger never mentioned how he died to anybody we know. She doesn't even drink any more than she did then, but there's something different about her, I guess, because after he died she could never change but always had to go on acting herself.

"The *church*," Parkhearst began again, getting up and looking out into the black windows. "What do you think of the *church?*"

"All those photographs of rich people?" Fenton said.

"Yes," Parkhearst nodded seriously. "And those fake poses of her. She knows she is not the woman in those photos, of course, because she wasn't the woman in her own mind Russell said she was.

"Grainger knows the truth about herself," Parkhearst continued, "but it only makes things more impossible for her. And it's really only money that keeps her alive, and it's going, nearly gone."

"You make me sicker than I was," Fenton said suddenly. "Why do you find out all these things about people when they are so sad?"

"I don't know," Parkhearst said softly.

"How do you know all these things?" Fenton said almost desperately. "Do you know about me like that too?" He laid his head down on the table and didn't wait for Parkhearst's answer.

Parkhearst said nothing.

Then Fenton got up. "I got to go back."

"Where?" Parkhearst was curious and anxious.

"The *All Night Theater.*"

"Why don't you tell me about the *All Night Theater* some time?" Parkhearst asked.

"There ain't nothing to tell. It's what it says, it goes on all night."

"It's like the park then," Parkhearst had a very quiet voice.

Fenton did not say anything, drinking his coffee from the saucer.

"It's morning," Parkhearst announced more cheerfully.

"You can't tell when it's morning in a city place," Fenton said.

"You told me that before," Parkhearst said, "but that is only because you're Fenton that you think that."

The next day, Parkhearst woke up with a headache and the feeling of rags on his tongue. He knew without looking that Bella had gone to work.

He thought of the greatwoman almost at once and before he thought of Fenton. He would have to go to see her at once. She would still be unconscious, the wreck of her evening undisturbed yet by the maids.

His face looked old and thin and brown in the looking glass, old for twenty-nine. Yet how old did that look, except older than Fenton Riddleway?

Then all the part about Grainger and Russell and Russell's resembling Fenton or Fenton's resembling Russell came back.

"I suppose in Grainger's mind," he said aloud to himself, "she thinks she has already taken him over, away from me. Of course it's true. I've given her everybody she ever had."

He had forgotten Russell only because he had never counted him.

A not unusual thing was to smell flowers in front of Grainger's house. Today their perfume was stronger than usual. There was the silence of early day inside of the house, but there was evidence that the maids had come and gone, and noiselessly enough to have left her still sleeping in the front parlor.

The flowers, he noticed, were only roses. Grainger lay on the divan, a queer frayed coverlet over her. A tiny smile covered her mouth.

"Is the Queen of Hell conscious?" he said in a voice that struggled with both eagerness and contempt.

He began kissing her on the eyelids. "Open those big blue eyes."

Grainger opened her eyes, her smile vanished, and the accusing frown returned. "You cheap son of a bitch," she said groggily. "You never loved Russell. You never even would talk about him. You didn't understand his greatness. His going never even moved you."

"Shall I make you some breakfast now?" he wondered.

"You hated Russell."

He kissed her fingers.

"You make me sick. You cheap son of a bitch," she said, looking at him kiss her fingers. "I ought to hate you. Russell hated you. He said you were lacking in the fundamental. That boy you dragged here last night, what's his name? . . ."

Parkhearst told her.

". . . he hates you too. You know so damn much. You sit around seeing things so that you can write them down in a hundred years."

Parkhearst went on holding her fingers as though he were giving her the energy to go on.

He looked longingly at some hot coffee on a nearby table, then letting her hands fall slowly, he got up and went over to the table and poured himself a cup and began sipping.

"And why do we all love you, though, when you stink with cheapness, dishonor, not having probably one human hair on your body. Maybe I love you the most. . . ."

"Don't forget my wife," he said, and the expression *my wife* as he said it had a different quality than that of any other husband who had ever said the words.

"*Your wife!*" she said, getting up and staring at him. "She owns you, but I wouldn't call that loving. Anyhow, she's overpaid. . . ."

"Overpaid?" he said, his mouth dropping slightly.

They were both silent, as though even for them frankness had overstepped itself.

"What was I saying to you when we ran into this quiet period?" she began again.

"About my wife getting too much for her money," he said exhaustedly.

"Who is this Fenton?" she changed topics. "What did you bring him here for?"

"I thought he would be a change for you. You really ordered him anyhow, and have forgotten it."

"I never ordered *him*," she said carefully, drawing the silk coverlet up to her eyebrows. "Did you think he would remind me of Russell?" she put the question with coy crafty innocence, and he felt he would laugh.

"No, Grainger, it didn't occur to me at the time."

"Don't lie to me as though I were your wife!" she lashed at him. "If he hadn't looked a *little* like Russell would you have brought him here then?"

"Yes, I would, Grainger." He smarted now under her attack. "I brought him here because he was so much just himself. This boy is better than Russell," he took final courage to throw at her.

"I'm glad you said *boy*." Grainger was quiet under his blasphemy. "He's a child, really. And I'm an old woman."

Parkhearst waited for her.

"How did you find him?" she went on, muttering now, less irritation in her voice.

"How do I find everybody?" he said, a kind of dull bitterness in his voice.

"I never find anybody at all," she said. "Are you jealous because I did something for him?" she wanted to know suddenly.

"Yes, I suppose," he said. "But after all I wanted to bring him here. I was willing to take the risk."

She saw the flowers for the first time.

"Do you know why I buy all these flowers?" she asked him.

"Of course," he said, impatient at her always changing the subject so abruptly.

"No, you don't," she said with a ridiculous emphasis. "Tell me why I have them then, if you know. . . ."

"Why do you have that church upstairs?" he said.

"Church?" she said, somewhat distracted and looking at him with her back to the window. He had forgotten that this was his private word and that he had not ever used it for her; and yet he had employed it with such force of habit, she knew it was his word and that he must say it all the time when out of her presence.

Recovering from her shock over the word, she began to talk about the flowers again: "I can see now you don't know everything after all."

"If there hadn't been any Russell, of course you wouldn't have flowers," he raised his voice as he would have had he lived an ordinary domestic life with ordinary people.

"Should I go to see him?" She changed to a new line of thought.

He stared at her with almost real anger.

"Should I return his call or not?" she roared. "Don't start being Christ with me again or something will happen."

"It's too silly even for you to say," he told her. "Returning a call to Fenton." His voice, though, softened a bit.

"He is very beautiful, isn't he?" she said. "More than Russell was."

"Grainger, you know we never agree with one another about who is beautiful or who is anything."

"He's more beautiful than Russell," she went on, both musing and commanding. "But there's something not right with him that Russell never had. There was nothing really wrong with Russell."

He looked up briefly at her as though something important had finally been said.

"When should I go visit him?" she asked him eagerly.

"We can't go today." Parkhearst acted bored. "Bella's coming home this afternoon from work."

"I wish you would quit mentioning Bella," she complained. "It's all you talk about . . . You get me involved with this new boy, and then you go off with your wife, and leave me without anything."

"Grainger, don't be a complete idiot all the time."

"*I'll* go," she said. "You'll stay home and entertain that Bella and *I'll* go. And every minute," she vituperated, "you'll be thinking of me and him together."

Parkhearst laughed a little, and then the pain of the scene which she had just presented to his imagination bore down with unaccustomed weight.

"You don't even know where he lives," he said. "I can just see you going in there in your finery."

He laughed such a nasty laugh that Grainger found herself listening to it as attentively as one of the "concerts."

The next thing Fenton remembered was standing in front of a wrestling arena known as Fair City. He was in front of a little wooden gate with his hands put through the partitions as though asking somebody for an admission ticket. It was still early morning, almost no one was on Sixty-third Street; and so removing his hands from the partitions at last, he began walking in the direction of the house.

Right in front of the house he stopped. He heard several voices singing something vaguely sacred. "It's niggers," he said peevishly, rubbing the back of his neck. He raised his eyes to the *Come and See Resurrection Church*. He leaned his head then gently over onto the pavement so that it was within a few inches of the curb and some of the coffee he had drunk came up easily. Then he got up and unlocked the door to the house and went inside.

He felt he must look creased and yellow as he opened Claire's door.

Claire was sitting on the kitchen chair but hardly glanced up at Fenton and only nodded in answer to his brother's greeting.

The sound of the colored spiritualists was just faintly audible here.

"How can they shout when it's morning?" Fenton asked, and then as Claire did not say any more, he asked, "I don't suppose anybody called?"

Claire merely stared at him.

"Ain't you all right?" Fenton said, going over to the chair and touching him.

"Dooon't," the boy cried, as though he had touched him on a raw nerve.

"Claire! Are you sick?" Fenton wanted to know.

"Don't touch my head," Claire told him, and Fenton took his hand away.

"Let me get you into bed, and I'll go for coffee and rolls," Fenton told him and he helped him into the cot.

"I don't want none," Claire said and he closed his eyes.

"You didn't notice my new clothes," Fenton complained.

"Yes, I did," Claire replied without opening his eyes.

"Do you like them?" Fenton said, looking around, as though to find some part of the room that would reflect his image.

"Kind of, yeah," Claire answered.

"I'll go for something for you now," Fenton encouraged him, but he didn't go. He kept staring at the deep pallor of Claire. He looked around the room as though there might be something there that would extend help to them.

Fenton looked at himself as he sat there on the chair in his new clothes. He wondered if he was changing; there was something about the wearing of those clothes that made him feel almost as if his body had begun to change, that his soul had begun to change into another soul. A new life was beginning for him, he dimly recognized. And with the new life, he knew, Claire would be less important. He knew that Claire would not like Grainger or Parkhearst and would not go to visit them or be with them. He knew that Claire actually never wanted to leave this room again. He had come to the last stages of his journey. Fenton tried not to think of this but it was too difficult to avoid: Claire had come as far now as he could. . . . There could be no more journeying around for him. And Fenton knew that as long as Claire was Claire he would not let him lead the "new life" he saw coming for him. There would be trouble, then, a great deal of trouble.

He wanted desperately to be rid of Claire and even as he had this feeling he felt more love and pity for him than ever before. As he sat there gazing at Claire, he knew he loved him more than any other being. He was almost sure that he would never feel such tenderness for any other person. And then this tenderness would be followed by fury and hatred and loathing, so that he was afraid he would do something violent, would strike the sick boy down and harm him.

"Claire," he said looking at him in anguish. "What are we going to do about this?"

Claire moved his closed eyes vaguely. "Don't know," Claire replied.

Fenton smiled to think that Claire did not ask what *this* was. Well, the boy was past caring, and it was plain enough what *this* was: *this* was everything that faced and surrounded them. It was plain, all right, what it was. Their trouble had made them both one.

"What do you want me to do?" Fenton said, his desperation growing. "Tell me what to do."

"We can't go away now, can we?" Claire said, and his voice was calmer but weaker.

Fenton considered this, taking out from his pants cuff a cigarette butt which he had begun in the greatwoman's house, lighting it swiftly with a kitchen match, and inhaling three powerful drags all at once.

Claire opened his eyes slowly and stared at his brother, waiting for the answer.

"No, we can't go away anywhere," Fenton said.

"Isn't there any place to go but here?" Claire asked.

"This is as far as we can get. Anyhow for the winter. . . . We have to stick in here now."

Claire closed his eyes again.

"Unless, of course, you want to go and live at Grainger's with me," Fenton said.

"What would I do there in her big house?" Claire said angrily, his eyes opening and closing.

"She would get a special room for you, where you could do anything you want. She could buy you anything you want, take you anywhere and show you anything. You would never know how happy you could be."

"What are *you* going to do there?" Claire wondered with surprise. . . .

"I'm going to marry her."

"Marry?" Claire sat up briefly in bed, but his strength could not hold him up, and falling back flat, he uttered: "You're not old enough."

"I'm more than old enough," Fenton laughed. "You've seen me enough times to know that. I got to make use of what I have, too. She thinks I look like her old husband."

"I ain't going to go there. . . . I ain't going to leave this house," Claire said.

"Well, suit yourself," Fenton said. "But I'm going over there. . . . The only thing is I don't believe any of it. It's a dream I keep having. Not one of those real pleasant dreams you have when you open a package and something beautiful falls out. In this dream even bigger more wonderful things seem like they're going to happen, getting married to a rich woman and living in a mansion and dressing up like a swell and all that, but at the same time it's all scary spooky and god-damned rotten. . . ."

"It's rotten, all right," Claire said. "You don't have to tell nobody that twice."

"Well, when there ain't nothing else you got to stoop down and pick up the *rotten*. You ought to know that."

"Not me. I don't have to pick it up if I don't want to."

"Well, then you can stick here till you choke to death on it," Fenton said passionately.

They both stopped as if listening to the words he had just said. They contained enough of some sort of truth and the truth was so terrible they had to listen to it as though it were being repeated on a phonograph for them.

"When do you aim on going?" Claire said suddenly, his voice older and calmer.

"In a day or so," Fenton warned him.

"Well it could be sooner. . . . You don't mind if I just stay here, do you?" Claire implored him.

"There's nothing to stop you staying here, of course," Fenton said irritably, twisting the hair around his ear. "This house don't have no owner, no tenants, nobody going to bother you but the spooks." He hurried on, talking past the pain that registered on Claire's face when he heard the words. "But I ain't coming dragging my ass over here every day just to see how you are when you could be living like a king."

"You don't need to come over and see me on account of I ain't asking you to," Claire said.

"Well, then don't be sorry if something happens to you. . . ."

"Nothing ain't going to happen and you know it," Claire shouted. "Why would anything happen to *me?*"

"Well, that's because you don't know nothing about cities is all," he said. "Do you know how many murders are done right in this one town?"

Claire did not answer for a moment and then said, "Those are rich people they murder. Like that old woman you're going to move in with. She's a likely murder person now. And you too if you get to be her husband."

"That's where you're wrong," Fenton said. "Most of the murders they do in this town are on bums, young boys and men that don't have no home and come from nowhere, these they find with their throats cut and their brains mashed out in alleys and behind billboards. Damned few rich people are ever found murdered in this town."

"You think you can scare me into moving into your old woman's house, don't you?" Claire said. "Well, you can do to her all you want to, but I ain't going to be there to watch you . . . fuck her."

"Now listen to that dirty-mouthed little bugger talk, would you. What would Mom think if she knew her religious little boy talked like a cocksucker?" He slapped Claire across the face. ". . . after all I done for you," Fenton finished.

"Go be with that old woman, why don't you, and leave me alone," Claire warned him. "I don't need you nor her. I don't need nobody."

"You'll come bellyachin' around trying to get in touch with me, you'll come crawling like you always do some night when you get the shit scared out of you in this house, hearing the sounds that you can't explain, and maybe *seeing* something too. . . ."

Claire could not control the look of terror that appeared at Fenton's words.

"Claire," Fenton changed suddenly to a tone of imploring, "you got to listen to reason. You *can't* live in this old house alone. . . . Something *will* happen to you. Can't you see that. . . ."

"Why will it?" Claire said, his terror abating a little, searching in himself for some secret strength.

"Things happen here. Everybody knows that. Now listen, Claire," Fenton went on. "Grainger would be very good to you and you could be happy there with her, you don't know how happy you would be. You haven't ever been happy or comfortable before so you don't know what you're talking about. Anyhow, Claire, I can't leave you here. I can't leave you here. . . . I'd have to do something else first. . . ."

"I don't see why not," he said. "I would rather be dead than go there."

"You would not rather be dead. You're a tough little bastard and you would rather be alive and you know it. . . . I'm not going to leave you here, Claire. I'm going to take

you with me and you may just as well make up your mind to
it now. . . . Hear?"

"You won't even get to drag me because I'm not
going. . . ."

Fenton's anguish grew. He knew he could not leave Claire
and he knew Claire's determination would be hard to break.
He felt suddenly an uncontrollable urge of violence against this
puny, defiant, impossible little brother. If he had only not
taken him from West Virginia in the first place. Or if he had
only died as the doctor had said he would a long time ago. He
knew that he *did* want to go on to the "new life" with Grainger
and Parkhearst. He wanted to change, he wanted to wear
Russell's clothes, he wanted the life that was just in sight and
which Claire was now preventing. He knew that as long as
there was Claire, whether he went with him or stayed in the
house hardly mattered, because he knew that as long as there
was Claire there was part of his old life with him, and he
wanted to destroy all that behind him and begin all over again.
Claire was a part of his old life, part of his disbelief in himself,
the disbelief he could ever change and be something different.
Claire did not even believe he could be married and love a
woman. And though Claire was younger, he could exert this
terrible triumph of failure over him.

Whether Claire stayed in the old house or followed him
to Grainger's, he would exert a power of defeat over him.

Then suddenly Fenton realized that he did not want
Claire to come with him. He preferred him to stay in the old
house. And at the same time he knew that if he stayed he
would never have a moment's peace. . . .

There was no way out that he could see. He could only
stand there staring at Claire with impotence and rage.

"All right for you," Fenton said at the end. "All I can say
is watch out, watch out something don't happen now to you."

A tent production of *Othello* was to take place that night
near Sixty-third Street, the young man who had approached
Fenton was telling him, and as somebody was following

him he would welcome Fenton's company and protection.

"Who is Hayden Banks?" Fenton wondered, looking at the handbill which described the dramatic spectacle about to take place.

"Hayden Banks," replied the young man, "is one of the greatest living actors. You are probably seeing him just before he is to gain his international reputation. London is already asking for him. Few actors can touch him. He is playing, of course, Othello himself. The costumes are by a friend of mine, and I will introduce you to a good many of the cast, if you like."

"I don't know if I want that," Fenton said.

"You *will* go with me to the performance," the young man said.

Fenton did not say anything. He had to go somewhere, of course, there could be no doubt about that.

"I wish you would come with me because I'm afraid of the man who is following me. Don't look back now. You see, I'm in trouble," he explained. "You look like a good kind of bodyguard for me and if you come with me I'm less likely to get into . . . trouble. . . . And I can't disappoint Hayden Banks. This is the last night of *Othello,* but I have been afraid to go out all week because this Mexican is following me. I'm in awful trouble with him."

Fenton half turned around but he saw nobody in particular behind him, a crowd of people who all seemed to be following them.

"I'll go with you," Fenton said. Then he looked at the young man carefully. He was the most handsome young man he had ever seen, almost as beautiful as a girl in boy's clothes. He had never seen such beautiful eyelashes. And at the same time the young man looked like Grainger. He might have been Grainger's brother. He almost wanted to ask him if he was Grainger's brother, but of course Grainger could not have a brother. . . .

"You don't know what it is, being followed."

"What will he do if he catches you?"

The young man stared at him. Fenton could not tell whether he was telling the truth or making this up, but there was a look of fear on his face that must be genuine at least.

"I wish you wouldn't use the word *catch,*" the young man said.

"Are you afraid he will . . . hurt you," Fenton changed *kill* to *hurt* before he spoke.

"I'm afraid of the worst," the young man replied. "And you'll be an awfully good boy to come with me."

Fenton nodded.

The young man signalled a taxi and, waiting, said, "Those are awfully interesting clothes you have on. I've never seen clothes like that before. They remind me of some pictures of my father, wedding pictures."

Fenton looked down at himself as though seeing the clothes on himself for the first time. "These are clothes of a friend of mine," he explained.

"Get in," the young man urged as the taxi pulled up beside them. "Get in and don't stare at the crowd like that."

"Was I staring?" Fenton said, like a man awakened from sleepwalking.

"Staring into the crowd like that might incite him. You have an awful look when you stare," the young man said, looking more carefully now at Fenton. "I hope I am going to be safe with *you* now. I don't usually pick up people on the street like this. And maybe you don't like Shakespeare." He began to examine Fenton now more carefully that he felt free of the danger of being followed.

Fenton could see that his anxiety was genuine, but even so the way he said things seemed womanish and unreal, a little like Parkhearst. Both these men said things as though nothing was really important except the gestures and the words with which they said them. When he listened to either this young man or Parkhearst, Fenton felt that the whole of life must be merely a silly trifling thing to them, which bored them, and which they wanted to end, a movie they felt was too long and overacted.

"What is your name?" the young man said suddenly.

Fenton told him and the young man replied, "This is the most interesting name I have ever heard. Is it your own?"

Fenton looked down at his clothes and said it was.

"My name is Bruno Korsawski," he told Fenton.

They shook hands in the dark of the taxi and Bruno held Fenton's hand for many seconds.

"You may have saved my life," Bruno explained.

Soon they reached a vast lot deserted except for a giant circus tent before which fluttered, propelled by a giant cooling machine, banners reading

HAYDEN BANKS THE GENIUS OF THE SPOKEN WORD IN OTHELLO.

In addition to the angry puffing face of Hayden Banks on the posters was a picture of a rather old looking young man dressed, as Fenton thought, like a devil you might expect to see in an old valentine, if valentines had devils, but he lacked horns and a tail.

Fenton remembered vaguely having read *The Merchant of Venice* and he had heard from someplace that Othello had to do with a black man who tortured a white woman to death. He felt a vague curiosity to see Hayden Banks, however. There was nobody around the huge empty tent tonight, and the whole scene reminded him of the conclusion of a county fair which he had seen in West Virginia.

Bruno Korsawski was the kind of man who introduced all of his new friends to all of his old friends. His life was largely a series of introductions, as he was always meeting new people, and these new people had to be introduced to the old people. His idea of the world was a circle, a circle of friends, closed to the rest of men because of his world's fullness. He had thought that Fenton would be one of his circle. However, the introductions did not go off too well.

They went at once to the star's dressing room. A purple

sign with strange heavy tulips drawn on it announced *Mr. Hayden Banks.*

"You dear!" Hayden cried on seeing Bruno. "You look absolutely imperial."

Mr. Hayden Banks did not really look human, Fenton thought, and it was not only the deformity of his makeup.

"This is my friend Fenton Riddleway."

Mr. Banks bowed, and Fenton could not think of anything to say to him. . . .

"Don't you love his name?" Bruno said to Mr. Hayden Banks.

"It's incomparably the best I've heard," Mr. Banks replied. "Uncommonly good. But you've got to forgive me now, I haven't put on my beard yet, and without my beard I'm afraid some of you may mistake me for Desdemona.

"It's been so charming seeing you." Hayden Banks held out his hand to Fenton, and then whispering in Fenton's ear, he said, "You charmer you."

Fenton again could not think of anything to say, and in the hall Bruno said angrily to him, "You didn't open your mouth.

"I guess I'm used to people who talk well and a lot," Bruno explained apologetically as they went to their seats, which were in the first row. "You see what influence can do for you." Bruno pointed. "The best seats: compliments of Hayden Banks."

A small string orchestra was playing, an orchestra which Bruno explained was absolutely without a peer for its interpretation of the Elizabethan epoch. "They stand untouched," he stated, still speaking of the orchestra.

Whether it was the nearness of the actors or the oppressive heat of the tent or the general unintelligibility of both what the actors said and what they did, Fenton became sleepy, and he could not control a weakness he had for breaking wind, which considerably upset Bruno, although nobody else in the small audience seemed to hear. Perhaps Fenton's slumber was due also to the influence of the *All Night Theater,* and drama for Fenton was a kind of sleeping powder.

When Hayden Banks made his appearance, there was a tremendous ovation from the first few rows of the tent, and for a while Fenton watched this tall bony man beat his chest with complete lack of restraint and such uncalled-for fury that Fenton was amazed at such enormous energy. He could think of nothing in his own life that would have allowed him to pace, strut and howl like this. He supposed it belonged to an entirely different world where such things were perhaps done. The more, however, the great Moor shouted and complained about his wife's whoring, the more sleepy Fenton became. It was, however, something of a surprise to hear him fret so much about a whore and have so many rich-looking people nodding and approving of the whole improbable situation.

"He kills Desdemona," Bruno explained, watching Fenton doze with increasing displeasure.

"Would you buy me a drink now?" Fenton asked Bruno during intermission.

At the bar, the bartender asked Fenton if he was old enough, and Bruno said, "I can vouch for him, Teddy," and exchanged a knowing look with the bartender.

"There is one thing," Bruno began to Fenton after he had nodded to literally scores of friends and acquaintances: "I wonder if you couldn't control yourself a little more during the soliloquies at least."

Fenton knew perfectly well to what Bruno referred but he chose to say, "What are those?"

"During the performance, dear," Bruno went on, "you're making noises which embarrass me since I am among friends who know me and know I brought you as a guest."

"My farts, then?" Fenton said without expression.

"Brute!" Bruno laughed gaily.

"Would you buy me another whiskey now?" Fenton asked him.

When they returned to their seats Fenton immediately dozed off and did not waken until the last act which, whether due to his refreshing sleep or to the fact the actors seemed to talk less and do more, was rather frighteningly good to him.

Hayden Banks seemed to murder the woman named Desdemona (Aurelia Wilcox in real life) with such satisfaction and enjoyment that he felt it stood with some of the better murder shows he had seen at the *All Night Theater*. He applauded quite loudly, and Bruno, smiling, finally held his hand and said, "Don't overdo it."

After the performance, Bruno invited Fenton to meet the entire cast, and as drinks were being served now in the dressing room, Fenton drank four or five additional whiskies to the congratulations of nearly all present. At times Fenton would have sober moments and remember Aurelia Wilcox patting his hair or Hayden Banks giving him a hug and kiss, or the young man who played Iago and who looked even more like a valentine devil off the stage whispering in his ear.

"Hayden says we're to go on to his apartment and wait for him there," Bruno explained finally to Fenton, showing him at the same time a tiny key to the great man's rooms.

"You were extremely rude to Hayden Banks. You act like a savage when you're with people. I've never met anybody like you. What on earth *is* West Virginia if you are typical?"

They were in Hayden Banks' apartment and Fenton, instead of replying to Bruno's remarks, was looking about, comparing it with Grainger's mansion. The walls had been painted so that they resembled the ocean, and so skilfully done that one actually thought he was about to go into water. Fenton stared at the painting for a long while, noticing in the distance some small craft, a dwarf moon and the suggestion of dawn in the far distance.

"Arden Carruthers did that painting," Bruno said. "Arden Carruthers is one of the most promising of the younger artists and this mural will be worth a small fortune some day."

Bruno was smoking something strange smelling which Fenton recognized as one of the persistent odors of the *All Night Theater*. As he smoked, he drew nearer to Fenton, and his expression of critical disapproval of the boy suddenly vanished.

"What are you clenching your fists for, as though you were going into the prize ring?" Bruno said.

Fenton sniffed at the cigarette and then suddenly knew what it must be. It was what had changed Bruno.

"You are very beautiful looking. The Italian Renaissance all over again in your face," Bruno said. He kept standing right over Fenton as though he were a bird that was going to come down on top of his head. He kept staring right into the crown of his head.

Fenton suddenly reached out and with violence seizing Bruno's wrist cried, "Give me some of that," so that the cigarette nearly fell from his fingers.

"Have you ever had any?" Bruno wanted to know.

"Give me some," Fenton said again, remembering now with terrifying insistence the smell in the *All Night Theater*. He felt that he could really dominate this man now as much as he could Claire. At the same time he was terribly afraid. He felt that something decisive and irrevocable was about to happen.

"Just smoke a little of it and don't inhale as deep as I did," Bruno said nervously. "I don't think you know how."

Fenton took the cigarette and began inhaling deeply.

"Now stop," Bruno said. "I don't have a warehouse of those."

"No wonder somebody was following you," Fenton laughed.

"I wonder which one of us is more scared of the other," Bruno said finally, and he sat down at Fenton's feet.

Fenton was about to say that he was not afraid of anybody, but Bruno began babbling about Fenton's shoes. "Where on earth did you get *those?* They're privately manufactured!" He stared at Fenton with renewed respect and interest. "You didn't get *those* in West Virginia."

Bruno stared at Fenton again.

"You haven't killed anybody, have you?" he said finally.

Fenton stared at him and he went on agitatedly, "Why you've finished that entire cigarette. I hope you know what you've done and what it was. I'm not responsible for you, remember."

"Who the fuck is responsible?" Fenton said.

"Don't use that language," Bruno sniggered, and then got up swiftly and sat down beside Fenton. He began kissing his hair, and then slowly unbuttoning his shirt. He took off all his clothes, as from a doll, piece by piece, without resistance or aid, but left on at the last the privately manufactured shoes. . . .

The next thing Fenton remembered he was standing naked in the middle of the room, boxing; he was boxing the chandelier and had knocked down all the lamps, he had split open Bruno's face and Bruno was weeping and held ice packs to his mouth.

Then the next thing he remembered was Bruno standing before him with Hayden Banks who looked exactly like the murdered Desdemona. Bruno had a gun in his hand and was ordering him to leave.

"Don't you ever come back if you don't want to go to jail," Bruno said, as Fenton went out the door dressed in clothes that did not look like his own.

Morning is the most awful time. And this morning for Fenton was the one that shattered everything he had been or known; it marked the limits of a line, not ending his youth but making his youth superfluous, as age to a god.

He seemed to be awake and yet he had the feeling he had never been awake. He was not even sure it was morning. He was back in the old house, in Claire's room, and though he was staring at Claire he knew that his staring was of no avail, that he already knew what had happened and the staring was to prevent him from telling himself what he saw. He could not remember anything at that moment, he had even forgotten Bruno Korsawski and the production of *Othello* starring some immortal fruit.

Then the comfortable thought that it was breakfast time and that he would go out and get Claire his rolls and coffee. He was so happy he was here with Claire and he realized again how necessary Claire was to him, and how real he was compared to the Parkhearsts and the Brunos and the Graingers.

"Claire," he said softly. He went over to the bed and began shaking him. The room seemed suddenly deadly cold and he thought of the winter that would come and how uninhabitable this deserted old wreck would be. . . . And Claire, he recognized, almost as with previous knowledge, was as cold as the room. And yet he was not surprised. . . .

He sat there suddenly wondering why he was not surprised that Claire was cold. And at the same time he was surprised that he could be so cold. He shook him again.

"Claire," he said.

He began to be aware of a splitting headache.

He got up and turned on the sickly light. He was careful somehow not to get too close to Claire now that he had turned on the light, but stood at a safe distance, talking to him, telling him how he was going to get him some breakfast.

"Some good hot coffee will make you feel like a new boy, Claire," he said.

And then suddenly he began to weep, choking sobs, and these were followed by laughter so unlike his own that he remained frozen with confusion.

"I'm going right now, hear?" he said to Claire. "I'll be right back with the coffee. . . ." Then he laughed again. The silence of the room was complete.

He hurried to the lunch stand and then ran all the way back with the steaming coffee and rolls.

He bent down over Claire but was somewhat careful not to look at his face. His head ached as though the sockets of his eyes were to burst. He kept talking to Claire all the time, telling him how they were going back to West Virginia as soon as he got a little money saved up; they would buy a stock farm later and raise Black Angus cattle, and have a stable of horses. It was not impossible, Claire, he said.

He held Claire's head up but still without looking and tried to pour coffee down his throat. "This coffee's strong enough to revive a stiff," he laughed, ignoring the coffee's running down the boy's neck, ignoring that none of the coffee had even got into his mouth.

"Eat this bread," he said and put some to Claire's mouth. He pressed the small piece of roll heavily against the blue lips, smashing it to the coffee-moistened cold lips.

"Eat this, drink this," Fenton kept saying, but now he no longer tried to administer the bread and coffee. "Eat and drink."

We have to go back, Claire. We want to go back to West Virginia, you know you do.

Then as though another person had entered the room and commanded him, Fenton stood up, and pulled the light down as far as he could to search mercilessly the face and body of Claire.

The light showed Claire's neck swollen and blue with marks, the neck broken softly like a small bird's, the hair around his neck like ruffled young feathers, the eyes had come open a little and seemed to be attempting to focus on something too far out of his reach. The brown liquid of the coffee like blood smeared the paste of the offering of bread around his mouth.

Fenton looked down at his hands.

After that he did not know what happened, or how long he stayed in the room, trying to feed Claire, trying to talk to him, trying to tell him about Black Angus in West Virginia.

Slowly the sound of Fenton's own voice worked him from the stupor he had been in, saying again and again, "You're dead, you little motherfucker. Dead as mud and I don't have no need sitting here staring you down."

For a good many days he walked all over the city, riding street cars when they were full so that he could shove his way in without paying, eating in cheap lunch stands when they were full and running out the back door without paying the bill. He found he could steal fruit and candy from grocery stands without much trouble. In the evening he would go to the Square in front of a large gray library and listen to the revivalists and the fanatics.

Older men sometimes invited him to a beer, men he met in the crowds in front of the speaker, but as he drank with them his mind would wander and he would say things which chilled further talk, so that after a while absently he would look around and find himself alone looking down at his hands.

There was no respite for his misery during which time he slept in hallways, covering himself with newspapers he collected in alleys. By day he would go down to the docks and watch crews unload cargo, or he would go into a large museum where they kept the bones of prehistoric animals which he knew never existed. These big-boned monsters calmed some of his crushing grief.

But at last there came to him an idea which gave him some solace, if not any real hope or restoration. It was that Claire must be put in a sheltered place. He must have a service, a funeral. The thought did not occur to him that Claire was really dead until then; before he had only thought how he had killed him. And the thought that anybody *knew* he had killed Claire or was looking for him never occurred to him. What had happened to both him and Claire was much too terrible and closed in for the rest of the world to know or care about.

It was night when he returned to the house. He had vaguely remembered going upstairs weeks before and finding an old chest up there, an old cedar chest, perhaps, or merely an old box. He walked up the stairs now, using matches to guide his way. He heard small footsteps scamper about or it might have been only the echo of his own feet.

He stood in the immense vacant attic with its suffocating smell of rotting wood, its soft but ticklingly clammy caress of cobwebs, the feeling of small animal eyes upon him and the imperceptible sounds of disintegration and rot. How had he known there was a chest up here? As he thought of it now he could not remember having seen it. Yet he knew it was here.

He put himself on hands and knees and began groping for

the presence of it. He came across a broken rocking chair. His kitchen matches lit up pictures on the wall, one of a girl in her wedding dress, another of a young man in hunting costume, one of Jesus among thieves. Another picture was a poem concerning Mother Love. At the extreme end of the attic and in a position which must have been directly above the room where he and Claire had lived and where Claire now lay dead was a chest; it was not a fragrant cedar chest, such as he had hoped, but an old white box with broken hinges and whose inside lid was covered with a filthy cloth.

But even more disappointing was that inside was a gauzy kind of veil, like a wedding veil and his eye turned wearily to the picture of the girl in her wedding costume as though this veil might be the relic of that scene. But whatever the veil was, it might serve this cause. It was not a fit resting place for Claire, but it would have to do.

He hurried now downstairs and into the room, with the sudden fear that Claire might have disappeared. He sat down beside him, and his agony was so great he scarcely noticed the overpowering stench, and at the same time he kept lighting the kitchen matches, but perhaps more to keep his mind aware of the fact of Claire's death than to scare off the stink of death.

It took him all night to get himself ready to carry Claire up, as though once he had put him in the chest, he was really at last dead forever. For part of the night he found that he had fallen asleep over Claire's body, and at the very end before he carried him upstairs and deposited him, he forced himself to kiss the dead stained lips he had stopped, and said, "Up we go then, motherfucker."

• Daddy Wolf •

YOU aren't the first man to ask me what I am doing so long in the phone booth with the door to my flat open and all. Let me explain something, or if you want to use the phone, I'll step out for a minute, but I am trying to get Operator to re-connect me with a party she just cut me off from. If you're not in a big hurry would you let me just try to get my party again.

See I been home 2 days now just looking at them 2 or 3 holes in the linoleum in my flat, and those holes are so goddam big now — you can go in there and take a look — those holes are so goddam big that I bet my kid, if he was still here, could almost put his leg through the biggest one.

Maybe of course the rats don't use the linoleum holes as entrances or exits. They could come through the calcimine in the wall. But I kind of guess and I bet the super for once would back me up on this, the rats are using the linoleum holes. Otherwise what is the meaning of the little black specks in and near each hole in the linoleum. I don't see how you could ignore the black specks there. If they were using the wall holes you would expect black specks there, but I haven't found a single one.

The party I was just talking to on the phone when I got cut off was surprised when I told her how the other night after my wife and kid left me I came in to find myself staring right head-on at a fat, I guess a Mama rat, eating some of my uncooked cream of wheat. I was so took by surprise that I did not see which way she went out. She ran, is all I can say, the minute I come into the room.

I had no more snapped back from seeing the Mama rat when a teeny baby one run right between my legs and disappeared ditto.

183

I just stood looking at my uncooked cream of wheat knowing I would have to let it go to waste.

It was too late that evening to call the super or anybody and I know from a lot of sad experience how sympathetic he would be, for the rats, to quote him, is a *un-avoidable probability* for whatever party decides to rent one of these you-know-what linoleum apartments.

If you want something better than some old you-know-what linoleum-floor apartments, the super says, *you got the map of Newyorkcity to hunt with.*

Rats and linoleum go together, and when you bellyache about rats, remember you're living on linoleum.

I always have to go to the hall phone when I get in one of these states, but tonight instead of calling the super who has gone off by now anyhow to his night job (he holds 2 jobs on account of, he says, the high cost of chicken and peas), I took the name of the first party my finger fell on in the telephone book

This lady answered the wire.

I explained to her the state I was in, and that I was over in one of the linoleum apartments and my wife and kid left me.

She cleared her throat and so on.

Even for a veteran, I told her, this is rough.

She kind of nodded over the phone in her manner.

I could feel she was sort of half-friendly, and I told her how I had picked her name out from all the others in the telephone book.

It was rough enough, I explained to her, to be renting an apartment in the linoleum district and to not know nobody in Newyorkcity, and then only the other night after my wife and kid left me this Mama rat was in here eating my uncooked cream of wheat, and before I get over this, her offspring run right between my legs.

This lady on the wire seemed to say *I see* every so often but I couldn't be sure on account of I was talking so fast myself.

I would have called the super of the building, I explained

to her, in an emergency like this, but he has 2 jobs, and as it is after midnight now he is on his night job. But it would be just as bad in the daytime as then usually he is out inspecting the other linoleum apartments or catching up on his beauty sleep and don't answer the door or phone.

When I first moved into this building, I told her, I had to pinch myself to be sure I was actually seeing it right. I seen all the dirt before I moved in, but once I was in, I really *seen*: all the traces of the ones who had been here before, people who had died or lost their jobs or found they was the wrong race or something and had had to vacate all of a sudden before they could clean the place up for the next tenant. A lot of them left in such a hurry they just give you a present of some of their belongings and underwear along with their dirt. But then after one party left in such a hurry, somebody else from somewhere moved in, found he could not make it in Newyorkcity, and lit out somewhere or maybe was taken to a hospital in a serious condition and never returned.

I moved in just like the others on the linoleum.

Wish you could have seen it then. Holes everywhere and that most jagged of the holes I can see clear over here from the phone booth is where the Mama rat come through, which seems now about 3,000 years ago to me.

I told the lady on the phone how polite she was to go on listening and I hoped I was not keeping her up beyond her bedtime or from having a nightcap before she did turn in.

I don't object to animals, see. If it had been a Mama bird, say, which had come out of the hole, I would have had a start, too, as a Mama bird seldom is about and around at that hour, not to mention it not nesting in a linoleum hole, but I think I feel the way I do just because you think of rats along with neglect and lonesomeness and not having nobody near or around you.

See my wife left me and took our kid with her. They could not take any more of Newyorkcity. My wife was very scared of disease, and she had heard the radio in a shoe-repair store telling that they were going to raise the V.D. rate, and she said to me just a few hours before she left, *I don't think I am going to stay on here, Benny, if they are going to have one of them health epidemics.* She didn't have a disease, but she felt she would if the city officials were bent on raising the V.D. rate. She said it would be her luck and she would be no exception to prove the rule. She packed and left with the kid.

Did I feel sunk with them gone, but Jesus it was all I could do to keep on here myself. A good number of times at night I did not share my cream of wheat with them. I told them to prepare what kind of food they had a yen for and let me eat my cream of wheat alone with a piece of warmed-over oleo and just a sprinkle of brown sugar on that.

My wife and kid would stand and watch me eat the cream of wheat, but they was entirely indifferent to food. I think it was partly due to the holes in the linoleum, and them knowing what was under the holes of course.

We have only the one chair in the flat, and so my kid never had any place to sit when I was to home.

I couldn't help telling this party on the phone then about my wife and *Daddy Wolf.*

I was the one who told my wife about *Daddy Wolf* and the *Trouble Phone* in the first place, but at first she said she didn't want any old charity no matter if it was money or advice or just encouraging words.

Then when things got so rough, my wife did call *Daddy Wolf.* I think the number is CRack 8-7869 or something like that, and only ladies can call. You phone this number and say *Daddy Wolf, I am a lady in terrible trouble. I am in one of the linoleum apartments, and just don't feel I can go on another day. Mama rats are coming in and out of their holes with their babies, and all we have had to eat in a month is cream of wheat.*

Daddy Wolf would say he was listening and to go on, and then he would ask her if she was employed anywhere.

Daddy Wolf, yes and no. I just do not seem to have the willpower to go out job-hunting any more or on these house-to-house canvassing jobs that I have been holding down lately, and if you could see this linoleum flat, I think you would agree, Daddy Wolf, that there is very little incentive for me and Benny.

Then my wife would go on about how surprised we had both been, though she was the only one surprised, over the high rate of V.D. in Newyorkcity.

You see, Daddy Wolf, I don't hold a thing back, I have been about with older men in order to tide my husband over this rough financial situation we're in. My husband works in the mitten factory, and he just is not making enough for the three of us to live on. He has to have his cream of wheat at night or he would not have the strength to go back to his day-shift, and our linoleum apartment costs 30 smackers a week.

I leave the kid alone here and go out to try and find work, Daddy Wolf, but I'm telling you, the only job I can find for a woman of my education and background is this house-to-house canvassing of Queen Bee royal jelly which makes older women look so much more appealing, but I hardly sell more than a single jar a day and am on my feet 12 hours at a stretch.

The kid is glad when I go out to sell as he can have the chair to himself then. You see when I and his Daddy are home he either has to sit down on my lap, if I am sitting, or if his Daddy is sitting, just stand because I won't allow a little fellow like him to sit on that linoleum, it's not safe, and his Daddy will not let him sit on his lap because he is too dead-tired from the mitten factory.

That was the way she explained to *Daddy Wolf* on the *Trouble Phone,* and that went on every night, night after night, until she left me.

Daddy Wolf always listened, I will give him credit for that. He advised Mabel too: *go to Sunday school and church and quit going up to strange men's hotel rooms. Devote yourself only to your husband's need, and you don't ever have to fear the rise in the V.D. rate.*

My wife, though, could just not take Newyorkcity. She was out selling that Queen Bee royal jelly every day, but when cold weather come she had only a thin coat and she went out less and less and that all added up to less cream of wheat for me in the evening.

It is a funny thing about cream of wheat, you don't get tired of it. I think if I ate, say, hamburger and chop suey every night, I would get sick and tired of them. Not that I ever dine on them. But if I did, I would — get sick and tired, I mean. But there's something about cream of wheat, with just a daub of warm oleo on it, and a sprinkle of brown sugar that makes you feel you might be eatin' it for the first time.

My wife don't care for cream of wheat nearly so much as I do.

Our kid always ate with the old gentleman down the hall with the skullcap. He rung the bell when it was supper time, and the kid went down there and had his meal. Once in a while, he brought back something or other for us.

It's funny talking to you like this, Mister, and as I told this lady I am waiting to get re-connected with on the phone, if I didn't know any better I would think either one of you was *Daddy Wolf* on the *Trouble Phone*.

Well, Mabel left me, then, and took the kid with her.

It was her silly fear of the V.D. rate that really made her light out. She could have stayed here indefinitely. She loved this here city at first. She was just crazy about Central Park.

Newyorkcity was just the place for me to find work in. I had a good job with the Singer sewing-machine people in one of their spare-parts rooms, then I got laid off and was without a thing for over 6 months and then was lucky to find this job at the mitten factory. I raise the lever that sews the inner lining to your mittens.

I don't think it is Mabel and the kid leaving me so much sometimes as it is the idea of that Mama rat coming through the holes in the linoleum that has got me so down-in-the-dumps today. I didn't even go to the mitten factory this A.M., and I have, like I say, got so down-in-the-dumps I almost felt like calling *Daddy Wolf* myself on the *Trouble Phone* like she did all the time. But knowing he won't talk to nobody but ladies, as a kind of next-best-thing I put my finger down haphazard on top of this lady's name in the phone book, and I sure appreciated having that talk with her.

See *Daddy Wolf* would only talk with my wife for about one and a half minutes on account of other women were

waiting to tell him their troubles. He would always say *Go back
to your affiliation with the Sunday school and church of your choice,
Mabel, and you'll find your burdens lighter in no time.*

Daddy said the same thing to her every night, but she
never got tired hearing it, I guess.

Daddy Wolf told Mabel she didn't have to have any fear at
all of the V.D. rate on account of she was a married woman
and therefore did not have to go out for that relationship, but
if she ever felt that *desire* coming over her when her husband
was gone, to just sit quiet and read an uplifting book.

Mabel has not had time, I don't think, to write me yet,
taking care of the kid and all, and getting settled back home,
and I have, well, been so goddam worried about everything.
They are talking now about a shut-down at the mitten factory
so that I hardly as a matter of fact have had time to think about
my wife and kid, let alone miss them. There is, as a matter of
fact, more cream of wheat now for supper, and I splurged
today and bought a 5-pound box of that soft brown sugar that
don't turn to lumps, which I wouldn't ever have done if they
was still here.

The old gent down the hall with the skullcap misses my
kid, as he almost entirely kept the boy in eats.

He never speaks to me in the hall, the old man. They
said, I heard this somewhere, he don't have linoleum on his
floor, but carpets, but I have not been invited in to see.

This building was condemned two years ago, but still isn't
torn down, and the old man is leaving as soon as he can find
the right neighborhood for his married daughter to visit him
in.

Wait a minute. No, I thought I seen some action from
under that one hole there in the linoleum.

Excuse me if I have kept you from using the phone with
my talk but all I can say is you and this lady on the phone have
been better for me tonight than *Daddy Wolf* on the *Trouble Phone*
ever was for my wife.

Up until now I have usually called the super when I was
in one of these down-moods, but all he ever said was *Go back*

where you and Mabel got your own people and roots, Benny. You can't make it here in a linoleum apartment with your background and education.

He has had his eyes opened—the super. He has admitted himself that he never thought Mabel and me could stick it out this long. (He don't know she is gone.)

But I won't give up. I *will not* give up. Mabel let a thing like the hike in the V.D. rates chase her out. I tried to show her that that was just statistics, but she always was superstitious as all get-out.

I judge when this scare I've had about the Mama rat dies down and I get some sleep and tomorrow if I go back to the mitten factory I will then really and truly begin to miss Mabel and the kid. The old man down the hall already misses the kid. That kid ate more in one meal with him than Mabel and me eat the whole week together. I don't begrudge it to him, though, because he is growing.

Well, Mister, if you don't want to use the phone after all, I think I will try to have Operator re-connect me with that party I got disconnected from. I guess as this is the hour that Mabel always called *Daddy Wolf* I have just automatically caught her habit, and anyhow I sure felt in the need of a talk.

Do you hear that funny clicking sound? Here, I'll hold you the receiver so as you can hear it. Don't go away just yet: I think Operator is getting me that party again, so stick around awhile yet.

No, they cut us off again, hear? there is a bad connection or something.

Well, like I say, anyhow Mabel and the kid did get out of here, even if it was superstition. Christ, when I was a boy I had every one of those diseases and it never did me no hurt. I went right into the army with a clean bill of health, Korea, home again, and now Newyorkcity.

You can't bullshit me with a lot of statistics.

Mabel, though, goddam it, I could knock the teeth down her throat, running out on me like this and taking the kid.

WHERE IS THAT GODDAM OPERATOR?

Hello. Look, Operator, what number was that I dialed and talked so long. Re-connect me please. That number I just got through talking with so long. I don't know the party's name or number. Just connect me back, will you please. This here is an emergency phone call, Operator.

• HOME BY DARK •

EVERY day his grandfather bought him a new toy of a cheap kind, and a little racing car made out of chocolate. The boy ate the racing car slowly and almost dutifully as he and his grandfather sat on the immense porch and talked about how the birds know when to leave for the South.

"Have we ever been South?" the boy asked his grandfather, after he had finished the chocolate racing car and wiped his hands carefully on his cowboy handkerchief.

"No," the old man said. "Not since your parents died."

"Why don't we go?" the young boy said.

"There would be no reason to," the old man replied.

The birds that had been twittering on the huge lawn that surrounded the great white house in which he lived with his grandfather suddenly rose together in a flock as if hearing an inaudible signal, and disappeared into a clump of trees far off.

"There they all go," the boy told his grandfather.

"There they go," the old man repeated.

"Are you glad they're gone?" the young boy wondered.

"They're not really gone. Not South," the old man told the boy. "It isn't time yet—it's only July."

"Oh, I knowed they hadn't gone South," the boy told his grandfather. "I saw them yesterday do it. They practice like this all day long. They twitter and twitter and twitter, then they all get silent and then *zoom*, they all fly off like they knowed it was time."

"*Knew*," the grandfather corrected.

"Yes, *knew*," the boy nodded, and put his hand gently on his grandfather's hand.

"Birds are really strange creatures," the old man admitted. "They remember always where to go, where to build their nests, where to return to. . . ." He shook his head.

"They know to go South when it's cold," the boy agreed.
"Except the sparrows. They stay all winter, poor little fellows.
They are tough. They don't have no more feathers than the
other birds, yet they stay right on, don't they?"

The grandfather nodded.

"Maybe, though, they *do* have more feathers and we can't
see them," the boy added, thinking.

"That could be," the old man told his grandson, and he
brought his cane up now painfully, and then pressed down
with it with his hand.

The boy waited a little for his grandfather to say
something more, and the old man, sensing the boy's need for
words, said: "Did you like your chocolate racing car?"

"It was sweet and bitter and sweet all at the same time,
and then at the very end it was soapy."

"Soapy?" the grandfather wondered.

The boy nodded.

"Well, then there was something wrong with it," the old
man complained faintly.

"No," the boy said airily. "That's the way the sweet and
the bitter get after you have them both together. See," he said
pulling on his grandfather's cane a little, "after you taste the
sweet you taste the bitter and after you taste the sweet again
you taste the sweet and the bitter, and it's only soapy for a
second?"

"I see," the grandfather nodded.

"And then it's all sweet!" The boy laughed, and he
jumped up and down on the porch steps, making strange little
sounds imitating nobody knew what.

"And I lost a tooth!" the boy told his grandfather.

"Cook told me," the old man informed him.

"Tonight when I go to bed, I am going to put it under my
pillow and when I wake up in the morning do you know what
is going to be under where I slept all night?"

The grandfather smiled and shook his head.

"A pot of gold," the boy told him.

"What will you do with it?" the grandfather asked.

"I might turn into a bird and go South then," the boy told him.

"But you wouldn't want to leave your old granddad and Cook," the grandfather chided.

The boy thought a moment and said, "I would fly back for supper."

"Well, it will be interesting to see your pot of gold tomorrow," the old man agreed.

"You really think I will get it then?" the boy asked.

"All wishes like that come true," the grandfather said somewhat gravely. "It's because they're a . . . a *pure* wish."

"A *pure* wish?" the boy wondered, scratching his nose. "What's that?"

"Well, like pure candy; you've had that, you know."

The boy shook his head.

"Your chocolate racing car is pure candy," the grandfather said, unsure this was so, and no conviction in his voice.

"Oh," the boy answered.

"All you really wished for, you see," the grandfather explained, "was to have your wish come true. You really hadn't thought what you would do with your wish and your pot of gold."

"Yes," the boy agreed, but his attention wandered.

"So tonight when you go to sleep you must just think that you want the pot of gold, and that is all you want. And don't wish for it too hard, you know."

"No?" the boy raised his voice.

"Not too hard. That would frighten the good fairy away."

"The good fairy?" the boy wondered.

"Yes. Who did you think brought your pot of gold?"

"I thought," the boy felt his way. "I thought . . . somebody dead."

"What?" the old man said, and he moved his cane again so that now it pointed down to the grass where the birds had gathered in a flock.

"Cook didn't really tell me who did bring it," the boy said, studying the confusion on his grandfather's face.

"Yes," the old man said absently, and then looking at his grandson he said, "well, it's really the good fairy, I expect. Don't you know about her?"

The boy shook his head.

"Well, she is the one who's supposed to bring the gold." And the old man laughed rather loudly.

"Do you believe in her?" the boy asked.

"The good fairy?" the old man said, and he began to laugh again, but stopped. "Yes, I do," he said after a pause and with a sleepy serious expression.

The grandfather fished his heavy gold watch out of his vest pocket and looked at its face.

"Seven P.M.," he said.

"Seven P.M.," the boy repeated. "One hour to bedtime."

"That's right," the grandfather said, and he put his hand on the boy's head.

"Why don't you want to go South?" the young boy wondered, suddenly.

"Well," the old man stirred in his chair. "Memories, I suppose, you know." But then looking at his grandson he knew the boy did *not* know, and he said, "It's a long story."

"You don't remember why?" the boy asked.

"When you're older I will talk about it," the old man began. "You see there's so much explanation to it, and well, I'm very old, and it tires me out when I make long explanations."

"What is *explanation*—just telling everything, then?"

"Yes," the old man smiled. "And if I told you why I don't want to go South why we'd be here for days!"

"But we are anyhow!" the boy exclaimed. "We're always just standing and sitting and standing and talking here or watching the birds."

The old man was silent.

"Ain't we?" the boy said.

"Well, if I was a bird I would *never* go South," the old man spoke almost as if to himself.

The boy waited and then when his grandfather said no

more he told him: "I would always come home at dark, I think, if I was a bird."

"Yes, sir, *tomorrow,*" the old man's voice sounded, taking on warmth, "you'll have your pot of gold!"

"Hurray!" the small boy shouted, and he ran around the old man's chair making sounds now that were those of a jet.

"What will you buy me tomorrow?" the boy asked his grandfather.

"But tomorrow you will have your own pot of gold!" the grandfather told his grandson. "You'll be rich!"

"Will I then?" the boy wondered.

"Don't you believe you'll have it?" the old man interrogated.

"No," the boy said softly.

"But you must believe," the grandfather warned him.

"Why?" the boy asked, looking closely into his grandfather's face.

"You must always believe in one thing, that one thing."

"What is *that one thing?*" the boy asked, an almost scared look on his face.

"Oh, it's hard to say," the old man admitted failure again.

"Not like going South now, don't tell me again," the boy complained.

"No, this is even harder to explain than going South, but I will try to tell you."

The old man drew his grandson closer to him and arranged the collar of the boy's shirt. He said: "There is always one thing a person believes and wants to believe even if he doesn't believe it."

"Ahem," the boy said, standing on only one leg.

"Do you see?" the old man asked, his face soft and smiling.

"Yes," the boy replied, his voice hard.

"All right, then," the old man went on. "There is this one thing you want and you want it more than anything in the world. You see?"

"Like the birds knowing where to fly, you mean?" the boy was cautious.

"Yes," the old man doubted this, and then said, "but more like your pot of gold."

"Oh," the boy replied.

"You want this one thing, and you have to go on believing in it, no matter what."

"Well, what is the thing?" the boy smiled broadly now, showing the place in his mouth where he had lost his tooth, which was a front one.

"Only the person who knows can tell!" the grandfather said loudly as though this were a joke now.

"But am I old enough to know?" the boy said, puzzled and surprised.

"You're old enough and you should tell me now," the grandfather encouraged him.

"So," the boy paused, screwing his eyes shut, and he stood first on one foot and then on another. "I would like my father and mother both to be alive again, and all of us, including you, living South."

The old man opened his mouth and closed it again.

"Isn't that the right answer?" the boy said, worried.

"Yes, of course," the old man hurriedly agreed.

"You don't act like it was the right answer," the boy complained.

"Well, it is, anyhow. The only thing was — I was thinking about wishes that are about the future, you see."

"Oh," the boy was disappointed. Then in a kind of querulous voice he said, "My wish wasn't the future?"

"It's so hard to explain," the grandfather laughed, and he roughed up the boy's hair.

"Well," the boy said, "let's talk about things we can tell each other."

The grandfather laughed.

The light was beginning to die slowly in the trees, and a full rounded moon began to show in the near distance.

Suddenly the boy said *Oh* in a scared voice.

"What is it?" the grandfather was concerned.

"I think I lost my tooth," the boy said.

"You did?" the grandfather was even more alarmed now than the boy.

"I did, I lost it." He felt suddenly in his pockets.

"When we were talking about the birds, you know, I throwed my hand out . . . and the tooth must have been in my hand."

"You *threw* your hand out. Well, then it's in the grass," the grandfather said.

"Yes," the boy agreed.

The old man got out of his chair and his grandson helped him silently down the twelve steps that led to the long walk about which extended the immense lawn where the tooth had been thrown.

They searched patiently in the long grass, which had needed cutting for some time.

"It was such a little tooth," the boy said, as though he realized this fact for the first time.

The old man could not bend over very far, but his eyes, which were still keen, looked sharply about him for the tooth.

"Oh, what shall I ever do!" the boy said suddenly.

"But it will turn up!" the old man cried, but there was the same note of disappointment and fear in his voice, which, communicating itself to the boy, caused the latter to weep.

"You mustn't cry," the grandfather was stern. "It won't do at all!"

"But the pot of gold and all!" the boy cried.

"It doesn't matter at all," the grandfather said, and he touched the boy on the face.

"But you told me it did," the boy wept now.

"I told you *what?*" the old man said.

"You told me there was just that one thing you should want to believe in."

"But you've only lost your tooth," the old man replied. "And we'll find it. It isn't lost forever. The gardener will find it when he comes."

"Oh, I'm afraid not," the boy said, wandering about now

picking up the grass by the handfuls, looking and watching about him in the fading light.

"If we only hadn't let Cook take the flashlight we might locate it with that," the grandfather said, a few minutes later, when the light was quite gone.

The boy now just stood in one place staring down at the grass.

"I think we'll have to give up the search for tonight," the grandfather finally said.

"But this is the only night I can have my wish!" the boy cried. "This is the ONLY night."

"Nonsense," the grandfather told him. "Not true at all."

"But it is, it is," the boy contradicted his grandfather, gravely.

"How do you know?" the grandfather wondered.

"My mother told me," the boy said.

"But you don't . . . you don't remember her!" the grandfather stared into the growing dark.

"She told me in my sleep," the boy said, his voice plain, unemphatic.

The grandfather looked at his grandson's face but the dark hid it and its expression from him.

"Let's go up the steps now," the grandfather told him.

The small boy helped the old man up the twelve steps, and at the last one the old man laughed, making fun of his fatigue.

"Don't ever get old now, don't you ever do that," he laughed.

The grandfather sat down heavily in the chair, his cane thrown out as though commanding something, or somebody.

"We'll find your tooth tomorrow, or we'll all be hanged," the grandfather said cheerily. "And we won't let Cook take our flashlight again, will we?"

The boy did not answer. He stood as he stood every night beside his grandfather, looking out over the western sky, tonight half-seeing the red harvest moon rise.

"I will buy you something different tomorrow," the

grandfather said, "so that it will be a real surprise. Do you hear?"

The boy said yes.

"You're not crying now," the grandfather said. "That's good."

The boy nodded.

"I'm glad you're brave too, because a boy should not cry, really, no matter even . . . Well, he should never cry."

"But I don't know what to believe in now," the boy said in a dry old voice.

"Fiddlesticks," the old man said. "Now come over here and sit on my lap and I will talk to you some more."

The boy moved slowly and sat down on his grandfather's lap.

"Ouch," the grandfather said playfully when he felt how heavy the boy was.

"Just the two of us," the old man said. "Just the two of us here, but we're old friends, aren't we. Good, good old friends."

He pushed the boy's head tight against his breast so he would not hear the sounds that came out now like a confused and trackless torrent, making ridiculous the quiet of evening, and he closed his own eyes so that he would not see the moon.

· About Jessie Mae ·

I DON'T visit Jessie Mae's any more because of her untidiness," Myrtle said to Mrs. Hemlock as the two women walked through the garden, where they had been talking, toward Mrs. Hemlock's kitchen, where Myrtle was going to copy down a special recipe for the older woman.

"But I didn't know it had gone so far," Mrs. Hemlock said with mild disbelief.

"I didn't say it had gone *too* far now," Myrtle told her. "Nothing is under any order or control, that's all."

"And that I can believe," Mrs. Hemlock agreed.

"You see, Jessie Mae's never had to do anything for herself," Myrtle explained.

Mrs. Hemlock stared at her friend's youthful face, in the late morning Florida light, the desire for *more* written on her own expectant mouth and heavy double chin.

"You know Jessie Mae was *twice* an heiress," and Myrtle hit the word as hard as possible in order to begin at the beginning of her knowledge.

"I knew she had everything, of course," Mrs. Hemlock said in somewhat hushed tones now, as though a matter of considerable delicacy had been disclosed. She looked down at her apron suddenly and removed a long ravelling which had come to rest there.

Myrtle looked quickly at Mrs. Hemlock's apron and said, "That's cunning."

"It's Portuguese or Spanish or something," Mrs. Hemlock smiled, opening the back screen to her kitchen.

"You know, you have beautiful things, Mrs. Hemlock," Myrtle said.

Mrs. Hemlock laughed pleasantly.

"I love to come to *your* house," Myrtle told her.

"But I can't understand Jessie Mae's being that *untidy,*" Mrs. Hemlock seemed very surprised, and she pointed quickly to a large easy chair which she had brought into her kitchen specially for her many visitors. Myrtle sat down with a great sigh of pleasure.

"This chair!" Myrtle groaned loudly and pretended to collapse from their long earlier talk in the garden.

Mrs. Hemlock smiled at this compliment, too, and chuckled mildly, her double chin moving slightly as if she were singing a lullaby.

"I'm Jessie Mae's distant cousin, you know," Myrtle said suddenly.

Mrs. Hemlock paused a second because she was not sure she knew this or not. But dimly, from many years back in certain St. Augustine circles, a faint recollection stirred in her brain.

"I remember," Mrs. Hemlock nodded, and opening the refrigerator she moved swiftly for such a stout woman to hand Myrtle a tall cool glass of fruit punch, thickly frosted, and non-alcoholic.

"You jewel!" Myrtle almost squealed. "You think of everything. And you *have* everything."

Mrs. Hemlock could not conceal her pleasure again. Her heavy, healthy face flushed slightly from the additional praise.

"I'm alone and I have to keep busy at something," Mrs. Hemlock glanced at her kitchen.

"But most women wouldn't bother," Myrtle said. "You're *always* cooking. And so generous in sending around things to we neighbors. Why you're making us all fat, too!" Myrtle laughed loudly.

Mrs. Hemlock started at this, but then she laughed pleasantly also.

"I suppose eating is a sin," Mrs. Hemlock pretended seriousness.

"Nothing that gives one pleasure like this is," Myrtle was firm on this point, and Mrs. Hemlock could see Myrtle was thinking of Jessie Mae again.

"Well!" Mrs. Hemlock exclaimed, drinking now some of her own fruit punch and hoping Myrtle would go back to her first subject, "It's nice we're all a bit different."

"It's wonderful," Myrtle said, referring to the drink. "And I suppose it's a secret recipe . . ."

"No, no," Mrs. Hemlock deprecated this, but acted abstracted now, almost as if tasting something in the drink which she had not remembered putting there. Then suddenly she broke out: "I didn't know, as a matter of fact, you *were* Jessie Mae's distant cousin."

Myrtle put down her glass of juice on the kitchen table, which was provided with a handsome imported linen tablecloth, fresh and spotless.

"I really had forgotten, that is," Mrs. Hemlock said in a kind of apology.

"I'm really one of the last of her own people," Myrtle spoke indifferently, but with a certain tone which implied that the relationship might be important for others to remember.

"Jessie Mae is of course basically a fine person," Mrs. Hemlock stated, fearful now that she had perhaps stressed the untidiness too much, even though Myrtle had brought the whole subject up in the garden.

"Mrs. Hemlock, Jessie Mae's in terrible shape!" Myrtle suddenly changed any direction toward or need for apology, and she stared at her drink as if she had promised herself not to touch it again.

Mrs. Hemlock moistened her lips critically, as if she, too, did not require the refreshment now of the punch.

"Is Jessie Mae *worried* or something?" Mrs. Hemlock felt her way in the break which had come into the conversation.

"Worried, my foot," Myrtle sprang suddenly at this suggestion, and she picked up her glass again and tasted the punch.

"She lives to worry other people, if you want to know. . . . Or if you really think about it, too much money and not enough to do . . . Do you know she has a maid to *dress* her now!"

Mrs. Hemlock's heavy face was suffused with the flush of pleasure. And although she had stood until now in her professional guise as hostess, she decided to sit down. She sat directly in front of Myrtle and said: "She *doesn't!*"

Myrtle looked almost cross at Mrs. Hemlock, for she felt the latter's exclamation was hardly necessary even in a rhetorical sense.

"I don't think Jessie Mae does a thing for herself any more," Myrtle was definite on this. "She has, you know, eight servants."

"And yet her house remains so—" and Mrs. Hemlock was going to describe the untidiness again but Myrtle had already gone ahead with:

"Jessie Mae orders everything there is to be done. And you can bet your bottom dollar that if there's untidiness she orders that too!"

Mrs. Hemlock gasped quietly and lowered her head as if to take in all the meaning of the statement, but Myrtle did not see fit to let her contemplate anything at that moment.

"She keeps these eight servants busy, let me tell you. For every one of the rooms in her house, and there must be twenty if there's one—they're all in *use!*"

Mrs. Hemlock's eyes came open wide and then closed, and her mouth closed hard too like one who had found more put in it than she had been ready for.

"That's only the beginning!" Myrtle cried.

Mrs. Hemlock's eyes came open now and there was such a look of perfect satisfaction on her face that Myrtle's own expression softened and glowed with the reflected pleasure from her older friend.

"You *don't* know about her!" Myrtle intoned with happiness, sure at last of Mrs. Hemlock's ignorance.

"I was only at her house in the old days, when she entertained General Waite so much," Mrs. Hemlock said, coolly mater-of-fact, a hint of total abdication in her tone. "Jessie Mae's brother was more or less head of the house then."

"Well, Corliss liked to act like he was," Myrtle took this

statement up. "But Jessie Mae was running the whole place even then, and running him too. He died of her bossing, many people think."

"Then, of course, I've been there several times to tea, and to her art fairs," Mrs. Hemlock put in rather firmly before stepping down altogether.

"Oh those are nothing, my dear, I'm sorry to say. You see you have to spend the night to know how it really is!" Myrtle was suddenly indignant now, but Mrs. Hemlock could see that her indignation was over the principle of Jessie Mae's behavior.

For just a second Mrs. Hemlock looked at her large red recipe book lying open to the place where Myrtle was to fill in the instructions for baking Bavarian cookies. But then she moved her eyes away from the book back directly into Myrtle's face. She wanted Myrtle to know now that she didn't know anything about Jessie Mae, and that she wanted more than anything else to find out all there was.

Myrtle saw this expression on Mrs. Hemlock's face, and put her hands in her lap as a signal they could begin in earnest.

"Jessie Mae's trouble is she won't have anything planned or in order, until she wants it. And she doesn't know what she wants until the moment she does want it!"

Myrtle suddenly stopped there like one who has not quite caught the meaning of her own words. Mrs. Hemlock stared at her and her mouth came open again, and it was this open-mouthed expression and the immense interest on Mrs. Hemlock's face, together with the wonderful health and cleanliness of the latter, and the wonderful comfort and luxury of her kitchen that made Myrtle want to stay on here, perhaps indefinitely. She did not know when things had been better for a talk.

"More punch?" Mrs. Hemlock said in her most encouraging tone.

"I'd love more!"

"And some of my ice box fudge bars with it!" Mrs. Hemlock coaxed, almost a bit hysterical with the pleasure which the Jessie Mae story was giving her.

"I'd love some fudge bars too," Myrtle said, absent-mindedly, still hesitating, it was obvious, whether to give all she knew about their common acquaintance now, or perhaps hold some last bit still back, for another time, or forever.

"As I say," Mrs. Hemlock spoke in her matter-of-fact voice, afraid whatever she said would spoil the "more" that might come, "as I say, I was never a *friend* of Jessie Mae's, but I've known her for twenty-five years."

Myrtle did not even consider this but thanked Mrs. Hemlock for the fudge bars and the second glass of punch.

"I could eat these all day," Myrtle said chewing softly, not to be hurried or budged. She made a sound of pleasure.

"I wonder you don't win prizes with your culinary genius, Mrs. Hemlock," Myrtle purred, deliberating. "You should be famous."

The older woman bowed her head in pleasure and the blush of her health and good living covered her face and throat.

But both women waited for the signal to begin again, calmly now, but with tremendous expectation.

"I know everything about her," Myrtle said suddenly.

One would not have known Mrs. Hemlock had broken their talk by going to the icebox for the fudge bars. It was almost as though Jessie Mae herself were there before them on the TV screen, helpless and exposed for all their comments.

"I lived with her for a month!" Myrtle said after she had quit chewing on the fudge bars. "In 1952!"

Mrs. Hemlock waited.

"A month, mind you!"

"Then of course you do know," Mrs. Hemlock said in a voice close to awe.

"I was afraid every minute," Myrtle said.

Mrs. Hemlock showed a slight lack of comprehension.

"You spoke of her untidiness, Mrs. Hemlock," Myrtle swept on. "Well," she laughed, "you wouldn't think that that was largely connected with her leaving her jewels everywhere.

She left thousands and thousands of dollars worth of diamonds in my room."

Mrs. Hemlock shook her head.

"Then one evening I discovered in the top bureau drawer of my room enough other jewels for the Queen herself!"

Mrs. Hemlock began to say something but Myrtle hardly paused long enough to allow her friend to tense her mouth.

"I couldn't stand that kind of untidiness, if you please, and besides I'm not so sure her untidiness, as we call it, wasn't purposeful."

"Well!" Mrs. Hemlock managed to cry.

"It's part of her way of getting even!"

"But what would she want to get even for when she's got everything!" Mrs. Hemlock propelled the question into the room and beyond into the garden.

"You don't know everything," Myrtle cautioned again. "She hates me, she hates women even more. And she's not only untidy. You started to use the right word when we were outside. She's *dirty!*"

Mrs. Hemlock let out a moan of weak remonstrance.

"I could tell you things," Myrtle said, "but we're here in a beautiful tidy house with such wonderful things to eat. I won't."

Myrtle had suddenly stopped talking, and she lay back in her chair, leaving Mrs. Hemlock with a look of complete and unexpected emptiness on her red face.

Then, perhaps of a second mind, Myrtle said: "Her whole life is to get back at everybody. Hence the servants. Hence the parties at which nothing is quite right. Hence the jewels strewn everywhere to make everybody feel they are suspected of stealing. Who wants to go to a house where jewels are strewn everywhere. Why it makes the closest of us to her wince! And don't think she doesn't accuse people of taking them. And not just the servants!"

"Why, she sounds . . . *gone,*" Mrs. Hemlock had groped for the word but did not look satisfied when she had got it.

"No," Myrtle corrected politely, smiling quickly, "Jessie

Mae is just hateful . . . She's not *gone* as you say. A man, a strong old-fashioned type over her would have gone a long way to getting the house tidied up and the jewels either sold or put in a vault. But she's never had a strong hand over her, and since the day her old father died, she's done just as she pleased every second . . ."

"Really, I never!" Mrs. Hemlock began.

"But the thing nobody seems to know," Myrtle said, sitting up still more straight, and her face a peculiar shade, "and the thing nobody can believe even when you tell them is that the whole house is nothing but an excuse for dogs!"

Mrs. Hemlock's chin trembled but she said nothing.

"Jessie Mae has thirty pedigreed dogs in those rooms upstairs if she has one!"

Mrs. Hemlock closed her eyes again, but she could not conceal the pleasure that rested on her mouth and chin.

Myrtle waited until her friend opened her eyes and then she said: "Jessie Mae sleeps downstairs, where she made her brother sleep before her. The dogs live upstairs, and there's a servant on duty for every room of them."

"You're funning!" Mrs. Hemlock used an old word and an old tone that sounded like *Amen*.

"And when I stayed there that month," Myrtle said, her mouth dry from the exertion, "she let me see the whole performance, since I had to sleep downstairs with her in any case. After all the visitors and the bores had left, she let the dogs out of their upstairs rooms, and then they would romp and tear and romp and tear, and that old woman ran and romped right along with them, laughing and shouting at them, and the dogs all yelping and carrying on like a pack of wild animals after her until you wouldn't know which acted the nuttier, she or the dogs."

"Good God!" Mrs. Hemlock turned a deep orange now, and she fanned her face with her fat hand.

"I usually never talk about Jessie Mae to anybody," Myrtle intoned.

"Of course," Mrs. Hemlock nodded, a tone of firm moral philosophy in her voice.

"But you've been so kind and considerate, to all of we neighbors," Myrtle almost scolded, "and especially to me, that I think of you, Mrs. Hemlock, as a confidante."

"Thank you, Myrtle. I'm touched," Mrs. Hemlock managed to get out.

"It's the truth. You've been an angel. Why you've baked for us and sent us things. This could be another Delmonico's!" she waved with her hand. "I've never tasted such cooking. And the comparison between your wonderful generosity and neatness and normal ways always comes as such a distinct contrast with Jessie Mae, who is, after all, my cousin, but who never does anything for anybody, and who just isn't anyhow the kind of person you want to visit."

Myrtle stopped, perhaps in realization she had told more than she had ever known she knew.

"But the poor old thing," Mrs. Hemlock ventured.

"Well, with all her wealth why doesn't she try to straighten herself out, for pity's sake. She could help so many people if she cared about anybody but herself."

Myrtle waited now finally for Mrs. Hemlock to speak, but the older woman sat there quietly, a fudge bar still untasted in her hand, thinking about Jessie Mae's running up and down with the dogs.

"I'm not surprised now the house looked so bad," Mrs. Hemlock said at last, but with a kind of dreamy expression that lacked conviction.

Myrtle was so tired she just lay back in the chair.

"Would you like a nice home-made devilled ham sandwich with a good cup of strong coffee?" Mrs. Hemlock said invitingly. "You look *awfully* tired, Myrtle."

"Why, I'd love one, of course . . . But shouldn't I fill in that recipe for you first," Myrtle said, and she took out of her apron pocket a piece of paper which contained her directions for baking Bavarian cookies.

"I think you deserve a sandwich first. Copying is awfully tiring too."

"Well, you know me and your cooking," Myrtle giggled.

"Why, I would have *never* known that about Jessie Mae if you hadn't just happened to be walking through the garden to-day," Mrs. Hemlock said, and she began to boil the water for the coffee.

"I know you won't tell anybody," Myrtle said. "Because as you know, she *is* part of my family, though you'd never know it the way she acts."

"I understand, of course," and Mrs. Hemlock smiled from above her pink chin. "But it *does* explain at last the . . . *untidiness*. My stars, yes."

Mrs. Hemlock was firm on that point.

Myrtle nodded abstractedly and both women were silent now waiting for the coffee to be ready.

• THE LESSON •

THIS is not lady's day at the pool," Mr. Diehl said. "I can't admit her."

"But she pleaded so."

Mr. Diehl was about to give his lesson to a young man and wanted no women in the pool. He knew that if a woman entered the pool during the lesson she would distract the young man, who was already nervous about learning to swim. The young man was quite upset already, as he was going to have to go to a country house where there was lots of swimming and boating, and if he didn't know how, his hosts would be very put out with him. They might never invite him again. At any rate that was his story, and besides, he was the commander's son.

"But my grandmother always wants as many people to come into the pool as possible," the girl said. Her grandmother owned the pool.

"I have worked for your grandmother for a long time," Mr. Diehl, the swimming instructor said, "and I'm sure that she would not want a woman in the pool at this hour who does not belong to the club and so far as I know doesn't even know how to swim."

"Well, I asked her that," the girl said.

"And what did she say?" the swimming instructor wanted to know.

"She said she could swim."

"Just the same she can wait until the lesson is over. It takes only half an hour."

"I told her that, but she wanted to go in the pool right away. She has gone downstairs to change."

"For Christ's sake," Mr. Diehl said.

His pupil, the commander's son, was already splashing around in the shallow water, waiting for the lesson.

"Go and tell her in a half hour."

The girl looked as though she was not going to tell the woman.

"If your grandmother were here she would back me up on this," Mr. Diehl said.

"But she's not here and my instructions were to do as best I thought."

"As best you thought," Mr. Diehl considered this, looking at the girl. She was sixteen, but he knew she had a slow mind and he wondered what had ever made Mrs. Schuck leave the pool in the hands of such an immature person.

"Look," Mr. Diehl said. "Just go and tell the woman that I can't have her in the pool while I am giving this special lesson."

"Well, I can't forbid her the pool very well, now, can I. If she wants to come in! This club isn't that exclusive and she knows one of the members."

"I don't care if she knows the man who invented swimming, she can't come in. Is that clear?"

"Mr. Diehl, you forget that I am the granddaughter of the owner of the pool."

"I am responsible for what goes on in the water, am I not?"

"Yes, I'll go along with you there."

"All right then," Mr. Diehl said, as though having made his point. "Go tell her I can't have her in the water until after the lesson. Can't you do that?"

"No," the girl said. "I can't tell that to a perfectly good customer."

"You have this pool mixed up with a public dance hall or something. This is not exactly a money-making organization, as your grandmother must have told you. It is a club. Not open to everybody. And this unknown woman should not have been allowed in here anyhow. Not at all."

"I know better," the girl said. "Many nice people come here just for an occasional swim."

"Not unless they are known," Mr. Diehl said.

"But she knows a member," the girl pointed out.

"Who is the member?" Mr. Diehl wanted to know.

"Oh, I can't remember," the girl told him.

"But I know every member by name," Mr. Diehl was insistent. "I've been swimming instructor here now for nine years."

"I know, I know," the girl said. "But this woman has every right to come in here."

"She's not coming in the water."

"Well, I don't know what to tell her. She's already putting on her suit."

"Then she can take it right off again," Mr. Diehl said.

"But not here, though," the girl tried a joke. Mr. Diehl did not laugh.

"What I'm trying to get you to see, Polly," Mr. Diehl said, and it was the first time he had ever called her by name, "is that this is a pretty high-class place. Do you know by chance who that boy is who is waiting for the lesson."

Mr. Diehl waited for the girl to answer.

"I don't know who he is," she replied.

"That is Commander Jackson's son."

"And he doesn't know how to swim?"

"What has that got to do with it?" the swimming instructor said.

"Well, I'm surprised is all."

"Look, time is slipping away. I don't want to have any more argument with you, Polly. But I'm sure your grandmother would back me up on this all the way if she were here. Is there any way we can reach her by telephone?"

"I have no idea where she went."

"Well, this strange woman cannot come into the pool now."

"I am not going down to the locker room and tell her to put her clothes back on, so there," Polly said.

She was very angry, but she had also gotten a little scared.

"Then I'm going to have to tell your grandmother how nasty you've been."

"How nasty *I've* been?"

Mr. Diehl went up to the girl and put his hands on her shoulder as he often did to his students. "Look here now," he said. He did not realize how he was affecting the girl and how the water fell from him on her blouse. She looked at his biceps as they moved almost over her mouth and the way his chest rose and fell. She had always lowered her eyes when she met him in the hall, avoiding the sight of his wet, dripping quality, the many keys held in his hand, his whistle for the days when they practiced champion swimming. He had seemed to her like something that should always remain splashing about and breathing heavily in water.

"Polly, will you please cooperate with me," Mr. Diehl said.

"I don't think I can," she said.

He put down his arms in a gesture of despair. "Will you please, please just this once go down to the ladies' dressing room and tell that woman that you've made a mistake and that she can't come into the pool just now?"

Polly looked out now into the water where the commander's son was floating around by holding on to a rubber tire.

"I just can't tell her," Polly said, turning red.

"You can't tell her," Mr. Diehl observed. Then: "Look, do you know who the commander is?"

"Well, doesn't everybody?" Polly answered.

"Do you know or don't you?" Mr. Diehl wanted to know. Some more water fell from him as he gesticulated, wetting her blouse and her arms a little, and she was sure that water continued to fall from him no matter how long he had been out of the pool. She could hear him breathing and she could not help noticing his chest rise and fall as though he were doing a special swimming feat just for her in this room.

"Polly!" he said.

"I can't! I can't!" she cried.

He could see now that there was something else here, perhaps fear of something, he could not tell, he did not want to know.

"You're not going to run into any difficulty in just telling her, are you, that you didn't know the rules and that she will have to wait until the lesson is over."

"I can't and I won't," Polly said, and she refused to look at him.

The commander's son was watching them from the middle of the shallow part of the pool, but he did not act as though he was impatient for the lesson to begin, and Polly remembered what a severe instructor Mr. Diehl was said to be. Sometimes while she had sat outside in the reception room she had heard Mr. Diehl shout all the way from the pool.

"Look, do we have to go all over this again?" Mr. Diehl said. "You know the commander."

"I know the commander, of course," she said.

"Do you know he is the most influential member of the club here?"

Polly did not say anything.

"He built this pool, Polly. Not your grandmother. Did you know that?"

She felt that she might weep now, so she did not say anything.

"Are you hearing me?" Mr. Diehl wanted to know.

"*Hearing* you!" she cried, distracted.

"All right now," he said, and he put his hand on her again and she thought some more drops of water fell from him.

"I can't see how anybody would know," she said. "How would the commander know if a young woman went into his pool. And what would his son out there care."

"His son doesn't like people in the pool when he is taking a lesson," Mr. Diehl explained. "He wants it strictly private, and the commander wants it that way too."

"And the commander pays you to want it that way also."

"Polly, I'm trying to be patient."

"I'm not going to tell her she can't come in," Polly said.

She stood nearer now to the edge of the pool away from his moving arms and chest and the dripping water that she felt still came off them.

"Step away from the edge, please, Polly," he said, and he took hold of her arm drawing her firmly over to him, in his old manner with special pupils when he was about to impart to them some special secret of swimming.

"Don't always touch me," she said, but so faintly that it was hardly a reproach.

"Polly, listen to me," Mr. Diehl was saying to her. "I've known you since you were a little girl. Right?"

"Known me?" Polly said, and she felt the words only come vaguely toward her now.

"Been a friend of your family, haven't I, for a good long time. Your grandmother knew me when I was only a boy. She paid for some of my tuition in college."

"College," Polly nodded to the last word she had heard, so that he would think she was listening.

"You'll feel all right about this, Polly, and you will, I know, help me now that I've explained it to you."

"No, I can't," she said, awake again.

"You can't what?" Mr. Diehl said.

"I can't is all," she said but she spoke, as she herself recognized, like a girl talking in her sleep.

The hothouse heat of the swimming pool and the close presence of Mr. Diehl, a man she had always instinctively avoided, had made her forget in a sense why they were standing here before the water. Somewhere in a dressing room, she remembered, there was a woman who in a little while was going to do something wrong that would displease Mr. Diehl, and suddenly she felt glad this was so.

"Mr. Diehl, I am going," she said, but she made no motion to leave, and he knew from her words that she was not going. They were going on talking, he knew. It was like his students, some of them said they could never be champions, but they always were. He made them so. Some of the timid ones said they could never swim, the water was terror to them, but they always did swim. Mr. Diehl had never known failure with anything. He never said this but he showed it.

"Now you listen to me," Mr. Diehl said. "All you have to

do is go and tell her. She can sit outside with you and watch television."

"The set isn't working," Polly said, and she walked over close to the edge of the pool.

"Please come over here now," Mr. Diehl said, and he took hold of her and brought her over to where he had been standing. "Polly, I would never have believed this of you."

"Believed what?" she said, and her mind could not remember now again why exactly they were together here. She kept looking around as though perhaps she had duties she had forgotten somewhere. Then as she felt more and more unlike herself, she put her hand on Mr. Diehl's arm.

"Believed," he was saying, and she saw his white teeth near her as though the explanation of everything were in the teeth themselves—"believed you would act so incorrigible. So bad, Polly. Yes, that's the word. Bad."

"Incorrigible," she repeated, and she wondered what exactly that had always meant. It was a word that had passed before her eyes a few times but nobody had ever pronounced it to her.

"I would never want your grandmother to even know we have had to have this long argument. I will never tell her."

"I will never tell her," Polly said, expressionless, drowsily echoing his words.

"Thank you, Polly, and of course I didn't mean to tell you you didn't have to. But listen to me."

She put her hand now very heavily on his arm and leaned there.

"Are you all right, Polly," he said, and she realized suddenly that it was the first time he had ever really been aware of her being anything at all, and now when it was too late, when she felt too bad to even tell him, he had begun to grow aware.

"Polly," he said.

"Yes, Mr. Diehl," she answered and suddenly he looked down at her hand on his arm, it was pressing there, and he had become, of course, conscious of it.

He did not know what to do, she realized, and ill as she felt, the pleasure of having made him uncomfortable soothed her. She knew she was going to be very ill, but she had had at least, then, this triumph, the champion was also uncomfortable.

"You'll go and tell her then," Mr. Diehl said, but she knew now that he was not thinking about the woman anymore. The woman, the lesson, the pool had all lost their meaning and importance now.

"Polly," he said.

"I will tell her," she managed to say, still holding him tight.

"Polly, what is it?" he exclaimed.

He took her arm off him roughly, and his eyes moved about the room as though he were looking for somebody to 'help. His eyes fell cursorily upon the commander's son, and then back to her, but it was already too late, she had begun to topple toward him, her hands closed over his arms, and her head went pushing into his chest, rushing him with a strength he had seldom felt before.

When they fell into the water it was very difficult for him to get hold of her at all. She had swallowed so much water, and she had struck at him so hard, and had said words all the time nobody could have understood or believed but him. It was her speaking and struggling, as he said later, which had caused her to swallow so much water.

He had had to give her partial artificial respiration, a thing he had not done really in all his life, although he had taken all the courses in it as befitted a champion swimmer.

"Get out of the pool for God's sake and call somebody," Mr. Diehl yelled to the commander's son, and the boy left off hanging to the rubber tire, and slowly began to climb out of the shallow water.

"Get some speed on there, for Christ's sake," he said.

"Yes, sir," the commander's son replied.

"I can't be responsible for this whole goddam thing," he shouted after the retreating boy.

"Now see here, Polly, for Christ's sake," Mr. Diehl began looking down at her.

She opened her eyes and looked at him.

"You certainly pulled one over me!" he cried looking at her, rage and fear on his mouth.

She lay there watching his chest move, feeling the drops of water falling over her from his body, and smelling behind the strong chemical odor of the pool the strong smell that must be Mr. Diehl himself, the champion.

"I'll go tell her now," Polly said.

Mr. Diehl stared at her.

"She must never come here at all," Polly said. "I think I see that now."

Mr. Diehl stretched out his hand to her to lift her up.

"Go away, please," she said. "Don't lean over me, please, and let the water fall from you on me. Please, please go back into the pool. I don't want you close now. Go back into the pool."

• ENCORE •

HE'S in that Greek restaurant every night. I thought you knew that," Merta told her brother.

"What does he do in it?" Spence said, wearily attentive.

"I don't go to Greek restaurants and I don't spy on him," she said.

"Then how do you know so certainly he is there every night?"

"How do you know anything? He's not popular at the college. He says he likes to talk to Spyro, the restaurant owner's son, about painting. I don't know what they do!"

"Well, don't tell me if you don't know," her brother said. He got up and took his hat to go.

"Of course," she continued anxiously stepping in front of him to delay his going, "it isn't so much that Spyro is all at fault, you know. There are things wrong with Gibbs, too. As I said, he's not popular at the college. He wasn't asked to join a fraternity, you know. And the restaurant has made up for that, I suppose. It's always open for him day or night."

"Maybe you should make your own home more of a place he could bring his friends to," Spence said, a kind of cold expressionless tone in his voice.

"You would say that," she repeated almost without emotion. "I don't suppose you ever half considered what it is, I mean this home. It's not a home. It's a flat, and I'm a woman without a husband."

"I know, I know Merta. You've done it all alone. Nobody's lifted a finger but you." His weariness itself seemed to collapse when he said this, and he looked at her with genuine feeling.

"I'm not trying to get your pity. I wanted to tell somebody what was going on at Spyro's is all. I needed to talk to somebody."

"I think Spyro's is the best place he could go," Spence said.

"And Spyro's awful father and grandfather!" she cried as though seeing something from far back of dread and ugliness.

"The Matsoukases?" Spence was surprised at her vehemence.

"Yes, the Matsoukases! With their immense eyes and black beards. Old Mr. Matsoukas, the grandfather, came here one evening, and tried to get fresh with me."

"I can hardly believe it," Spence said.

"You mean I am making it up," she accused him.

"No, no, I just can't visualize it."

"And now," she returned to the only subject which interested her, "Gibbs is there all the time as though it was his home."

"Do you talk to him about it, Merta?"

"I can't. I can't tell him and nag him about not going to the Greek restaurant at night. It's glamor and life to him, I suppose, and I suppose it *is* different. A different sort of place. The old man hasn't allowed them to put in juke boxes or television or anything, and you know Gibbs likes anything funny or different, and there isn't anything funny or different but maybe Spyro's. None of the college crowd goes there, and Gibbs feels he's safe there from their criticism and can drink his coffee in peace."

"Well it sounds so dull, drinking coffee in a seedy Greek restaurant, I don't see why a mother should worry about her son going there. And call me out of bed to talk about it!"

"Oh Spence," she said urgently again, "he shouldn't go there. Don't you see? He shouldn't be there."

"I don't see that at all," Spence said. "And Merta, I wish you would quit calling me up at this hour of the night to talk about your son, who is nearly a grown man by now. After all I have my profession to worry about too. . . ."

She stared at him.

"I had to talk with somebody about Spyro," she said.

"Oh, it's Spyro then you wanted to talk about," Spence

said, the irritation growing in his manner.

"Spyro," she said vaguely, as though it were Spence who himself had mentioned him and thus brought him to mind. "I never cared much for that young man."

"Why not?" Spence was swift to hold her to anything vague and indirect because he felt that vagueness and indirectness was her method.

"Well, Spyro does all those paintings and drawings that are so bizarre."

"Bizarre," he paused on the word. "They're nearly *good*, if you ask me."

"I don't like Spyro," she said.

"Why don't you invite him here, if your son likes him?" he put the whole matter in her hands.

"When I work in a factory all day long, Spence. ... ."

"You don't feel like doing anything but working in a factory," he said irritably.

"I thought my own brother would be a little more understanding," she said coldly angry.

"I wish you would be of Gibbs," he told her.

"Oh Spence, please, please."

"Please, nothing. You always have a problem, but the problem is you, Merta. You're old and tired and complaining, and because you can't put your finger on what's wrong you've decided that there's something wrong with your son because he goes, of all places, to a Greek restaurant and talks to Spyro who draws rather well and who is now making a portrait of your son."

"Spence! Don't tell me that!"

"You dear old fool, Merta," he said and he put on his hat now, which she looked at, he thought, rather critically and also with a certain envy.

"That's a nice hat," she forced herself to say at last.

"Well a doctor can't look like a nobody," he said, and then winced at his own words.

"What you should do, Merta," he hurried on with another speech, "is get some sort of hobby, become a lady bowler, get on the old women's curling team, or meet up with some gent your own age. And let your son go his own way."

"You are comforting," Merta said, pretending to find humor in his words.

"Was that Spence leaving just now?" Gibbs said, putting down some books.

Merta held her face up to be kissed by him, which he did in a manner resembling someone surreptitiously spitting out a seed.

"And how was Spyro tonight?" she said in a booming encouraging voice whose suddenness and loudness perhaps surprised even her.

He looked at her much as he had when as a small boy she had suddenly burst into the front room and asked him what he was being so very still for.

"Spyro is doing a portrait of me," he told her.

"A portrait," Merta said, trying hard to keep the disapproval out of her voice.

"That's what it is," Gibbs said, sitting down at the far end of the room and taking out his harmonica.

She closed her eyes in displeasure, but said nothing as he played "How High the Moon." He always played, it seemed, when she wanted to talk to him.

"Would you like Spyro to come visit us some day?" she said.

"Visit us?"

"Pay a call," she smiled, closing her eyes.

"What would he pay us a call for?" he wondered. Seeing her pained hurt look, he expanded: "I mean what would he get to see here."

"Oh me," she replied laughing. "I'm so beautiful."

"Spyro thinks you don't like him," Gibbs said, and while she was saying *Tommyrot!* Gibbs went on: "In fact, he thinks everybody in this town dislikes him."

"They *are* the only Greeks, it's true," Merta said.

"And we're such a front family in town, of course!" he said with sudden fire.

"Well, your Uncle Spence is somebody," she began, white, and her mouth gaping a little, but Gibbs started to play on the harmonica again, cutting her off.

She tried to control her feelings tonight, partly because she had such a splitting headache.

"Would you like a dish of strawberry jello?" Merta said above the sound of the harmonica playing.

"What?" he cried.

"Some strawberry jello," she repeated, a little embarrassment now in her voice.

"What would I want that for?" he asked, putting down the harmonica with impatience.

"I suddenly got hungry for some, and went out there and made it. It's set by now and ready to eat."

There was such a look of total defeat on her old gray face that Gibbs said he would have some.

"I've some fresh coffee too," she said, a touch of sophistication in her voice, as if coffee here were unusual and exotic also.

"I've had my coffee," he said. "Just the jello, thank you."

"Does Spyro always serve you coffee?" she said, her bitterness returning now against her will as they stood in the kitchen.

"I don't know," he said belligerently.

"But I thought you saw him every evening," she feigned sweet casualness.

"I never notice what he serves," Gibbs said loudly and indifferently.

"Would you like a large dish or a small dish of jello?" she said heavily.

"Small, for Christ's sake," he told her.

"Gibbs!" she cried. Then, catching herself, she said, "Small it will be, dear."

"What have you got to say that you can't bring it out!" he suddenly turned on her, and taking the dish of jello from her hand he put it down with a bang on the oilcloth covering of the tiny kitchen table.

"Gibbs, let's not have any trouble. Mother has a terrible headache tonight."

"Well, why don't you go to bed then," he said in his stentorian voice.

"Perhaps I will," she said weakly. She sat down and began eating right out of the jello bowl. She ate nearly all the rubbery stiff red imitation strawberry jello and drank in hurried gulps the coffee loaded with condensed milk.

"Spence gave me hell all evening," she said eating. "He thinks I would be happier if I found a fellow!"

She laughed but her laughter brought no response from Gibbs.

"I know I have nothing to offer anybody. Let's face it."

"Why do you have to say *let's face it?*" Gibbs snapped at her.

"Is there something wrong grammatically with it?" she wondered taking her spoon out of her mouth.

"Every dumb son of a bitch in the world is always saying *let's face it.*"

"And your own language is quite refined," she countered.

"Yes, let's face it, it is." he said, a bit weakly, and he took out the harmonica from his pocket, looked at it, and put it down noiselessly on the oilcloth.

"I've always wanted to do right by you, Gibbs. Since you was a little boy, I have tried. But no father around, and all . . ."

"Mom, we've been over this ten thousand times. Can't we just forget I didn't have an old man, and you worked like a team of dogs to make up for everything."

"Yes, let's do. Let's forget it all. For heaven's sake, I'm eating all this jello," she said gaily.

"Yes, I noticed," he said.

"But I want to do for you," she told him suddenly again with passion, forgetting everything but her one feeling now, and she put out her hand to him. "You're all I have, Gibbs."

He stared at her. She was weeping.

"I've never been able to do anything for you," she said. "I know I'm not someone you want to bring your friends home to see."

"Mom, for Christ's sake," he said.

"Don't swear," she said. "I may not know grammar or English, but I'm not profane and I never taught you to be. So there," she said, and she brought out her handkerchief and wiped her eyes, making them, he saw, even older and more worn with the rubbing.

"Mom," he said, picking up the harmonica again, "I don't *have* any friends."

"No?" she said laughing a little. Then understanding his remark more clearly as her weeping calmed itself, she said, commanding again, "What do you mean now by that?"

"Just what I said, Mom. I don't have any friends. Except maybe Spyro."

"Oh that Greek boy. We would come back to him."

"How could I have friends, do you think. After all. . . ."

"Don't you go to college like everybody else," she said hurriedly. "Aren't we making the attempt, Gibbs?"

"Don't get so excited. I don't care because I don't have any friends. I wasn't accusing you of anything."

"You go to college and you ought to have friends," she said. "Isn't that right?"

"Look, for Christ's sake, just going to college doesn't bring you friends. Especially a guy like me with. . . ."

"What's wrong with you," she said. "You're handsome. You're a beautiful boy."

"Mom, Je-sus."

"No wonder that Greek is painting you. You're a fine-looking boy."

"Oh it isn't that way at all," he said, bored. "Spyro has to paint somebody."

"I don't know why you don't have friends," she said. "You have everything. Good looks, intelligence, and you can speak and act refined when you want to . . ."

"You have to be rich at that college. And your parents have to be . . ."

"Is that *all* then?" she said, suddenly very white and facing him.

"Mom, I didn't mean anything about you. I didn't say any of this to make you feel . . ."

"Be quiet," she said. "Don't talk."

"Maybe we *should* talk about it, Mom."

"I can't help what happened. What was *was*, the past is the past. Whatever wrong I may have done, the circumstances of your birth, Gibbs . . ."

"Mom, please, this isn't about you at all."

"I've stood by you, Gibbs," she hurried on as if testifying before a deaf judge. "You can never deny that." She stared at him as though she had lost her reason.

"I'd like to have seen those rich women with their fat manicured husbands do what I've done," she said now as though powerless to stop, words coming out of her mouth that she usually kept and nursed for her long nights of sleeplessness and hate.

She stood up quickly as if to leave the room.

"With no husband and no father to boot in this house! I'd like to see *them* do what I did. God damn them," she said.

Gibbs waited there, pale now as she was, and somehow much smaller before her wrath.

"God damn everybody!" she cried. "God damn everybody."

She sat down and began weeping furiously.

"I can't help it if you don't have friends," she told him, quieting herself with a last supreme effort. "I can't help it at all."

"Mom," he said. He wanted to weep too, but there was something too rocklike, too bitter and immovable inside him to let the tears come loose. Often at night as he lay in his bed knowing that Merta was lying in the next room sleepless, he had wanted to get up and go to her and let them both weep together, but he could not.

"Is there anything I could do to change things here at home for you?" she said suddenly wiping away the tears, and tensing her breast to keep more of the torrent from gathering inside herself. "Anything at all I can do, I will," she said.

"Mom," he said, and he got up and as he did so the harmonica fell to the linoleum floor.

"You dropped your little . . . toy," she said tightening her mouth.

"It's not a toy," he began. "This is," he began again. "You see, this is the kind the professionals play on the stage . . . and everywhere."

"I see," she said, struggling to keep the storm within her quiet, the storm that now if it broke might sweep everything within her away, might rage and rage until only dying itself could stop it.

"Play something on it, Gibbs darling," she said.

He wanted to ask her if she was all right.

"Play, play," she said desperately.

"What do you want me to play, Mom?" he said, deathly pale.

"Just play any number you like," she suggested.

He began then to play "How High the Moon" but his lips trembled too much.

"Keep playing," she said beating her hands with the heavy veins and the fingers without rings or embellishment.

He looked at her hands as his lips struggled to keep themselves on the tiny worn openings of the harmonica which he had described as the instrument of the professionals.

"What a funny tune," she said. "I never listened to it right before. What did you say they called it?"

"Mom," he said. "Please!"

He stretched out his hand.

"Don't now, don't," she commanded. "Just play. Keep playing."

• Night and Day •

THE chestnut man will be here before too long," Cleo said, "and I will buy you a lot of nice chestnuts before bedtime. But you must be a good boy, you must not tell Grandy things Mama says when we're alone together. After lunch tomorrow maybe he will take you out for a walk around the park. Won't that be nice?"

But he just sat there, on the new Persian rug, with his little train and engine, also new like the rug, and also gifts from Grandy, and would not answer her.

There was always the difficulty of his going to sleep, and the best thing was to just let him lie in bed talking to the animals on the wall, talking sometimes half the night.

One night, when Grandy made her tell him she was going to have the animals painted off the walls if he didn't behave, he had put up a fuss and said he was going to tell Grandy what she had called the old man the night he had not given her enough money. After that he got to talk to the kangaroo for an hour and told him what Mama had called Grandy, and then he told his other favorite, the elephant that stood on the weighing machine, and finally he told the South American foxes.

Tonight the chestnut man had not come, and when there was unexpectedly no sound from the little room upstairs, Cleo, once the tension had let up, began crying a little and said to Grandy: "His father will never know what bringing up a child means. And wouldn't care maybe if he knew."

Grandy patted her hand lightly.

"Where do you suppose Bruce is anyhow," she said, coldly angry. "It's going on two years."

"Cleo," Grandy said, "you know as well as I the only thing you can do."

They sat down then to their supper of cold chicken, cheese

233

casserole, and cup after cup of coffee ready to strengthen her.

She had just put some food into her mouth when the door upstairs opened and he screamed.

Going up immediately to his room and sitting down with the perfunctory motions of a sleepwalker, she said: "Why can't you control yourself for just one meal."

"Where is Grandy?" he wondered.

"Grandy is reading the paper," she told him.

"I want to see Grandy."

"Well, he is too old and tired to come up the steps all the time."

"Tell Grandy to come up."

"You go to sleep."

She went down again and sat with Grandy and he began to smooth her hair as was his custom.

"Please, please," Cleo said when he kissed her loudly. "Let's try to be a little more careful now."

"Has he been careful?"

"Bruce?" she said, knowing, of course, that it was Bruce he meant.

Grandy watched her as though commanding her to give the answer he wanted.

"I loved Bruce, Grandy. I really did."

"He deserted *you*," Grandy said.

"Oh, now, father, father." She was weak with him.

"I know my own son," he told her. "Bruce ran out on you."

"There is no proof of that, father." Then: "Oh, *Bruce, Bruce,*" she said, pretending she was saying this to herself.

"Bruce is no-account, never was, and it's infantile to ever expect his return."

"You shouldn't even think such a thing about your own boy," Cleo said unemphatically.

"Have Grandy come up now!" the small voice from upstairs called.

"He listens to everything we say and do," Cleo told the old man.

"And understands nothing, just like Bruce."

"But you *love* him, don't you," she said, fear in her voice, and her face suddenly red under the lamplight.

"Who?" Grandy roared.

"Who but the boy!" she said rather hotly.

"You know who I love," he told Cleo, and he put his hand on her lap. "And I know who you love."

"Oh, Grandy, Grandy." She was pliant and soft again.

"Why must it always be *Grandy*," the old man said. "Why can't it be . . ."

"Have Grandy come up, Mama; have him do that now. I am so lonesome."

"Talk to the little kangaroo until you go to sleep, lover," she called up. "Tell the little kangaroo your thoughts."

"No, I'm tired of *him*," the child said. "I want a new animal for telling my thoughts to," he called angrily.

"He wants a police dog," Cleo told the old man.

"They want everything," he replied, holding her hand tightly.

"Like some other people in this world," Cleo said, not removing her hand.

"You can't go on like this," Grandy emphasized to her, peremptorily removing his hand from hers and placing it on her cheek, where it stroked back and forth insinuatingly near her ear like a mouth whispering messages.

"What would our lives be like, if I did this terrible thing," Cleo said.

"You've already gone more than half the way," Grandy said.

"Oh, Grandy," she cried, and she pushed her face into his vest and cried a little.

"If Bruce ever knew, my God, my God." Her voice came muffled and weak from against his chest.

"And what do you think Bruce might be doing tonight?" He was cool and unmoved.

"Well, he's not with my *mother*," she gasped, weakly impetuous, as though this were her last outburst of concern, for immediately after she sank back into his arms, and he kissed her with real feeling.

"Where are you now?" The voice came from upstairs.

"Oh, is he out of his bed, do you think?" Cleo asked, jumping up.

"Sit down, Cleo," the old man commanded. "Nothing is going to surprise us. You're jumpy as a cat. Do sit down, and don't get up again."

"I wish that boy had a nurse sometimes."

"He could have," Grandy told her.

"Oh, dear, dear. What *is* it all about?"

"Don't talk like one of those religious philosophers now," Grandy said to her. "You know and I know what is going to happen." He kissed her on the mouth.

"I don't know, and you can't make me," she said weakly. He kissed her again.

"What is it, then, my *age*?" he asked ironically.

"Your age?" She laughed. "Have I ever known a younger man?" She touched his mouth, and he clasped her hand tightly at this.

"Younger than Bruce," he said, and his coy, crafty wink made her tense.

"Grandy, we might destroy everything!" she cautioned.

"You forget Bruce has already done that. How long has he been gone?" He began counting with that theatrical manner he so often assumed now.

"I can't helping thinking Bruce loved me," she said ignoring his manner.

"And his supposed love is enough."

"But for God's sake," she said getting up and pacing about the room. "You're his *father!* Grandy, you're Bruce's father!"

"How many times have you seen Bruce in the last two years—do you remember?" he asked now, his theatrical manner stronger than ever.

"He's been gone, of course, a little more than a year this time."

"*This* time!" Grandy stood up now and walked over to

her. He embraced her with passion. Everything else he did resembled different people doing different things sucessively. But his embraces were his own. Perhaps that is what made her go on with them.

"More than a year, Cleo!" he said, almost shaking her. "Do you realize how ridiculous that is. Your own husband. Why a year? Why a month? Why even a fortnight? Why should that be?" He actually shook her now. "Why?"

"Please, please, don't wake the child again now. He's been quiet for nearly half an hour."

"Bruce can take *him!*" he said with great suddenness.

"Grandy!" she cried. "Why, you must know me better than that. Why, Grandy!"

She moved out of his orbit, her mouth trembling with surprise, her face a hot, red moon of hurt and confusion.

"Of course, I didn't mean that just as it sounded."

"You did too." She turned on him. "How dare you! Grandy, how dare you!"

She wept a little and, finding no handkerchief, she accepted the one he handed her.

"Give up that little thing upstairs," she began. "I hate you for that talk." Then softening a little again: "Oh, Grandy, Grandy, what *am* I going to do?"

"Do you want to answer this question," he cleared his throat, the actor playing now the counselor-at-law, closing the case. "Where would you have been this past year without my help? How would the little prince upstairs have eaten and slept, do you think? Who would have had the artist to paint the animals on his bedroom wall?"

"Stop all of this talk at once," she said without conviction. "Oh, Grandy." She collapsed.

He held her hand as though this gesture were the source of his power and her weakness.

"You're not a working-woman type, Cleo," he told her, his mouth to her ear now. He kissed her softly and insistently.

"I'm not very clever, if that's what you mean," she said, wiping her tears on his handkerchief again.

"You're not clever in the world's view. You're not a modern woman, Cleo. You belong at home with a man who can take care of you. You aren't meant to make your own way. . . . But that's right what you're going to be doing, if you go on with Bruce! My patience . . ." He thundered now.

"Oh, no, Grandy," she sobbed. "Don't speak like this. We have to think . . ."

"You've said that for months. What do we have to think about?"

"Maybe there are circumstances we don't understand," she begged him. "Maybe there's something happened to Bruce we don't know about."

"You forget you're talking about my son."

"That doesn't mean anything here," she said, some of her old thoughts awakening suddenly, only to fade to extinguishment under his touch.

"I know Bruce better than anybody in the world," he emphasized.

"You know him as a man," she said.

"I'm his father," Grandy said.

"You're a man." She was implacable.

"All right, you love Bruce then," he told her.

"I didn't say that. I didn't say that at all." A wave of weakness, impotence, idiocy swept over her again.

"Then what do you mean?" He was insistent.

"All I meant," she said, her breath coming heavily and fear changing her voice so that it resembled both a child's and an old woman's, "all I meant is, are we being fair to *them,* are we . . ."

"Tell me this," he said, holding her hand with savage firmness. "Does Bruce love you?"

She drew back, as though this question, never posed before, had swept away everything of the little she had held back for herself.

"Grandy, please, do we have to be so . . . so specific?"

"Yes, Cleo, yes."

"What was your question then?" she said, reaching for her cigarettes.

"Here," he commanded, "take one of mine."

"I'd rather have one of my . . ."

He put the cigarette in her mouth and lit it.

"Now, Cleo, I also can be of another mind. . . ."

"About what?" she said, looking at him with her terrified, young-innocent-girl face.

"There is a limit to *my* time, *my* endurance. And I'm not going to live forever, after all. I want life now. Not tomorrow. And I've waited . . ."

"Grandy, just don't do anything rash yet. Please wait, things will straighten out, I know. . . ."

"Have you ever thought that I might have somebody else, too?" he said.

"Yes," she said, trying to steady the fear that made her voice muffled as though she were speaking to him through a curtain. "I've thought of that, Grandy . . . many times." She lifted her tear-stained face to him.

"Think of it tonight with special clearness," he ordered her.

"I will, Grandy," she said, the tears falling again now, and she noticed that he did not caress her, did not hold out a hand to her. He had given her the question, the final decision; he was not going to do more. She saw that she must answer.

"It's the most difficult thing in the world, Grandy."

"Bawling's not going to help you, not going to get you anywhere." He was like another man now, and she saw something in him at that moment, vague and far away, which must have destroyed happiness for her with his son Bruce.

"I must know *now*," he told her.

"Oh, Grandy, no." She wept now, unashamed, uncontrolled.

"Of course," she said incoherently, "it's you, Grandy."

"And if it's me, then, it can't be him."

"You mean Bruce," she said, looking up from her hands which she had put over her face, hopefully expectant.

"I mean the kid!" He was clear and complete.

"What are you saying," she said, suddenly calm, her tears suddenly gone, a white toneless face, stripped of every emotion, looking at him.

"I want to marry *you*. Let Bruce have the kid."

"He's not a kid," she said.

"Well, what the hell is he?"

"He's still almost an infant." She walked up and down the room.

"And you will go to work to support him then?"

She did not say anything.

"I asked you a question, Cleo. Will you go to work in a factory or office to support him?"

"I never knew before how cruel you really are, and *were*."

"I've waited for you for at least two years, and I can't wait any longer." His voice quieted down slowly.

"I think I am beginning to see how it would be," she said and walked to the other side of the room and sat down.

"What was the meaning of that cryptic remark?"

"There was nothing cryptic in it, and it was more than a remark. I think it was a decision."

"You've made a decision?" He smiled knowingly.

"I think I have," she said.

He laughed.

"I must try to be calm, though," she told him. "I must say only what I mean and no more."

"That would be unusual for you." He used all his bitterness.

"Would it, Grandy?" She looked at him and as he gazed at her he hardly recognized her. She hardly, perhaps, recognized herself.

"What then have I been doing these years?" she said. "My God, yes, what."

"Now, Cleo, what is this?" he said going over to the chair where she was sitting.

"Don't come near me," she ordered him, and there was a

strength in the way she motioned to him with trembling, thin hands covered with his rings.

"I see everything, of course, I've always seen it," she told him. "I think I see myself."

"You sound just like Bruce now," he said. "The goddam old preacher in him has come out in you."

"Just words," she said. "Just your old words." She stood up. "Words from an old goat," she cried, looking at his white hair.

"Cleo," he admonished, with gay good humor. "Realize what you are saying, my dear."

"What does that mean, realize what I'm saying. I'm *realizing* you, for the love of God. Don't you know that?"

"And what does that mean?" he said, and his disguise, or disguises, suddenly to her seemed to fall like pieces of cardboard at their feet. She felt she almost heard a sound of collapse in the room.

"An old old goat on his last legs, making a bargain as hard . . . as hard . . ." she said.

"Cleo, you know if you finish saying this, there can be nothing more for the two of us. Consider well what you are going to say."

He held up his hand.

"Oh the theater of *that!*" She almost spat, her handsome face suddenly ugly.

At that moment they heard the bare feet and saw the child come into the room, or rather they did not see him. They both looked and looked away as though, after all, he had been there from the beginning.

The boy clasped his mother around the waist, but she went on talking, her hand, which had always fallen automatically on his curls when he went up close to her, suddenly now raised at the old man.

"You hit Grandy! Mama you hit Grandy!" the child cried, and he ran between her and his grandfather.

"Stop, don't touch him," she told the child. She went over to where the boy stood and brought him back to her.

"He's not your Grandy any more," she roared at him.

"Cleo, I can and I will make trouble for you if you speak in front of that boy."

"You old goat," she cried, and her hand now fell on the head of her son.

"You whoring old goat!"

• MRS. BENSON •

I DON'T know why Mrs. Carlin entertained," Mrs.
Benson admitted. "She didn't like it, and she couldn't do
it."

"I had to sit an entire hour under one of those potted palms
she had in her house," Mrs. Benson's daughter, Wanda, recalled.
"There was a certain odor about it — whether from the soil, or
the plant, or the paper about the container. I felt terribly uncomfortable."

The two women, Wanda Walters, unmarried and thirty,
from Philadelphia, and her mother, who lived in Europe, and
had been married many times, and who was now Mrs. Benson,
had nearly finished their tea, in an English tearoom within walking distance from the American Express, in Paris.

Mrs. Benson had known the English tearoom for many
years, though she could never exactly remember its French
name, and so could not ever recommend it to her friends, and
she and her daughter, when they had their yearly reunions in
Paris, always came to it. Their meeting in Paris this year had
been rather a prolonged one, owing to Wanda's having failed
to get a return passage to the States, and it had been a summer
that was hot, humid, and gray — and not eventful for either of
them.

This year, too, they found themselves going less and less
anywhere at all, and they were somewhat embarrassed — at least,
Mrs. Benson said *she* was — to find that they spent the better part
of the day in the English tearoom, talking, for the most part,
about people they had both known in Philadelphia twenty-odd
years ago, when Wanda had been "little," and when Mrs.
Benson — well, as she said, had at least had a different name!

It was the first time in many years, perhaps *the* first, that
Mrs. Benson had really talked with her daughter at length about
anything (they had always *traveled* before, as the older woman

said), and certainly the first time in Wanda's memory that they had talked at all about "back home," as Mrs. Benson now called it with a chilly, condescending affection. And if their French or American friends happened by now, Mrs. Benson, if not Wanda, expressed by a glance or word a certain disappointment that their "talk" must be interrupted.

Mrs. Benson had made it a fixed practice not to confide in her daughter (she had once said to a close friend of hers: "I don't know my daughter, and it's a bit too late to begin!"), but the name *Mrs. Carlin,* which had come into their conversation so haphazardly, as if dropped from the awning of the café, together with the gloominess of their Paris, had set Mrs. Benson off. *Mrs. Carlin* came to open up a mine of confidences and single isolated incidents.

This was interesting to Wanda because Mrs. Benson had always been loath to "tell," to reminisce. Mrs. Benson hated anecdotes, regarding them as evidence of senility in the old, and cretinism in the young, and though there were other people "back home," of course, Mrs. Carlin could easily carry them through for the rest of Paris, and the potted palms, which had so dismayed Wanda, seemingly set Mrs. Benson "right" at last.

"I don't suppose you remember when they were popular," Mrs. Benson referred to the palms. "But they were once nearly everywhere. I've always disliked them, and, I think, perhaps, I even vaguely *fear* them."

"I don't think Mrs. Carlin *liked* them," Wanda said abruptly, so abruptly that Mrs. Benson dropped a long ash from her cigarette into her tea, and then called the waiter.

"How on earth do you know Mrs. Carlin didn't like them?" Mrs. Benson flushed slightly and then paused while the waiter brought her a fresh cup.

Wanda paused also. She felt that her mother did not *want* to know that she knew anything about Mrs. Carlin, and Wanda, in any case, was not very much interested in explaining what she did mean.

"I simply meant this," Wanda felt she must explain,

under the *look* her mother gave her. "The part of the house Mrs. Carlin used for *entertainment* could not have reflected *anybody's* taste."

Mrs. Benson opened her eyes wide, and brought her mouth into a kind of cupid's bow. Then, in a voice quieter than her expression, she said: "I'd have to say, Wanda, that you were right!

"But how on earth did you *know?*" Mrs. Benson suddenly brought out, and she looked at her daughter as if a fresh light had been thrown on the latter's character also.

"What I think I meant," Wanda began again, tearing apart one of the tiny envelopes of sugar that lay beside her spoon, "Mrs. Carlin was, as we both know, more than a *little* wealthy . . . "

Mrs. Benson cleared her throat, but then decided, evidently, not to speak, and her silence was as emphatic as she could make it.

"That is," Wanda went on slowly, "she could *afford* to entertain rather shabbily."

"Rather *shabbily?*" Mrs. Benson considered this. "That is a terribly queer word for *her.*"

"But you yourself . . ."

"I don't like potted palms," Mrs. Benson pushed through to what was, as her face showed, the important matter here, "and I don't like all those original early 19th-century land-scapes with cattle," she became now as firm as if in court, "but as to her house being *shabby* . . ."

"*Depressing* then," Wanda said. "It was certainly depressing."

Mrs. Benson laughed, guardedly indulgent. "You're so hard on the poor dear," she said in a tone of voice unlike her own.

"But I thought you thought as I did," Wanda cried. "About *her,* at least!" Displeasure and boredom rang in her voice, but there was an even stronger expression there of confusion and doubt.

"I do, and I don't," Mrs. Benson put endearment and

confidence now into her voice. Then, unaccountably, she
looked at her rings. She had many. They were, without doubt,
too genuine, if anything, and as they shone in the later afternoon light, they made her mother look, Wanda felt, both very
rich and very old.

"I think you're right, though," Wanda heard Mrs.
Benson's voice continuing, "right about Mrs. Carlin's not
caring whether she impressed *people* or not."

"I don't know if I quite meant that," Wanda told her
mother, but under her breath now. "I mean only she didn't
care whether they *enjoyed* themselves or not at her house."

They were both silent for a moment, as if surprised at the
difficulties which had suddenly sprung up from nowhere,
difficulties that were so obscure in themselves, and yet which
offered some kind of threat of importance.

"The potted palms were a fright, of course," Mrs. Benson
seemed either conciliatory or marking time. "And even for
potted palms, they were dreadful." She touched her daughter's
arm lightly. "They looked *dead.*"

Going on, Mrs. Benson added: "I always thought of old-
fashioned small-town Greek candy-kitchens when I saw those
palm trees at Mrs. Carlin's. And her strange little painted-
glass player piano, too!"

"I never saw *that,*" Wanda admitted. She looked away
from her mother's expression.

"Oh, you've forgotten it, is all," Mrs. Benson said. "It
played for *all* the guests, that player piano . . . at least once."
She laughed. "Mrs. Carlin seldom invited anybody twice."

Mrs. Benson had a peculiar, oblique, faraway look in her
eyes, a look Wanda did not remember quite ever having seen
on her mother's face before—indeed, on anybody's face.

Then, suddenly clearing her throat, Mrs. Benson
coughed ceremoniously, struggling perhaps with a decision.

The one thing, Wanda remembered again, the thing that
her mother disliked so much in others, was stories, *anecdotes*—
indeed any narration which was prolonged beyond the length

of a paragraph. But usually when Mrs. Benson cleared her throat *and* coughed, she was going to tell something which was important and necessary, if not long, or anecdotal.

But then, quickly, as if she had been given a reprieve of some kind, Mrs. Benson cried: "Oh, it's all so *nothing!*" and poured herself some tea.

"But what else was there?" Wanda cried, annoyance and curiosity both in her voice. Mrs. Benson shook her head.

"You did have something special, I believe," Wanda was positive.

"Oh, not actually," Mrs. Benson said. Then, with her faraway look again, she managed to say, "I *was* remembering an afternoon — oh, a long, long time ago at Mrs. Carlin's. . . . But in a *different* part of the house, you see."

Wanda waited, suddenly touched with something stronger than curiosity. But she knew that if she so much as moved now, Mrs. Benson might remember her own horror of anecdotes, and would close up tight.

"I dread to think how long ago that actually was," Mrs. Benson continued carefully, and her eyes then strayed out to the street, where a bus was slowing down to stop for a woman and a small child.

Mrs. Benson waited for the woman and child to board the bus, then commencing again: "I can't believe that it was so long ago as 1935, I mean, or along in there. . . . But, Mrs. Carlin had already begun to entertain her guests in one part of the house . . . and to *live* herself in another! She had begun dividing up her life in that way!"

She smiled at Wanda, almost in the manner of one who had finished her story there.

Wanda nodded only enough to let her mother know she was listening.

"I don't care much for this *tea,* today," Mrs. Benson said suddenly in an unexpectedly loud voice, and she looked up and about the room.

When Wanda said nothing, but showed that she was waiting, Mrs. Benson drank some more of the tea she did not

like, and said: "Mrs. Carlin had never, I think, been particularly interested in *me,* as distinct from the others, until your
father left me. . . . Evidently, *she* had never been too happy in
her marriage, either . . . I gathered that from something she
once let drop. . . .

"However," Mrs. Benson said, raising the empty tea cup,
and looking up under at the bottom of it hurriedly, "however,
she wanted me to see things. I knew that. She wanted me to
see the things — the part of the house, you understand, that the
others never saw."

Wanda nodded, a kind of fleeting awareness in her face.

"That was when she called me, well *aside,* I suppose one
would have to say, and said something to me like, '*I want to
really have you in some time, Rose.*' "

It came as a sort of shock to Wanda to hear her mother's
Christian name. She had not only not heard it for many
years — she had actually forgotten it, so separate had their two
lives, and their very names, become.

But Mrs. Benson had gone right on now through her
daughter's surprise, or shock: "At first I hadn't quite
understood what Mrs. Carlin meant, you see. . . . She had
taken hold of my arm, gently, and led me out of the room
where she had always entertained the *others.* We got into a
small gold elevator, and were gone in a minute. . . . When we
got out, well — let me assure you, there wasn't a potted palm
in the place!

"It was another house, another atmosphere, another place
and time!"

A look of something like pain crossed Wanda's face, but
her mother missed this in her final decision to "tell."

"It was a bit incredible to me then, and it's more so now,"
Mrs. Benson anticipated her daughter's possible incredulity,
or indifference.

Pausing briefly, it was Mrs. Benson's turn now to study
her daughter's face critically, but evidently, at the last, she
found nothing on the younger woman's face to stop her.

Still, Mrs. Benson waited, looking at nothing in

particular, while the waiter removed the empty cups, wiped the marble swiftly with a small cloth, bowed vaguely, and muttering part of a phrase, left.

Mrs. Benson commented perfunctorily on the indulgence of French waiters and French cafés, pointing out how wonderful it was to be able to stay *forever* when one wanted to.

Outside the light was beginning to fail, and a slight breeze came across to them from the darkening boulevard.

Wanda moved suddenly and unceremoniously in her chair, and Mrs. Benson fixed her with a new and indeterminate expression.

Raising her voice, almost as if to reach the street, Mrs. Benson said: "A week after Mrs. Carlin had showed me the 'real' part of the house, she invited me again, in an invitation she had written in her own hand, and which I must have somewhere, still. . . . I had never had a *written* invitation before from her, nobody had . . . always telephoned ones. . . . It was a dark January afternoon, I recall, and I was feeling, well, at that time, pretty low. . . . In the *new* part of the house — and I couldn't get over this time its *immensity* — tea was never mentioned, thank God, and we had some wonderful ancient Portuguese brandy. . . . But as we sat there talking, I kept hearing something soft but arresting. . . ."

Mrs. Benson stopped now in the guise of one who hears only what she is describing.

"Looking back away from Mrs. Carlin," Mrs. Benson said, "In the furthest part of the room, I was quite taken aback to see some actual *musicians.* Mrs. Carlin had an entire small string orchestra playing there for her. . . . You know, I thought I was mistaken. I thought it was perhaps a large oil, a mural, or something. . . . But Mrs. Carlin touched my hand just then, and said, '*They're for you, Rose.*' "

Mrs. Benson pressed her daughter's hand lightly at that, as if to convey by some touch *part* of the reality of that afternoon.

"I think she wanted to *help* me," Mrs. Benson said in a flat plain voice now, and with a helpless admission of anticlimax.

"Your father—as I've said, had just *gone,* and I think she knew how everything stood."

Mrs. Benson avoided her daughter's glance by looking at her hands, which she held before her again now, so that there was the sudden quick scintillation again, and then went on: "When Mrs. Carlin took me to the door that day, I knew she wanted to say something else, something still more *helpful,* if you will, and I was afraid she was going to say what in fact she did."

Wanda's open-eyed expression made her mother suddenly smile.

"It was nothing sensational, my dear, or alarming! Mrs. Carlin was never *that!*"

"Well, for heaven's sake, then," Wanda cried.

"I said it was nothing sensational." In Mrs. Benson's dread of the *anecdote*—the inevitable concomitant of old age—she had so often told people nothing at all, and safety still, of course, lay in being silent. But as Wanda watched Mrs. Benson struggle there, postponing the telling of what she would have liked so much to tell, she realized in part what the struggle meant: Mrs. Benson had invariably all her life told her daughter *nothing.*

But Mrs. Benson had gone on again: "Mrs. Carlin was still beautiful then, and as I see now, *young.* . . . And I rather imagine that when she was very young, and when there had been, after all, a Mr. Carlin . . ."

A look from Wanda sped Mrs. Benson on: "I don't know *why* I treasure what Mrs. Carlin said to me," she hurried faster now. "But it is one of the few things that any other human being ever said to me that I do hold on to."

Mrs. Benson looked at the *addition* which the waiter had left, and her lips moved slightly over what was written there.

"Mrs. Carlin said to me," she went on, still looking at the waiter's bill, although her eyes were closed, "'You're the only one who could *possibly* be asked in here with me, my dear. . . . I couldn't have the *others,* and I knew I couldn't have them. . . . They're not for *us* . . . And if you should ever feel you would like to *stay on*,' Mrs. Carlin said, *'why don't you, my dear?'* "

"She actually thought so well of you!" Wanda said, and then hearing the metallic hardness of her own voice, lowered her eyes in confusion.

"Of course, that was a long time ago," Mrs. Benson said vaguely, more of a cold edge now in her voice. "She wouldn't want *anyone* there now," she added.

"She is such a recluse then?" Wanda asked. Mrs. Benson did not answer. She had taken some francs out of her purse and was staring at them.

"Some of this money," she pointed out, "have you noticed? It comes to pieces in one's hands. I hardly know what to do with some of the smaller notes."

"These little reunions in Paris are such a pleasure, Mother," Wanda said in a rather loud, bright voice.

"Are they, my dear?" Mrs. Benson answered in her old firm manner. Then, in a sudden hard voice: "I'm so glad if they are."

The two women rose from the table at the same time, Mrs. Benson having deposited some of the notes on the marble-topped table, and they moved toward the front of the café, and into the street.

• SERMON •

LADIES and people, you must realize, or you would not be sitting here before me, that I am the possessor of your ears. Don't speak, I will talk. You have sat here before, and have heard things men, or, in some cases, ladies told you. I have no intention of telling you the same things, but will proceed just as though you were all in the privacy of your own bathhouses. I was not called here to entertain you. You could entertain yourselves if you weren't here. The fact you are here means something. (I will not mention the fact of my being here.) We face one another across the hostile air, you waiting to hear and to criticize, and I half-staring at some of you and not seeing the rest of you, though perhaps wanting to. Some of you are rude. Many of you are old and homely, others are not up to the speech I have in readiness. We *all* of us know *all* of this. It is in the *air* I look through to see you. Yet we all feel we have to go on. You have left the comfort of your living rooms and bathhouses to be here. I have come because I am a speaker and had to. None of us are really happy, none of us are in the place he feels he might want to be. Many of you feel there must be a better place for you than the one you are occupying now. There is a feeling of everything being not quite right. You feel if you only knew more or could do more you would be somewhere else. The fact is, however, you are wrong.

I say this looking at all of you now. You are wrong, and I am powerless to add or subtract from that fact. You came originally wrong, and you have been getting worse in every way since that day. There is, in fact, no hope for you, and there never was. Even if you had never been born there would have been no hope for you. It was hopeless whether you arrived or not. Yet you all arrived, you got here, you are *here*. And it is all so meaningless, because you all know there is a better place for you than here. And that is the trouble.

You will not accept the *hereness*. You will not accept me. Yet I am the only thing there is under the circumstances, but you reject me, and why — well I will tell you why. Because you have nothing better to do or be than the person you are now, occupying the particular chair you now occupy and which you are not improving by occupying. You have improved nothing since you came into this situation. You have tried to improve yourself, of course, or things connected with yourself, but you have only finished in making everything worse, you have only finished in making yourself worse than when you were sent, worse than what you were when you were born, worse even than what you were before you entered this great Amphitheater.

There is, in short, no hope for you, as I said earlier. You are bad off and getting more so, and sadly enough when you get in the worst shape of all so that you think you will not be able to go on for another second, the road ahead is still worse yet. For there is no hope for you even when things get so impossibly terrible that you will kill yourself. For that is no solution. In death you will only begin where you left off, but naturally, in worse shape.

Yet you continue to sit here watching me, like skinned tadpoles whose long-dead brains still send messages to your twitching feet. You twitch as you listen to me but you hear nothing. You have never heard anything.

And now you are waiting for the message, the solution to all my speech. You have been thinking, "What He says is terrible and frightening, but now will come the Good Part, the part with the meaning . . ." Ladies and people, listen to me. I have no Good Part to give you. My only message, if it can be called one, and I do not call it one, I call it nothing, my message to you is there is no message. You have made a terrible mistake in coming to the Amphitheater tonight to hear Me, yet you would have made a mistake no matter what you did tonight for the simple reason that you have no choice but to make mistakes, because you have no plans. You are going somewhere because you think you have to . . . That is what you are doing, and how therefore could you do anything but make mistakes. You continue to act and you have nothing to act with but the actions. Hence you are doomed to lectures and books hoping to save yourselves in the evening. Another attempt at action. You are doomed because you will go on trying to be other than you are and therefore you succeed always in continuing as you have been. There is no choice. You are listening even now with your pathetic tadpole faces because you know you are not getting my words. Give up trying, dear auditors. Be without trying to be. Lie back in your seats and let the air have its way with you. Let it tickle you in the spots where you are always fighting its insistent moisture. Don't let it retreat. Let things be. Don't try to be improved by my speech, because nothing can improve you. Surrender to what you are continuing *against,* and perhaps you will not have to go ahead with everything. And I know how weary you are of going ahead. Oh, don't I know it.

You are beginning to look at the Giant Clocks, meaning you have stood all you can for one night. I do not pity or sympathize with you and at the same time I do, because you do not belong here, as I said earlier. Nobody belongs here. It has all been a mistake your coming here. I, of course, am a Mistake, and how could my coming be a success. Yet in a sense it *is,* ladies and people, for the simple reason that I have prepared no speech and have not thought about what I am saying to you. I knew it would be hopeless. I knew when I saw your faces that you would only listen to what you say to yourself in your bathhouses or your laundry cleanup kitchens. You knew everything anyhow and have continued to improve on what has already been done. Hence you are hopeless.

I have talked here tonight in the hope you would not hear, because if you didn't you might not so thoroughly disgust yourselves, and therefore me. But you have sat in exactly the rapport or lack of it which I expect from the human tadpole. You have been infinitely repulsive to me, and for that I thank you, because by being infinitely repulsive you have continued continuity and what more could any speaker ask. What if you had become while I was talking. The whole world would have changed, of course. You would have all become alive. But the truth of the continuum is that it is continuous. You have not failed History, the continuous error. You have gone on with it, but *continuing*.

And so I say to you, pale and yet red tadpoles, you are hopeless and my words are spoken to tell you not to hope. You have nothing with which to win. It is doom itself that I see your bloated eyes and mouths begging for. How could I say anything to you then but to return to you the stale air which you have been breathing in my face all evening. I return it to you, therefore, not in flatulence, that would be to flatter you, but in air in return. And I thank you. I *mean* this. I thank you one and all, ladies and people. I take pleasure in my activity though I know you do not, are not expected to take any and would be miserable if my pleasure became real to you. And so farewell, or rather good-by, because we will meet again. There is no escape from it. That is why we are all so repulsive to one another: infinitely so. Life is immortal. Its eggs are too numerous for it but to spawn at the mere touch, and therefore with real emotion I say *So be it.* Come whenever you can, I am always here. Good-by, and yet not good-by.

GOD

• Everything Under the Sun •

I DON'T like to make things hard for you," Jesse said to Cade, "but when you act like this I don't know what's going to happen. You don't like nothing I do for you anyhow."

The two boys, Jesse and Cade, shared a room over the south end of State Street. Jesse had a job, but Cade, who was fifteen, seldom could find work. They were both down to their last few dollars.

"I told you a man was coming up here to offer me a job," Cade said.

"You can't wait for a man to come offering you a job," Jesse said. He laughed. "What kind of a man would that be anyhow."

Cade laughed too because he knew Jesse did not believe anything he said.

"This man did promise me," Cade explained, and Jesse snorted.

"Don't pick your nose like that," Jesse said to Cade. "What if the man seen you picking."

Cade said the man wouldn't care.

"What does this man do?" Jesse wondered.

"He said he had a nice line of goods I could sell for him and make good money," Cade replied.

"Good money selling," Jesse laughed. "My advice to you is go out and look for a job, any job, and not wait for no old man to come to teach you to sell."

"Well nobody else wants to hire me due to my face," Cade said.

"What's wrong with your face?" Jesse wanted to know. "Outside of you picking your nose all the time, you have as good a face as anybody's."

"I can't look people in the eye is what," Cade told him.

Jesse got up and walked around the small room.

257

"Like I told you," Jesse began the same speech he always gave when Cade was out of work, "I would do anything for you on account of your brother. He saved my life in the goddam army and I ain't never going to forget that."

Cade made his little expression of boredom which was to pinch the bridge of his nose.

"But you got to work sometimes!" Jesse exploded. "I don't get enough for two!"

Cade grimaced, and did not let go the bridge of his nose because he knew this irritated Jesse almost as much as his picking did, but Jesse could not criticize him for just holding his nose, and that made him all the angrier.

"And you stay out of them arcades too!" Jesse said to Cade. "Spending the money looking at them pictures," Jesse began. "For the love of . . ." Suddenly Jesse stopped short.

"For the love of what?" Cade jumped him. He knew the reason that Jesse did not finish the sentence with a swear word was he went now to the Jesus Saves Mission every night, and since he had got religion he had quit being quite so friendly to Cade as before, cooler and more distant, and he talked, like today, about how good work is for everybody.

"That old man at the trucking office should have never told you you had a low IQ," Jesse returned to this difficulty of Cade's finding work.

But this remark did not touch Cade today.

"Jesse," Cade said, "I don't care about it."

"You don't care!" Jesse flared up.

"That's right," Cade said, and he got up and took out a piece of cigarette from his pants cuff, and lit a match to the stub. "I don't believe in IQs," Cade said.

"Did you get that butt off the street?" Jesse wanted to know, his protective manner making his voice soft again.

"I ain't answering that question," Cade told him.

"Cade, why don't you be nice to me like you used to be," Jesse said.

"Why don't *I* be nice to *you!*" Cade exclaimed with savagery.

Suddenly frightened, Jesse said, "Now simmer down." He was always afraid when Cade suddenly acted too excited.

"You leave me alone," Cade said. "I ain't interferin' with your life and don't you interfere with mine. The little life I have, that is." He grunted.

"I owe something to you and that's why I can't just let you be any old way you feel like being," Jesse said.

"You don't owe me a thing," Cade told him.

"I know who I owe and who I don't," Jesse replied.

"You always say you owe me on account of my brother saved your life just before he got hisself blowed up."

"Cade, you be careful!" Jesse warned, and his head twitched as he spoke.

"I'm glad he's gone," Cade said, but without the emotion he usually expressed when he spoke of his brother. He had talked against his brother so long in times past in order to get Jesse riled up that it had lost nearly all meaning for both of them. "Yes, sir, I don't care!" Cade repeated.

Jesse moved his lips silently and Cade knew he was praying for help.

Jesse opened his eyes wide then and looking straight at Cade, twisted his lips, trying not to let the swear words come out, and said: "All right, Cade," after a long struggle.

"And if religion is going to make you close with your money," Cade began looking at Jesse's mouth, "close and *mean,* too, then I can clear out of here. I don't need you, Jesse."

"What put the idea into your head religion made me close with my money?" Jesse said, and he turned very pale.

"You need me here, but you don't want to pay what it takes to keep me," Cade said.

Jesse trembling walked over to Cade very close and stared at him.

Cade watched him, ready.

Jesse said, "You can stay here as long as you ever want to. And no questions asked." Having said this, Jesse turned away, a glassy look on his face, and stared at the cracked calcimine of their wall.

"On account of my old brother I can stay!" Cade yelled.

"All right then!" Jesse shouted back, but fear on his face. Then softening with a strange weakness he said, "No, Cade, that's not it either," and he went over and put his arm on Cade's shoulder.

"Don't touch me," Cade said. "I don't want none of that *brother* love. Keep your distance."

"You behave," Jesse said, struggling with his emotion.

"Ever since you give up women and drinking you been picking on me," Cade said. "I do the best I can."

Cade waited for Jesse to say something.

"And you think picking on me all the time makes you get a star in heaven, I suppose," Cade said weakly.

Jesse, who was not listening, walked the length of the cramped little room. Because of the heat of the night and the heat of the discussion, he took off his shirt. On his chest was tatooed a crouched black panther, and on his right arm above his elbow a large unfolding flower.

"I did want to do right by you, but maybe we *had* better part," Jesse said, crossing his arms across his chest. He spoke like a man in his sleep, but immediately he had spoken, a scared look passed over his face.

Cade suddenly went white. He moved over to the window.

"I can't do no more for you!" Jesse cried, alarmed but helpless at his own emotion. "It ain't in me to do no more for you! Can't you see that, Cade. Only so much, no more!"

When there was no answer from Cade, Jesse said, "Do you hear what I say?"

Cade did not speak.

"Fact is," Jesse began again, as though explaining now to himself, "I don't seem to care about nothing. I just want somehow to sit and not move or do nothing. I don't know what it is."

"You never did give a straw if I lived or died, Jesse," Cade said, and he just managed to control his angry tears.

Jesse was silent, as on the evenings when alone in the dark, while Cade was out looking for a job, he had tried to figure out what he should do in his trouble.

"*Fact* is," Cade now whirled from the window, his eyes brimming with tears, "it's all the other way around. I don't need you except for money, but you need me *to tell you who you are!*"

"What?" Jesse said, thunderstruck.

"You know goddam well *what*," Cade said, and he wiped the tears off his face with his fist. "On account of you don't know who you are, that's why."

"You little crumb," Jesse began, and he moved threateningly, but then half remembering his nights at the Mission, he walked around the room, muttering.

"Where are my cigarettes?" Jesse said suddenly. "Did you take them?"

"I thought you swore off when you got religion," Cade said.

"Yesh," Jesse said in the tone of voice more like his old self, and he went up to Cade, who was smoking another butt.

"Give me your smoke," he said to Cade.

Cade passed it to him, staring.

"I don't think you heard what I said about leaving," Cade told Jesse.

"I heard you," Jesse said.

"Well, I'm going to leave you, Jesse. God damn you."

Jesse just nodded from where he now sat on a crate they used as a chair. He groaned a little like the smoke was disagreeable for him.

"Like I say, Jesse," and Cade's face was dry of tears now. "It may be hard for me to earn money, but I know who I am. I may be dumb, but I'm *all together!*"

"Cade," Jesse said sucking on the cigarette furiously. "I didn't mean for you to go. After all, there is a lot between us."

Jesse's fingers moved nervously over the last tiny fragment of the cigarette.

"Do you have any more smokes in your pants cuff or anywhere?" Jesse asked, as though he were the younger and the weaker of the two now.

"I have, but I don't think I should give any to a religious man," Cade replied.

Jesse tightened his mouth.

Cade handed him another of the butts.

"What are you going to offer me, if I do decide to stay," Cade said suddenly. "On account of this time I'm not going to stay if you don't give me an offer!"

Jesse stood up suddenly, dropping his cigarette, the smoke coming out of his mouth as though he had all gone to smoke inside himself.

"What am I going to offer you?" Jesse said like a man in a dream. "What?" he said sleepily.

Then waving his arms, Jesse cried, "All right! Get out!"

And suddenly letting go at last he struck Cade across the mouth, bringing some blood. "Now you git," he said. "Git out."

Jesse panted, walking around the room. "You been bleedin' me white for a year. That's the reason I'm the way I am. I'm bled white."

Cade went mechanically to the bureau, took out a shirt, a pair of shorts, a toothbrush, his straight razor, and a small red box. He put these in a small bag such as an athlete might carry to his gym. He walked over to the door and went out.

Below, on the sidewalk, directly under the room where he and Jesse had lived together a year, Cade stood waiting for the streetcar. He knew Jesse was looking down on him. He did not have to wait long.

"Cade," Jesse's voice came from the window. "You get back here, Cade, goddamn you." Jesse hearing the first of his profanity let loose at last, swore a lot more then, as though he had found his mind again in swearing.

A streetcar stopped at that moment.

"Don't get on that car, Cade," Jesse cried. "Goddam it."

Cade affected impatience.

"You wait now, goddam you," Jesse said putting on his rose-colored shirt.

"Cade," Jesse began when he was on the street beside his

friend. "Let's go somewhere and talk this over. . . . See how I am," he pointed to his trembling arm.

"There ain't nowhere to go since you give up drinking," Cade told him.

Jesse took Cade's bag for him.

"Well if it makes you unhappy, I'll drink with you," Jesse said.

"I don't mind being unhappy," Cade said. "It's *you* that minds, Jesse."

"I want you to forgive me, Cade," Jesse said, putting his hand on Cade's arm.

Cade allowed Jesse's arm to rest there.

"Well, Jesse," Cade said coldly.

"You see," Jesse began, pulling Cade gently along with him as they walked toward a tavern. "You see, I don't know what it is, Cade, but you know everything."

Cade watched him.

They went into the tavern and although they usually sat at the bar, today they chose a table. They ordered beer.

"You see, Cade, I've lied to you, I think, and you're right. Of course your brother did save my life, but you saved it again. I mean you saved it more. You saved me," and he stretched out his trembling arm at Cade.

Jesse seeing the impassive look on Cade's face stopped and then going on as though he did not care whether anybody heard him or not, he said: "You're all I've got, Cade."

Cade was going to say *all right now* but Jesse went on speaking frantically and fluently as he had never spoken before. "You know ever since the war, I've been like I am . . . And Cade, I need you that's why . . . I know you don't need me," he nodded like an old man now. "But I don't care now. I ain't proud no more about it."

Jesse stopped talking and a globule of spit rested thickly on his mouth.

"I'm cured of being proud, Cade."

"Well, all right then," Cade finally said, folding his arms and compressing his mouth.

"All right?" Jesse said, a silly look on his face, which had turned very young again.

"But you leave me alone now if I stay," Cade said.

"I will," Jesse said, perhaps not quite sure what it was Cade meant. "You can do anything you want, Cade. All I need is to know you won't really run out. No matter what I might some day say or do, you stay, Cade!"

"Then I don't want to hear no more about me getting just any old job," Cade said, drinking a swallow of beer.

"All right," Jesse said. "All right, all right."

"And you quit going to that old Mission and listening to that religious talk.'"

Jesse nodded.

"I ain't living with no old religious fanatic," Cade said.

Jesse nodded again.

"And there ain't no reason we should give up drinking and all the rest of it at night."

Jesse agreed.

"Or women," Cade said, and he fumbled now with the button of his shirt. It was such a very hot night his hand almost unconsciously pushed back the last button which had held his shirt together, exposing the section of his chest on which rested the tattooed drawing of a crouched black panther, the identical of Jesse's.

"And I don't want to hear no more about me going to work at all for a while," Cade was emphatic.

"All right, then, Cade," Jesse grinned, beginning to giggle and laugh now.

"Well I should say *all right*," Cade replied, and he smiled briefly, as he accepted Jesse's hand which Jesse proffered him then by standing up.

• Goodnight, Sweetheart •

PEARL Miranda walked stark naked from her classroom in the George Washington School where she taught the eighth grade, down Locust Street, where she waited until some of the cars which had stopped for a red traffic light had driven on, then hurried as fast as her weight could allow her down Smith Avenue.

She waited under a catalpa tree, not yet in leaf, for some men to pass by on the other side of the street. It was fairly dark, but she could not be sure if they would see her.

Hurrying on down Smith Avenue then, she passed a little girl, who called out to her, though the child did not recognize her.

The house she at last turned into was that of Winston Cramer, who gave piano lessons to beginners, and whom she herself had taught in the eighth grade nearly twenty years before.

She rang the doorbell.

She could see Winston beyond the picture window sitting in an easy chair engaged in manicuring his nails.

She rang and rang, but he did not move from his sitting position.

A woman from across the street came out on the porch and stood there watching.

Pearl rapped now on the door, and called Winston's name softly. Then she saw him get up. He looked angry.

"I discontinued the subscription," she heard his cross high voice. "I don't want the *News*—" and he caught sight of her.

He stood looking at her, immobile behind the glass of the door. Then he opened the door cautiously.

"Miss Miranda?"

"Let me in, for pity's sake," she answered him. "It's all right to open the door."

The woman across the street went on standing on her porch looking over at the Cramer house.

"Miss Miranda," Winston could only go on repeating when she was inside.

"Go and get me a bathrobe or something, Winston. For pity's sake." She scolded with her eyes.

Winston stood on for a minute more, trying to keep his gaze only on her face.

She could hear him mumbling and making other silly sounds as he went upstairs.

Pearl Miranda lowered the shade for the picture window, and then seeing the shade up on a smaller side window, she lowered it also. She picked up a music album and held this over her.

"For God Almighty's sake," Winston said when he handed her a bathrobe.

She put it on with some difficulty, and Winston did not help her. She sat down.

"What can I get for you?" he wondered.

"Usually they give people brandy in such cases," Miss Miranda said. "Cases of exposure," she spoke with her usual precise culture and refinement. "But I think you remember my views on drinking."

"I don't drink either, Miss Miranda," Winston told her.

"Some hot milk might be all right." She seemed to speak condescendingly now. "In the case of a chill coming on." Looking down at her bare feet, she inquired, "Do you have any house slippers, by chance."

"I have some that were my mother's," Winston told her.

That will be fine she was about to say, but he was already racing up the steps.

When he came back, he acted a bit more like himself, and he helped her on with the tickly, rabbit-lined house slippers.

"What happened to you?" he asked, looking up at her from his kneeling posture before her.

"Get me the hot milk first," she told him.

He turned to go out into the kitchen, then wheeling

around he said: "Miss Miranda, are you really all right?"

She nodded.

"Shouldn't I call the doctor?"

She shook her head vigorously.

He came back into the room, his left hand slowly stealing up to his throat. "You were assaulted, weren't you?" he asked.

"No, Winston, I was not," she replied. "Now please fix me my milk." She spoke to him much as she would have twenty years ago in her classroom.

Miss Miranda sank back into the warmth and mild comfort of the bathrobe and slippers while he was in the kitchen. She could hear him muttering to himself out there as he went about the task of warming the milk. She supposed all lonely people muttered to themselves, and it was one of the regrettable habits she could never break in herself.

Waiting, she looked at his Baldwin piano loaded with Czerny practice books. Another stack of music books sat on his piano stool.

She felt depressed thinking of Winston earning his living sitting all day and part of the evening hearing ungifted children play scales. It was not a job for a man.

Then she thought of how her own sister had felt sorry for her having to teach the eight grade.

"I'm shaking more now than when you walked in," Winston mumbled inaudibly, bringing in a little Mexican tray with a steaming pot of milk and a cup.

"Doesn't that look nice," Miss Miranda said.

"I'll get you a napkin, too." And he left the room again.

"Don't bother," Miss Miranda called out after him, but not vigorously, for she wanted a napkin.

She hiccuped a bit drinking the hot milk.

Winston cleared the exercise books from the piano stool, sat down and watched her drink the hot milk.

"Just a touch of cinnamon maybe?" He pointed to her cup.

She shook her head.

"I just took a pie out of the oven a couple of hours ago,"

he informed her. "Would you like a piece?"

"What flavor is it, Winston?" Miss Miranda wondered.

"Red raspberry," he told her. "Fresh ones."

She studied his face a second. "I might at that," she spoke as if consulting with a third party.

"Do you do all your own cooking, Winston?"

"Since Mother died, yes," he said. "But even in her day I did quite a bit, you know."

"I bet you're a good cook, Winston. You were always a capable boy." Her voice lowered as she said the second sentence.

"I haven't really talked to you since the eighth grade," Winston reminded her in a rather loud voice.

"I expect not." Miss Miranda drank some more of the milk. "My, that hits the spot."

"Wouldn't you like another hot cup?"

"Yes, I think I would," she replied.

He took the tray and all and went out into the kitchen.

Miss Miranda muttered when he had gone, and held her head in her hands, and then suddenly, as if in pain, she cried out, "God!"

Then she straightened out her face and got calm, her hands folded on her bathrobe, for Winston's return.

He handed her a new cup of milk, and she thanked him.

"You're not hurt now, Miss Miranda," he ventured again. He looked very scared.

"I've had a trick played on me is all, Winston." She opened her eyes at him wide.

Somehow, however, she did not seem to be telling the truth, and as she did not look away, Winston looked down at the floor, an expression of sorrow and disappointment about his mouth and eyes. Then he got up from the piano stool and went over to an easy chair and plumped himself down.

"You gave me a start." He put his hand across his chest.

"Now don't you give out on me," she said.

"You don't want me to call the police or anybody?" he asked, and she could see how upset he was getting.

"Just calm down, now. Of course I don't want the police. We'll handle this our own way."

"You said it was a joke, Miss Miranda."

She nodded.

There was a long silence.

"Ready for your raspberry pie?" he asked weakly.

She wiped her hands carefully on the linen napkin. "You could have just given me a paper napkin, Winston," she told him. "Do you have to do your own laundry, too?"

He mumbled something which sounded like *I'm afraid I do.* "I'll get you that pie." He went out of the room.

He came back, after a rather lengthy absence, with a generous piece of red raspberry pie on a hand-painted plate.

"A pretty, pretty sight," Miss Miranda said.

She bit into her piece of pie and said *Mmmm.*

"I wish you would let me do something for you," he almost whined.

"Now sit down, Winston, and be quiet. Better do nothing than do the wrong thing," she admonished.

"I know you haven't done anything wrong, of course," Winston said, and his voice sounded prophetic of weeping.

"Now, I'll explain everything just as soon as I have eaten your pie here," she told him. "But it's all nothing to be concerned about."

"Did anybody see you come in here?" he wondered.

She chewed on for a few seconds. "I suspect they may have. Who lives across the street from you there?" She pointed with her fork in the direction of the house in question.

"Not Bertha Wilson," Winston exclaimed.

"A woman came out on that porch. I think she saw me. Of course I know Bertha Wilson," Miss Miranda said.

"Oh, gosh." Winston raised his voice. He looked at her now almost accusingly. "It's all so unusual," he cried, thinking something much more extreme than his words gave inkling of.

"Winston, you've got to keep calm," Miss Miranda told him. "I *had* to come in here tonight. You know that."

"I don't begrudge you coming in here," he said, and he

was more in possession of himself.

"Then let's both be calm and collected." She handed him the empty pie plate. "What beautiful work people did when they painted their own china." She nodded at the plate.

"My Aunt Lois hand-painted all of Mother's china."

He left the room with the plate, and there was complete silence everywhere for a few minutes. Then she heard the water running in the kitchen, and she realized he was doing the dishes.

"He's a neat one," she said out loud.

She shook her head then, though she did this about something else than his neatness, and she cried, "God!" again.

In about a quarter of an hour, he came on back into the living room, sat down, crossed his legs, and said, "Now."

"I don't think I'm even going to have a chill." She smiled at him.

Winston was looking at her narrowly, and she thought he was less sympathetic. There was a look of irritability on his face. His mouth had set.

"How long has it been since you lost your mother?" Miss Miranda said.

"Two years this April," he replied without expression.

Miss Miranda shook her head. She opened the linen napkin out and put it over the lap of the bathrobe.

"What happened tonight was a joke," she said, and stopped.

"Did many people see you cross over the school playground?" he wondered.

"The school playground?"

"There are the fewest trees there to hide under," he explained.

"I couldn't tell if anybody saw me or not," she said.

"Miss Miranda, if you were . . . *harmed,* you must have me call the doctor."

"You want me to leave?" she inquired. "I will—"

"I didn't mean leave," he protested.

"Please be calm, Winston," she asked him.

"I am calm, Miss Miranda. . . . But gosh almighty, nobody can just sit here and act like nothing happened to you. . . . I never heard of such a thing as tonight!"

She sat thinking how it all must seem to him. At the height of her predicament she had not had time to think.

"I'm unhurt, Winston, except for the exposure, and I told you I can see I'm not going to have a chill."

"I can go over to your house and get your clothes."

She nodded pleasantly. "Tomorrow," she said.

"Tonight!" He was emphatic.

"This young man who looked like one of my own former students came into my classroom at six o'clock tonight," she began her story. "I was cleaning the blackboard."

Winston watched her, his face drained of blood.

"He asked me if I remembered him, and I said I didn't, though his face was familiar. . . . He then asked if I remembered Alice Rodgers. Of course, I remembered her. We just expelled her last term, you know. She had gotten herself and nearly every boy in the eighth grade in all that trouble. You remember reading about it all in the paper . . .

"Do you remember all that about Alice Rodgers?" Miss Miranda asked him.

Winston half-nodded.

"This young man, oh, he couldn't have been more than twenty . . . certainly not more than your age at the most, Winston . . . he said, 'I think you ought to have to pay for what you did to Alice Rodgers, ruining her name and reputation.'

"'I only wanted to make a real future for Alice Rodgers,' I told him.

"'In the reformatory?' he asked with an ugly grin."

Miss Miranda stopped, perhaps expecting Winston to help her on, but he did nothing.

"Then," Miss Miranda said, "he asked me to take off my clothes. He had a gun, you see."

Winston got up and walked in the direction of the next room.

"Where are you going?" Miss Miranda cried.

He looked back at her, asked her to excuse him, and then came back and sat down.

"He said he would use the gun if I didn't do exactly as he said," she spoke in a matter-of-fact tone.

Miss Miranda was looking at Winston, for she was certain that he was not listening to what she said.

"He took all my clothes away from me, including my shoes, and keys, and then, saying he hoped I would remember Alice Rodgers for the rest of all our lives, he walked out, leaving me to my plight. . . ."

Winston was looking down at the carpet again.

Miss Miranda's voice continued: "I called out to him from the bannister to come back. 'How will I get home?' I called after him."

Her voice now trailed off. Suddenly she held her head in her hands and cried, "Oh, God! God!"

"Are you in pain?" Winston looked up sleepily from the carpet.

"No," Miss Miranda replied quickly.

"My head's in a whirl," Winston told her.

"I don't remember that young man at all," Miss Miranda went on. "But you know, Winston, after you've taught so many years, and when you're as old as I am, all young people, all old people, too, look so much alike."

"Miss Miranda, let me call somebody! We should inform —"

"No," she told him. "I won't hear of it. Now, please be calm and don't let what has happened upset you. I want to stay here tonight."

"This young man you describe. He didn't harm you in any way?"

"He did not," Miss Miranda said in the voice of one who defends.

She looked at Winston.

Without warning, he began to gag. He rushed out of the parlor to a small room near the kitchen.

He evidently did not have time to close the door behind him. She could hear him vomiting.

"Oh, dear," Miss Miranda said.

She came into the bathroom and watched him. He was straining very hard over the toilet bowl.

"Winston, I am going to hold your head," she advised him. He made no motion.

She held his head while he vomited some more.

When he had stopped, she took a fresh wash cloth off the rack, and wiped his mouth.

"I've had the virus," he explained.

Suddenly he turned to the bowl again and vomited.

"Poor lad," she said, wiping his mouth again with the cloth.

"You must lie down now," she admonished him.

He walked toward an adjoining room where there was a double bed, and lay down on it.

She helped him off with his shoes, and put the covers partly over him.

"I'm afraid it was me who upset you," she apologized.

"No, Miss Miranda, it's the virus. Can't seem to shake it off. I catch it off and on from my pupils. First from one, then the other."

"Just rest quietly," she said.

When he had dozed off, she exclaimed again, "God! God!"

She must have dozed off, too, in her chair by the double bed, for some time later she awoke with a start and heard him vomiting again in the bathroom, and she hurried in to hold his head.

"Winston, poor lad," she said, feeling his hair wet with sweat.

"How could you stand to watch me be sick like that," he wondered later when they were back in the bedroom.

"I've taught public school for thirty years," she reminded him.

"Miss Miranda," he said suddenly, "you were raped tonight, weren't you?"

She stared at him.

"You've got to let me call the doctor." He wiped his mouth.

"I was not . . . raped," she denied his statement.

He watched her.

"That fellow just asked you to take off your clothes?"

She nodded.

"On account of Alice Rodgers." He echoed her story.

"I had testified against Alice in court," she added, "and they sent her to the reformatory."

"Well, if it's your story," he said.

"I wouldn't lie to you," Miss Miranda said.

"Nobody will believe you," he told her.

"Aren't you talking too much, Winston?" Miss Miranda showed concern for his health.

He did not answer.

"Bertha Wilson saw you across the street," he said sleepily.

"She was looking in my direction all right," Miss Miranda admitted.

"She must have seen you then."

"Oh, it was quite dark, Winston, after all."

"Bertha's got real X-ray eyes."

"Well, so she saw me," Miss Miranda said. "I had to come in somewhere."

"Oh, it's all right," Winston said. "Nobody will think anything about *us*."

"Oh God!" Miss Miranda cried suddenly.

Winston raised himself on his elbows.

"You in pain, Miss Miranda? Physical pain?"

She stifled back her sobs.

"Miss Miranda," Winston began. "That young man that came into your classroom tonight . . . are you listening to me . . . that young man was Fred Rodgers. Alice Rodgers' older brother."

Miss Miranda went on making the stifling sounds.

"Did you hear what I said, Miss Miranda?"

She nodded.

"Alice Rodgers' older brother," he repeated. "I know him. Listen, Miss Miranda, I know he wouldn't stop at just taking away your clothes. Don't you think I have any sense at all?"

He looked away from the look she gave him then.

"Knowing Fred Rodgers the way I do, Miss Miranda, I know he wouldn't stop at what you said he did. He had it in for you for sending his sister to the reform school."

"I'm nearly sixty years old, Winston," Miss Miranda said in the pool of darkness that was her chair. "I'd rather we didn't talk about it, if you don't mind."

"You've got to call the doctor," he said.

Miss Miranda looked down at the long lapel of her bathrobe.

"You had blood on you, too," Winston told her.

A moment later, he screamed and doubled up with pain in the bed.

"Winston, for pity's sake."

"I think I got an attack of appendicitis," he groaned. "Ouch, ouch, ouch." He touched his stomach.

"Do you want a doctor then!" she cried, as if he had betrayed her.

He lay back in the bed and groaned. His face went a kind of green, then yellow, as if suddenly illuminated by a searchlight.

"Dear God. God!" Miss Miranda cried.

"I may get all right," Winston told her, and he smiled encouragement at her from out of his own distress.

"Oh, what shall I do. What *shall* I do," she cried.

"I guess we both will have to have the doctor," Winston told her.

"I can't tell him, Winston. . . . I'm sixty years old."

"Well, you let *him* do the worrying now, Miss Miranda."

"You knew this Fred Rodgers?" She cried a little now. Winston nodded.

"I never taught him, though." She sighed. Suddenly she cried again, "Dear God. God!"

"You try to be calm, Miss Miranda," he comforted her.

He seemed almost calm now himself.

"Why don't you lay your head down on the bed, you look so bad," he told her.

"Oh, aren't we in the worst situation, Winston," she said. She cried a little.

She laid her head down on the bed, and he patted her hair a moment.

"I don't know how many people saw me," she said.

Winston lay back, easier now. His pain had quit.

Miss Miranda, suddenly, as if in response to his pain's easing, began to tremble violently.

"Get into bed," he told her. "You've got a chill coming on."

He helped her under the covers.

She screamed suddenly as he put her head down on the pillow.

"Just try to get as quiet as possible, Miss Miranda." He helped her cover up.

She was trembling now all over, crying, "Oh, God! At sixty!"

"If you can just get a good night's rest," he comforted her.

"Dear God. Oh, God!"

"In the morning the doctor will fix you up."

"I can never go back and teach those children," she said.

Winston patted her hand. His nausea had left him, but he had a severe headache that throbbed over his temples.

"What is that woman's name across the street again?" Miss Miranda questioned him.

"You mean Bertha Wilson."

Miss Miranda nodded.

"I taught her in the eighth grade. Way back in 1930, just think."

"I wouldn't think about it, Miss Miranda."

"Wouldn't think about what?"

"Anything."

"I can't believe this has happened," she told Winston.

"The doctor will come and fix us both up."

"I don't see how I can have the doctor or go back to school or anything," she wept.

She began crying hard now, and then after a while she got quiet.

"Go to sleep," he said.

He had thought to go upstairs and sleep in the bedroom that had been his mother's, but he didn't know whether he had the strength to get up there, and in the end he had crawled back under the covers next to Miss Miranda, and they both lay there close to one another, and they both muttered to themselves in the darkness as if they were separated by different rooms from one another.

"Good night," he said to her.

She looked up from her pillow for a moment.

"Good night, sweetheart," he said again, in a much lower voice.

She looked at the wall against which he had said the last words. There was a picture of his mother there, pretty much as Miss Miranda remembered her.

"God," Miss Miranda whispered. "Dear God."

• Some of These Days •

WHAT my landlord's friends said about me was in a way the gospel truth, that is he was good to me and I was mean and ungrateful to him. All the two years I was in jail, nonetheless, I thought only of him, and I was filled with regret for the things I had done against him. I wanted him back. I didn't exactly wish to go back to live with him now, mind you, I had been too mean to him for that, but I wanted him for a friend again. After I got out of jail I would need friendship, for I didn't need to hold up even one hand to count my friends on, the only one I could even name was him. I didn't want anything to do with him physically again, I had kind of grown out of that somehow even more while in jail, and wished to try to make it with women again, but I did require my landlord's love and affection, for love was, as everybody was always saying, his special gift and talent.

He was at the time I lived with him a rather well-known singer, and he also composed songs, but even when I got into my bad trouble, he was beginning to go downhill, and not to be so in fashion. We often quarreled over his not succeeding way back then. Once I hit him when he told me how much he loved me, and knocked out one of his front teeth. But that was only after he had also criticized me for not keeping the apartment tidy and clean and doing the dishes, and I threatened him with an old gun I kept. Of course I felt awful bad about his losing this front tooth when he needed good teeth for singing. I asked his forgiveness. We made up and I let him kiss me and hold me tight just for this one time.

I remember his white face and sad eyes at my trial for breaking and entering and possession of a dangerous weapon, and at the last his tears when the judge sentenced me. My landlord could cry and not be ashamed of crying, and so you didn't mind

279

him shedding tears somehow. At first, then, he wrote me, for as the only person who could list himself as nearest of kin or closest tie, he was allowed by the authorities to communicate with me, and I also received little gifts from him from time to time. And then all upon a sudden the presents stopped, and shortly after that, the letters too, and then there was no word of any kind, just nothing. I realized then that I had this strong feeling for him which I had never had for anybody before, for my people had been dead from the time almost I was a toddler, and so they are shadowy and dim, whilst he is bright and clear. That is, you see, I had to admit to myself in jail (and I choked on my admission), but I had hit bottom, and could say a lot of things now to myself, I guess I was in love with him. I had really only loved women, I had always told myself, and I did not love this man so much physically, in fact he sort of made me sick to my stomach to think of him that way, though he was a good-looker with his neat black straight hair, and his robin's-egg-blue eyes, and cheery smile. . . . And so there in my cell I had to confess what did I have for him if it was not love, and yet I had treated him meaner than anybody I had ever knowed in my life, and once come close to killing him. Thinking about him all the time now, for who else was there to think about, I found I got to talking to myself more and more like an old geezer of advanced years, and in place of calling on anybody else or any higher power, since he was the only one I had never met in my twenty years of life who said he cared. I would find myself saying like in church, *My landlord,* though that term for him was just a joke for the both of us, for all he had was this one-room flat with two beds, and my bed was the little one, no more than a cot, and I never made enough to pay him no rent for it, he just said he would trust me. So there in my cell, especially at night, I would say *My landlord,* and finally, for my chest begin to trouble me about this time and I was short of breath often, I would just manage to get out *My lord.* That's what I would call him for short. When I got out, the first thing I made up my mind to do was find him, and I was going to put all my efforts behind the search.

And when there was no mail now at all, I would think over all the kind and good things he done for me, and the thought would come to me which was blacker than any punishment they had given me here in the big house that I had not paid him back for his good deeds. When I got out I would make it up to him. He had took me in off the street, as people say, and had tried to make a man of me, or at least a somebody out of me, and I had paid him back all in bad coin, first by threatening to kill him, and then by going bad and getting sent to jail. . . . But when I got out, I said, I will find him if I have to walk from one ocean shore to the other.

And so it did come about that way, for once out, that is all I did or found it in my heart to do, find the one who had tried to set me straight, find the one who had done for me, and shared and all.

One night after I got out of jail, I had got dead drunk and stopped a guy on Twelfth Street, and spoke, *Have you seen my lord?* This man motioned me to follow him into a dark little theater, which later I was to know all too well as one of the porno theaters, he paid for me, and brought me to a dim corner in the back, and then the same old thing started up again, he beginning to undo my clothes, and lower his head, and I jumped up and pushed him and ran out of the movie, but then stopped and looked back and waited there as it begin to give me an idea.

Now a terrible thing had happened to me in jail. I was beat on the head by another prisoner, and I lost some of the use of my right eye, so that I am always straining by pushing my neck around as if to try to see better, and when the convict hit me that day and I was unconscious for several weeks and they despaired of my life, later on when I come to myself at last, I could remember everything that had ever happened in my whole twenty years of life except my landlord's name, and I couldn't think of it if I was to be alive. That is why I have been in the kind of difficulty I have been in. It is the hardest thing in the world to hunt for somebody if you don't know his name.

I finally though got the idea to go back to the big building where he and I had lived together, but the building seemed to be under new management, with new super, new tenants, new everybody. Nobody anyhow remembered any singer, they said, nor any composer, and then after a time, it must have been though six months from the day I returned to New York, I realized that I had gone maybe to a building that just looked like the old building my landlord and I have lived in, and so I tore like a blue streak straightaway to this "correct" building to find out if any such person as him was living there, but as I walked around through the halls looking, I become somewhat confused all over again if this was the place either, for I had wanted so bad to find the old building where he and I had lived. I had maybe been overconfident of this one also being the correct place, and so as I walked the halls looking and peering about I become puzzled and unsure all over again, and after a few more turns, I give up and left.

That was an awesome fall, and then winter coming on and all, and no word from him, no trace, and then I remembered a thing from the day that man had beckoned me to come follow him into that theater, and I remembered something, I remembered that on account of my landlord being a gay or queer man, one of his few pleasures when he got an extra dollar was going to the porno movies in Third Avenue. My remembering this was like a light from heaven, if you can think of heaven throwing light on such a thing, for suddenly I knowed for sure that if I went to the porno movie I would find him.

The only drawback for me was these movies was somewhat expensive by now, for since I been in jail prices have surely marched upwards, and I have very little to keep me even in necessities. This was the beginning of me seriously begging, and sometimes I would be holding out my hand on the street for three-fourths of a day before I got me enough to pay my way into the porno theater. I would put down my three bucks, and enter the turnstile, and then inside wait until my eyes got used to the dark, which because of my prison illness took nearly all of ten minutes, and then I would go up to each aisle looking for my landlord. There was not a face I didn't examine carefully. . . . My interest in the spectators earned me several bawlings-out from the manager of the theater, who took me for somebody out to proposition the customers, but I paid him no mind. . . . But his fussing with me gave me an idea, too, for I am attractive to men, both young and old, me being not yet twenty-one, and so I began what was to become regular practice, letting the audience take any liberty they was in a mind to with me in the hopes that through this contact they would divulge the whereabouts of my landlord.

But here again my problem would surface, for I could not recall the very name of the person who was most dear to me, yes that was the real sore spot. But as the men in the movie theater took their liberties with me, which after a time I got sort of almost to enjoy, even though I could barely see their faces, only see enough to know they was not my landlord, I would then, I say, describe him in full to them, and I will give them this much credit, they kind of listened to me as they went about getting their kicks from me, they would bend an ear to my asking for this information, but in the end they never heard of him nor any other singer, and never knowed a man who wrote down notes for a living.

But strange as it might seem to anybody who will ever see these sheets of paper, this came to be my only connection with the world, my only life — sitting in the porno theater. Since my only purpose was to find him and from him find my own way back, this was the only thoroughfare there was open for me to reach him. And yet I did not like it, though at the same time even disliking it as much as I did, it give me some little feeling of a resemblance to warmth and kindess as the unknown men touched me with their invisible faces and extracted from me all I had to offer, such as it was. And then when they had finished me, I would ask them if they knew my landlord (or as I whispered to myself, my lord). But none ever did.

Winter had come in earnest, was raw in the air. The last of the leaves in the park had long blown out to sea, and yet it was not to be thought of giving up the search and going to a warmer place. I would go on here until I had found him or I would know the reason why, yes, I must find him, and not give up. (I tried to keep the phrase *My lord* only for myself, for once or twice when it had slipped out to a stranger, it give him a start, and so I watched what I said from there on out.)

And then I was getting down to the last of the little money I had come out of jail with, and oh the porno theater was so dear, the admission was hiked another dollar just out of the blue, and the leads I got in that old dark hole was so few and far between. Toward the end one man sort of perked up when I mentioned my landlord, the singer, and said he thought he might have known such a fellow, but with no name to go on, he too soon give up, and said he guessed he didn't know after all.

And so I was stumped. Was I to go on patronizing the porno theater, I would have to give up food, for my panhandling did not bring in enough for both grub and movies, and yet there was something about bein' in that house, getting the warmth and attention from the stray men that meant more to me than food and drink. So I began to go without eating in earnest so as to keep up my regular attendance at the films. That was maybe, looking back on it now, a bad mistake, but what is one bad mistake in a lifetime of them.

As I did not eat now but only give my favors to the men in the porno, I grew pretty unsteady on my feet. After a while I could barely drag to the theater. Yet it was the only place I wanted to be, especially in view of its being now full winter. But my worst fears was now realized, for I could no longer afford even the cheap lodging place I had been staying at, and all I had in the world was what was on my back, and the little in my pockets, so I had come at last to this, and yet I did not think about my plight so much as about him, for as I got weaker and weaker he seemed to stand over me as large as the figures of the film actors that raced across the screen, and at which I almost never looked, come to think of it. No, I never watched what went on on the screen itself. I watched the audience, for it was the living that would be able to give me the word.

"Oh come to me, come back and set me right!" I would whisper, hoping someone out of the audience might rise and tell me they knew where he was.

Then at last, but of course slow gradual-like, I no longer left the theater. I was too weak to go out, anyhow had no lodging now to call mine, knew if I got as far as a step beyond the entrance door of the theater, I would never get back inside to its warmth, and me still dressed in my summer clothes.

Then after a long drowsy time, days, weeks, who knows? my worse than worst fears was realized, for one — shall I say day? — for where I was now there was no day or night, and the theater never closed its doors — one time, then, I say, they *come* for me, they had been studying my condition, they told me later, and they come to take me away. I begged them with all the strength I had left not to do so, that I could still walk, that I would be gone and bother nobody again.

When did you last sit down to a bite to eat? A man spoke this direct into my ear, a man by whose kind of voice I knew did not belong to the porno world, but come from some outside authority.

I have lost all tract of time, I replied, closing my eyes.

All right, buddy, the man kept saying, and *Now, bud,* and then as I fought and kicked, they held me and put the strait-jacket on me, though didn't they see I was too weak and dispirited to hurt one cruddy man jack of them.

Then as they was taking me finally away, for the first time in months, I raised my voice, as if to the whole city, and called, and shouted, and explained: *"Tell him if he comes, how long I have waited and searched, that I have been hunting for him, and I cannot remember his name. I was hit in prison by another convict and the injury was small, but it destroyed my one needed memory, which is his name. That is all that is wrong with me. If you would cure me of this one little defect, I will never bother any of you again, never bother society again.*

I will go back to work and make a man of myself, but I have first to thank this former landlord for all he done for me."

He is hovering between life and death.

I repeated aloud the word *hovering* after the man who had pronounced this sentence somewhere in the vicinity of where I was lying in a bed that smelled strong of carbolic acid.

And as I said the word *hovering,* I knew his name. I raised up. Yes, my landlord's name had come back to me. . . . It had come back after all the wreck and ruin of these weeks and years.

But then one sorrow would follow upon another, as I believe my mother used to say, though that is so long ago I can't believe I had a mother, for when they saw that I was conscious and in my right mind, they come to me and begun asking questions, especially *What was my name.* I stared at them then with the greatest puzzlement and sadness, for though I had fished up his name from so far down, I could no more remember my own name now when they asked me for it than I could have got out of my straitjacket and run a race, and I was holding on to the just-found landlord's name with the greatest difficulty, for it, too, was beginning to slip from my tongue and go disappear where it had been lost before.

As I hesitated, they begun to persecute me with their kindness, telling me how they would help me in my plight, but first of all they must have my name, and since they needed a name so bad, and was so insistent, and I could see their kindness beginning to go, and the cruelty I had known in jail coming fresh to mind, I said, "I am Sidney Fuller," giving them you see my landlord's name.

"And your age, Sidney?"

"Twenty, come next June."

"And how did you earn your living?"

"I have been without work now for some months."

"What kind of work do you do?"

"Hard labor."

"When were you last employed?"

"In prison."

There was a silence, and the papers was moved about, then: "Do you have a church or faith?"

I waited quite a while, repeating his name, and remembering I could not remember my own, and then I said, "I am of the same faith as my landlord."

There was an even longer silence then, like the questioner had been cut down by his own inquiry, anyhow they did not interrogate me any more after that, they went away and left me by myself.

After a long time, certainly days, maybe weeks, they announced the doctor was coming.

He set down on a sort of ice-cream chair beside me, and took off his glasses and wiped them. I barely saw his face.

"Sidney," he began, after it sounded like he had started to say something else first, and then changed his mind. "Sidney, I have some very serious news to impart to you, and I want you to try to be brave. It is hard for me to say what I am going to say. I will tell you what we have discovered. I want you, though, first, to swallow this tablet, and we will wait together for a few minutes, and then I will tell you."

I had swallowed the tablet it seemed a long time ago, and then all of a sudden I looked down at myself, and I saw I was not in the straitjacket, my arms was free.

"Was I bad, Doctor?" I said, and he seemed to be glad I had broke the ice, I guess.

"I believe, Sidney, that you know in part what I am going to say to you," he started up again. He was a dark man, I saw now, with thick eyebrows, and strange, I thought, that for a doctor he seemed to have no wrinkles, his face was smooth as a sheet.

"We have done all we could to save you, you must believe us," he was going on as I struggled to hear his words through the growing drowsiness given me by the tablet. "You have a sickness, Sidney, for which unfortunately there is today no cure. . . ."

He said more, but I do not remember what, and was glad when he left, no, amend that, I was sad I guess when he left.

Still, it didn't matter one way or another if anybody stayed or lit out.

But after a while, when I was a little less drowsy, a new man come in, with some white papers under his arm.

"You told us earlier when you were first admitted," he was saying, "that your immediate family is all dead. . . . Is there nobody to whom you wish to leave any word at all? . . . If there is such a person, we would appreciate your writing the name and address on each of these four sheets of paper, and add any instructions which you care to detail."

At that moment, I remembered my own name, as easily as if it had been written on the paper before me, and the sounds of it placed in my mouth and on my tongue, and since I could not give my landlord's name again and as the someone to whom I could bequeath my all, I give the inquirer with the paper my own real name:

James De Salles

"And his address?" the inquirer said.

I shook my head.

"Very well, then, Sidney," he said, rising from the same chair the doctor had sat in. He looked at me some time, then kind of sighed, and folded the sheaf of papers.

"Wait," I said to him then, "just a minute. . . . Could you get me writing paper, and fountain pen and ink to boot. . . ."

"Paper, yes. . . . We have only ball-point pens, though. . . ."

So then he brought the paper and the ball-point, and I have written this down, asking another patient here from time to time how to say this, or spell that, but not showing him what I am about, and it is queer indeed isn't it, that I can only bequeath these papers to myself, for God only knows who would read them later, and it has come to me very clear in my sleep that my landlord is dead also, so there is no point in my telling my attendants that I have lied to them, that I am really James

De Salles, and that my lord is or was Sidney Fuller.

But after I done wrote it all down, I was quiet in my mind and heart, and so with some effort I wrote my own name on the only thing I have to leave, and which they took from me a few moments ago with great puzzlement, for neither the person was known to them, and the address of course could not be given, and they only received it from me, I suppose, to make me feel I was being tended to.

• Mr. Evening •

YOU were asking the other day, Pearl, what that very tall young Mr. Evening—the one who goes past the house so often—does for a living, and I think I've found out for you," Mrs. Owens addressed her younger sister from her chair loaded with hand-sewn cushions.

Mrs. Owens continued to gaze out the big front window, its heavy shutter pulled back now in daylight to allow her a full view of the street.

She had paused long enough to allow Pearl's curiosity to whet itself while her own attention strayed to the faces of passersby. Indeed Mrs. Owens's only two occupations now were correcting the endless inventory of her heirlooms and observing those who passed her window, protected from the street by massive wrought-iron bars.

"Mr. Evening is in and out of his rooming house frequently enough to be up to a good deal, if you ask me, Grace," Pearl finally broke through her sister's silence.

Coming out of her reverie, Mrs. Owens smiled. "We've always known he was busy, of course." She took a piece of newsprint from her lap, and closed her eyes briefly in the descending rays of the January sun. "But now at last we know what he's busy at." She waved the clipping gently.

"Ah, don't start so, child." Mrs. Owens almost laughed. "Pray look at this, would you," and she handed the younger woman a somewhat lengthy "notice" clipped neatly from the *Wall Street Journal*.

While Pearl put on thick glasses to study the fine print, Mrs. Owens went on as much for herself as her sister: "Mr. Evening has always given me a special feeling." She touched her lavaliere. "He's far too young to be as idle as he looks, and on the other hand, as you've pointed out, he's clearly busier than

291

those who make a profession of daily responsibility."

"It's means, Grace," Pearl said, blinking over her read-ing, but making no comment on it, which was a kind of des-perate plea, it turned out, for information concerning a certain scarce china cup, circa 1910. "He has means," Pearl repeated.

"Means?" Mrs. Owens showed annoyance. "Well, I should hope he has, in his predicament." She hinted at even further knowledge concerning him, but with a note of displeasure creeping into her tone at Pearl's somewhat offhand, bored manner.

"I've telephoned him to appear, of course," Mrs. Owens had decided against any further "Preparation" for her sister, and threw the whole completed plan at her now in one fling. "On Thursday, naturally."

Putting down the "notice" Pearl waited for Mrs. Owens to make some elaboration on so unusual a decision, but no elaboration came.

"But you've never sold anything, let alone shown to anybody!" Pearl cried, after some moments of deeply troubled cogitation.

"Who spoke of selling!" Mrs. Owens tightened an ear-ring. "And as to showing, as you say, I haven't thought that far. . . . But don't you see, poor darling"—here Mrs. Owens's voice boomed in what was perhaps less self-defense than self-explanation—"I've not met anybody in half a century who wants heirlooms so bad as he." She tapped the clipping. "He's worded everything here with one thought only in mind—my seeing it."

Pearl withdrew into incomprehension.

"Don't you see this has to be the case!" Here she touched the "notice" with her finger. "Who else has the things he's enumerated here? He's obviously investigated what I have, and he could have inserted this in the want ads only in the hope it would catch my eye."

"But you're certainly not going to invite someone to the house who merely wants what you have!" Pearl found herself for the first time in her life not only going against her sister in opinion, but voicing something akin to disapproval.

"Why, you yourself said only the other night that what we needed was company!" Mrs. Owens put these words adroitly now in her sister's mouth, where they could never have been.

"But Mr. Evening!" Pearl protested against his coming, ignoring or forgetting the fact she had been quoted as having said something she never in the first place had thought.

"Don't we need somebody to tell us about heirlooms! I mean *our* heirlooms, of course. Haven't you said as much yourself time after time?"

Mrs. Owens was trying to get her sister to go along with her, to admit complicity, so to speak, in what she herself had brought about, and now she found that Pearl put her mind and temper against even consideration.

"Someone told me only recently"—Pearl now hinted at a side to her own life perhaps unknown to Mrs. Owens—"that the young man you speak of, Mr. Evening, can hardly carry on a conversation."

Mrs. Owens paused. She had not been inactive in making her own investigations concerning their caller-to-be, and one of the things she had discovered, in addition to his being a Southerner, was that he did not or would not "talk" very much.

"We don't need a conversationalist—at least not about *them*." Mrs. Owens nearly snapped, by *them* meaning the heirlooms. "What we need is an appreciator, and the *muter* the better, say I."

"But if that's all you want him for!"—Pearl refused to be won—"why, he'll smell out your plan. He'll see you're only showing him what he can never hope to buy or have."

A look of deep disappointment tinged with spleen crossed Mrs. Owens's still-beautiful face.

"Let him *smell* out our plan, then, as you put it," Mrs. Owens chided in the wake of her sister's opposition, "we won't care! If he can't talk, don't you see, so much the better. We'll have a session of 'looking' from him, and his 'appreciation' will perk us up. We'll see him taking in everything, dear love, and it will review our own lifelong success. . . . Don't be so down on it now. . . . And mind you, we won't be here quite forever," she ended, and a certain hard majestical note in her voice was not lost on the younger woman. "The fact," Mrs. Owens summed it all up, "that we've nothing to give him needn't spoil for us the probability he's got something to give us."

Pearl said no more then, and Mrs. Owens spoke under her breath: "I haven't a particle of a doubt that I'm in the right about him, and if it should turn out I'm wrong, I'll shoulder all the blame."

Whatever particle of a doubt there may have been in Mrs. Owens's own mind, there was considerable more of doubt and apprehension in Mr. Evening's as he weighed, in his rooming house, the rash decision he had made to visit formidable Mrs. Owens in — one could not say her business establishment, since she had none — but her background of accumulation of heirlooms, which vague world was, he could only admit, also his own. Because he had never known or understood people well, and he was the most insignificant of "collectors," he was at a loss as to why Mrs. Owens should feel he had anything to give her, and since her "legend" was too well known to him, he knew she, likewise, had nothing at all to give him, except, and this was why he was going, the "look-in" which his visit would give him. Whatever risk there was in going to see her, and there appeared to be some, he felt, from "warnings" of a queer kind from those who had dealt with her, it was worth something just to get inside, even though again he had been informed by those in the business it would be doubtful if he would be allowed to mention "purchase" and in the end it was also doubtful he would be allowed even a close peek.

On the other hand, if Mrs. Owens wanted him to tell her something — this crossed his mind as he went toward her huge pillared house, though he could not imagine even vaguely what he could have to tell her, and if she was mad enough to think him capable of entertaining her, for after all she was a lonely ancient lady on the threshold of death, he would disabuse her of all such expectations almost as soon as they had met. He was uneasy with old women, he supposed, though in his work he spent more time with them than with other people, and he wanted, he finally said out loud to himself, that hand-painted china cup, 1910, no matter what it might cost him. He fancied she might yield it to him at some atrocious illegal price. It was no more improbable, after all, than that she had invited him in the first place. Mrs. Owens never invited anybody, that is, from the outside, and the inside people in her life had all died or were incapacitated from paying calls. Yes, he had been summoned, and he could hope at least therefore that what everybody else told him was at least thinkable — purchase, and if that was not in store for him, then the other improbable thing, "viewing."

But Mr. Evening could not pretend. If his getting the piece of china or even more improbably other larger heirlooms, kept from daylight as well as human eyes, locked away in the floors above her living room, if possession meant long hours of currying favor, talking and laughing and dining and killing the evening, then no thank you, never. His inability to pretend, he supposed, had kept him from rising in the antique trade, for although he had a kind of business of his own here in Brooklyn, his own private income was what kept him afloat, and what he owned in heirlooms, though remarkable for a young dealer, did not make him a figure in the trade. His inconspicuous position in the business made his being summoned by Mrs. Owens all the more inexplicable and even astonishing. Mr. Evening was, however, too unversed both in people and the niceties of his own profession to be either sufficiently impressed or frightened.

Meanwhile Pearl, moments before Mr. Evening's arrival gazing out of the corner of her eye at her sister, saw with final and uncomfortable consternation the telltale look of anticipation on the older woman's face which demonstrated that she "wanted" Mr. Evening with almost the same inexplicable maniacal whim which she had once long ago demonstrated toward a certain impossible-to-find Spanish medieval chair, and how she had got hold of the latter still remained a mystery to the world of dealers.

• I •

"Shall we without further ado, then, strike a bargain?" Mrs. Owens intoned, looking past Mr. Evening, who had arrived on a bad snowy January night.

He had been reduced to more than his customary kind of silent social incommunicativeness by finally seeing Mrs. Owens in the flesh, a woman who while reputed to be so old, looked unaccountably beautiful, whose clothes were floral in their charm, wafting sachets of woody scent to his nostrils, and whose voice sounded like fine chimes.

"Of course I don't mean there's to be a sale! Even youthful you couldn't have come here thinking that." She dismissed at once any business with a pronounced flourish of white hands. "Nothing's for sale, and won't be even should we die." She faced him with a lessening of defiance, but he stirred uncomfortably.

"Whatever you may think, whatever you may have been told" — she went now to deal with the improbable fact of their meeting — "let me say that I can't resist their being admired" (she meant the heirlooms, of course). She unfolded the piece of newsprint of his "notice." "I could tell immediately by your way of putting things" — she touched the paper — "that you knew all about them. Or better, I knew you knew all about them by the way you left things undescribed. I knew you could admire, without stint or reservation." She finished with a kind of low bow.

"I'm relieved" — he began to look about the large high room — "that you're not curious then to know who I am, to know about me, that is, as I'm afraid I wouldn't be able to satisfy your curiosity on that score. That is to say, there's almost nothing to tell about me, and you already know what my vocation is."

She allowed this speech to die in silence, as she did with an occasional intruding sound of traffic which unaccountably reached her parlor, but then at his helpless sinking look, she said in an attempt, perhaps, to comfort: "I don't have to be curious about anything that holds me, Mr. Evening. It always unfolds itself, in any case.

"For instance," she went on, her face taking on a mock-wrathful look, "people sometimes try to remind me that I was once a famous actress, which though being a fact, is irrelevant, and, more, now meaningless, for even in those remote days, when let's say I was on the stage, even then, Mr. Evening, these" — and she indicated with a flourish of those commanding white hands the munificent surroundings — "these were everything!

"One is really only strictly curious about people one never intends to meet, I think, Mr. Evening," Mrs. Owens said.

She now rose and stood for a moment, so that the imposition of her height over him, seated in his low easy chair, was emphasized, then walking over to a tiny beautiful peachwood table, she looked at something on it. His own attention, still occupied with her presence, did not move for a moment to what she was bestowing a long, calm glance on. She made no motion to touch the object on the table before her. Though his vision clouded a bit, he looked directly at it now, and saw what it was, and saw there could be no mistake about it. It was the pale rose shell-like 1910 hand-painted china cup.

"You don't need to bring it to me!" he cried, and even she was startled by such an outburst. Mr. Evening had gone as white as chalk.

He searched in vain in his pockets for a handkerchief, and noting his distress, Mrs. Owens handed him one from the folds of her own dress.

"I won't ever beg of you," he said, wiping his brow with

the handkerchief. "I would offer you anything for the cup, of course, but I can't beg."

"What will you do then, Mr. Evening?" She came to within a few inches of him.

He sat before her, his head slightly tilted forward, his palms upturned like one who wishes to determine if rain is beginning.

"Don't answer"—she spoke in loud, gay tones—"for nobody expects you to do anything, beg, bargain, implore, steal. Whatever you are, or were, Mr. Evening—I catch from your accent you are Southern—you were never an actor, thank fortune. It's one of the reasons you're here, you are so much yourself.

"Now, mark me." Mrs. Owens strode past his chair to a heavy gold-brocaded curtain, her voice almost menacing in its depth of resonance. "I've not allowed you to look at this cup in order to tempt you. I merely wanted you to know I'd read your 'notice,' which you wrote, in any case, only for me. Furthermore, as you know, I'm not bargaining with you in any received sense of the word. You and I are beyond bargaining with one another. Money will never be mentioned between us, papers, or signatures—all that goes without saying. But I do want something," and she turned from the curtain and directed her luminous gray eyes to his face. "You're not like anybody else, Mr. Evening, and it's this quality of yours which has, I won't say won me, you're beyond winning anybody, but which has brought an essential part of myself back to me by your being just what you are and wanting so deeply what you want!"

Holding her handkerchief entirely over his face now so that he spoke to her as from under a sheet, he mumbled, "I don't like company, Mrs. Owens." His interruption had the effect of freezing her to the curtain before her. "And company, I'm afraid, includes you and your sister. I can't come and talk, and I don't like supper parties. If I did, if I liked them, that is, I'd prefer you."

"What extraordinary candor!" Mrs. Owens was at a loss

where to walk, at what to look. "And how gloriously rude!"
She considered everything quickly. "Good, very good, Mr.
Evening. . . . But *good* won't carry us far enough!" she cried,
and her voice rose in a great swell of volume until she saw with
satisfaction that he moved under her strength. The handkerchief fell away, and his face, very flushed, but with the eyes
closed, bent in her direction.

"You don't have to talk"—Mrs. Owens dismissed this as
if with loathing of that idea that he might—"and you don't
have to listen. You can snore in your chair if you like. But if
you come, say, once a week, that will more than do for a start.
You could consider this house as a kind of waiting room, let's
say, for a day that's sure and bound to come for all, and
especially us. . . . You'd wait here, say, on Thursday, and we
could offer you the room where you are now, and food, which
you would be entitled to spurn, and all you would need do is
let time pass. I could allow you to see, very gradually"—she
looked hurriedly in the direction of the cup—"a few things here
and there, not many at a visit, of course, it might easily
unhinge you in your expectant state"—she laughed—"and certainly I could show you nothing for quite a while from up
there," and she moved her head toward the floors above. "But
in the end, if you kept it up, the visits, I mean, I can assure
you your waiting would 'pay off,' as they say out there. . . . I
can't be any more specific." She brought her explanation of the
bargain to an abrupt close, and indicated with a sweeping
gesture he might stand and depart.

• **II** •

Thursday, then, set aside by Mrs. Owens for Mr. Evening to
begin attendance on the heirlooms, loomed up for the two of
them as a kind of fateful, even direful, mark on the calendar;
in fact, both the mistress of the heirlooms and her viewer were
ill with anticipation. Mr. Evening's dislike of company and

being entertained vied with his passion for "viewing." On the other hand, Mrs. Owens, watched over by a saddened and anguished Parl, felt the hours and days speed precipitously to an encounter which she now could not understand her ever having arranged or wanted. Never had she lived through such a week, and her fingers, usually white and still as they rested on her satin cushions, were almost raw from a violent pulling on and off of her rings.

At last Thursday, 8:30 PM, came, finding Mrs. Owens with one glass of wine—all she ever allowed herself, with barely a teaspoon of it tasted. Nine-thirty struck, ten, no Mr. Evening. Her lips, barely touched with an uncommon kind of rouge, moved in a bitter self-deprecatory smile. She rose and walked deliberately to a small ebony cabinet, and took out her smelling bottle, which she had not touched for months. Opening it, she found it had considerably weakened in strength, but she took it with her back to her chair, sniffing its dilute fumes from time to time.

Then about a quarter past eleven, when she had finished with hope, having struck the silk and mohair of her chair several castigating blows, the miracle, Mr. Evening, ushered in by Giles (who rare for him showed some animation), appeared in his heavy black country coat. Mrs. Owens, not so much frosty from his lateness as incredulous that she was seeing him, barely nodded. Having refused her supper, she had opened a large gilt book of Flaxman etchings, and was occupying herself with these, while Pearl, seated at a little table of her own in the furthest reaches of the room, was dining on some tender bits of fish soaked in a sauce into which she dipped a muffin.

Mr. Evening, ignored by both ladies, had sat down. He had not been drinking, Mrs. Owens's first impression, but his cheeks were beet-red from cold, and he looked, she saw with uneasy observation, more handsome and much younger than on his first call.

"I hate snow intensely." Mrs. Owens studied his pants cuffs heavy with flakes. "Yet going south somewhere"—it was not clear to whom she was speaking from this time on—"that would be now too much in the way of preparation merely to avoid winter wet. . . . At one time traveling itself was home to me, of course," she continued, and her hands fell on a massive yellowed ivory paper-opener with a larger than customary blade. "One was put up in those days, not hurled over landscape like an electric particle. One wore *clothes*, one 'appeared' at dinner, which was an occasion, one conversed, *listened*, or merely sat with eyes averted, one rose, was looked after, watched over, if you will, one was often more at home *going* in those days than when one remained home, or reached one's destination."

Mrs. Owens stopped, mortified by a yawn from Mr. Evening. Reduced to a kind of quivering dumbness, Mrs. Owens could only restrain herself, remembering the "agreement."

A butler appeared wearing green goggles and at a nearly imperceptible nod from Mrs. Owens picked up a minuscule marble-topped gold inlaid table, and placed it within a comfortable arm's reach of Mr. Evening. Later, another servant brought something steaming under silver receptacles from the kitchen.

"Unlike the flock of crows in flight today"—Mrs. Owens's voice seemed to come across footlights—"I can remember *all* my traveling." She turned the pages of Flaxman with critical quickness. "And that means in my case the globe, all of it, when it was largely inaccessible, and certainly infrequently commented or written upon by tradespeople and typists." She concentrated a moment in silence as if remembering perhaps how old she was and how far off her travel had been. "I didn't miss a country, however unrecommended or unlisted by some guide or hotel bursar. There's no point in going now or leaving one's front door when every dot on the map has been ground to dust by somebody's heavy foot. When everybody is *en route*, stay home! . . . Pearl, my dear, you're not looking at your plate!"

Pearl, who had finished her fish, was touching with

nearsighted uncertainty the linen tablecloth with a gleaming fork. "Wear your glasses, dear child, for heaven's sake, or you'll stab yourself!"

Mr. Evening had closed his eyes. He appeared like one who must impress upon himself not to touch food in a strange house. But the china on his table was stunning, though obviously brand-new and therefore not "anything." At last, however, against his better judgment, he lifted one of the cups, then set it down noiselessly. Immediately the butler poured him coffee. Against his will, he drank a tablespoon or so, for after the wet and cold he needed at least a taste of something hot. It was an unbelievable brew, heady, clear, fresh. Mrs. Owens immediately noted the pleasure on his face, and a kind of shiver ran through her. Her table, ever nonpareil, might win him, she saw, where nothing in her other "offerings" tonight had reached him.

"After travel was lost to me," Mrs. Owens went on in the manner of someone who is dictating memoirs to a machine, "the church failed likewise to hold me. Even then" (one felt she referred to the early years of another century), "they had let in every kind of speaker. The church had begun to offer thought and problems instead of merging and repose. . . . So it went out of my life along with going abroad. . . . Then my eyes are not, well, not so bad as Pearl's, who is blind without glasses, but reading tires me more and more, though I see the natural world of objects better perhaps now than ever before. Besides, I've read more than most, for I've had nothing in life but time. I've read, in sum, everything, and if there's a real author, I've been through him often more than twice."

Mr. Evening now tried a slice of baked Alaska, and it won him. His beginning the meal backwards was hardly intentional, but he had looked so snowy the butler had poured the coffee first, and the coffee had suggested to the kitchen the dessert course instead of the entrée.

Noting that Mr. Evening did not touch his wine, Mrs. Owens thought a moment, then began again, "Drinking has never been a consolation to me either. Life might have been more endurable, perhaps, especially in this epoch," and she looked at her glass, down scarcely two ounces. "Therefore spirits hardly needed to join travel in the things I've eliminated. . . ." Gazing upwards, she brought out, "The human face, perhaps strangely enough, is really all that has been left to me," and after a moment's consultation with herself, she looked obliquely at Mr. Evening, who halted conveying his fork, full of meringue, to his mouth. "I need the human face, let's say." She talked into the thick pages of the Flaxman drawings. "I can't stare at my servants, though outsiders have praised their fetching appeal. (I can't look at what I've acquired, I've memorized it too well.) No, I'm talking about the unnegotiable human face. Somebody," she said, looking nowhere now in particular, "has that, of course, while, on the other hand, I have what he wants badly, and so shall we say we are, if not a match, confederates of a sort."

Time had passed, if not swiftly, steadily. Morning itself was advancing. Mr. Evening, during the entire visit, having opened his mouth chiefly to partake of food whose taste alone invited him, since he had already dined, took up his napkin, wiped his handsome red lips on it, though it was, he saw, an indignity to soil such a piece of linen, and rose. Both Mrs. Owens and her sister had long since dozed or pretended to doze by the carefully tended log fire. He said good night therefore to stone ears, and went out the door.

• III •

It was the fifth Thursday of his visits to Mrs. Owens that the change which he had feared and suspected from the start, and which he was somehow incapable of averting, came about.

Mrs. Owens and her sister had ignored him more and more on the occasion of his "calls," and an onlooker, not in on the agreement, might have thought his presence was either distasteful to the ladies, or that he was too insignificant — an impecunious relative, perhaps—to merit the bestowal of a glance or word.

The spell of the pretense of indifference, of not recognizing one another, ended haphazardly one hour when Pearl, without any preface of warning, said in a loud voice that strong light was being allowed to reach and ruin the ingrain carpet on the third floor.

Before Mrs. Owens could take in the information or issue a command as to what might be done, if she intended indeed to do anything about protecting the carpet from light, she heard a certain flurry from the direction of the visitor, and turning saw what the mention of this special carpet had done to the face of Mr. Evening. He bore an expression of greed, passionate covetousness, one might even say a deranged, demented wish for immediate ownership. Indeed his countenance was so arresting in its eloquence that Mrs. Owens found herself, going against her own protocol, saying, "Are you quite all right, sir?" But before she had the words out of her mouth he had come over to her chair without waiting her permission.

"Did you say ingrain carpet?" he asked with great abruptness.

When Mrs. Owens, too astonished at his tone and movement, did not reply, she heard Mr. Evening's peremptory: "Show it to me at once!"

"If you have not taken leave of your senses, Mr. Evening," Mrs. Owens began, bringing forth from the folds of her red cashmere dress an enormous gold chain, which she pressed, "would you be so kind, I might even say, so decent, as to remember our agreement, if you cannot remember who I am, and in whose house you are visiting."

Then, quickly, in a voice of annihilating anger, loud enough to be heard on a passing steamship: "You've not waited long enough, spoilsport!"

Standing before her, jaws apart, an expression close to that of an idiot who has been slapped into brief attention, he could only stutter something inaudible.

Alarmed by her own outburst, Mrs. Owens hastened to add, "It's not ready to be shown, my dear, special friend."

Mrs. Owens took his hands now in hers, and kissed them gently.

Kneeling before her, not letting go her chill handclasp, looking up into her furrowed rouged cheeks, "Allow me one glimpse," he beseeched.

She extricated her hands from his and touched his forehead.

"Quite out of the question." She seemed almost to flirt now, and her voice had gone up an octave. "But the day will come"—she motioned for him to seat himself again,—"before one perhaps is expecting it. You have only hope ahead of you, dear Mr. Evening."

Obeying her, he seated himself again, and his look of crestfallen abject submissiveness, coupled with fear, comforted and strengthened Mrs. Owens so that she was able to smile tentatively.

"No one who does not live here, you see, can see the carpet." She was almost apologetic for her tirade, certainly she was consoling.

He bent his head.

Then they heard the wind from the northeast, and felt the huge shutter on the front of the house struggle as if for life. The snow followed soon after, hard as hail.

Tenting him to the quick, Mrs. Owens studied Mr. Evening's incipient immobility, and after waiting to see whether it would pass, and as she suspected, noted that it did not, she rang for the night servant, gave the latter cursory instructions, and then sat studying her guest until the servant returned with a tiny decanter and a sliver of handsome glass, setting these by Mr. Evening, who lightly caressed both vessels.

"Alas, Mr. Evening, they're only new," Mrs. Owens said.

He did not remember more until someone put a lap robe over his knees, and he knew the night had advanced into the glimmerings of dawn, and that he therefore must have slept upright in the chair all those hours, fortified by nips from the brandy, which, unlike the glass that contained it, was ancient.

When morning had well advanced, he found he could not rise. A new attendant, with coal-black sideburns and ashen cheeks, assisted him to the bathroom, helped him bathe and then held him securely under the armpits while he urinated a stream largely blood. He stared into the bowl but regarded the crimson pool there without particular interest or alarm.

Then he was back in the chair again, the snow still pelted the shutters, and the east wind raved like lunatics helpless without sedation.

Although he was certain Mrs. Owens passed from time to time in the adjoining room — who could fail to recognize her tread, as dominating and certain as her resonant voice — she did not enter that day either to look at him or inquire. Occasionally he heard, to his acute distress, dishes being moved and, so it seemed, placed in straw.

Once or twice he thought he heard her clap her hands, an anachronism so imperial he found himself giggling convulsively. He also heard a parrot screech, and then almost immediately caught the sound of its cage being taken up and the cries of the bird retreating further and further into total silence.

Some time later he was served food so highly seasoned, so copiously sprinkled with herbs and spices that added to his disinclination to partake of food, he could not identify a morsel of what he tasted.

Then Giles reappeared, with a sterling-silver basin, a gleaming tray of verbena soap, and improbably enough, looking up at him, his own straight razor, for if it was one thing in the world of manhood he had mastered, it was to shave beautifully with a razor, an accomplishment he had learned from his captain in military school.

"How did they get my own things fetched here, Giles?" he inquired, with no real interest in having his question answered.

"We've had to bring everything, under the circumstances," Giles replied in a hollow vestryman's voice.

Mr. Evening lay back then, while he felt the servant's hands tuck a blanket about his slippers and thighs.

"Mrs. Owens thinks it's because your blood is thinner than we Northerners that the snow affects you in this way." Giles offered a tentative explanation of the young man's plight.

Suddenly from directly overhead, Mr. Evening heard carpenters, loud as if in the room with him, sawing and hammering. He stirred uncomfortably in his stocking feet.

In the hall directly in line with his chair, though separated by a kind of heavy partition, Mrs. Owens and two gentlemen of vaguely familiar voices were doing a loud inventory of "effects."

Preparations for an auction must be in progress, Mr. Evening decided. He now heard with incipient unease and at the same time a kind of feeble ecstasy the names of every rare heirloom in the trade, but these great objects' names were loudly hawked, checked, callously enumerated, and the whole proceedings were carried off with a kind of rage and contempt in the voice of the auctioneer so that one had the impression the most priceless and rarest treasures worthy finally of finding a home only in the Louvre were being noted here prior to their being carted out in boxes and tossed into the bonfire. At one point in the inventory he let out a great cry of "Stop it!"

The partition in the wall opened, and Mrs. Owens stood staring at him from about ten feet away; then after a look of what was meant perhaps to be total unrecognition or bilious displeasure, she closed the sliding panel fast, and the inventory was again in progress, louder, if anything, than before, the tone of the hawker's voice more rasping and vicious.

Following a long nap, he remembered two strangers, dressed in overalls, enter with a gleaming gold tape; they stooped down, grunting and querulous, and made meticulous if furtive movements of measuring him from head to toe, his sitting posture requiring them, evidently, to check their results more than once.

Was it now Friday night, or had the weekend already passed, and were we arrived at Monday?

The snow had continued unabated, so far as his memory served, though the wind was weaker, or more fitful, and the shutters nearly silent. He supposed all kinds of people had called on him at his lodgings. Then Giles appeared again, after Mr. Evening had passed more indistinct hours in his chair, and the servant helped him into the toilet, where he passed thick clots of blood, and on his return to his chair Mr. Evening found himself face to face with his own large steamer trunk and a pair of valises.

While he kept his eyes averted from the phenomenal appearance of his luggage, Giles combed and cut his long chestnut hair, trimmed the shagginess of his eyebrows, and massaged the back of his neck. Mr. Evening did not ask him if there was any reason or occasion for tonsorial attention, but at last he did inquire, more for breaking the lugubrious silence than for getting any pertinent answer, "What was the carpentering upstairs for, Giles?"

The servant hesitated, stammered, and in his confusion came near nipping Mr. Evening's ear with the barber's shears, but at last answered the question in a loud whisper: "They're remodeling the bed."

The room in which he had sat these past days, however many, four, six, a fortnight, perhaps, the room which had been Mrs. Owens's and her sister's on those first Thursday nights of his visits, was now only his alone, and the two women had passed on to other quarters in a house whose chambers were, like its heirlooms, difficult, perhaps impossible, to number.

Limited to a kind of speechless listlessness — he assumed he must be very ill, though he did not wonder why no doctor came — and passing several hours without attendance, suddenly, in pique at being neglected, he employed Mrs. Owens's own queer custom and clapped his hands peremptorily. A dark-skinned youth with severe bruises about his temples appeared and, without inquiry or greeting, adjusted Mr. Evening's feet on a stool, poured him a drink of something red with a bitter taste, and, while he waited for the sick man to drink, made a gesture of inquiry as to whether Mr. Evening wished to relieve himself.

More indistinct hours swam slowly into blurred unremembrance. At last the hammering, pounding, moving of furniture, together with the suffocating fumes of turpentine and paint, all ceased to molest him.

Mrs. Owens, improbably, appeared again, accompanied by Pearl.

"I am glad to see you better, Mr. Evening, needless to say," Mrs. Owens began icily, and one could see at once that she appeared some years younger, perhaps strong sunlight — now pouring in — flattered her, or could it be, he wondered, she had had recourse to plastic surgery during his illness, at any rate, she was much younger, while her voice was harsher, harder, more actresslike than ever before.

"Because of your splendid recovery, we are therefore ready to move you into your room," Mrs. Owens went on, "where, I'm glad to report, you'll find more than one ingrain carpet spread out for you to rest your eyes on. . . . The bed," she added after a careful pause, "I do hope will meet with your approval" (here he attempted to say something contradictory, but she indicated she would not allow it), "for its refashioning has cost all of us here some pains to make over." Here he felt she would have used the word *heirloom,* but prevented herself from doing so. She said only, in conclusion, "You're over, do you realize, six foot six in your stocking feet!"

She studied him closely. "We couldn't let you lie with your legs hanging out of the bedclothes!

"Now, sir" — Mrs. Owens folded her arms — "can you move, do you suppose, to the next floor, provided someone, of course, assists you?"

The next thing he remembered was being helped up the interminable winding staircase by a brace of servants, while Mrs. Owens and Pearl brought up the rear, Mrs. Owens talking away: "Those of us who are Northerners, Mr. Evening, have of course the blood from birth to take these terribly snowy days, Boreas and his blasts, the sight of Orion climbing the winter night, but our friends of Southern birth must be more careful. That is why we take such good care of you. You should have come, in any case, from the beginning and not kept picking away at a mere Thursday call," she ended on a scolding note.

The servants deposited Mr. Evening on a large horsehair sofa which in turn faced the longest bed he had ever set eyes on, counting any, he was certain, he had ever stared at in museums. And now it must be confessed that Mr. Evening, for all the length of him, had never from early youth slept in the kind of bed that his height and build required, for after coming into his fortune, he had continued to live in lodging houses which did not provide anything adequate for his physical measurements. Here at Mrs. Owens's, where his living was all unchosen by him, he now saw the bed perfectly suited for his frame.

A tiny screen was thrown up around the horsehair sofa, and while Mrs. Owens and Pearl waited as if for a performance to begin, Cole, a Norwegian, as it turned out, quietly got Mr. Evening's old business clothes off, and clad him in gleaming green and shell silk pajamas, and in a lightning single stride across the room carried the invalid to the bed, propped him up in a layer of cushions and pillows so that he looked as a matter of fact more seated now than when he had spent those days and nights in the big chair downstairs.

Although food had been brought for all of them, seated in different sections of the immense room, that is for Pearl, Mrs. Owens, and Mr. Evening, only Pearl partook of any. Mr. Evening, sunk in cushions, looked nowhere in particular, certainly not at his food. Mrs. Owens, ignoring her own repast (some sort of roast game), produced from the folds of her organdy gown a jewel-studded lorgnette, and began reading aloud in droning monotone a list of rare antiques, finally naming with emphasis a certain ormolu clock, which caused Mr. Evening to cry out, "If you please, read no more while I am dining!" although he had not touched a morsel.

Mrs. Owens put down the paper, waved it against her like

a fan, and having put away her lorgnette came over to the counterpane of the bed.

She bent over him like a physician and he closed his eyes. The scent which came from her bosom was altogether like that of a garden by the sea.

"Our whole life together, certainly," she began, like one talking in her sleep, "was to have been an enumeration of effects. I construed it so at any rate. . . . I had thought," she went on, "that you would be attentive. . . . I procured these special glasses"—she touched the lorgnette briefly—"and if I may be allowed an explanation, I thought I would read to you since I no longer read to myself, and may I confess it, while I lifted my eyes occasionally from the paper, I hoped to rest them by letting them light on your fine features. . . . If you are to deprive me of that pleasure, dear Mr. Evening, say so, and new arrangements and new preparations can be made."

She pressed her hand now on the bed, as if to test its quality.

"I do not think even so poor an observer and so indifferent a guest as yourself can be unaware of the stupendous animation, movement, preparation, the entire metamorphosis indeed which your coming here has entailed. Mark me, I am willing to do more for you, but if I am to be deprived of the simple and may I say sole pleasure left to me, reading a list of precious heirlooms and at the same time resting my eyes from time to time on you, then say so, then excuse me, pray, and allow me to depart from my own house."

Never one endowed with power over language, Mr. Evening, at this, the most dramatic moment in his life, could only seize Mrs. Owens's pliant bejeweled hand in his rough, chapped one, hold her finger to his face, and cry, "No!"

"No what?" she said, withdrawing her hand, a tiny indication of pleasure, however, moving her lips.

Raising himself up from the hillock of cushions, he got out, "What about the things I was doing out there," and he pointed haphazardly in the direction of where he thought his shop might possibly lie.

Mrs. Owens shook her head. "Whatever you did out there, Mr. Evening"—she looked down at him—"or, rather, amend that, sir, to this; you are now doing whatever and more than you could have ever done elsewhere. . . . This is your home!" she cried, and as if beside herself, "Your work is here, and only here!"

"Am I as ill as everything points to?" He turned to Pearl, who continued to dine.

Pearl looked to her sister for instructions.

"I don't know how you could be so self-centered as to talk about a minor upset of the urinary tract as illness"—Mrs. Owens raised her voice—"especially when we have prepared a list like this"—she tapped with her lorgnette on the inventory of antiques—"which you can't be ass enough not to know will one day be yours!"

Mrs. Owens stood up and fixed him with her gaze.

Mr. Evening's eyes fell then like dropping balls to the floor, where the unobtainable ingrain carpets, unobserved by him till then, rested beneath them like live breathing things. He wept shamelessly and Mrs. Owens restrained what might have been a grin.

He dried his eyes slowly on the napkin which she had proffered him.

"If you would have at least the decency to pretend to drink your coffee, you would see your cup," she said.

"Yes," she sighed, as she studied Mr. Evening's disoriented features as he now caught sight of the 1910 hand-painted cup within his very fingertip, unobserved by him earlier, as had been the ingrain carpets. "Yes," Mrs. Owens continued, "while I have gained back my eyesight, as it were"—she raised her lorgnette briefly—"others are to all practical purposes sand-blind . . . Pearl"—she turned to her sister—"you may be excused from the room.

"My dear Mr. Evening," Mrs. Owens said, her voice materially altered once Pearl had disappeared.

He had put down the 1910 cup, perhaps because it seemed unthinkable to drink out of anything so irreplaceable,

and so delicate that a mere touch of his lips might snap it.
"You can't possibly now go out of my life." Mrs. Owens
half-stretched out her hand to him.

He supposed she had false teeth, they were too splendid
for real, yet all of her suddenly was splendid, and from her person again came a succession of wild fragrance, honeysuckle,
jasmine, flowers without names, one perfume succeeding
another in enervating succession, as various as all her priceless
heirlooms.

"Winter, even to a Southerner, dear Mr. Evening, can
offer some tender recompense, and for me, whose blood, if I
may be allowed to mention it again, is incapable of thinning."
Here she turned down the bedclothes clear to his feet. The
length of his feet and the beautiful architecture of his bare in-
step caused her for a moment to hesitate.

"I'm certain," she kept her words steady, placing an icy
hand under the top of his pajamas, and letting it rest, as if in
permanent location on his breast, "that you are handsome to
the eye all over."

His teeth chattered briefly, as he felt her head come down
on him so precipitously, but she seemed content merely to rest
on his bare chest. He supposed he would catch an awful cold
from it all, but he did not move, hearing her say, "And after
I'm gone, all—all of it will be yours, and all I ask in return,
Mr. Evening, is that all days be Thursday from now on."

He lay there without understanding how it had occurred,
whether a servant had entered or her hands with the quickness
of hummingbirds had done the trick, but there he was naked
as he had come into the world, stretched out in the bed that
was his exact length at last and which allowed him to see just
what an unusually tall young man he was indeed.

• LILY'S PARTY •

AS HOBART came through the door of Crawford's Home Dinette, his eyes fell on Lily sitting along at one of the big back tables, eating a piece of pie.

"Lily! Don't tell me! You're supposed to be in Chicago!" he ejaculated.

"Who supposed I was to be?" Lily retorted, letting her fork cut quickly into the pie.

"Well, I'll damn me if—" He began to speak in a humming sort of way while pulling out a chair from under her table, and sitting down unbidden. "Why, everybody thought you went up there to be with Edward."

"Edward! He's the last person on this earth I would go anywhere to be with. And I think you know that!" Lily never showed anger openly, and if she was angry now, at least she didn't let it stop her from enjoying her pie.

"Well, Lily, we just naturally figured you had gone to Chicago when you weren't around."

"I gave your brother Edward two of the best years of my life." Lily spoke with the dry accent of someone testifying in court for a second time. "And I'm not about to go find him for more of what he gave me. Maybe you don't remember what I got from him, but I do. . . ."

"But where were you, Lily? . . . We all missed you!" Hobart harped on her absence.

"I was right here all the time, Hobart, for your information." As she said this, she studied his mouth somewhat absent-mindedly. "But as to your brother, Edward Starr," she continued, and then paused as she kept studying his mouth as if she found a particular defect there which had somehow escaped scrutiny hitherto. "As to Edward," she began again, and then stopped, struck her fork gingerly against the plate, "he was a

315

number-one poor excuse for a husband, let me tell you. He left me for another woman, if you care to recall, and it was because of his neglect that my little boy passed away. . . . So let's say I don't look back on Edward, and am not going to any Chicago to freshen up on my recollections of him. . . ."

She quit studying his mouth, and looked out the large front window through which the full October moon was beginning its evening climb.

"At first I will admit I was lonesome, and with my little boy lying out there in the cemetery, I even missed as poor an excuse for a man as Edward Starr, but believe you me, that soon passed."

She put down her fork now that she had eaten all the pie, laid down some change on the bare white ash wood of the table, and then, closing her purse, sighed, and softly rose.

"I only know," Lily began, working the clasp on her purse, "that I have begun to find peace now. . . . Reverend McGilead, as you may be aware, has helped me toward the light. . . ."

"I have heard of Reverend McGilead," Hobart said in a voice so sharp she looked up at him while he held the screen door open for her.

"I am sure you have heard nothing but good then," she shot back in a voice that was now if not deeply angry, certainly unsteady.

"I will accompany you home, Lily."

"You'll do no such thing, Hobart. . . . Thank you, and good evening."

He noticed that she was wearing no lipstick, and that she did not have on her wedding ring. She also looked younger than when she had been Edward Starr's wife.

"You say you have found peace with this new preacher." Hobart spoke after her retreating figure. "But under this peace, you hate Edward Starr," he persisted. "All you said to me tonight was fraught with hate."

She turned briefly and looked at him, this time in the

eyes. "I will find my way, you can rest assured, despite your brother and you."

He stayed in front of the door of the dinette and watched her walk down the moonlit-white road toward her house that lay in deep woods. His heart beat violently. All about where he stood were fields and crops and high trees, and the sailing queen of heaven was the only real illumination after one went beyond the dinette. No one came down this small road with the exception of lovers who occasionally used it for their lane.

Well, Lily was a sort of mystery woman, he had to admit to himself. And where, then, did the rumor arise that she had been to Chicago. And now he felt she had lied to him, that she had been in Chicago after all and had just got back.

Then without planning to do so, hardly knowing indeed he was doing so, he began following after her from a conveniently long distance down the moonlit road. After a few minutes of pursuing her, he saw someone come out from one of the ploughed fields. The newcomer was a tall still-youthful man with the carriage of an athlete rather than that of a farmer. He almost ran toward Lily. Then they both stopped for a moment, and after he had touched her gently on the shoulder they went on together. Hobart's heart beat furiously, his temple throbbed, a kind of film formed over his lips from his mouth rushing with fresh saliva. Instead of following them directly down the road, he now edged into the fields and pursued them more obliquely. Sometimes the two ahead of him would pause, and there was some indication the stranger was about to leave Lily, but then from something they said to one another, the couple continued on together. Hobart would have liked to get closer to them so that he might hear what they were saying, but he feared discovery. At any rate, he could be sure of one thing, the man walking with her was not Edward, and also he was sure that whoever he was he was her lover. Only lovers walked that way together, too far apart at one time, too weaving and close together another time: their very breathing appeared uneven and heavy the way their bodies swayed. Yes, Hobart realized, he was about to see love being made, and it

made him walk unsteadily, almost to stumble. He only hoped
he could keep a rein on his feelings and would not make his
presence known to them.

When he saw them at last turn into her cottage he longed
for the strength to leave them, to go back home to forget Lily,
forget his brother Edward, whom he was certain Lily had been
"cheating" all through their marriage (even *he* had been
intimate once with Lily when Edward was away on a trip, so
that he had always wondered if the child she bore him in this
marriage might not have been after all his, but since it was
dead, he would not think of it again).

Her cottage had a certain fame. There were no other
houses about, and the windows of her living room faced the
thick forest. Here she could have done nearly whatever she
liked and nobody would have been the wiser, for unless one
had stood directly before the great window which covered
almost the entire width of her room, any glimpse within was
shut out by foliage, and sometimes by heavy mist.

Hobart knew that this man, whoever he was, had not
come tonight for the purpose of imparting Jesus' love to her
but his own. He had heard things about this young preacher
Reverend McGilead, he had been briefed on his "special"
prayer meetings, and had got the implication the man of the
cloth had an excess of unburned energy in his makeup. He
shouted too loud during his sermons, people said, and the
veins in his neck were ready to burst with the excess of blood
that ran through him.

From Hobart's point of observation, in the protection of
a large spruce tree, nothing to his surprise he saw whom he
believed to be the young preacher take her in his arms. But
then what happened was unforeseen, undreamed of indeed,
for with the rapidity of a professional gymnast, the preacher
stripped off his clothing in a trice, and stood in the clear illumination of her room not covered by so much as a stitch or
thread. Lily herself looked paralyzed, as rodents are at the sudden appearance of a serpent. Her eyes were unfocused on
anything about her, and she made no attempt to assist him as

he partially undressed her. But from the casual way he acted, it was clear they had done this before. Yes, Hobart confessed to himself, in the protective dark of the tree under which he stood, one would have expected certainly something more gradual from lovers. He would have thought that the young preacher would have talked to her for at least a quarter of an hour, that he would have finally taken her hand, then perhaps kissed her, and then oh so slowly and excitingly, for Hobart at least, would have undressed her, and taken her to himself.

But this gymnast's performance quite nonplussed the observer by the spruce tree. For one thing, the gross size of the preacher's sex, its bulging veins and unusual angry redness, reminded him of sights seen by him when he had worked on a farm. It also recalled a surgical operation he had witnessed performed by necessity in a doctor's small, overcrowded office. The preacher now had pushed Lily against the wall, and worked vigorously at, and then through, her. His eyes rolled like those of a man being drawn unwillingly into some kind of suction machine, and saliva suddenly poured out of his mouth in great copiousness so that he resembled someone blowing up an enormous balloon. His neck and throat were twisted convulsively, and his nipples tightened as if they were being given over to rank torture.

At this moment, Hobart, without realizing he was doing so, came out from his hiding place, and strode up to the window, where he began waving his arms back and forth in the manner of a man flagging a truck. (Indeed Lily later was to believe that she thought she had seen a man with two white flags in his hands signaling for help.)

Lily's screams at being discovered broke the peace of the neighborhood, and many watchdogs from about the immediate vicinity began barking in roused alarm.

"We are watched!" she was finally able to get out. Then she gave out three uncadenced weak cries. But the preacher, his back to the window, like a man in the throes of some grave physical malady, could only concentrate on what his body dictated to him, and though Lily now struggled to be free of him, this only secured him the more tightly to her. Her cries now rose in volume until they reached the same pitch as that of the watchdogs.

Even Hobart, who had become as disoriented perhaps as the couple exhibited before him, began making soft outcries, and he continued to wave his arms fruitlessly.

"No, no, and no!" Lily managed now to form and speak these words. "Whoever you are out there, go, go away at once!"

Hobart now came directly up to the window. He had quit waving his arms, and he pressed his nose and mouth against the pane.

"It's me," he cried reassuringly. "Hobart, Edward Starr's brother! Can't you see?" He was, he managed to realize, confused as to what he now should do or say, but he thought that since he had frightened them so badly and so seriously disturbed their pleasure, he had best identify himself, and let them know he meant no harm. But his calling to them only terrified Lily the more, and caused her young partner to behave like someone struggling in deep water.

"Hobart Starr here!" the onlooker called the them, thinking they may have mistaken him for a housebreaker.

"Oh merciful Lord," Lily moaned. "If it is you, Hobart Starr, please go away. Have that much decency—" She tried to finish the sentence through her heavy breathing.

The preacher at this moment tore off the upper part of Lily's dress, and her breasts and nipples looked out from the light into the darkness at Hobart like the troubled faces of children.

"I'm coming into the house to explain!" Hobart called to them inside.

"You'll do no such thing! No, no, Hobart!" Lily vociferated back to him, but the intruder dashed away from the window, stumbling over some low-lying bushes, and then presently entered the living room, where the preacher was now moaning deeply and beginning even at times to scream a little.

"What on earth possessed you." Lily was beginning to speak when all at once the preacher's mouth fell over hers, and he let out a great smothered roar, punctuated by drumlike rumblings from, apparently, his stomach.

Hobart took a seat near the standing couple.

The preacher was now free of Lily's body at last, and he had slumped down on the floor, near where Hobart was sitting, and was crying out some word and then he began making sounds vaguely akin to weeping. Lily remained with her back and buttocks pressed against the wall, and was breathing hard, gasping indeed for breath. After her partner had quit his peculiar sobbing, he got up and put on his clothes, and walked out unsteadily into the kitchen. On the long kitchen table, the kind of table one would expect in a large school cafeteria, Hobart, from his chair, could spy at least fifteen pies of different kinds, all "homemade" by Lily expressly for the church social which was tomorrow.

He could see the preacher sit down at the big table, and cut himself a piece of Dutch apple pie. His chewing sounds at last alerted Lily to what was happening, and she managed to hurry out to the kitchen in an attempt to halt him.

"One piece of pie isn't going to wreck the church picnic. Go back there and entertain your new boyfriend, why don't you," the preacher snapped at her attempt to prevent him eating the piece of pie.

"He's Edward Starr's brother, I'd have you know, and he's not my boyfriend, smarty!"

The preacher chewed on. "This pie," he said, moving his tongue over his lips cautiously, "is very heavy on the sugar, isn't it?"

"Oh, I declare, hear him!" Lily let the words out peevishly, and she rushed on back into the living room. There she gazed wide-eyed, her mouth trying to move for speech, for facing her stood Hobart, folding his shorts neatly, and stark naked.

"You will not!" Lily managed to protest.

"Who says I don't!" Hobart replied nastily.

"Hobart Starr, you go home at once," Lily ordered him. "This is all something that can be explained."

He made a kind of dive at her as his reply, and pinioned her to the wall. She tried to grab his penis, clawing at it, but he had perhaps already foreseen she might do this, and he caught her by the hand, and then slapped her. Then he inserted his membrum virile quickly into her body, and covered her face with his freely flowing saliva. She let out perfunctory cries of expected rather than felt pain as one does under the hand of a nervous intern.

At a motion from her, some moments later, he worked her body about the room, so that she could see what the preacher was doing. He had consumed the Dutch apple pie, and was beginning on the rhubarb lattice.

"Will you be more comfortable watching him, or shall we return to the hall?" Hobart inquired.

"Oh, Hobart, for pity's sake," she begged him. "Let me go, oh please let me go." At this he pushed himself more deeply inwards, hurting her, to judge by her grimace.

"I am a very slow comer, as you will remember, Lily. I'm slow but I'm the one in the end who cares for you most. Tonight is my biggest windfall. After all the others, you see, it is me who was meant for you. . . . You're so cozy too, Lily."

As he said this, she writhed, and attempted to pull out from him, but he kissed her hard, working into her hard.

"Oh this is all so damned unfair!" She seemed to cough out, not speak, these words. "Ralph," she directed her voice to the kitchen, "come in here and restore order. . . ."

As he reached culmination, Hobart screamed so loud the preacher did come out of the kitchen. He was swallowing very hard, so that he did remind Hobart of a man in a pie-eating contest. He looked critically at the two engaged in coitus.

A few minutes later, finished with Lily, Hobart began putting on his clothes, yawning convulsively, and shaking his head, while Ralph began doggedly and methodically to remove his clothing again, like a substitute or second in some grueling contest.

"Nothing more, no, I say no!" Lily shouted when she saw Ralph's naked body advancing on her. "I will no longer cooperate here."

He had already taken her, however, and secured her

more firmly than the last time against the wall.

Hobart meanwhile was standing unsteadily on the threshold of the kitchen. He saw at once that the preacher had eaten two pies. He felt un-understandably both hungry and nauseous, and these two sensations kept him weaving giddily about the kitchen table now. At last he sat down before a chocolate meringue pie, and then very slowly, finickily, cut himself a small piece.

As he ate daintily he thought that he had not enjoyed intercourse with Lily, despite his seeming gusto. It had been all mostly exertion and effort, somehow, though he felt he had done well, but no feeling in a supreme sense of release had come. He was not surprised now that Edward Starr had left her. She was not a satisfier.

Hobart had finished about half the chocolate meringue when he reckoned the other two must be reaching culmination by now for he heard very stertorous breathing out there, and then there came to his ears as before the preacher's intense war whoop of release. Lily also screamed and appealed as if to the mountain outside, *I perish! Oh, perishing!* And a bit later, she hysterically supplicated to some unknown person or thing *I cannot give myself up like this, oh!* Then a second or so later he heard his own name called, and her demand that he save her.

Hobart wiped his mouth on the tablecloth and came out to have a look at them. They were both, Lily and Ralph, weeping and holding loosely to one another, and then they both slipped and fell to the floor, still sexually connected.

"Gosh all get out!" Hobart said with disgust.

He turned away. There was a pie at the very end of the table which looked most inviting. It had a very brown crust with golden juice spilling from fancily, formally cut little air holes as in magazine advertising. He plunged the knife into it, and tasted a tiny bit. It was of such wonderful flavor that even though he felt a bit queasy he could not resist cutting himself a slice, and he began to chew solemnly on it. It was an apricot, or perhaps peach, pie, but final identification eluded him.

Lily now came out into the kitchen and hovered over the

big table. She was dressed, and had fixed her hair differently,
so that it looked as if it had been cut and set, though there were
some loose strands in the back which were not too becoming,
yet they emphasized her white neck.

"Why, you have eaten half the pies for the church social!"
she cried, with some exaggeration in her observation, of
course. "After all that backbreaking work of mine! What on
earth will I tell the preacher when he comes to pick them up!"

"But isn't this the preacher here tonight?" Hobart waving
his fork in the direction of the other room motioned to the man
called Ralph.

"Why, Hobart, of course not. . . . He's no preacher, and
I should think you could tell . . ."

"How did I come to think he was?" Hobart stuttered out,
while Lily sat down at the table and was beginning to bawl.

"Of all the inconsiderate selfish thoughtless pups in the
world," she managed to get out between sobs. "I would have
to meet up with you two, just when I was beginning to have
some sort of settled purpose."

Ralph, standing now on the threshold of the kitchen, still
stark naked, laughed.

"I have a good notion to call the sheriff!" Lily threatened.
"And do you know what I'm going to do in the morning? I'm
going back to Edward Starr in Chicago. Yes siree. I realize
now that he loved me more than I was aware of at the time."

The two men were silent, and looked cautiously at one
another, while Lily cried on and on.

"Oh, Lily," Hobart said, "even if you do go see Edward,
you'll come home again to us here. You know you can't get the
good loving in Chicago that we give you, now don't you?"

Lily wept on and on repeating many times how she would
never be able to explain to the church people about not having
enough pies on hand for her contribution to the big social.

After drying her tears on a handkerchief which Hobart
lent her, she took the knife and with methodical fierce energy
and spiteful speed cut herself a serving from one of the still-
untouched pies.

She showed by the way she moved her tongue in and out of her mouth that she thought her pie was excellent.

"I'm going to Chicago and I'm never coming back!" As she delivered this statement she began to cry again.

The "preacher," for that is how Hobart still thought of him, came over to where Lily was chewing and weeping, and put his hand between the hollows of her breasts.

"Now don't get started again, Ralph. . . . No!" she flared up. "No, no, no."

"I need it all over again," Ralph appealed to her. "Your good cooking has charged me up again."

"Those pies *are* too damned good for a church," she finally said with a sort of moody weird craftiness, and Ralph knew when she said this that she would let him have her again.

"Hobart" — Lily turned to Edward's brother — "why don't you go home. Ralph and I are old childhood friends from way back. And I was nice to you. But I am in love with Ralph."

"It's my turn," Hobart protested.

"No, no." Lily began her weeping again. "I love Ralph."

"Oh hell, let him just this once more, Lily," the "preacher" said. Ralph walked away and began toying again with another of the uncut pies. "Say, who taught you to cook, Lily?" he inquired sleepily.

"I want you to send Hobart home, Ralph. I want you to myself. In a bed. This wall stuff is an outrage. Ralph, you send Hobart home now."

"Oh why don't you let the fellow have you once more. Then I'll really do you upstairs." Meanwhile, he went on chewing and swallowing loudly.

"Damn you, Ralph," Lily moaned. "Double damn you."

She walked over to the big table and took up one of the pies nearest her and threw it straight at the "preacher."

The "preacher"'s eyes, looking out from the mess she had made of his face, truly frightened her. She went over to Hobart, and waited there.

"All right for you, Lily," the "preacher" said.

"Oh, don't hurt her," Hobart pleaded, frightened too at the "preacher" 's changed demeanor.

The first pie the "preacher" threw hit Hobart instead of Lily. He let out a little gasp, more perhaps of surprised pleasure than hurt.

"Oh now stop this. We must stop this," Lily exhorted. "We are grown-up people, after all." She began to sob, but very put-on like, the men felt. "Look at my kitchen." She tried to put some emphasis into her appeal to them.

The "preacher" took off his jockey shorts, which he had put on a few moments earlier. He took first one pie and then another, mashing them all over his body, including his hair. Lily began to whimper and weep in earnest now, and sat down as if to give herself over to her grief. Suddenly one of the pies hit her, and she began to scream, then she became silent.

There was a queer silence in the whole room. When she looked up, Hobart had also stripped completely, and the "preacher" was softly slowly mashing pies over his thin, tightly muscled torso. Then slowly, inexorably, Hobart began eating pieces of pie from off the body of the smeared "preacher." The "preacher" returned this favor, and ate pieces of pie from Hobart, making gobbling sounds like a wild animal. Then they hugged one another and began eating the pies all over again from their bare bodies.

"Where do you get that stuff in my house!" Lily rose, roaring at them. "You low curs, where do you—"

But the "preacher" had thrown one of the few remaining pies at her, which struck her squarely in the breast and blew itself red all over her face and body so that she resembled a person struck by a bomb.

Ralph hugged Hobart very tenderly now, and dutifully ate small tidbits from his body, and Hobart seemed to nestle against Ralph's body, and ate selected various pieces of the pie from the latter.

Then Lily ran out the front door and began screaming *Help! I will perish! Help me!*

The dogs began to bark violently all around the neighborhood.

In just a short time she returned. The two men were still closely together, eating a piece here and there from their "massacred" bodies.

Sitting down at the table, weeping perfunctorily and almost inaudibly, Lily raised her fork, and began eating a piece of her still-unfinished apple pie.

• On the Rebound •

FRANKLY, gentlemen," Rupert Douthwaite reflected one gray afternoon in January to a few of us Americans who visited him from time to time in his "exile" in London, "no one in New York, no one who counted, ever expected to see Georgia Comstock back in town," and here Rupert nodded on the name, in his coy, pompous but somewhat charming way, meaning for us to know she was an heiress, meaning she had "everything," otherwise he would not be mentioning her. "She sat right there." He pointed to a refurbished heirloom chair which had accompanied him from New York. "I would never have dreamed Georgia would sue for a favor, least of all to me, for, after all"—he touched a colorful sideburn—"if you will allow me to remind you, it was I who replaced Georgia so far as literary salons were concerned." He groaned heavily, one of his old affectations, and took out his monocle, one of his new ones, and let it rest on the palm of his hand like an expiring butterfly. "Georgia's was, after all, the only bona fide salon in New York for years and years—I say that, kind friends, without modification. It was never elegant, never grand, never *comme il faut,* granted, any more than poor Georgia was. She was plain, mean, and devastating, with her own consistent vulgarity and bad taste, but she had the energy of a fiend out of hot oil and she turned that energy into establishing the one place where everybody had to turn up on a Thursday in New York, whether he liked it or not.

"When the dear thing arrived, then, at my place after her long banishment, I was pained to see how much younger she'd gotten. It didn't become her. I preferred her old, let's say. It was obvious she'd had the finest face-lifting job Europe can bestow. (You know how they've gone all wrong in New York on that. You remember Kathryn Combs, the film beauty. One eye's higher than the other now, dead mouth, and so on, so that I always feel when Kathryn's about I'm looking into an open casket.) But Georgia! Well, she hardly looked forty.

"Now mind you, I knew she hadn't come back to New York to tell me she loved me — the woman's probably hated me all my life, no doubt about it, but whatever she'd come for, I had to remind myself she had been helpful when Kitty left me." Rupert referred openly now to his third wife, the great New York female novelist who had walked out on him for, in his words, a shabby little colonel. "Yes," he sighed now, "when all the papers were full of my divorce before I myself hardly knew she had left me, Georgia was most understanding, even kind, moved in to take care of me, hovered over me like a mother bird, and so on. I had been ready to jump in the river, and she, bitch that she is, brought me round. And so when she appeared five years to the day after New York had kicked her out, and with her brand-new face, I saw at once she had come on a matter as crucial to her as my bust-up had been with Kitty, but I confess I never dreamed she had come to me because she wanted to begin all over again (begin with a salon, I mean of course). Nobody decent begins again, as I tried to tell her immediately I heard what she was up to. She'd been living in Yugoslavia, you know, after the New York fiasco. . . .

"When she said she did indeed want to begin again, I simply replied, 'Georgia, you're not serious and you're not as young as you look either, precious. You can't know what you're saying. Maybe it's the bad New York air that's got you after the wheat fields and haymows of Slavonia.'

"'Rupert, my angel,' she intoned, 'I'm on my knees to you, and not rueful to be so! Help me to get back and to stay back, dearest!'

"'Nonsense'— I made her stop her dramatics —'I won't hear of it, and you won't hear of it either when you're yourself again.'

"I was more upset than I should have been, somehow. Her coming and her wish for another try at a salon made me aware what was already in the wind, something wicked that

scared me a little, and I heard myself voicing it when I said,
'Everything has changed in New York, sweety, since you've
been away. You wouldn't know anybody now. Most of the old
writers are too afraid to go out even for a stroll anymore, and
the new ones, you see, meet only on the parade ground. The
salon, dear love, I'm afraid, is through.'

"'I feel I can begin again, Rupert, darling.' She ignored
my speech. 'You know it was everything to me, it's everything
now. Don't speak to me of the Yugoslav pure air and haymows.'

"Well, I looked her up and down, and thought about
everything. There she was, worth twenty million she'd in-
herited from her pa's death, and worth another six or seven
million from what the movies gave her for her detective novels,
for Georgia was, whether you boys remember or not, a
novelist in her own right. Yet here she was, a flood of grief.
I've never seen a woman want anything so much, and in my
day I've seen them with their tongues hanging out for just
about everything.

"'Let me fix you a nice tall frosty drink like they don't
have in Zagreb, angel, and then I'm going to bundle you up
and send you home to bed.' But she wouldn't be serious.
'Rupert, my love, if as you said I saved you once' (she
overstated, of course), 'you've got to save me now.'

"She had come to the heart of her mission.

"'What did I do wrong before, will you tell me,' she
brought out after a brief struggle with pride. 'Why was I driven
out of New York, my dear boy. Why was I blacklisted, why
was every door slammed in my face.' She gave a short sob.

"'Georgia, my sweet, if you don't know why you had to
leave New York, nobody can tell you.' I was a bit abrupt.

"'But I don't, Rupert!' She was passionate. 'Cross my
heart,' she moaned. 'I don't.'

"I shook my finger at her.

"'You sit there, dear Douthwaite, like the appointed
monarch of all creation whose only burden is to say no to all
mortal pleas.' She laughed a little, then added, 'Don't be
needlessly cruel, you beautiful thing.'

" 'I've never been that,' I told her. 'Not cruel. But, Georgia, you know what you did, and said, the night of your big fiasco, after which oblivion moved in on you. You burned every bridge, highway, and cowpath behind you when you attacked the Negro novelist Burleigh Jordan in front of everybody who matters on the literary scene.'

" 'I? Attacked him?' she scoffed.

" 'My God, you can't pretend you don't remember.' I studied her new mouth and chin. 'Burleigh's grown to even greater importance since *you* left, Georgia. First he was the greatest black writer, then he was the greatest Black, and, now, God knows what he is, I've not kept hourly track. But when you insulted him that night, though your ruin was already in the air, it was the end for you, and nearly the end for all of us. I had immediately to go to work to salvage my own future.'

" 'Ever the master of overstatement, dear boy,' she sighed.

"But I was stony-faced.

" 'So you mean what you say?' she whined, after daubing an eye.

" 'I mean only this, Georgia,' I said, emphasizing the point in question. 'I took over when you destroyed yourself' (and I waited to let it sink in that my own salon, which had been so tiny when Georgia's had been so big, had been burgeoning while she was away, and had now more than replaced her. I was *her* now, in a manner of speaking).

" 'Supposing then you tell me straight out what I said to Burleigh.' She had turned her back on me while she examined a new painting I had acquired, as a matter of fact, only a day or so before. I could tell she didn't think much of it, for she turned from it almost at once.

" 'Well?' she prompted me.

" 'Oh, don't expect me to repeat your exact words after all the water has flowed under the bridge since you said them. Your words were barbarous, of course, but it was your well-known tone of voice, as well as the exquisitely snotty timing of what you said, that did the trick. You are the empress of all bitches, darling, and if you wrote books as stabbing as you talk, you'd have no peer. . . . You said in four or five different rephrasings of your original affidavit that you would never kiss a black ass if it meant you and your Thursdays were to be ground to powder.'

" 'Oh, I completely disremember such a droll statement.' She giggled.

"Just then the doorbell rang, and in came four or five eminent writers, all of whom were surprised to see Georgia, and Georgia could not mask her own surprise that they were calling on me so casually. We rather ignored her then, but she wouldn't leave, and when they found the bottles and things, and were chattering away, Georgia pushed herself among us, and began on me again.

"At last more to get rid of her than anything else, I proposed to her the diabolic, unfeasible scheme which I claimed would reinstate her everywhere, pave the way for the reopening of her Thursday salon. I am called everywhere the most soulless cynic who ever lived, but I swear by whatever any of you hold holy, if you ever hold anything, that I never dreamed she would take me on when I said to her that all she'd be required to do was give Burleigh the token kiss she'd said she never would, to make it formal and she'd be back in business. You see, I thought she would leave in a huff when she heard my innocent proposal and that in a few days New York would see her no more—at least I'd be rid of her. Well, say she'd quaffed one too many of my frosty masterpieces, say again it was the poisonous New York air, whatever, I stood dumbfounded when I heard her say simply, 'Then make it next Thursday, darling, and I'll be here, and tell Burleigh not to fail us, for I'll do it, Rupert, darling, I'll do it for you, I'll do it for all of us.'

"The next day I rang to tell her of course that she wasn't to take me seriously, that my scheme had been mere persiflage, etc. She simply rang off after having assured me the deal was on and she'd be there Thursday.

"I was so angry with the bitch by then I rang up big black Burleigh and simply, without a word of preparation, told him. You see, Burleigh and I were more than friends at that time, let's put it that way." Rupert smirked a bit with his old self-assurance. "And," he went on, "to my mild surprise, perhaps, the dear lion agreed to the whole thing with alacrity.

"After a few hours of sober reflection, I panicked. I called Burleigh back first and tried to get him not to come. But Burleigh was at the height of a new wave of paranoia and idol worship and he could do no wrong. He assured me he wanted to come, wanted to go through with our scheme, which he baptized divine. I little knew then, of course, how well he had planned to go through with it, and neither, of course, did poor Georgia!

"Then, of course, I tried again to get Georgia not to come. It was like persuading Joan of Arc to go back to her livestock. I saw everything coming then the way it did come, well, not *everything*." Here he looked wistfully around at the London backdrop and grinned, for he missed New York even more when he talked about it, and he hadn't even the makings of a salon in London, of course, though he'd made a stab at it.

"I didn't sleep the night before." Rupert Douthwaite went on to describe the event to which he owed his ruin. "I thought I was daring, I thought I had always been in advance of everything—after all, *my* Thursdays had been at least a generation ahead of Georgia's in smartness, taste, and éclat, and now, well, as I scented the fume-heavy air, somebody was about to take the lead over from me.

"Everybody came that night—wouldn't you know it, some people from Washington, a tiresome princess or so, and indeed all the crowned heads from all the avenues of endeavor managed to get there, as if they sensed what was to come off. There was even that fat man from Kansas City who got himself circumcised a few seasons back to make the literary scene in New York.

"Nobody recognized Georgia at first when she made her entrance, not even Burleigh. She was radiant, if slightly drawn, and for the first time I saw that her face-lifting job wasn't quite stressproof, but still she only looked half her age, and so she was a howling success at first blush.

"'Now, my lovely' — I spoke right into her ear redolent of two-hundred-dollar-an-ounce attar of something — 'please bow to everybody and then go home — my car is downstairs parked directly by the door, Wilson is at the wheel. You've made a grand hit tonight, and now go while they're all still cheering.'

"'I'm going through with it, love.' She was adamant, and I saw Burleigh catch the old thing's eye and wink.

"'Not in my house, you won't,' I whispered to her, kissing her again and again in deadly desperation to disguise my murderous expression from the invited guests. 'After all,' I repeated, 'my little scheme was proposed while we were both in our cups.'

"'And it's in cups where the truth resides, Douthwaite, as the Latin proverb has it,' and she kissed me on the lips and left me, walking around the room as in her old salon grandeur days, grasping everybody's outstretched hand, letting herself be embraced and kissed. She was a stunning, dizzy success, and then suddenly I felt that neither she nor Burleigh had any intention of doing what they had agreed to do. I was the fool who had fallen for their trap.

"When I saw what a hit she was making, I took too many drinks, for the more accolades she got, the angrier and more disturbed I became. I wasn't going to let Georgia come back and replace me, whatever else might happen.

"I went over to where Burleigh was being worshipped to death. He turned immediately to me to say, 'Don't you come over here, Ruppie, to ask me again not to do what I am sure as greased lightning I'm going to do, baby,' and he smiled his angry smile at me.

"'Burleigh, dearest,' — I took him by the hand — 'I not only want you to go through with it bigger and grander but megatons more colossal than we had planned. That's the message I have to give you,' and I kissed and hugged him quietly.

"I couldn't be frightened now, and what I had just proposed to him was a little incredible even for me, even for me drunk, I had gone all out, I dimly realized, and asked for an assassination.

"But the more I saw Georgia's success with everybody, the more I wanted the horror that was going to happen. And then there was the size of her diamond. It was too much. No one wore diamonds that big in the set we moved in. She did it to hurt me, to show me up to the others, that whereas I might scrape up a million, let's say, she had so much money she couldn't add it all up short of two years of auditing.

"Time passed. I looked in the toilet where Burleigh was getting ready, and hugged encouragement.

"Then I felt the great calm people are said to feel on learning they have but six months to live. I gave up, got the easiest seat and the one nearest to the stage, and collapsed. People forgot me.

"Still the hog of the scene, Georgia was moving right to where she knew she was to give her comeback performance.

"Some last-minute celebrities had just come in, to whom I could only barely nod, a duchess, and some minor nobility, a senator, a diva, and somehow from somewhere a popular film critic of the hour who had discovered he was not homosexual, when with a boom and a guffaw Burleigh sails out of the john wearing feathers on his head but otherwise not a stitch on him.

"I saw Georgia freeze ever so slightly—you see, in our original scheme nothing was said about nakedness, it was all, in any case, to have been a token gesture, she had thought— indeed *I* had thought, but she stopped, put down her glass, squared her shoulders like a good soldier, and waited.

"Burleigh jumped up on my fine old walnut table cleared for the occasion. Everybody pretended to like it. Georgia began to weave around like a rabbit facing a python. Burleigh turned his back to her, and bent over, and with a war whoop extended his black biscuits to her. She stood reeling, waiting for the long count, then I heard, rather than saw, owing to heads in the way, her kissing his behind, then rising I managed to see him proffer his front and middle to her, everything there waving, when someone blotted out my view again, but I gathered from the murmur of the crowd she had gone through with it, and kissed his front too.

"Then I heard her scream, and I got up in time to see that Burleigh had smeared her face with some black tarlike substance and left a few of his white turkey feathers over that.

"I believe Georgia tried to pretend she had wanted this last too, and that it was all a grand charade, but her screams belied it, and she and Burleigh stood facing one another like victims of a car accident.

"It had all failed, I realized immediately. Everybody was sickened or bored. Nothing was a success about it. Call it wrong timing, wrong people, wrong actors or hour of the evening, oh explain it any way you will, it was all ghastly and cruddy with nonsuccess.

"I stumbled over to the back of my apartment, and feeling queasy, lay down on the floor near the rubber plant. I thought queerly of Kitty, who had, it seemed, just left me, and I — old novelist *manqué* — thought of all those novels I had written which publishers never even finished reading in typescript, let alone promised to publish, and I gagged loudly. People bent down to me and seemed to take my pulse, and then others began filing out, excusing themselves by a cough or nod, or stifling a feeble giggle. They thought I had fainted from chagrin. They thought I had not planned it. They thought I was innocent but ruined.

"I have never seen such a clean, wholesale, bloody failure. Like serving a thin, warm soup and calling it baked Alaska.

"I didn't see anybody for weeks. Georgia, I understand, left for Prague a few days later. Only Burleigh was not touched by anything. Nothing can harm him, bad reviews, public derision, all he has to do is clap his hands, and crowds hoist him on their shoulders, the money falls like rain in autumn.

"Burleigh has his own salon now, if you can call his big gatherings on Saturday a salon, and Georgia and I both belong to a past more remote than the French and Indian Wars.

"To answer your first question, Gordon" — Rupert turned now to me, for I was his favorite American of the moment — "I've found London quieting, yes, but it's not my world exactly, sweety, since I'm not in or of it, but that's what I need, isn't it, to sit on the sidelines for a season and enjoy a statelier backdrop? I don't quite know where Georgia is. Somebody says it's Bulgaria."

• In This Corner . . . •

WHEN he was 42, Hayes's second wife, like his first, died unexpectedly. She had left instructions that there were to be no special services for her, that she should be cremated and her ashes scattered over the water. The farewell note did not say what water, and her husband one late evening threw the ashes into the river near the docks in Brooklyn. Once they had been disposed of he felt a loosening of tension such as he had not experienced since boyhood. This was followed by a kind of exaltation so pronounced he was nonplused. He breathed deeply and looked out over the dark river on which a small tugboat with green and orange lights was gliding in perfect silence.

A few moments later he found himself whistling.

When he got to his flat near Middagh Street, he opened the seldom-used store room which contained his archery set and his punching bag. He got his boxing gloves out, and punched the bag until he was tired. That night he slept with the deep unconsciousness he had experienced as a soldier on furlough.

It was beginning to get nippy, for they were in late September, and yet he went to his Wall Street job without bothering to put on his jacket or tie.

For some time now, whenever he got off at the Bowling Green subway stop, he had been noticing a young man, almost a boy, holding up a stack of missionary tracts. Today, on a sudden impulse, Hayes bought up all the tracts the boy had for sale. The vendor did not seem too pleased at this unusual generosity, but managed a husky thanks.

The next time he got off at his subway stop, he looked immediately for the young man with the tracts, but when he went up to him, the boy turned away abruptly and began talking with a vendor of Italian ices. Hayes did not feel nervy enough to buy any more tracts.

There was an unexpected killing frost, which was supposed to have set some kind of record, and the next day,
shivering from the change in weather, Hayes, as he came from
underground, caught sight of the boy with the tracts sitting on
a little folding chair. He had no tracts in his hands, and was
wearing only a thin summer shirt, very light trousers, and
worn canvas shoes without socks.

As he was late for work, he hurried on, but that evening
as he left work he observed the young man still sitting on the
folding chair.

"Hello," Hayes called out. "Where's your tracts?"

The boy's lips moved fitfully, and then after considerable
effort, he got out the words: "I'm not with the missionary
society any more," and his eyes moved down to the pavement.

Hayes walked on toward the subway entrance without
having been able to make any rejoinder to the boy's explanation. Then all at once before descending he stopped and looked
back. The boy had followed Hayes with his eyes. The expression on his face was of such sad eloquence Hayes retraced his
steps, but could think of nothing to say. Studying the boy's
features he could not miss the evidence that the boy had been
crying.

"Supposin' we go over there and get something to eat,"
Hayes suggested, pointing to a well-known chop house.

"Suits me, but I don't have a dime to my name."

They sat in the back part of the restaurant, which was
nearly deserted at this hour owing to the fact that most of their
clientele were luncheon patrons.

"What looks good to you?" Hayes went on, shifting his
weight in the roomy booth, and watching the boy study the
elaborate pages of the menu.

"Oh, why don't you choose for me?" the boy finally said,
and handed over the bill of fare to his host.

"We'll have the deluxe steak platter," Hayes told the
waiter.

"So that's that," Hayes smiled awkwardly as they waited
for their order. The boy flushed under his deep tan, and

brushed a lock of his straw-colored hair from his eyes.

When the deluxe steak platters were set before them, the young man kept his knife and fork raised over the still sizzling Porterhouse, as if unsure how to begin. Then after the first hesitant motions, he was eating almost ferociously, his tongue and jaw moving spasmodically.

When the boy had finished, Hayes inquired: "Wouldn't you like my portion?"

"You don't want it?" the boy wondered blankly, looking down at the untasted steak.

"I had a very hearty lunch today," Hayes explained. He pushed his platter toward the boy. "Please don't let it go to waste."

"You're sure?"

Hayes nodded weakly.

"Well, then, if you say so." The boy grinned and began on the second platter. He ate it with even more relish.

"I love to see a young guy with a good appetite," Hayes congratulated him when he had finished.

"How about some dessert? Their pies are all baked here on the premises, you know."

The boy shook his head and put his right hand over his stomach.

"By the way, what is your name?" Hayes wondered bashfully.

"Clark," the boy raised his voice. "Clark Vail."

"And mine is Hayes." The older man stood up and extended his hand, and Clark followed suit. Their handclasp resembled somehow that of two contending athletes before the fray.

"Where do you live now that you're not with the missionary society?" Hayes wondered after they had finished their coffee.

Clark gave a start. "To tell the truth, nowhere." At a long look from Hayes, Clark lowered his eyes and said, "I've been sleeping . . . out."

"Out?" Hayes spoke with something like affront.

A kind of warmth was coming over Hayes. He felt little pearls of perspiration on his upper lip. He wanted to take out his handkerchief and dry himself but somehow he felt any movement at that moment would spoil what he wanted to say. Finally, he forced out:

"Clark, you are more than welcome to stay the night at my place. It's not too far."

Clark made no answer, and his mouth came open, then closed tightly.

"If you are sleeping out, I mean," Hayes went on. "I insist you come where you'll have a roof over your head."

They both rose at the same moment, as in a business meeting where a project had been approved.

Owing to the clatter and noise on the subway they did not speak again until they had got out at their stop.

"I live near the river," Hayes told the younger man.

"You have boxing gloves," Clark cried, picking the gloves up admiringly when they were inside his apartment. "Were you a boxer?"

"Amateur," Hayes colored. "Golden Gloves," he added almost inaudibly.

"I was in the CYO bouts a few times," Clark volunteered.

They both laughed embarrassedly.

"This is a big place you have here," Clark said wonderingly. "And you look out over the water and all the skyscrapers!"

"Excuse me if I take off my shoes," Hayes said. "They pinch."

"You have big feet like me," the boy looked at his friend's feet. He relaxed a bit.

"Want to try my shoes on for a fit?" Hayes joked.

Clark went over to the chair near where Hayes was seated, and picked up one of the shoes.

"Go on, try it on."

Finding the shoe more comfortable, Clark smiled broadly for the first time.

"Try the other while you're at it, Clark."

Clark obeyed.

"Walk around now to see if they feel all right."

Clark walked around the room in Hayes's shoes. He looked as carefree and joyful as a boy who is walking on stilts.

"They're yours, Clark," Hayes told him. When the young man acted perturbed, Hayes walked over to a partly closed door, and opened it fully to reveal inside a whole closetful of shoes.

"Look at my collection," Hayes quipped. "Two dozen pairs of shoes, and every one pinches!"

Clark laughed. "These do fit," he said, looking down at his feet. "But I don't think I should have such expensive shoes."

"Well if you don't, I do." Hayes's voice had a kind of edge in it. At that moment, their eyes met. Hayes's right hand raised, and then fell heavily against his thigh.

"I'm glad you chose to come here tonight," he managed to say. He had meant to say *come home,* but instead changed it to *here.*

Hayes rose very slowly then like a man coming out of a deep slumber and walked in his stocking feet over to where Clark, seated in a big armchair, was looking at his new shoes.

Hayes put his hand briefly on the boy's yellow hair. "I know I need a haircut," Clark looked up trustfully at his friend.

"I like your hair just this length," Hayes told him.

Clark's lips trembled, and his eyes closed briefly.

"You should never have to sleep . . . out," Hayes managed to say. His hand moved from the boy's hair to his cheek. To his relief, the boy took his hand and pressed it.

"I have only the one bed, Clark. Come on and look."

They walked over to the next room where a four-poster faced them.

"Big enough for four people," Clark's voice came out rather loud.

"Could you stand to share it? Be frank now. If not, I can always sleep on the davenport."

"Sure, share," Clark agreed.

Hayes strode over to a big chiffonier and pulled out from one of the drawers a pair of pajamas.

"Here, Clark, you can put these on. Whenever you want to turn in, that is."

"To tell the truth, that bed looks good to me." Clark sat down on a small stool and took off his new shoes. He yawned widely.

There was a long silence.

"Do you want to change in the bathroom?" Hayes wondered when the boy sat motionless holding his pajamas.

"No, no," Clark rose from where he was sitting, and then as if at a command seated himself again.

"It's just that. . . ."

"What?" Hayes prompted him, a kind of urgency in his tone.

"It's the *change* in everything, all around me. From being out there!" Hayes saw with acute uneasiness that there were tears in his friend's eyes.

"Talk about *change*," Hayes began huskily. "Your coming here has changed a lot."

As if this speech of Hayes were a signal, very quickly Clark undressed, and even more quickly stepped into the fresh pajamas which gave off a faint smell of dried lavender.

"Remember, though, if you would be more comfortable alone," Hayes reminded him of his offer to go sleep on the davenport.

Hayes's eyes rested on the boy's pajamas, which had several buttons missing, revealing the white skin of his belly.

"Don't you worry, Hayes," the boy told him. "I'm so dead tired I could lie down in a bed with a whole platoon."

Hayes began taking off his own clothes. He deposited his shirt, undershirt, and trousers on a little chest.

"I can see you was a boxer, all right," Clark noted. "You're pretty husky still."

Hayes smiled, and went to the bed and pulled back the comforter and the sheets under it. Then he helped himself in on the right side of the bed.

"Would you mind if I prayed before I get in?" Clark wondered.

Hayes was so taken by surprise he did not reply for a moment. Then he nodded emphatically.

Clark knelt down on the left side of the bed, and raised his two hands clasped together. Hayes could only hear a few words, like *I thank thee O Father for thy kindness and thy care.*

When they were both under the covers, Hayes extinguished the little lamp on the stand beside the bed.

They could hear the boat whistles as clearly as if they were standing on the docks, and they could see out the windows the thousands of lights from the skyscrapers from across the water.

To his sharp disbelief, Hayes felt the younger man take his left hand in his right, and the boy brought it then against his heart and held it there.

"Clark," Hayes heard his own voice coming from it seemed over water.

The boy in answer pressed his friend's hand tighter.

Hardly knowing what he was doing, as when in the morning he would sometimes rise still numbed with slumber, Hayes turned his head toward the boy and kissed him lightly on the lips. Clark held his hand even tighter, painfully tighter. He felt the young man's soft sweet spittle as he kissed him all over his face, and then lowered his lips and kissed his throat, and pressed against his Adam's apple.

Hayes had the feeling the last twenty-five years of his life had been erased, that he had been returned to the Vermont countryside where he had grown up, that he had never been married, had never worked in a broker's office, and ridden dirty ear-piercing subways or had rented a flat in a huge impersonal building designed for multi-millionaires.

He helped Clark off with his pajamas and turned a kind

of famished countenance against the boy's bare chest, and to his lower body.

"Yes, oh yes," the boy cried under the avalanche of caresses.

In the morning, Hayes realized he had overslept. It was nearly nine o'clock by his wristwatch, and he would never be able to get to the office in time. The place where Clark had slept beside him was vacant, so that he assumed the young man was in the bathroom. He waited, then, hearing nothing, he walked down the hall. The door to the bath was open, the room vacant. The apartment, he knew, was also vacant, vacant of the one he had loved so deliriously.

"Clark?"

Hayes felt a kind of stab in his abdomen, as if a practiced fist had hit him with full force.

After such a night when he had felt such unexpected complete happiness, and when he had felt sure the young man, despite the great difference in their ages, had returned his love—how could Clark then have left him? A rush of even greater anguish hit him when he saw that the shoes he had given Clark were resting under the chair near the closet.

He knew then Clark had left him for good, left him, that is, for dead.

He did not bother to shave or wash before going to work. Several of the secretaries looked at him wonderingly. They probably though he had been out on a tear. His boss, an elderly man who favored Hayes, was, as usual, out of the office on a trip somewhere.

He finally made no attempt to keep his mind on his work, but stared out at the vast gray canyons of buildings facing him from the windows. Each time he signed some letter or memorandum for a secretary, he would mutter to himself that at five o'clock he would begin his search for Clark.

"And if I don't find him," he said aloud to himself, "what will I do then?"

One thing he saw was certain: if he did not find him, he could not live.

The sudden unforeseen upheaval in his life was just as difficult to understand as if he had fallen under a subway train and lost his arms and legs. He went over the implausibility, the impossibility even of it all, a 42-year-old man, married twice, had taken a young man home, and never having loved any man before, had fallen somehow ecstatically in love, had confessed his love, as had the young man, and then after this happiness, it had all been taken from him. He had been ushered to the gates of some unreachable paradise, and waking had found himself in an empty hell.

His search went on day and night. Often he did not go to work at all, and he did not even bother to call his employer. He quit shaving and soon sported a rather attractive beard.

He looked crazily and brazenly into the face of every young man who crossed his path, hoping it would be Clark. He wore out one pair of shoes after another. He no longer was aware that his shoes pinched, and taking off a pair at night he saw with indifference that his feet were not only afflicted with new calluses and corns, but that his toes were bleeding from so much walking. Had he seen his toes had been severed, it could not have meant less to him.

"Clark, Clark," he would cry at night. He could still smell the boy's hair against the adjoining pillow.

One night while walking late on the promenade, two men approached him and asked him something. Hayes was so lost in his own misery he paid no attention to them. The next moment he was aware they were ripping off his jacket, and robbing him. After taking all he had they beat him with what seemed to be brass knuckles and then knocked him to the pavement.

He lay there for a long time. He felt his jaw aching horribly, and he noticed that he had lost a tooth. The physical pain he found more bearable than his loss of Clark.

He knew then that he would kill himself, but he did not know what means to choose: the wheels of the subway, jumping from his building, or swallowing countless pain-killing pills.

The elderly widows of his building were very much alarmed by the change in "young Mr. Hayes," as they called him. They blamed it on the death of his wife.

The mugging he had received left several deep gashes on his forehead and cheek which did not heal. He did not want to go to a doctor, but whenever he touched the wounded places, they would open and a thin trickle of blood would run down his face. He spitefully welcomed this purely physical anguish. It made his losing Clark at least momentarily less excruciating.

The loss of Clark was equaled only by his failure to understand why the boy had deserted him. What had he done wrong to drive him away when they had felt such great happiness in one another's arms?

In late November a heavy wet snow began falling. Hayes went out only in a light windbreaker, and no hat. He walked to the end of the promenade and then as he was about to turn and go further north down the steep hill on Columbia Heights, he slipped and fell. The sudden sharp blow to his head and face opened his still unhealed cuts and abrasions.

He lay as if lifeless with the snow quickly covering his face and hair. A few persons began stopping and looking down at him. Soon others began to gather.

A policeman got out of a squad car and hurried over to where he lay. When he saw the policeman, Hayes rose on one elbow, and made every effort to get up.

The cop kept asking him if he was going to be all right, or if he thought he should go to the emergency room of a hospital.

Hayes managed somehow to get on his feet, and, shaking off the accumulation of snow, assured the policeman and the onlookers that he was all right. But his eye fell on someone in the crowd the sight of whom almost caused him to fall to the pavement again. There, watching him with a kind of lunatic fear, was Clark.

Hayes moved quickly away from the last of the onlookers and sat down on one of the benches thick with snow. He was as a matter of fact not certain Clark had really been there staring at him. He decided that he had sustained a slight concussion and it had made him imagine Clark's presence. He held his face in his hands, and felt the wet snow descending on his mouth and throat.

Presently he was aware someone was standing close over him. He removed his hands from his face. It was Clark, no mistake.

All at once a great anger took over, and he rose and cried: "Well, what's your excuse?"

When Clark did not respond, he moved close to him, and taking a swipe with his right hand he hit the boy a fierce blow knocking him to the pavement.

Standing over him, Hayes muttered again, *What's your excuse?*

Then he must have blacked out, for when he came to himself he was again seated on the wet snow-covered bench, and Clark was standing over him, saying, "Can I sit beside you, Hayes?"

"What ever for?"

"Please."

"Well," Hayes snarled, "to quote the way you talk, *suit yourself.*"

Clark sat down beside him, but Hayes moved vengefully away from him.

"The reason I left, Hayes," the boy began, "the reason has nothing to do with you, understand. It's only what's missing in me . . . I wanted to stay — stay forever," he gulped and could not go on.

But Hayes's anger was only getting more intense.

"That's a lot of bull, if I ever heard any," the older man

roared. "You missionary people are all alike, aren't you. All nuts. You should all be locked up from meddling with the rest of the human race."

"I'm not a missionary person, as you call it. I never was, Hayes. They took me in, true, but I couldn't believe in what they believed. I couldn't believe in their kind of love, that is."

"Love," Hayes spat out. "Look at me when you say that. See what it did to me. . . ."

Hayes stopped all at once. He could see that Clark's own mouth and jaw were bleeding, evidently from Hayes's blow.

"I have done lots of soul-searching," the boy was going on as if talking to himself. "But the reason, Hayes, I left, you ain't heard, and maybe you won't believe me. See," he almost shouted, "I left because I felt such great happiness with you was . . . well, more than I could bear. I thought my heart would break. And I feared it couldn't last. That something would spoil it. When I first left you I thought I'd come back at once, of course, once I got myself together. But a kind of paralysis took over. The night with you was the happiest in my life. And you were in the best thing ever. I couldn't take such happiness after the life I have led. I couldn't believe it was real for me."

"Bull, bull," Hayes cried. He rose, the anger flashing out of his eyes, but as he moved toward the street where he lived he fell headlong and hurt himself on the paving stones. He was too weak to rise, too weak also to resist Clark picking him up.

"Hayes, listen to me . . . you've got to let me help you home."

Hayes swore under his breath. Then, as if remembering Clark had been a missionary, he used all the foul language and curses he could recall from his army days.

Impervious to all the insults and abuse, Clark helped him home, holding him under his arms. Hayes tried a last time to shake him off at the front entrance, but Clark insisted on coming up to his apartment with him.

Hayes fell almost unconscious on his bed.

"If you could only believe me," Clark kept saying. He

began taking off Hayes's wet clothing. Then he went into the kitchen and heated some water, and put it in a basin he found under the sink.

He began wiping Hayes's face of dirt and blood and snow. When he had finished these ablutions he took off Hayes's shoes and socks. He drew back for a moment at the sight of his naked feet, for they looked as if they had been run over, and at his touch the toes streamed with blood. He wiped them gently, bathing them again and again though Hayes winced and even cried out from the discomfort.

All at once Hayes raised up for he felt Clark kissing his feet.

"No, no," Hayes cried. "Don't humiliate me all over again."

"Let me stay," Clark begged him. "Hayes, let me stay with you."

"No," Hayes growled. "I don't want you."

Hayes could feel the boy's lips on his bare feet.

"You need someone," Clark beseeched him.

"Not you, not you."

Clark covered his friend's feet, and came up to the bed and lay down beside him. He refused to budge from this position, and then slowly without further remonstrance from Hayes he put his head over Hayes's heart, and kissed him softly.

At these kisses, Hayes began weeping violently. Almost like an athlete who has been told he must give up his place to another younger, more promising candidate, he yielded then any attempt to dispute Clark's claim.

Clark removed all of his own clothing now, and held Hayes to him in an almost punishing embrace. Still weeping, indeed almost more violently, Hayes nonetheless began to return Clark's kisses.

Then slowly began a repetition of their first evening of lovemaking, with perhaps even more ardor, and this time Hayes's cries could be heard beyond their own room, perhaps clear to the river and the boats.

"And tomorrow, I suppose, when I wake up, you'll have cleared out again," Hayes said, running his fingers through the boy's hair.

"No, Hayes," Clark said with a bitter contriteness. "I think you know now wild horses couldn't drag me from your side. Even if you was to tell me to leave you, I'd stay this time."

"And do you swear to it on that stack of tracts you used to peddle?" Hayes asked him.

"I'll swear to it on my own love of you," the boy confessed. . . . "Cross my heart, Hayes, cross my heart."

Printed September 1991 in Santa Barbara
& Ann Arbor for the Black Sparrow Press
by Graham Mackintosh & Edwards Brothers Inc.
Text set in Baskerville by Words Worth. Design
by Barbara Martin. This edition is published
in paper wrappers; there are 300 hardcover
trade copies; 150 hardcover copies have
been numbered & signed by the author;
& 35 numbered copies have been handbound
in boards by Earle Gray each with an
original drawing by James Purdy.

Ken Fitch

JAMES PURDY was born in Ohio on 14 July 1923. He was educated at the University of Chicago, the University of Puebla, Mexico and the University of Madrid. He worked as an interpreter in Latin America, France and Spain. He taught at Lawrence College, Appleton, Wisconsin from 1949 to 1953 and has been a full-time writer since 1953. His first book of fiction, *63: Dream Palace,* was published in England in 1957 to great critical acclaim. Since that time he has published thirteen novels, six books of stories and plays and five volumes of poetry. His books have appeared in translation in over thirty countries. He currently lives in Brooklyn where he is finishing a new novel concerning the life of New York composers.